REGENCY
Brides

REGENCY
Brides

*Love Crosses England's Social Barriers
in Three Historical Novels*

Kimberley
COMEAUX

BARBOUR
PUBLISHING

The Vicar's Daughter © 2003 by Kimberley Comeaux
The Engagement © 2004 by Kimberley Comeaux
Remember Me © 2005 by Kimberley Comeaux

ISBN 1-59789-368-4

All scripture quotations are taken from the King James Version of the Bible.

Cover image © Michael Boys/Corbis

Published by Barbour Publishing, Inc., P.O. Box 719, Uhrichsville, Ohio 44683, www.barbourbooks.com

Our mission is to publish and distribute inspirational products offering exceptional value and biblical encouragement to the masses.

 Member of the
Evangelical Christian
Publishers Association

Printed in the United States of America.
5 4 3 2 1

Dear Reader,

Ever since I read Jane Austen's *Pride and Prejudice* in the eighth grade, I've been intrigued by the English Regency era. All their rules of conduct and courtly manners were so foreign, yet fascinating to a modern American girl. Through the years I've read and re-read anything I could find on this era, watched every BBC & Masterpiece Theatre movie I could find, and even traveled to England to see the beautiful castles and historical ruins for myself.

So after I finished up a western series I'd written for Heartsong Presents, I decided to write my own Regency romance stories and show how God worked through six people, amidst a society that would often disguise immorality with false modesty and courteous protocol.

The first two stories take place in England, but for the third story, I couldn't resist bringing them to my home state of Louisiana. During this period, wars were fought and glorious plantations were built amidst the wild swamps where Indians and alligators reigned. Though our hero and heroine experience quite a culture shock, they still somehow manage to find love!

I hope you enjoy reading about Christina and Nicholas, Catherine and Cameron, and finally Helen and North, as much as I had creating them and even vicariously living through them. Maybe something that they experienced in their Christian journey will encourage or inspire you in your own.

God Bless,
Kimberley Comeaux

The Vicar's Daughter

To my husband, Brian,
for taking me to England and inspiring this story; and to my son,
Tyler, who shares my love of history.

Chapter 1

C hristina Wakelin quickly realized the situation had developed into quite a dilemma. When she'd seen the poor old yellow cat, crying while it clung in terror to the unsteady limb near the top of the tree, she'd wanted only to help it down.

So without a care for how unseemly it might be for a young lady to climb a tree or for the fact the tree just happened to be on the estate of Lord Nicholas Thornton, the Earl of Kenswick, she set forth to rescue the poor creature.

If only she'd heeded her friend's warning, she would not be in this predicament! Helen, who stood staring up at Christina with worry marring her pretty face, had pleaded several times for her to give up the foolish mission and climb down.

She should have taken the advice earlier, however, because now she could not. Not only was the cat stuck in the tree, Christina feared that she was, too. But the fact remained—the cat needed rescuing, and she must try to save it.

"Please, Christina! Do come down," Helen told her in an overloud whisper. "What if Lord Kenswick finds you frolicking around in his tree? He hasn't been exactly friendly and sociable since his return. I do not want to even consider what he might do!"

Christina carefully moved her hand to get a better grip on the branch as she hugged it with both her arms and legs. "Helen, I do not think he could do anything that could be worse than falling out of this tree." She winced as her arm slipped, scraping the tender skin of her wrist. "I don't suppose you could climb up here and help me?"

"I can scarcely go up a flight of stairs without feeling faint from the height; you know that!"

Christina groaned with frustration over her inability to think of a way to get down from her perch and save the cat at the same time.

"Meeoow," the scruffy animal cried again as it peered at her with big golden eyes.

"Do not carry on so, cat. You are the reason I am in this situation in the—ow!—first place!" Christina slipped again, this time scraping the palms of both hands.

"Don't tell me you are conversing with that animal," Helen said from below. "What if Lord Kenswick should happen to hear you? Why, he'd think you were not only a nuisance but mad, as well."

Christina tried again to reach out for the cat, but the contrary animal kept backing away, going farther onto the weaker part of the limb. "Since Lord Kenswick has not been seen since his return to Malbury these last four months, I'd say you worry in vain. Besides, Helen, I do not understand this dismal fascination you have for the earl. One would think him a monster by your comments."

"He is a scoundrel, Christina! I dare say there is not one in all of England who has not heard of his exploits. He drinks excessively and frequents gaming halls, and it's been rumored he has participated in two duels. *Two*, Christina!" she emphasized, her voice showing how scandalous she thought it was. "His own fiancée threw him over because she found him in the company of another woman of questionable reputation."

"Perhaps you did not listen to my father's sermon last Sunday when he spoke of how we should not judge our brothers," Christina gently reminded her friend, as she dared to look down at her. Christina was the daughter of the village vicar, a man whose heart-stirring sermons brought parishioners from as far away as Nottinghamshire, ten miles away. "And besides, while I do not know the particulars of his engagement or the duels, I think we can safely assume he has not been gambling or calling someone to pistols since his return!"

Christina tried not to think about how unsteady the branch seemed as she scooted out a little farther. This time she could touch the cat but not quite grab it.

"Christina!" Helen cried out again, this time sounding more alarmed. "Can you not let the cat be and come down? I do believe the branch is bending!"

"Nonsense! I've almost got him," she replied, though she could feel the branch giving way herself.

Just as she had the cat by the scruff of its neck, her attention was caught by someone walking from the house toward them.

"Oh, dear! Helen, it's Lord Kenswick, and he's headed this way!" she cried in a hushed tone.

Helen's eyes grew round with fright. "Say it isn't so, Christina! What are we to do?"

"You must run, Helen. Leave the grounds before he sees you!"

"But what about you?"

"Surely he won't see me up here. I'll climb down just as soon as it is safe."

Helen looked doubtful, but she didn't argue further. Casting a worried last look up to her friend, she started running toward the opening in the fence through which they'd slipped.

Christina turned her eyes back toward the earl. He appeared to be quite a dour, brooding gentleman, not at all like he'd been when he left Malbury years ago. Even his appearance was vastly changed, older and somehow wilder. His black hair was tousled about his face and falling unfashionably past his collar, framing features that were stern and proud with defined cheekbones and a straight, noble nose. He walked with a definite limp that Christina knew must have been a product of the war.

Despite his grim countenance, he was smartly dressed in a dark green riding coat over a tan waistcoat, and his buckskins tucked into polished black Hessian boots encased his long legs. A snow-white cravat about his neck cinched the look and made him appear very much the lord of the estate.

He was nearly at her tree now, and she found herself holding her breath and praying he wouldn't look up. Christina's heart nearly stopped when he paused briefly and looked around, as if he were looking for something.

It seemed to Christina an eternity passed before he finally started to walk away. And just as she thought she might escape his notice, the old tomcat let out a long, mournful meow Lord Kenswick would have to be deaf not to hear.

Apparently his hearing was fine, because he immediately turned and looked up into the tree—and directly at her.

His brooding expression turned thunderous. "What. . . ?" he growled in unbelief. "You up there, who are you and what are you doing on my estate?"

Christina swallowed and hoped she could somehow talk her way out of this situation without her father finding out. "Uh, I beg your pardon, my lord. I did not mean to trespass, but—"

"I suppose you didn't mean to climb my tree either?"

"Well, no, I didn't actually mean to, but—"

"Yet here you are, trespassing on my land and my privacy," he interrupted, his face stony and unreadable. "Come down at once. Although I should call for the constable, I must find out your identity and return you to your parents."

Christina had many faults, but her worst, as her father frequently reminded her, was her inability to bridle her temper or her tongue. "I would appreciate it if you would refrain from interrupting me and let me explain! Had you looked at my situation up here with a rational mind, you would see I am not alone but am attempting to rescue this poor, unfortunate cat!" Unable to lift her hands without falling, she nodded toward the animal that sat looking at her as if it didn't have a care in the world.

"That is *my* unfortunate cat," he said, surprising her.

"Yours?" He did not look like the sort of man who would be a pet owner. "Then what is his name, pray?"

She saw that her question disconcerted him for a moment. "Well, he doesn't have one. I just call him Cat."

"I am not sure that I believe—"

Before Christina could finish her statement, the cat leaped from the limb

11

and sailed down to the next limb, and then the next, until he landed perfectly in the Earl of Kenswick's arms. As she watched the big man cuddle the cat and fondly scratch those scruffy ears, she wished she could leap out of the tree herself and run away. How embarrassing to know her efforts were all for nothing; they served only to put her in an awful standing with Thornton and would probably get her in trouble with her father.

"My patience is wearing thin, madam. I want you out of the tree this minute," he barked at her, as he let the cat jump from his arms.

Christina bit her lip, trying to decide what to do. She finally decided to confess. "There's just a small problem, my lord."

"And that problem would be?"

"I'm afraid if I move, this branch will break."

He frowned. "Nonsense! The tree is as strong as any you'll find in—"

A loud crack belied his words, and Christina found herself airborne. Frantically she reached out, trying to stop herself, and latched onto a branch full of spring leaves, but not before scratching herself even more in the process. The rough wood cut into the skin of her palms where she held fast to the limb, and Christina knew she could not maintain a grip for much longer.

"Madam! Look down and see where I'm standing. You're not very far up now; so let go, and I'll catch you," Thornton called from below in an uncharacteristically gentle tone.

Tears began to well up as Christina forced herself to look down to where the man stood. *Not very far?* It looked a distance of miles from where she hung. She recalled his limp. "How. . . ?" she began, unsure how to ask it. "Your leg, sir. Won't it hurt?"

"Forget my leg and just let go." When she didn't respond, he shouted, "I said *now*, woman!"

The booming command worked better than any gentle coaxing could do. Christina closed her eyes and let go, screaming the whole way down until she hit something solid. Firm, strong arms wrapped around her, and she heard Lord Kenswick grunt at the impact. He stumbled a moment and then righted himself.

"You can open your eyes now," he told her with a dry, almost humoring voice.

She did, but she wanted to close them again when she realized the compromising position she found herself in. The earl cradled her legs with one arm and supported her shoulders with the other. With her arm around his neck, there could be no more than an inch separating their faces.

His glittering blue eyes stared into her own bright green ones, and for some reason, Christina found herself a little light-headed. There was something so disturbing about him, so compelling.

What would it be like, she wondered fancifully, *if he kissed me?*

"I should think we ought to be introduced first, don't you?"

With horrified shock, she gasped, realizing she'd spoken her thoughts aloud. Like a fly trying to free itself from a web, she scrambled out of his embrace, backed away from him, and began tugging at her dress and smoothing her hair. Hot waves of embarrassment swamped her, and she did what she always did when she got nervous.

She began to prattle.

"Well, that didn't turn out so bad, did it? I mean, the cat's fine, you don't seem too wounded from my crashing into you, and as you can see, I've sustained no broken bones, so I'll just run back to my home and leave you to your coveted solitude. I'm sure you're anxious for me to leave, since you all but said so just a minute ago when I was perched in your tree, so I'll say cheerio and—"

"Do be quiet, will you? You've already jarred every bone in my body. Don't add to it by giving me a headache," he snapped, making a show of rubbing his temple.

"Oh, dear! I knew I would wound you! What can I do? Do I need to fetch a servant?"

He put out a hand to stop her from fawning over him, and then he froze. A look of astonishment crossed his features. "I just realized who you are!" he exclaimed, not looking too happy about it. "The red hair, the penchant for getting yourself into messes, the rattling tongue. You're Christina Wakelin, the vicar's daughter!"

Christina was a little insulted that his last statement sounded remarkably like an accusation. "Very good, my lord, now I'll just leave and—"

"It was you who pushed Harriet Cummings into the pond the summer before I left for the war!" he charged, coming toward her with eyes narrowed.

"I thought she could swim," Christina said defensively. "I didn't mean to almost drown her."

"I suppose you didn't mean for me to get blamed for it either?"

Christina swallowed and took another step back. "Well, it was all sort of confusing after she fell in," she explained, knowing the excuse was weak. Actually, Harriet had been teasing Christina cruelly that whole day. Even now Christina didn't understand why Harriet seemed to hate her so much. But Christina, tired of being teased and too immature to think about the consequences, decided on a whim to exact her revenge when she'd seen Harriet walking with Nicholas Thornton along the lake's edge.

"I'm sorry I didn't come forward and take the blame, but that was so long ago, my lord. Surely you can't still be holding it against me. Harriet survived, after all." She tried to smile but erased it once she saw he was not placated by her apology.

"My father almost disowned me over the incident, and my brother was upset I'd ruined his sixteenth birthday party. Not to mention Harriet declared never to speak to me again."

Christina backed up until she hit another tree. "Well, she really wasn't a very good friend, then, was she?" she reasoned with a halfhearted smile.

"I didn't want her for a friend. I intended to begin courting her!"

"Oh, dear."

"That's just one instance. I have a dozen other memories of your mischief!" he emphasized.

"Surely you're not going to list them all," she pleaded, hating that he was correct in his allegations.

"That would take all day."

He looked so peeved that Christina briefly wondered if all the rumors about him were true. Was he such a cad that he would harm a lady?

"But that was so long ago, my lord! Surely you don't hold me accountable for things I did as a child," she reasoned.

He looked at her as if she had just told him the moon were made of cheese. "I don't *if* the person learns her lesson and grows up to be a responsible adult! Did I or did I not just find you in my tree? You, madam, have not changed."

"You're not going to challenge me to a duel, are you?" she asked, remembering the conversation she'd just had with her friend.

He shook his head as if he hadn't heard right. "I beg your pardon?"

"Never mind," she answered quickly, wishing she would think before she spoke. "My lord," she began again, "you are wrong in saying I haven't changed. I am a Christian woman and strive to—"

"Don't start handing me any drivel about religion! I lost any faith I might have had years ago."

Christina's heart broke at the bitterness that marred his face and laced his words. "But God can restore—"

"No one can take away the bitterness of war or the contempt I hold myself in for causing my father's death! And now word has come that my brother's ship has been lost at sea. . . ." He seemed to choke on the last sentence and quickly looked away, but not before Christina saw the sorrow that filled his eyes. "Now, if you don't mind, Miss Wakelin, I'll escort you home. But from now on, I'd appreciate you not trespassing or climbing any more of my trees."

Christina wanted to say something to make things better, but she thought it wise to hold her tongue. At least for now. But, being the crusader that she was, she knew she would not let this subject or this man be for long. There had to be a way to help him. Perhaps her father could provide her with answers.

"This isn't London, my lord. My home is only a stone's throw, so I shall see myself home and leave you to your solitude," she told him as she started to go. But when she had taken only a few steps, she turned back to where he stood looking at her. A strange expression filled his eyes as he stared at her, as if he were puzzled by something.

His eyes were the most beautiful shade of blue, and Christina thought she could stare into them for hours. But his sudden frown dispelled any fanciful thoughts she entertained about the earl. A bitter, disillusioned man was not someone to have romantic feelings for. Of course, a mere vicar's daughter had no business entertaining any sort of feelings for a titled man.

"You've changed your mind about needing an escort?" the earl spoke, breaking Christina from her thoughts.

She blinked, embarrassed she'd been staring at him for such a lengthy time. "I only wish to thank you for catching me. I could have come to great harm, had you not been there."

His face was one of cool indifference. "You are fortunate I did not know who you were, or I just might have let you hang there."

Christina could not help it; he seemed to be trying so hard to appear the mean-hearted villain that she started to laugh. "Then I thank you for having such a bad memory. Good day, my lord," she told him. Turning from his glowering face, made even angrier by her laughing, she ran to the back gate and off the estate.

Chapter 2

Nicholas Thornton, the sixth Earl of Kenswick, was not having a good day. He had not had a good day for the three days since his encounter with Christina Wakelin. It confounded him, and even irritated him, that he could not seem to get her out of his mind.

He, who had been in the company of the most refined women of England, of whom he had given no more than a passing glance, could not make himself forget the way her eyes sparkled with mischief when she stared down at him from atop the tree.

The past year had been hard on Nicholas. Because of his physical injury during the war, not to mention the injury his mind and soul had suffered, he'd been filled with bitterness and self-pity. He wasn't proud of how he had spent the last year of his life, living a less than sterling existence—frequenting places no gentleman would enter—but he hadn't been able to stop himself. It was as though he were on a path to self-destruction and couldn't seem to stop.

Which is why he returned to Kenswick Hall, hoping to shut himself away from the world, to find some sort of peace in his solitude. He felt so alone, with his father dead and his brother missing at sea.

Perhaps he was getting his just reward. He felt no hope for himself—no light at the end of his long, dark tunnel.

For exactly four weeks and nineteen days, his mood had grown darker, his attitude so beastly even his servants stayed clear of him.

And then Miss Wakelin climbed his tree, and for the first time in a very long time, he found himself concentrating on someone other than himself.

Perhaps it was because she acted so shockingly. He found himself admiring her daring to have climbed his tree just to save a cat. He had to admit, though, it was rare to see a gentleman's daughter, country-bred or no, so lacking in feminine graces. The vicar had always seemed so capable a person when it came to taking care of the parish. How did that capability not extend to the rearing of his only daughter?

It was a shame really, because Nicholas had to admit she was quite pretty, despite the wild red color of her hair. How would she ever attract a marriage offer behaving as if she were a child?

Not that it was any of his business, Nicholas reminded himself as he stepped onto the balcony overlooking his front lawn. He'd forget about her soon enough, and his solitary world would go back to normal.

"My lord," Pierce spoke from the doorway, breaking him from his thoughts. Nicholas turned, noticing that his butler regarded him with the same wary expression most of his staff had adopted around him.

"Yes, Pierce, what is it?" he asked briskly, irritated he was interrupted at all.

"Sir Walter Keen, the solicitor of your brother's estate, is here to see you. I've shown him to the library."

Nicholas replied curtly, "I believe my orders were to turn away anyone who called. You know I don't receive visitors."

He was surprised when Pierce remained in the doorway, nervously clearing his throat. "I beg your pardon, my lord, but I believe that you *must* see him."

Nicholas raised a haughty, dark eyebrow. " 'Must,' Pierce?"

"Sir Walter's word, my lord."

He wondered if he hid in the attic, would he be able to get through the day without interruptions? "Then tell him I'll be right down."

Fifteen minutes later, Nicholas opened the door to the library and was surprised to find not only Sir Walter but also a woman, whose plain dress made him guess she was a servant of some sort. It was the baby she held, however, that made Nicholas uneasy.

Sir Walter, a tall, broad-shouldered man, impeccably dressed, stood up as the earl entered. "I'm so sorry for this inconvenience, Lord Kenswick, but a matter of great importance has arisen."

Nicholas glanced over at the woman with the child as she stood and gave him a brief curtsy. He looked back to the solicitor. "It must indeed be an emergency that you had to bring your child along," he commented, before remembering Sir Walter was not a married man.

Sir Walter, apparently, was not one to be intimidated by class or sarcasm. He looked directly into the earl's eyes and told him what Nicholas did not want to hear. "This is not my baby, Thornton. He is your brother's child. Tyler Douglas Thornton he is so named, and now he is yours."

Nicholas looked with horror at the tiny, pink infant swaddled in a blanket. "Why cannot Anne, my late brother's wife, care for the child?"

"I regret to inform you that Mrs. Thornton did not make it through childbirth. Of course, you know both her parents are deceased, as well as any close relative, and since the baby seems to be your sole heir at the moment, the guardianship for the child falls to you, my lord."

"What about my aunt, Lady Wilhelmina Stanhope? She has a nice home in Stafford, and I'm sure—"

"And she is never there, my lord. She is abroad seven months of the year." He gave the earl a pitying look. "I'm afraid there is no one else."

"Have you utterly lost your senses, man? You cannot bring an infant and just drop it on my doorstep, expecting me to look after it. I know nothing about raising children!" he exclaimed. How could he be responsible for a helpless, innocent infant?

"I'm sure you can find a competent nanny to take care of the child. I've a list here, in case you need one."

Thornton took the list, crumbled it, and threw it across the room. "This is what I think of your list!" he said, taking a menacing step toward the attorney.

Sir Walter, maintaining his mild expression, sighed. "I hope, for your sake, you'll be able to find that list once I'm gone. You'll need it, I'm sure."

"I think not, since I'm going to make sure that. . .that child goes with you!" He glared at the man accusingly. "There is no possible way I can take care of this child!"

"I find one does what one must when situations arise, my lord." With that, Sir Walter walked past Nicholas to where the butler stood with his hat and coat ready.

Nicholas stared at the back of the retreating man with unbelieving eyes. "You cannot mean to leave, sir!"

"I do and I must. I have other matters to attend to." He donned his hat and nodded at the woman.

Before Nicholas could bark out another protest, the woman pushed the squirmy bundle into his arms and walked out with Sir Walter.

"Good day, Lord Kenswick," the solicitor said with a calmness that made Nicholas seethe.

"Now see here. . . !" His voice drifted to a stop when he realized the solicitor had already left the room.

"I cannot believe this!" he growled under his breath as he started toward the door.

But Pierce, acting out of character, boldly stepped into the doorway, blocking his path. "Shall I see the nursery is made ready for young Master Tyler?"

Nicholas felt a rising panic take over his body. "The only thing I want you to do, Pierce, is to move your body from my doorway!"

"For what purpose, my lord? The young master is a Thornton. Should not the best place for him be with his closest Thornton relative?"

"You overstep your boundaries, Pierce."

The old butler simply nodded his head calmly. "Yes, my lord."

Nicholas turned away from the butler and went to the window. He watched as Sir Walter's coach pulled away from Kenswick Hall, leaving him with a burden he could not even begin to fathom.

However, he could not deny Pierce's words. The babe was a Thornton and, therefore, since Nicholas had no desire to marry, the future Earl of Kenswick.

If there is a God, he thought, *He surely must be punishing me for all my misdeeds.*

Almost fearfully, he turned his attention to the child. *What did Sir Walter call him? Tyler Douglas.*

The baby looked at him at that moment and made a cooing sound. He was so tiny, so vulnerable—so innocent. Nicholas may have thought having a baby shoved upon him was highly unfair, but as he looked at those trusting blue eyes, he realized what was most unfair was that the babe should have him for a surrogate father. He, who could not even manage his own life, would now be in control of someone else's.

Even in war he'd not been so terrified.

He looked around and saw that his staff had gathered at the doorway, joining his rebellious butler. They exchanged nervous glances, but they didn't move.

One of the younger maids, whose name eluded Nicholas at the moment, shyly walked into the room. "Pardon me, m'lord, but I believe I know someone who might can 'elp you find a good nanny for the little one there."

Nicholas sighed. "Then by all means find this person and send her to meet me right away." He winced at the desperation he heard in his voice.

How could something so small disrupt his life so thoroughly?

"Right away, m'lord," she said and, after a quick curtsy, hurried from the room.

Noticing the group of staring servants, Nicholas scowled. "Well, don't just stand there as if there were nothing to do! Someone tell Jennings to ride out to Stafford and fetch my aunt if she is there. And would somebody please take this smelly child. . . ." His voice drifted off when he realized no one had stayed to honor his last request.

With a defeated sigh, he turned back to the window, thinking his life could not possibly get any worse.

For three days, Christina had not been herself. Usually she would go about her business, looking after her sick animals, helping her father with his duties as vicar, as well as researching different topics for her father's sermons. But for three days she could not concentrate on anything. She tried to do needlepoint but kept knotting the thread. She sat to play the piano but hit so many bad notes her father made her stop.

It was all *his* fault. That dreadful man, the Earl of Kenswick.

Oh, she knew their meeting had been all her fault initially, but when she'd been turned away from his door, when she'd called on him not once, but twice—well, that just infuriated her! To think she'd actually been feeling sorry for him. His butler informed her he wasn't receiving anyone, but she knew he must have given special instructions not to allow her inside the hall. How could he know she wanted to speak to him? She'd wanted only to invite him to church and perhaps help him see that there is a God after all.

Her other reason was to inquire about his cat. Because of her talent for mixing herbs, most folks in the area brought their sick pets to her; she wanted to offer her services in case his cat ever needed her.

It was a strange gift, to be sure, but one that was often needed in their small village, whether it was a limping workhorse or a sickly hound. The last three days, however, even her animal services had suffered, and she hadn't been able to cure Mrs. Walden's cat from a bout of sick stomach!

Why Thornton's blatant snubbing hurt Christina so much, she had no idea. Maybe it was that she just wanted to make up for her past mistakes. Maybe it was that she wanted to encourage him to attend one of her father's services so he could hear about how God loved him.

Maybe you just find him attractive! She quickly dismissed the thought since, of course, she'd never be attracted to such a rude, boorish man.

No, she was sure her motives were of a noble nature. He was a man made bitter because of war and the death of his father and brother. That was why he'd developed such a terrible reputation—why he fought those duels and broke off with his fiancée.

She would help him. Somehow, some way, she would show him God could truly give him a new life—a brand-new heart.

And that is what Christina prayed. She asked God to open a door of opportunity for her to be able to help Lord Kenswick.

A knock sounded at her door, and Mrs. Hopkins, their longtime housekeeper, walked into the parlor where Christina sat. "Miss Cooper to see you, ma'am."

"Polly! Do come in." Christina welcomed the girl with a smile as she walked into the room. "It's only ten in the morning. Did Mrs. Donaldson give you the day off?"

Polly smiled shyly at Christina as she tucked a wayward strand of hair back into her white ruffled cap. "Oh no, ma'am. I don't work for Mrs. Donaldson anymore. I found a post as a 'ousemaid at Kenswick 'all. That's why I've come 'ere."

Christina couldn't have been more surprised. Was this God's answer to her prayer? "Is there something I can help you with?" she queried, trying to appear nonchalant.

"Yes, ma'am. You see, Lord Kenswick is in need of a nanny, and I knew if anyone in the county knew where to find one, it would be you."

Christina could do nothing but stare at the young girl. Finally she found her voice. "I beg your pardon, did you say *nanny*?"

The man was a bigger cad than even Helen thought!

"Yes, you see, Lord Kenswick's sister-in-law died in childbirth just a few days ago, leaving behind the young master. He was brought to Kenswick 'all a few moments ago, since the earl is 'is nearest relative."

Perhaps she'd been a little hasty in judging the man, Christina thought guiltily. If he were willing to raise the child, then surely he couldn't be all that bad.

"Lord Kenswick tried to give him back to the man who brought 'im. You should 'ave seen 'im, ma'am. I've never seen the man in such a temper, although I've 'eard 'e's rarely in an agreeable mood. But when the earl tried to run after the man, the butler stopped 'im, reminding 'im of 'is duty." She widened her eyes and shook her head slowly. " 'E was none too 'appy about it though, truth be told!"

So maybe he was a little bit of a cad after all.

"Well," Christina said, standing to her feet. "We must see to this poor infant. I will endeavor to find a nanny, but in the meantime I will see that he is sufficiently taken care of."

Polly eyed her warily. "I'm not sure the earl would like that, ma'am. 'E doesn't allow anyone 'sides us servants into Kenswick 'all. And sometimes I think 'e'd rather we would just disappear and leave 'im alone!"

Christina marched to the door, grabbing her bonnet as she went. "How well I know, Polly. But no matter. I will see to the infant, and Lord Kenswick will just have to abide me!"

In an uncharacteristic fit of vanity, she checked her reflection in the hall mirror. She was wearing one of her better morning gowns, with its fashionable high waist and rounded neckline, the light blue color a perfect complement to her complexion. Her hair was a bit messy since, as usual, curly strands had come loose from her topknot, but at least with a bonnet she would look presentable.

As she finished tying the ribbon to her bonnet, Christina cast a quick look upward and smiled. "You not only work in mysterious ways, Lord, You work in a most hasty manner!"

"What's that, ma'am?" Polly asked.

"Oh, nothing, Polly. I was just thinking aloud," she replied. And as she marched toward Kenswick Hall, she felt somehow empowered, as though she'd been handed a mission only she could fulfill—a crusade to lead a man out of his self-indulgent life and into the light.

Chapter 3

Christina and Polly entered Kenswick Hall from the servants' entrance and walked through two long hallways before they entered the enormous main hall.

Since she was a little girl, Christina had loved the home with its grand chandeliers and richly dyed carpets. Many times over the years, the former earl and his wife had invited them for tea or for a small dinner party, and Christina relished the memories of how she'd felt among the tall marble columns and antique tapestries. Huge windows on either side of the door allowed sunlight to pour in and caused the crystal chandeliers to scatter splashes of color throughout the room.

It had truly been a beautiful and happy home.

Now it was a sad and dismal one, because other than the lamps set about the room, every piece of furniture was covered with white dust cloths. "What is all this, Polly? It looks as though the house is not in use!"

"That's the way the master 'as ordered it, ma'am. 'E says no use in showing off furniture no one's going to see," Polly answered matter-of-factly, as she stopped suddenly at a huge double door, causing Christina to bump into her.

"Oh! So sorry."

"It's all right, ma'am." Polly lifted her hand to knock on the door. "I'll just let 'im know you're 'ere."

"Wait!" she said suddenly, as she thought of how she'd been turned away from the hall in the last few days. "Did you tell him you were bringing me back here to the hall?"

Polly shook her white-capped head. "No, ma'am. I just said I knew someone who could 'elp 'im."

"Hmm," Christina said. "If that is the case, you'd do well to let me go in first." Polly opened her mouth to disagree, but Christina shook her head. "If you announce it is I you've brought to aid him, then I'm afraid he might not see me."

"But, ma'am," Polly tried to argue, but Christina ignored her and opened the door herself.

The scene that greeted her was one not even her imagination could have conjured up. There he was—the stern, unsmiling man she'd met earlier, the brooding creature who turned away visitors, the same person who ordered that

22

dust cloths remain on all his furniture—trying to change a diaper.

He was so focused on his task that he did not even hear her enter the room, and she took the opportunity to study him. No longer was his dress impeccable. His dress coat had been thrown over a chair, so he was wearing only his unbuttoned waistcoat, linen shirt, and fawn-colored britches. His cravat was untied and rumpled, and his dark curls looked as if he'd been running his hands through them.

"I do not understand how this simple little cloth could be so difficult to put on you," he muttered to the baby, his fingers fumbling with the thick material. "I daresay someone should devise a simpler way to go about this!"

"Well, if you could accomplish that, I promise every mother in England would rise up, throw King George off his throne, and put you in his place," she announced as she walked in his direction.

The earl's head snapped up at the sound of her voice, and a scowl creased his dark features. "First my tree and now my house. Tell me, Miss Wakelin, do you intrude on everyone's privacy here in Malbury, or do you single me out in particular?"

"Actually, my lord, I'm not intruding; I was invited." She pointed to the desk where the baby lay, waiting for him to finish the job. "I believe if you turn the cloth the other way you'll find it will fit much better."

He threw her another dark look before focusing on the child. He did as she told him and in no time had the diaper fastened snugly.

He looked a little bemused at what he'd just accomplished. "How could you know such a thing?"

Since Thornton made no effort to pick the infant up despite his squirming, Christina nudged the earl out of the way and lifted the child into her arms. "I am the daughter of a vicar," she answered. "I've stayed in the home of many a young mother who needed time to recover after the baby came."

Christina gently rocked back and forth as she looked into the eyes of the earl's nephew. He looked to be only about a month old, but already his head was full of inky black curls just like his uncle's. Her heart swelled as she bent to plant a kiss on the soft cheek and breathed in the sweet baby smell. One day, she thought, she would be holding one of her own. She prayed it would be so.

"How is your cat, my lord? I've been wondering how he has fared," she asked, though her eyes were still focused on the baby.

"Never mind about the cat! I have a problem on my hands, if you haven't noticed. And though I'd hoped for someone more experienced in these matters. . ." He paused to look her over with a critical eye. "I suppose you'll have to do."

Although Christina was the grandniece of a baronet, she rarely had the opportunity to be in the company of the upper classes. She had never had a "coming out" and had never attended a ball, because her father did not approve. Since her life was so full here in the gentle countryside, she had not been bothered by it. Now, standing before this boorish man, Christina was even more thankful of the vicar's disapproval if this were an example of how society behaved. Were they all this rude and obnoxious?

Christina smiled stiffly. "I am thrilled you approve."

He apparently missed the sarcasm, since he nodded, then backed away from her and started pacing the room. "The servant girl said you could help me find a nanny, and there is no time to waste. I trust you'll be able to procure someone by nightfall." He stopped in the middle of the room as he finished his sentence and looked at her, lifting an imperial eyebrow for emphasis.

"You must be joking!" she blurted. "Acquiring a nanny is a tedious and sometimes lengthy process, Lord Kenswick. Of course, I know a few women whom you could interview for the position, but you must choose one who is right for this household, as well as for the child."

Thornton narrowed his eyes. "I am not in the habit of repeating myself, Miss Wakelin, but I'll concede you might not be too bright, so therefore I'll make this one concession." Ignoring her outraged gasp, he continued. "I need someone by tonight. I don't care who it is or how far you have to travel to get her, as long as you have her here by nightfall. Is that clear?"

Christina tried hard to hold her tongue, but it proved to be too difficult. "Perhaps you are right. If I were a bright person, I would have recognized you for the mean-spirited cad you are and not come at all!" She held out the baby until he reluctantly took him. "I'll find you a nanny, and not because you are ordering me to do so, but because that poor child needs someone to look after him properly."

She swung around and headed for the door, angry with him for being so arrogant and demanding, and angry with herself for letting his behavior get to her.

"Wait!" he ordered in a tone that stopped her dead in her tracks. It was a voice she imagined he had used on the battlefield.

She turned back. *What now?* she wondered, bracing herself for another tirade.

He spoke only five words.

"Take this baby with you!"

∽

One thing Nicholas knew how to do was brood, and he did plenty of it in the hours he waited for the vicar's daughter to return.

His thoughts ran more to the negative than to the positive. *What if she couldn't find anyone?* he thought. Of course, he'd been unreasonable in his request, but he was a desperate man! A man who had no idea how he was going to raise an infant.

He tried to think of someone who might take the child, but he realized he'd severed most of the relationships with those families who might have helped him.

His behavior and broken engagement had cast him out of society's good graces. And since the *ton*, as the cream of all English society was referred to, had the ability to make or break someone's reputation, he realized it might cast a shadow on his nephew's future also.

That is, if the poor child survived growing up first.

There was always his aunt Wilhelmina. Perhaps she would agree to take the child on, despite the fact she traveled so much. Widowed at an early age, his aunt had never remarried nor had any children. Perhaps she would like the chance to raise a child.

But his aunt was not in England at the moment, and he had no idea when she would return.

It was ironic that the harder he tried to alienate himself from the world, the more responsibility the world dumped on his lap. He could, of course, live up to his reputation as a scoundrel and dump the child back at Sir Walter's door.

But, surprisingly, he couldn't even contemplate it. Maybe there was some decency left in him after all. A small part that still had honor.

He had no time to dwell on that thought, however, because his library door was pushed open at that moment without so much as a knock, and Miss Wakelin came sailing into the room.

Nicholas was struck dumb for a moment as he took in her flushed cheeks and her wild red hair streaming about her face. Never had he known someone (especially a female, for the ones in his acquaintance had been mild-mannered, dull creatures) who appeared to have such a zest for life. When she'd first gone, he asked his housekeeper about her, and she regaled him with tales of the way Miss Wakelin took care of the animals in town and helped the people in her father's congregation. She was never still, he was told, but always flitting about here and there, finding causes and projects to occupy her time.

She might be a bit odd, but she was also the most fascinating woman he'd ever met.

"Good news, my lord!" she exclaimed as she neared him, clasping her hands together. "I have hired a most suitable nanny, a Mrs. Sanborne, and she comes with high recommendations from the Duke of Northingshire himself!"

Guilt swept over Nicholas as she spoke, for he knew the Duke of Northingshire well. They'd been the best of friends before he went to war. North, as his peers called him, tried to speak to him after his father's death, but Nicholas spurned his offer of friendship.

He could use a good friend now.

But a desperate man couldn't let guilt stand in his way of finding decent help for his situation. Nodding briefly, he gestured toward the sitting area.

"Show her in then."

Apparently he did not give her the response she was looking for. "Is that all you can say to me? After the miles I have traveled and the people I have met to make sure your request was carried out?" she asked, clearly put out.

Maybe it was the red hair that caused her to be so passionate about everything. "What more do you want me to say, Miss Wakelin?"

"A simple thank-you wouldn't hurt."

"All right then, thank you. Now show her in, please."

Rolling her eyes, Miss Wakelin whirled around and strode toward the door. Watching her, Nicholas realized the lady amused him a great deal with her colorful nature. In fact, it was getting harder to maintain a bad mood with her constantly bursting into his life.

How was it possible to hate *and* love the way she made him feel at the same time? It was extremely irritating. *She* was extremely irritating.

When Miss Wakelin brought the older woman into the room, Nicholas first noticed she carried the baby competently in her arms. He noticed, secondly, that she wore the biggest smile he'd ever seen on a human being.

"Lord Kenswick! May I say what a stupendous honor it is for me to be in your service! Stupendous!" she gushed as she walked up to him, gently bouncing his nephew in her arms as she went. "Might I add what a stupendous little lad he looks to be. Why, just look at how pleasant a disposition he has! Stupendous, isn't he? Quite stupendous!" She looked up at him with a grin wider than the Thames, as if she expected him to respond to her cheerful greeting.

Frankly, he wasn't sure how to respond to the woman. He'd not been confronted with this much merriment since he was a boy, and he was sure he'd never heard the word *stupendous* used so many times in one day, much less a few seconds.

He looked over at Christina Wakelin. Her green eyes sparkled with mirth as she met his gaze, and he wondered if she had known the woman was such a talker when she'd hired her. Perhaps she knew a woman such as this would get on his nerves, and that was why she chose her.

He would have to keep his wits about him in dealing with Christina Wakelin. She was either extremely crafty or a complete innocent. Either way, she could be dangerous to his peace of mind.

Returning his attention to Mrs. Sanborne, he had to stop himself from flinching at her bright smile. *Just because she's cheerful does not mean she is incompetent,* he told himself.

And besides, in times of desperation, one could not be choosy.

"Yes, well, Mrs. Sanborne, I'm sure Miss Wakelin has filled you in on my situation. I'm glad you could come on such short notice," he told her briskly. "Of course, we need to discuss schedules and salary, but it can wait until the morning." He walked behind his desk and pulled a heavy rope hanging from the ceiling that rang for the servants.

It took only a few moments for his housekeeper to usher the new nanny out. Not before she, however, got in a few more sentences of gratitude and used that dreaded word five more times. He was left alone with Miss Wakelin.

"Well," Christina said in the awkward silence. "I guess since I've solved your little problem, I'll be on my way."

"Not so fast, Miss Wakelin," he countered, taking her arm as she tried to turn toward the door. Surprised, she spun back around and fell forward onto his chest. Nicholas steadied her, but he wasn't prepared for the feelings that coursed through him as he held her.

He looked down at her, and their eyes met. Unfortunately it was embarrassment and not attraction he saw in them as they widened under his inspection. "I daresay I have fallen on you again, my lord," she mumbled, as she scrambled from his arms and backed away. With cheeks rising to the color of her hair, she continued. "Was there something else you wanted to say?"

It took a moment for Nicholas to answer, because he was still reasoning in his mind that he could not possibly be attracted to the vicar's daughter. It had been too long since he'd been near a woman, he reasoned. *Yes, of course, that must be it.*

He'd sworn off women months ago. He meant to stand by his decision.

"You will, of course, come by tomorrow," he said in a voice harsher than he'd intended. "I'll leave it up to you to decide whether Mrs. Sanborne is the right nanny for my nephew."

Her embarrassment vanished at his words, but her cheeks were blazing now for a different reason. "I am weary, Lord Kenswick, of being ordered about as if I were one of your servants. I have done as you asked, gone above and beyond what any friend would do, considering we are not friends, but it ends right here." She thrust her chin in the air in a show of defiance. "I must insist you handle this situation on your own."

She turned back toward the door, and Nicholas did something he'd done only a few times in his life—he panicked. He could not allow her to leave him stranded (why this was important, he refused to ponder), so he found himself using the only ammunition at his disposal.

Blackmail.

"The church, Miss Wakelin, is it not a part of the Kenswick estate?"

Those words stopped her cold in her tracks. She turned around, gazing at him through wary eyes. "The church is, but our home is not. Our small estate was given to my father by my grandfather, Sir Charles Wakelin."

"I am sure your father enjoys his position as vicar here in Malbury. It would be a shame if something or someone should do anything to jeopardize it," he said evenly.

Of course he had no plans to make good on his threat, and he fully expected her to blow up at him and call his bluff.

She did neither. Instead, she studied him calmly, as if trying to see past his haughty facade and read his true thoughts.

When she finally did speak, her words cut him straight to the bone. "Lord Kenswick, you had only to ask for my help instead of yelling orders at me, and I would have been glad to comply. Truly, the events that have led to your withdrawal from society and your abandonment of all gentlemanly behavior must have been great, indeed, for you to treat a lady so abominably.

"I am also sorry you have no shame in using blackmail to get your way. But you must understand that God is greater than your threats and even greater than the building you are using for ammunition. That is all it is—just a building. God's Church is everyone who believes on Him. If you take away our walls, we will not cease to exist but will simply find another place to join together and worship Him."

Miss Wakelin was wrong. Nicholas was feeling his shame most acutely. "Miss Wakelin, I—"

"Say no more, my lord. I shouldn't have gotten angry at your suggestion, and I apologize. I've suddenly remembered why I came here today. I felt God had opened a door for me to help you. You see, I'd been praying He would ever since I fell out of your tree," she said with a sad smile. "God has, evidently, not closed the door, so you can count on me to assist you in any way I can. And, of course, I want to do all I can for young Tyler. I'll call directly after breakfast tomorrow."

So stunned was he that *she'd* apologized to *him*, he could not get out a reply before she quit the room.

Chapter 4

The morning came too quickly for Christina, who had not slept well at all during the night. What was it about the autocratic man that disturbed her so? He was much like all the other nobles she'd ever been acquainted with—self-absorbed, haughty, and so unaware of the lesser classes beneath them.

Not wanting to dwell on him more than she should, Christina chose a pale yellow day dress, accented with blue ribbon around its high waist and cap sleeves. The spring color brought a little cheer to her mood, and she determined by the time she walked downstairs to the breakfast table that she'd be her normal sunny self.

And she was, especially when she saw her friend Helen sitting at the table with her father.

"Helen!" Christina exclaimed as she took her seat to the left of her father and across from her friend. "What brings you to us so early?"

"Why, it's all over the village, Christina, so I had to come hear the news from your lips straightaway!" The fact that Helen said this as if she were shocked made Christina wary.

"Um, I'm not sure what you heard. . . ."

"I'd like to hear your explanation as well, daughter. I heard from Cook you arrived home at a late hour last night," Reverend Wakelin interjected. "What kind of mischief are you about now that concerns that scalawag, Thornton?"

Christina swallowed as she looked from Helen to her father. "I have only been assisting his lordship in procuring a nanny for his young nephew. Yesterday I traveled all over the shire until I found one suitable."

Helen's eyes glinted. "That's not what I heard from my maid, who got the news directly from one of Lord Kenswick's kitchen help! She said. . ." Helen paused for effect and leaned forward, causing the ribbons of her dress to dip into her orange marmalade. "She said you visited Lord Kenswick's home not once but twice yesterday!"

"Yes, but there was a perfectly good reason—"

"Lord Kenswick is not a gentleman I would see you associate with, Christina," her father interjected. "From all accounts, I would say he is considered the scoundrel of all English society."

Helen sniffed. "I tried to tell her the very same thing, Reverend Wakelin, but she quoted one of your sermons to me and demanded I not judge him."

A grin formed on the vicar's face, though Christina could tell he tried to hide it. "Ah, so you do listen to some of the things I preach about."

"Of course I do, Father, and I heed every word."

"If that is true, then it must have been someone else who trespassed on Lord Kenswick's property and climbed his tree," he responded dryly.

Christina threw a disgruntled look at Helen, who quickly threw up her hands in defense. "I never said a word!"

"Of course not," the vicar seconded. "I heard it from Cook, just this morning."

Christina took a careful sip of her hot tea. "I think the servants gossip entirely too much. Something should be done about it."

Her father only gave her an indulgent smile. "You only think so, daughter, when the gossip concerns you."

Christina sighed as she buttered her bread. "You have a point, Father—one that may not be entirely accurate, but a point all the same." She looked up to find her father giving her one of those I-can-see-right-through-you stares, so she felt the need to blurt, "Oh, all right. I suppose I should confess my true reasons for helping the Earl of Kenswick."

Helen slapped her hand on the table. "I knew it!" she declared with a triumphant smile. "I knew you were in love with the earl! I did not believe the excuse about the cat for a minute!"

Christina prudently didn't remind Helen it was she who'd sent Christina after it in the first place. "Helen, I do believe that is the silliest thing I've ever heard come from your lips. I'd sooner fall in love with that ragged cat of his than waste my feelings on him." She took another sip of tea and patted her mouth daintily with her napkin. "You can be assured Lord Kenswick feels exactly the same way about me. He was quite put out when he realized who I was that day at the tree."

Helen leaned back in her chair and smiled dreamily. "How romantic! He remembers you from childhood."

"You misunderstand me."

"I would imagine his lordship remembers how Christina used to follow him and his brother all around the village," Reverend Wakelin inserted dryly.

Christina put out a hand. "Please go no further. Lord Kenswick has already listed my numerous misadventures, and I'd rather not hear them again, thank you!"

"So, if it's not to secure Lord Kenswick for a husband, just what are your plans concerning him?" Helen asked.

Christina took a breath as she looked from her father to Helen. "I fear it concerns his spiritual condition," she began, and then told them about his life since he'd come home from war, how embittered and hopeless he seemed. "And the worst thing is he no longer has faith in God. From what I can understand, he feels God has abandoned him and his family. I feel it's my duty to help him see God loves him."

The teasing light from her father's eyes was soon replaced with concern. "Christina, I know you think you can help him—and that's extremely commendable of you—but I fear you'll be taking on more than you can handle. I wasn't joking when I said Thornton has garnered quite a bad reputation in London. Any sort of connection with him might not be prudent, no matter how noble the reason."

"But I've already given my word, Father. He's expecting me this morning."

Christina gazed imploringly at her father, a look that served her well when it came to winning an argument.

With a heavy sigh, Reverend Wakelin stood up from the table and stared down at both young women. "If you must go, then I insist Helen go with you," he said in no uncertain terms.

Helen, whose one goal in life was to marry a titled gentleman, was not going to pass up an opportunity to rub shoulders with one when presented, no matter how much of a scoundrel she believed Lord Kenswick to be. "Of course I'll go with her."

Stifling the moan Christina felt rising within her, she gave in to her father's demand. "Yes, that will be fine. I should have thought of it myself," she told them, all the while wondering how she was going to explain the presence of yet another person barging into Lord Kenswick's self-imposed solitude.

❧

Because Nicholas had trouble falling asleep the night before, it seemed only minutes had passed when he heard the discreet cough beside his bed. Which was odd, really, considering he'd ordered his bedroom strictly off limits as long as he occupied it. That especially meant the morning, so if he chose to sleep until noon, there'd be no one to bother him in his slumber.

He tried to turn away from the sound but to no avail. Another cough rang throughout his bedchamber—this time a bit louder and more than a bit closer.

"Go away," he commanded without moving or opening his eyes.

"I fear I cannot, my lord," came the starchy reply.

Nicholas realized this was a voice he did not recognize. Like a shot, he turned and sat up, glaring at the tall, skinny stranger with narrowed, wary eyes. "Who are you?" he demanded.

Undaunted, the young man straightened his stiff posture even more and thrust his pointed chin in the air. "The name is Smith, my lord, your new valet."

Nicholas wondered if perhaps he was still asleep and only dreaming he'd been awakened. Even better, maybe he'd dreamed all of yesterday—the baby, the nanny, and that annoying Miss Wakelin, too.

"Are you all right, my lord?"

He sighed, knowing that even in his sleep he could not dream up such a grating voice.

"I do not have a valet," Nicholas growled, ignoring the young man's question.

"You do today, my lord. Pierce, a cousin of mine on my mother's side, hired me just this morning. I was told to start right away."

"Well, it all makes perfect sense now," Nicholas grumbled, as he got out of bed and walked over to his washbasin. "Only one related to Pierce could annoy me as much as he does."

He grabbed a linen cloth from the dresser and wiped the moisture from his face. "You can go back downstairs and inform your cousin I have no need of your services, and if he keeps overstepping his bounds, I won't have need of his either!"

The young man shook his head. "My lord, it is my opinion that all gentlemen need a valet's services."

"This one does not, so take your opinions and leave, man!" he shouted.

"In order to properly bring up one's heir, a gentleman needs to bring order to his life so he can be a proper example. That is why my services are needed, my lord," Smith stated, as if he were quoting.

"Did Pierce tell you that?"

"My father did, my lord. He is the valet to the Duke of Northingshire."

"Wait a minute," Nicholas interjected. This was the second time in two days North's name had been mentioned. "Is he orchestrating this whole affair? Because if he is. . ."

"I beg your pardon, my lord?" Smith queried, his puzzlement authentic.

Nicholas stalked to the door that led to his dressing chamber. "Never mind; just leave. I'll deal with you *and* your annoying cousin after breakfast."

He slammed the thick oak door behind him, but he could hear Smith from the other side. "Very good, my lord. And I hope the blue coat I laid out for you meets with your approval. I thought it the most appropriate for meeting your nephew this morning."

Nicholas stared at the carefully laid out blue coat and black trousers. Just for spite, he knocked them aside and pulled a green one from his collection.

❧

A housemaid escorted Christina and Helen to the nursery on the second floor of the west wing upon their arrival. There they found Mrs. Sanborne rocking the baby.

Already, Christina could see the staff had been hard at work bringing life into the old room with fresh linens, newly polished furniture, and warm rugs in pastel shades on the wood floors.

"Ah, stupendous! My dear Miss Wakelin, I was hoping you'd pay us a visit," Mrs. Sanborne sang out in her enthusiastic way. Her bright eyes turned to

Helen. "And you've brought a friend! Why, that's stupendous!"

"This is Miss Helen Nichols. Helen, Mrs. Sanborne is young Tyler's new nanny." The two women nodded to one another, but Christina's eyes were all for the baby.

"Oh, do let me hold him, Mrs. Sanborne. I've thought of nothing else since I left here yesterday," she confessed, as the nanny gently handed Tyler into her arms.

Mrs. Sanborne grinned proudly. "My, you look quite stupendous holding that child. I must say, you should marry and have some of your own."

Helen took one of the baby's tiny hands into her own. "It has been difficult during the war for any of us country misses to procure a husband with all our men off fighting," she replied, her voice sad.

" 'Tis true," Mrs. Sanborne agreed. "But isn't it lucky his lordship was able to come home and be here for his dear nephew?"

"I don't think 'his lordship' appreciates his good fortune, though. I think it shall be up to us to help him realize it," Christina declared, as she bent to kiss the baby's soft cheek.

"I did not appreciate the silence of this old house until it was bombarded with the silly chatter of women and a crying baby," Thornton said from the doorway, his voice filled with disdain. He scanned the room until his eyes landed on Helen. "And who are you? It seems my house is overrun by strangers this morning."

Christina turned to him at the sound of his voice, and for a moment she felt her pulse quicken. And because she did not want to feel excitement where this rogue was concerned, she retaliated with sarcasm. She managed to execute an overly dramatic curtsy while holding the baby with one arm and fanning her skirt with the other. "My Lord Kenswick, we are so glad you have graced us with your estimable presence this morning, and, yes, we are all quite well. Thank you for inquiring."

Their eyes clashed and held—Christina's matching the challenge in the earl's stare.

The silence in the room grew thick. "My lord!" Mrs. Sanborne burst out. "How good of you to come see after your dear nephew. What a stupendous sleeper he is, too."

Seeing how Mrs. Sanborne's favorite word was affecting the earl, Christina felt laughter bubbling up within her. Though she tried to stifle it, she found she could not.

It was the proverbial straw on the camel's back. "Mrs. Sanborne, could you please cease in your use of that irritating word!" he barked out. "And have you no sense, Miss Wakelin, not to laugh in the face of a lion!"

Mrs. Sanborne abruptly stopped her chatter, and both she and Helen took several steps away from him. Truthfully, Christina wanted to run, but she'd sooner be stung by a hundred bees than let the earl see her fear.

"Woke up on the wrong side of the bed, did we?" Christina observed lightly. "Perhaps a little breakfast will set your mood aright. We wouldn't want to scare a poor, helpless baby with our voices, now, would we?"

They both looked down at Tyler, and to Christina's chagrin, he was looking at his frowning uncle with bright eyes, blowing bubbles from his tiny mouth.

Christina glanced up at Lord Kenswick, and for a moment she caught the smallest of smiles beginning to form on his lips. He must have felt her gaze, however, because he immediately frowned again and took a step back. "I'd say he's none the worse for wear," he muttered. Then, as if he were suddenly in a hurry to escape, he nodded stiffly and left the room.

Chapter 5

Soon after their encounter, the Earl of Kenswick sent his butler to inform the women that under no circumstances was he to be disturbed. Mrs. Sanborne would direct all problems to the new valet or send for Christina. He did not want reports on how his nephew was faring, nor did he want to visit him. He just wanted to be left alone.

Christina, of course, thought this was ludicrous and had no qualms about disobeying his order, but doing so was much harder than she anticipated.

In fact, nearly a fortnight had passed and not once had she gained an audience with the earl.

How was her plan ever going to work if she could not talk to him or get him to see his nephew? Doubts began to plague her. Maybe the earl really was a lost cause. Maybe not even *she* could reach him.

Every day she prayed God would give her guidance, and every time she prayed, she felt God did not want her to give up on him.

So she decided to persevere—and become a little devious. Several times she was able to catch him coming from the library or walking in the garden when he thought she had already left the estate. Still, he would either ignore her or tell her he had no desire to converse.

Christina became so dispirited at her thwarted attempts to help him that she stopped seeking him out. In fact, she came to the decision by week's end that she'd no longer go to Kenswick Hall except for the occasional visit to Mrs. Sanborne and the baby. The nanny was doing an excellent job, and it was silly to keep coming when there was no need.

On the particular morning she made her decision, Pierce appeared in the garden, telling Christina that Lord Kenswick wanted to speak with her in his study.

Curious and elated, Christina nodded to the butler and began to follow him, when Helen grabbed her by the arm. "Christina, you cannot think to meet with the earl alone. I must go with you!"

Christina knew she would not be able to speak to Lord Kenswick frankly if Helen was in the room. Besides, she'd waited so long to speak with him that she didn't want to share the moment with Helen. Of course, he would be upset to see Helen there, too, making him change his mind about seeing her altogether.

Quickly she thought of an alternative. "Pierce," she said, "is there a window in the study that overlooks the garden?"

Pierce frowned. "Yes, Miss Wakelin, 'tis over there directly in front of us."

"There, you see, Helen? You can stay outside with the baby and watch us from the window. I can assure you, all will be very proper."

"Oh, I see," Helen said slowly. "You want to speak to Lord Kenswick *alone.*"

"I don't believe you 'see' at all, Helen, and I know I don't like what you're trying to imply," Christina replied.

"If you say so," Helen said with a casual shrug.

Knowing she was not going to convince Helen there was nothing between the earl and herself, Christina sighed with frustration and headed toward the house.

Pierce led her to the study, where she found Lord Kenswick studiously looking over what appeared to be a ledger. He glanced her way and mumbled something about being with her in a moment, then returned his attention to his desk.

Christina squelched the hurt feelings that were once again aroused inside her. Forcing herself not to dwell on his snobbery, she realized it was the perfect time to open the heavy velvet curtains that covered the window. Not only would it allow Helen to see in, it would brighten the otherwise dark and depressing room. With purpose, she pushed the curtains aside, allowing the brilliant sunlight to fill the room.

The earl's response was immediate. "If I'd wanted the curtains open, I would have opened them. Close them. Now!"

Instead of obeying his command, Christina turned to look squarely at him. "Why?"

He blinked, clearly not expecting his wishes questioned. "I beg your pardon?"

"Why do you want them closed?"

"Because I don't like them opened."

Christina felt a shiver of apprehension run up her spine at his deceptively soft tone. Swallowing, she made herself stand firm. "From what I can tell, there is not much you do like."

For a moment, she thought she saw a slight smile curve his lips, but it was so brief, she supposed she must have imagined it. "You're right. There's not much I do like anymore. Now, close the curtain."

At those words, Christina put a hand to her chest and stepped toward him. "But that is so sad! How can you live like that?"

"I was living it very well until you came crashing into my life, disrupting my peace at every opportunity."

He sounded so much like a disgruntled little boy that Christina laughed. "I might have crashed into you once, but I'm not the one who dropped a baby on your doorstep." She folded her arms and gave him a direct look. "And let's not forget, I might have stayed out of your life had you not brought me back into it."

He stood and walked around his desk toward her. Christina felt momentarily breathless at how handsome he looked stepping into the sunlight. "Ah, but you accepted the invitation, as I recall, to have a go at making me see the error of my ways, or something like that, did you not?"

Christina prayed her admiration for him did not show in her face as she stared up at him. Focusing on his question, she replied bluntly, "It's hard to help someone who will not even talk to me." She looked away deliberately with a small shrug. "One might think you were a little afraid of being in my presence."

"All men are wary of women when they're on a mission to reform them," he said as he stepped around her and walked toward the window.

She turned to see that he was about to close the curtains. "No!" she cried as she ran after him, putting a hand on his arm to stop his movement. "I have the curtains open because I cannot be in here with you without some sort of chaperone. If you had good manners, you'd realize that very fact!"

He stopped but did not move his arm from her grasp. A puzzled expression filled his eyes. "Are you not alone with me right at this moment?"

"Not with Helen watching us from the window." She waved at her friend in the garden.

Thornton's eyes narrowed in contemplation. "Watching a couple through a glass pane does not exactly constitute a chaperone."

"I know that, but Helen is just a simple country miss and does not know all the rules of society. I fear I have taken advantage of her on that score," she admitted, feeling slightly ashamed of herself.

"Where as you are a sophisticated lady of society, hmm?"

If he thought to embarrass her, he was mistaken. "Of course I'm not. I've simply had the advantage of being tutored by an aunt who believes all young ladies should have knowledge of society's rules, whether they need it or not." She peered out the window at the two women playing with the baby.

Thornton gave a loud sigh and walked away from her. "Well, now that your reputation is safe, will you please have a seat so I can discuss something with you?"

Christina hid a smile at his disgruntled tone and sat where he indicated.

Lord Nicholas Thornton leaned back in his large cushioned chair and stared broodingly at her for a moment. "Whether you think I'm afraid of speaking to you or not, Miss Wakelin, I'd appreciate it if you'd cease in your efforts to track me down. It has become a little irritating to find you skulking about every corner that I—"

"Oh, I wouldn't call it skulking."

"In those lessons your aunt so generously taught you, I don't suppose there was a lesson on proper etiquette when conversing, was there?" he barked out, clearly irritated she'd interrupted him.

"Yes, I do believe there was," Christina said pleasantly, while picking up a small figurine from his desk. "I must not have felt up to listening that day, though. But, please, do continue."

He began to speak, but Christina's attention was fixated on the expertly carved tiger that was no more than three inches long. Great care had gone into creating each feature, from the expressive eyes to the menacing claws on all four paws.

"This is incredible!" she cried out. "Do you know the person who carved this?"

"I did," he said with a frown. "Now, can we get back to what I was—"

"You did? Unbelievable!"

"Why does that seem so unbelievable?"

"Oh, I didn't mean it that way," Christina said, realizing she must have hurt his feelings. "I just meant I never knew you had such a wonderful talent."

He dismissed her compliment with a wave of his hand. "It's nothing but a hobby. I've just had more time to indulge in my craft lately, which brings me back to what I was saying. My privacy is—"

"So you haven't just been brooding and feeling sorry for yourself. You've actually been expressing your feelings through art!" She held up the tiger to inspect it again. If he could create beautiful figurines like this, somewhere deep inside was a man who was worth saving—a man who saw beauty in life despite his bitterness and grief.

Her statement seemed to bother him. "I do not 'express' myself, as you call it. I was merely indulging in a hobby."

She tried to hide her disbelief. "Of course you were, my lord."

"What? No argument?"

"Why argue, when I know that *you* know I'm right."

He leaned forward, his hands palms down on the desk. "This is exactly why I need to speak with you. You seem to be on a quest to disrupt my life at every turn, and I would like to know why you feel so compelled to help me, as you call it."

She smiled at him, silently thanking God for the door He'd just opened before her. "The answer is simple, my lord. I'm trying to make you realize you are special to God and to your nephew. Too special to allow yourself to be locked away from the world."

❧

Nicholas sat stunned at her words. Not just because she had the audacity to speak to him so freely, but because her words touched something deep within his heart.

He'd told himself time and time again he didn't need anyone. He'd done and seen horrific things during the war, and he had allowed his self-pity, upon his return to England, to destroy his father's health. He'd been engaged to a nice young woman who didn't deserve the disservice he paid her by breaking their engagement. And he mourned a brother he should have spent more time with.

He'd convinced himself he deserved to be alone. Little did he realize the loneliness would consume him to the point of madness. In the past, he'd enjoyed the company of others—always surrounded by friends and fellow officers. To be constantly alone was not an easy state to maintain, no matter how much Nicholas thought he deserved it.

Especially with such a lovely, vivacious young woman within his household.

How often had he watched her from the window of his library as she played with his nephew or laughed with her friend? Christina Wakelin made him wish for things he had no right to wish—that he'd been a better man, maybe even a whole different person.

It was ironic that he, a man who once put such a high regard on his status and title, was attracted to a mere vicar's daughter.

He'd acknowledged that truth three days ago when she'd caught him down in the garden. She came walking up to him, holding his nephew, and cheerfully dumped the child in his arms.

Nicholas almost dropped him, he'd been so surprised. Fortunately he recovered fast enough to just as quickly transfer him back to Christina.

Couldn't she understand he was actually afraid he'd fail Tyler just as he had all the others in his life?

"I don't want anyone's help, Miss Wakelin. Now, if you'll excuse me, I—"

But Christina interrupted him. Maybe he'd hoped she would. "But Ty needs your help, Lord Kenswick. He's beginning to respond to our faces, and I think it would provide more of a balance in his life to see a man's face as well as a woman's." She stepped closer to the desk. "Every boy needs a father in his life, and you are the closest he will ever have."

The brunt of her words hit him squarely in the conscience. "I'll give you this much, Miss Wakelin, you certainly know what strings to pull to get what you want."

For the first time since she walked into his room, he saw her cheery smile turn into a frown. "You make me sound calculating, and I'm not that way at all!"

"I believe I would use the word *cunning*." He studied her thoughtfully. "Don't think I haven't noticed how you manage to make everyone around here do exactly what you want. Most of the time, you make them think it was their idea instead of yours."

"I simply treat people the way I would like to be treated, with kindness and concern. That is why they—" She suddenly stopped. "Wait one minute! Have you been spying on me?"

"I was observing, nothing more," he answered with a shrug. "I had to make sure you and Mrs. Sanborne were giving sufficient care to my only heir."

She stared at him and then seemed to accept his answer. "Since you seem to care a little for your nephew's welfare, can you agree to at least spend time with him once a day?"

"Only if you are there, too. I refuse to spend too much time in that Sanborne woman's presence."

Christina laughed. "I promise she's not as annoying as you think."

Nicholas shuddered. "I don't care. Either you are there, or there's no visit."

"Of course I will be there, but. . ." Christina paused, then continued cautiously. "I don't understand why you've just chastised me for forcing my presence on you, and now you are blackmailing me to be with you every day. I'm afraid I'm a little at sea, sir."

Nicholas felt like the idiot she just described. What was the matter with him? What had possessed him to make such a stipulation?

Because you are attracted to her, a little voice whispered in his mind. *Because she makes you feel more alive than you've felt in years.*

Something deep inside him wanted to reach out and take the friendship she was offering, but another feeling warred within him at the same time. Guilt and fear would not allow him to act on his attraction, but neither would they stop him from spending a little time in her sunny presence.

"You simply presented a good argument, and I have reconsidered. I've seen how good you are with the babe, and I thought he would be more comfortable with you in the room," he said by way of excuse.

Those green eyes of hers seemed to see too much as she studied him warily. He was terrified she could read his thoughts. But then she smiled at him and stood up from her chair. "That's a nice way of putting it."

He stood also. "Shall we meet after the noon hour?"

She was clearly surprised he wanted to meet so soon, but she agreed. "That will be fine, my lord. Until then," she answered with a small bow and left the room.

Chapter 6

I don't know what to do with 'em, miss. My papa says 'e'll be throwing 'em into the river 'n be done wi' 'em if I don't find 'em a 'ome," little William Potts told Christina. Tears made dirty streaks down his freckled cheeks. Six newborn puppies squirmed about in the weathered wooden crate he was holding.

Christina looked worriedly at Helen and then back at the puppies. She'd been summoned to her own home by their housekeeper just as she was about to go with Mrs. Sanborne to meet the earl. "William, these pups look too young to be given away. Where is the mother dog?"

"Got run over by a coach, she did."

"Oh, dear!" Christina cried, her heart always soft toward animals. *And to little boys,* she silently added as she looked at the six-year-old. "I suppose you want me to care for them?" she asked, although she already knew the answer. It wasn't the first time she'd had to nurse puppies whose mother had died or rejected them. Normally she had plenty of time for such things, but now she had so much on her mind.

As the boy nodded, Christina sighed. "I suppose I'll have to take them then." She took the crate from him and sent him on his way.

"Your father warned you there was no more room for animals, Christina!" Helen reminded her. "He's not going to be happy you've taken on more."

"I was just thinking the same thing," Christina admitted, smiling down at the defenseless little creatures. "I suppose I'll just have to find somewhere to put them at Kenswick," she said, as a plan formulated in her mind.

"Oh no, you cannot risk it. If Lord Kenswick finds out about them, he'll be furious."

"You're probably right."

"There's no probably to it! You know he will be!"

Christina threw Helen a confident look as she shifted the crate for a better hold. "Then we will just make sure he doesn't find out!"

Helen shook her head and groaned. "You have more temerity than brains! This will be worse than the tree incident; I just know it."

"I've come to realize the earl is not as bad as we first thought. He growls and frowns a lot, but he's mostly harmless." She turned and began walking back to her house so she could get some needed supplies. Helen followed her.

41

" 'Mostly harmless'?" Helen shrieked. "Do you call participating in two duels 'mostly harmless'?"

"Really, Helen, you bring that up so often, I think you must be a little fascinated by it."

"Nothing about that man fascinates me!" Helen stated firmly.

Christina thought Helen protested too much, but she decided not to pursue it. If anyone had a problem with being fascinated by the earl, it was she.

⁓

". . .and it is stupe. . .I mean, magnificent how Master Ty is learning to roll, and just yesterday he. . ." Mrs. Sanborne prattled on, but the earl had only one thing on his mind at the moment.

Christina had not come.

Hurt and angry, he barely heard what the nanny was saying to him. For ten minutes she'd talked nonstop, enumerating the tiniest details of what the child had been doing. He tried unsuccessfully, several times, to break into the conversation to ask where Christina was.

Finally he could take no more. "Where is she?" he interrupted in a booming voice.

Mrs. Sanborne swallowed hard before she spoke. "I beg your pardon, my lord?"

He made a sweeping motion toward the door with his hand. "Christina. Why isn't she here with you?"

Mrs. Sanborne's face cleared as she smiled. "Oh! Why, she was called back to her home just before our meeting. I apologize; she asked me to let you know, and I forgot."

The anger immediately faded, and in its place came a relief so fierce it astounded him. Pointedly ignoring that last feeling, he inquired, "I trust everything is all right with her? Her father is not ill?" He was more concerned than he wanted to be.

"I do not think so, but I cannot be sure," she answered with an apologetic smile.

Preoccupied, Nicholas walked over to the window and peered outside. "Did she say when she would return?"

"No, my lord." Nicholas heard a rustling sound and knew the woman had walked up behind him. "Would you not like to hold the baby for a moment, my lord?"

Nicholas turned, his eyes fastening on the baby, who already bore a remarkable resemblance to him and his brother. He nodded curtly to the nanny and stood still as she placed the baby into his arms. Nicholas had never felt more awkward and inadequate in his entire life. What did one *do* when holding an infant?

The baby must have sensed Nicholas's unease because he squirmed and cried.

Dismayed, Nicholas quickly gave him back to the nanny. "Here, take him," he ordered, but to his utter amazement—and irritation—she just shook her head and laughed.

"Oh, he's just not used to you yet. Bounce him a bit, and he'll be just fine," she assured him.

Nicholas scowled at the woman, only to be met with that same amused expression. First his butler, then his unwanted valet, and now the nanny. Did no one take his orders seriously anymore?

"Bounce him," she urged again, when he remained stock-still. "You might even try humming a tune. Babies like that, you know."

"I do not hum," he muttered, but as silly as it felt, he did begin to bounce the baby.

He didn't know what bouncing was supposed to accomplish, and apparently the baby didn't either, because he only cried harder.

Suddenly, like a miracle, the baby stopped crying. Incredulously Nicholas stared down at the infant and noticed something had caught Ty's eye. Following the direction of his gaze, he turned and saw Christina standing in the doorway.

Uncle and nephew together took in the sight of the vicar's daughter with her curly red hair, held back by a yellow ribbon. Her face was aglow from the outside air, and the sparkle in her green eyes seemed to be solely for him.

He quickly looked away, dismissing the direction his thoughts had taken, but he just as quickly looked back. This time, his eyes fastened on her yellow dress.

"Your dress has dirt on it," he observed with a disapproving frown.

Christina glanced down and shrugged. "Only a little. I'm sure Mrs. Hopkins can get it clean with no problem."

Nicholas had never known a female who wouldn't immediately change for even one tiny speck of dirt. Ladies, he observed, were generally vain creatures. They were educated mostly in music and art and had extensive knowledge of needlepoint, but beyond that they knew very little.

His own former fiancée had been more intelligent than the average lady but also very vain about her looks and her station. She was, after all, a duke's daughter. It was her right to be.

Or so Nicholas had thought at the time. But since becoming reacquainted with the vicar's daughter, he realized how shallow his former fiancée now seemed.

As guilty as he felt about it, he was sorely glad he would not have to marry Lady Katherine Montbatten.

His thoughts were broken when Christina came toward him. "I see you are getting acquainted with Ty, and look, he's even smiling!" she cried, as she smoothed her hand over his downy head.

Nicholas had trouble forming a response with her standing so close to him. She smelled like honeysuckle, and he found himself wanting to kiss her.

"I knew he would like you!"

He blinked and made himself get control of his wayward thoughts. Clearing his throat, he finally spoke. "If he likes me, he has a strange way of showing it. He was screaming the chandeliers down until you walked in here."

Just as he thought she might, Christina laughed at his dry words. She looked up at him, and their eyes met. A strange feeling came over Nicholas as he stared into those laughing eyes. There they were, the two of them, standing together with a baby between them. If anyone had walked into the room at that moment, they would have thought they came upon a couple of proud parents with their newborn son—a family.

Something, Nicholas had convinced himself, that would never be a part of his future.

He was allowing this snip of a girl to lure him into thinking he could be happy. That he could be. . .normal.

But he wasn't. He, the scoundrel and wastrel who had brought pain to his family and dishonor to his friends.

Christina believed that God loved him no matter what he had done. But Nicholas knew that even God could not forgive him.

How could He when Nicholas could not forgive himself?

Pushing the infant into the arms of a surprised Christina, he mumbled something about making an appointment with his steward and walked out as quickly as his injured leg would allow him to.

⟨≈⟩

Christina watched with concerned eyes as the earl made a mad dash for the door, as if wild boars were nipping at his heels. For a moment, he had seemed more open than ever.

But when their eyes had met and held for a few breathtaking seconds, she'd watched his expression change, as if a door suddenly closed on his happiness. All that remained was a face full of self-loathing, and Christina was positive she'd also seen fear.

Sighing, she kissed Ty's head before looking over at Mrs. Sanborne. The older woman was staring at the door with a confused look upon her usually smiling face.

"I'd hoped he would stay longer," she murmured before turning her gaze to Christina. "Do you suppose it was because I pushed him into holding the baby? I just thought that if he could hold the child, he might feel a bond or *something*."

Christina went to the woman and put a comforting hand on her arm. "It is not your fault, Mrs. Sanborne. It's just going to take a little time before Lord Kenswick adjusts to having a baby around."

The nanny smiled at her. "I suppose you're right." She reached out for the baby. "I'll just take Ty up to the nursery and put him down for his nap."

She left Christina alone in the library. Once she was out of sight, Christina headed for the east wing of the estate. She'd discovered a few days earlier that this particular wing of the hall had not been used for years. All the furniture was covered, and cobwebs hung thickly from the chandeliers and corners of the massive rooms.

It wasn't a strange thing for some of the hall not to be in use. Many titled families used only a small portion of their grand homes, some because of a lack of money and others because they didn't want to be bothered. Since Christina knew the Thorntons were one of the wealthiest families in England, she knew the reason for the neglect had to be the latter.

A shiver snaked up her back as she walked through the cool, darkened hallways, guided by the light of a single candle. She was glad to finally reach her destination.

The enormous carved door creaked as Christina pushed it open. Inside, Helen sat staring wide-eyed and apparently frightened out of her wits in the middle of an immense room, holding the crate of puppies.

Christina gasped in awe as she stepped into the grand ballroom, still beautiful even after years of neglect and busy spiders. Helen had thrown the heavy curtains back, and sunlight warmed the otherwise cool, damp room.

"Are you sure we won't be discovered here?" Helen asked anxiously, as Christina set about removing the milk she'd brought from her house.

"Of course I'm sure. I asked Pierce the best place to keep them, and he recommended this wing of the mansion. He also assured me no one ever comes here."

Helen let out a gasp of dismay. "You told Pierce!"

Christina dipped the edge of a rag into the milk, preparing to feed the puppies. "I had to ask someone, Helen. Besides, he told me he is indebted to me for the tonic I mixed up for him to get rid of the fleas on his cat. Our secret is quite safe."

And it seemed it would remain so since the night passed and the earl was still none the wiser. Pierce had even lit a fire in the huge fireplace to keep the pups warm and made sure they were fed first thing the next morning.

"I've grown quite fond of the little spotted one, miss. I fear I shall insist on bringing him home to the missus when he's old enough," Pierce confided to Christina when she arrived midmorning. She'd worried all night over the puppies' health and safety, but apparently it was all for naught. Pierce had turned out to be quite the guardian.

"Of course you shall have him. That just leaves the other five to worry about!" she exclaimed with exaggeration.

"Don't you worry about a thing, miss. I'll inquire around to see if anyone is interested," he assured her.

"Interested in what?" a deep voice spoke behind them.

Christina slowly turned to Lord Kenswick, searching his face for clues to how much he'd heard of their conversation. Pierce saved the day.

"Ah. I see you've decided to come down for breakfast, my lord. I'll send word to Cook that you'll be joining Miss Wakelin," he said in his usual emotionless manner as he headed toward the kitchens.

"But I didn't want breakfast," the earl said, but by that time, Pierce was already out of the room.

He turned his irate gaze to Christina, who put up a hand, shaking her head. "Don't look at me. I've already had my breakfast!"

Thornton sighed in frustration. "I've become convinced I should fire my whole household and hire new servants. It seems lately they all do the opposite of what I want at every turn!"

Christina had to smile at his exasperated tone. Despite his words, he actually seemed happier than she'd ever seen him. His countenance wasn't as dark and brooding as it was when she'd first met him. Just the fact that he was walking about and not hibernating in his chambers proved that a slight change was happening inside him.

"Most of them have been here at Kenswick since you were a young boy. Perhaps they are just trying to look after you the best they know how."

He brought his gaze back to her. "I don't need or want to be looked after."

Christina let her eyes roam over Nicholas Thornton's incredibly handsome features. It was true he presented a picture of a man who needed no one, but she could feel the sadness and loneliness radiating from him. He needed someone to look after him worse than anybody she'd ever known. He just didn't know it.

She would need God's guidance in how to help him realize it.

"Breakfast is served!" Pierce announced from the doorway and just as quickly disappeared again.

"It would seem the matter of wanting or needing to be looked after has been taken out of your hands," she told the earl with a grin.

The brooding Earl of Kenswick actually returned her smile, although sheepishly. "You could be right. Or Pierce could be using breakfast as an excuse to check up on you, since you seem to be alone in my presence without your chaperone about."

He held out his arm and with a raised eyebrow asked with mock formality, "Miss Wakelin, will you be so kind as to allow me to escort you to the morning room?"

Christina laughed softly as she put her hand on his arm. She knew she needed to see about the puppies, but she could not turn down his offer. He was in such a different mood that she felt drawn to him like never before. "Indeed, I shall," she answered, matching his tone, and together they went into the morning room.

He stayed in that pleasant mood all through breakfast, even after he noticed Pierce standing just inside the room to act as a chaperone. He merely nodded to the man, then took a big bite of the sticky bun on his plate. Only once did Lord Kenswick mention hearing a strange noise in the night that sounded like animal cries. Christina offered him some more marmalade to distract him, and that seemed to do the trick. He mentioned the cries no more.

In fact, Christina realized it was surprisingly easy to get the earl to forget he'd asked a question. If she thought it a little odd, she dismissed the thought as soon as it entered her mind. Why worry over nothing?

Chapter 7

Of course, Nicholas was not so easily distracted, nor was he a simpleton. He knew when wool was being pulled over his eyes; he just didn't know what, exactly, that was.

He spent all day thinking about it and finally came to the conclusion that Christina must have brought some sort of animal into the house. Pierce was evidently in on it since he'd been avoiding him all day.

Whatever it was, he hoped it wouldn't eat his cat.

But that was not the only thing preying on his mind. Right before Christina left in the afternoon, she'd casually invited him to church the next day.

He'd acted like a stiff-necked buffoon! He'd grown defensive, and instead of declining like a gentleman, he'd answered with a cold no and quickly left the room. He didn't know how to explain that going to church scared him. People expected things out of you when they saw you in church. They expected you to act more like a Christian should, being kind and giving to others.

Nicholas knew he had not been a kind man in many years, and the only thing he'd given to anybody was a lot of grief and pain.

No. Going to church would make everyone expect him to change, and he just didn't know how to do that.

No matter how much he wished it were so.

No matter how much he wanted to show Christina he could.

❧

Christina had no appetite as she sat down to dinner with her father that evening. If only she could have waited before blurting out such an invitation. The earl was just beginning to open up to her, and she had to go and ruin it by issuing an invitation to church too soon.

It was obvious he wasn't ready to discuss God yet, and she'd pushed too hard. If only she had her father's way of speaking to people. He had such a soothing manner even the angriest man could be calmed with just a few spoken words from the vicar.

"You've hardly touched your stew, daughter, and you know how Cook gets offended if you leave too much uneaten," her father teased, pulling her from her melancholy mood.

Christina managed to give him a small smile. "I'm sorry, Father. It's just that I think I made the earl upset today when I invited him to church, and I feel awful about it." She absently pushed the vegetables around in her bowl.

She looked up to find her father's worried eyes studying her carefully. "You have not taken a fancy to the earl, have you, Christina? You do spend quite a bit of time at Kenswick Hall these days."

Christina knew she could not lie to her father, but neither could she tell him the truth. "I only see the earl a couple of times a day, Papa. Most of the time I am with Helen, Mrs. Sanborne, and Ty," she carefully evaded. "It's just that I know if he could hear one of your sermons he would feel so much better."

The vicar shook his head. "Christina, one sermon is not going to fix what ails the Earl of Kenswick. God can change him, yes, but only if he allows Him to."

An idea began to form in Christina's mind. "What if you go and speak to him, Papa? From what I've gathered from the things he's said and what I've been told from the servants, he blames himself for his father's death. I also think he feels guilty for his behavior after he returned from the war." She pushed her bowl back and reached for her father's hand. "If you could speak to him, it might help him."

The vicar studied his daughter a moment before nodding his head reluctantly. "I will go, but I cannot promise anything. My concern, however, is more for you than for him. You must promise me you will not fill your head with any silly notions of romance between you and Lord Kenswick. Even if he did not have the reputation he has or the problems surrounding him, he would still be completely out of our class. Earls do not marry vicars' daughters, Christina. You must remember that."

Christina knew all this, of course. Hadn't she told herself the very same thing from the moment she'd fallen into his arms? Yet hearing her father say it so bluntly hurt just the same. "I harbor no such aspirations of being the Earl of Kenswick's wife, Papa. I am twenty-three and already past the age of desirability for a bride from even a man of my own station. Your fears are completely unjustified."

Her words, meant to calm, had just the opposite effect on her father. "You speak as though you have resigned yourself to being an old maid! That is ridiculous, Christina. There are many young men in our acquaintance who have shown interest in you. You are much too lovely to be put on the shelf, and I will not have you speak so!"

Christina smiled at his disgruntled expression. "I am lovely only to you, Papa. To those young men you speak of, I'm merely the vicar's strange daughter who spends too much time with animals and speaks her own mind too often."

"Then you must learn to control your tongue and spend more time indoors!" he declared, but Christina saw that he looked a little sheepish at the ridiculous statement. "What I mean is, you must show them the part of you I love so much—the loving, caring girl who would give away her own food before seeing even her enemy starve."

Christina rose from her seat and bent to kiss her father's bald, shiny head. "I will endeavor to appear more lovable in the future, Papa. I promise. Before you know it, all of Derbyshire will be lined up at our door asking for my hand!"

The vicar chuckled and playfully swatted her away. "Perhaps it's the earl I should be concerned about! You may end up causing the chap more problems than he already has."

⁂

The next morning, Nicholas knew right off it was not going to be a pleasant day. He had leftover guilt for turning down Christina's invitation, and he'd berated himself half the night for allowing himself to *feel* the guilt. What was wrong with him that her downcast expression would bother him so?

But that wasn't his only aggravation.

It was Sunday. Everyone in his household knew on Sunday he slept late, had his breakfast late, and then spent the entire day in his workshop, working on his carvings. Why his servants collectively forgot about this schedule was beyond his understanding.

He wondered if a mutiny were afoot, and if so, who was the leader?

It certainly wasn't his unwanted, yet still employed, valet, although he did a good job of beginning his Sunday on the wrong foot.

Smith had awakened him at seven and all but shoved him into a dark blue coat, dove gray vest, and britches. He was tugging on his black Hessians before he had the wits to inquire why he was wearing one of his finer suits.

"You'll want to look your best when you attend the service this morning, my lord," Smith answered, as if his going was a foregone conclusion.

A vessel started to pulse in his temple. "I beg your pardon, but in the very short time you've been here, have you ever known me to get up and attend church?" he barked, while running a hand through his hair in frustration.

Smith seemed oblivious to his disgruntled attitude, however, as he rummaged about the room, picking up Nicholas's bedclothes. "Ah, but Miss Wakelin had never invited you before yesterday, my lord."

"But I told her I would—" He stopped as something occurred to him. "How could you possibly know she even asked me? I don't remember you being there, Smith!"

Smith threw Nicholas an absent smile as he continued to busy himself about the room. "Oh, I wasn't, sir, but although it's not something you like to acknowledge, we servants do talk, my lord."

He knew Christina would never say anything, and besides, she wasn't a servant. Young Ty could do nothing but emit baby sounds, so that left only one person. "Mrs. Sanborne! I'll fire her, posthaste!"

"That wouldn't be wise, my lord. You'd be left with a baby you have no idea how to care for. Miss Wakelin would probably stop coming by because she'd be upset you dismissed a lady she's grown quite fond of, and the solitude you crave so mightily would be turned topsy-turvy."

Nicholas stared in amazement at the man who had insinuated himself into his life and household. "I'm all agog at your reasoning, Smith. It almost sounds a little like blackmail."

Smith bowed to Nicholas. "I would never presume to resort to blackmailing, your lordship." With that, he turned and walked to the bedroom door. "I'll inform Cook you'll be down in a moment." He offered another brief bow before leaving the room.

Stunned that he'd been hoodwinked yet again by his wily valet, it took a few seconds for Nicholas to respond. "I will eat breakfast, but I will not be attending church!" he shouted at the closed door, knowing Smith would probably not hear him.

He managed to get through breakfast without mishap and conveyed to Smith, Pierce, and any other servant within earshot that he was definitely *not* leaving the house.

But the moment he finished breakfast, Mrs. Sanborne breezed into the dining room and pushed his nephew into his arms. "I'm terribly sorry, my lord, but I fear I cannot look after Master Ty today. I just received a terribly frightening note from my daughter's husband. She's gone into labor with her first child, and she's terribly afraid and needs me there with her. I'm sure you understand, do you not, my lord?"

Nicholas opened his mouth to say he very much did not understand, when she rushed ahead of him. "That's terribly good of you, Lord Kenswick. Terribly good."

Nicholas looked down at his nephew with dismay. "But, Mrs. Sanborne, you cannot leave me. . . ." He stopped when he looked up and realized she'd already left the room.

He ran to catch her, but no amount of pleading or threats of termination would induce her to stay.

Nicholas was so perplexed that he stood out on the front steps of the hall for ten minutes after her carriage pulled away.

How was a person to know what babies wanted or needed? Were there instructions written down somewhere he could follow? His housekeeper had left the estate for some purpose or another. Not knowing what else to do, he went to the nursery and sat in the high-backed rocking chair.

So there he was, the sixth Earl of Kenswick, doing something he was sure none of his forebears had ever done—rocking an infant. For an hour or so, he fumed about the circumstances he found himself in. As he rocked back and forth, he promised himself he would add more servants to his small staff. With that settled in his mind, he calmed down a little and for the first time really noticed the baby in his arms.

The child looked so much like Thomas. So much so it hurt a little to hold him, knowing his brother never would. And then he thought of something else: What would it be like to hold his own son?

Of course, that wasn't a possibility for him, and it irritated him that he would even entertain such thoughts.

Christina. Christina Wakelin was the reason his priorities were so confused. His was a well-ordered solitary world until she came into his life.

The baby made a noise. Nicholas looked down at him, panicked that he was about to cry. What would he do then? There was no one to hand him to! But little Ty didn't cry. Instead, he looked up at Nicholas with a full gaze. A warm feeling spread throughout the earl's body, and an unfamiliar emotion squeezed at his heart as he studied the child. He might have determined never to marry and have children, but someone (God?) had seen fit to give him a child anyway.

What was next, a wife? Immediately, Christina Wakelin's teasing smile and shiny auburn hair flashed into his mind's eye. That shook him up more than any thought of children did.

She was the kind of woman who would brighten a man's life and fill his home with laughter and love. It would certainly not be a boring life with her in it!

If only he were a different man. If only. . .

"My lord, Reverend Wakelin is here to see you," Pierce announced at the nursery's door. "I've shown him to the parlor."

Isn't the vicar supposed to be at church? was his first thought. But a quick glance at a mantel clock revealed that it was much later than he'd surmised. Nicholas opened his mouth to reply that he was not receiving visitors but changed his mind when the baby started to make fussing noises. Seizing the opportunity, he quickly got up from the rocker and placed the baby into Pierce's arms.

"You don't mind seeing to the baby while I greet the vicar, do you, Pierce?" He gave the surprised man a triumphant smile. "Of course, you don't," he answered for him as he slipped out of the room.

As Nicholas entered the parlor, he made a quick study of Christina's father. He'd aged, of course, since the last time he'd seen him, but he was still the tall, stately-looking man he'd always been. There was a kindness in the vicar's eyes that had always warmed him as a child, listening to the Sunday sermons.

The vicar stood with a welcoming smile as he gave a brief bow to Nicholas. "Lord Kenswick," he greeted. "It's been quite a few years since we last met."

Nicholas returned the smile, though a bit warily. What could the vicar possibly want, and did Christina have anything to do with it?

"It has indeed, Reverend. Please have a seat," he directed, indicating the brocade-covered chairs near the massive marble fireplace. "To what do I owe the pleasure of your company?" he asked once they were seated.

"There's no need to pretend you are overjoyed to have me intrude on your time," the vicar stated dryly, though a kind grin lit his face. "Christina has spoken to me a little of what you've gone through these last few weeks, and may I start off by saying I am truly sorry for the loss of both your father and your brother. Your father was one of my dearest friends, and I still miss him terribly."

Nicholas nodded. "As do I, Reverend." He hesitated but found he had to ask, "So Christina asked you to come speak to me? I know she must be upset that I did not attend the services, but I—"

Reverend Wakelin held up his hand to stop the explanation. "Yes, she did ask me to come, but that is not why I agreed." He leaned forward, resting his elbows on his knees and looking seriously into Nicholas's eyes. "She wanted me to come and speak to you as your vicar, but I'm afraid I came as someone else. Christina's father."

Nicholas took a deep breath as he absorbed the vicar's words. Of course, he should have seen this coming. "I see," Nicholas said. "You think I might have had ulterior motives in asking Christina to help me."

Reverend Wakelin wasn't a man to beat around the bush. "That is it exactly."

"Then let me set your mind at ease, Reverend. Christina is completely safe in this household. I would never do anything to jeopardize her reputation."

"I'm afraid you already have," the vicar answered.

Chapter 8

That got Nicholas's attention. "I beg your pardon?"

"You have jeopardized Christina's reputation, and if it weren't for the fact they all know Christina well and love her as their own kin, it wouldn't just be jeopardized—it would be ruined." Reverend Wakelin took a deep breath and continued. "She is a young, unmarried woman, and you, sir, do not have the best reputation. Now, I am not one to listen to or believe gossip, but there is so much scandal attached to your name that I fear it can't all be just speculation. My parishioners are afraid you might have the power to lead her astray."

At those accusing words, Nicholas stiffened. "While it is true I have done things for which I am extremely ashamed of, sir, I would never do anything to harm Miss Wakelin. She has been too kind in her efforts to help me. I would not see her name sullied." He swallowed, looking away from the vicar's piercing gaze.

"Then there's only one thing to do," the vicar stated.

Nicholas's head snapped back toward the tall man across from him. "You want me to marry her! That is what all this is leading to, is it not? You feel I have compromised her, so I need to offer to make it right!"

"I should say not!" the vicar all but shouted at him, causing Nicholas to sit back in surprise. "Christina is much too carefree to be thrust into the life of a countess. I would see her married to a nice farmer or small landholder, not to the aristocracy! She would never fit."

The reasonable part of Nicholas agreed with the vicar that, indeed, she would be better suited to a simpler life. But another part of the earl was captivated by the thought of Christina being his bride. She'd brought so many changes to his life in the short time since he'd found her in his tree. And with the changes had come laughter and brightness to his dark world. He'd come to rely on her goodness even though he pretended he didn't want it.

What would it be like to have Christina as a wife?

But as he turned his eyes back to the serious stare of the vicar, he knew marrying Christina would never be possible. They not only came from two different social classes, but she was much too naive and innocent; whereas he, sadly, was not.

"Of course, you are right. I apologize for jumping to such an erroneous conclusion," he answered.

The vicar smiled slightly as if he'd glimpsed what was going through

Nicholas's head. "No harm done. I was merely going to say she must continue to have Helen as a chaperone, and you must never be seen together in public."

"Of course," he agreed. "As for the latter, haven't you heard, Reverend? I never leave the estate."

The vicar nodded, but if Nicholas thought this was the end of their conversation, he was mistaken. "Now that we have the subject of my daughter out of the way, I would like to ask you something about yourself."

Nicholas sighed, leaning back in his chair and throwing up his arms in surrender. "Of course you may ask, though I'm sure there's little you and the rest of England do not already know."

"I want to know how long you intend to hang on to the guilt that has taken over your life."

A shadow fell over Nicholas's face. He did not like the personal turn this conversation had taken. "Guilt?"

"Your father was ill long before you returned from the war and broke your engagement, you know. Several times I visited and prayed with him when he'd had an episode with his heart."

"But it was my bad behavior that pushed him over the edge, Reverend. I know it was!" Nicholas said harshly, his fists clenched on the arms of the chair.

"Do you not think he knew what the war had done to you? He saw the pain you endured with your leg; he knew the images of battle haunted your every dream and thought. We spoke of it and prayed that God would see you through it," the vicar tried to explain, but Nicholas would not believe it.

"Yet all God did was take my father from me!" Nicholas growled, as he stood and limped to the window, which he now kept open because of Christina. He deliberately put extra pressure on his leg so he could feel the pain and be reminded of why he'd made the choices he had.

The vicar stood and turned to where the earl was. "It was your father's time to go, and he was ready for it. His dying wish was to see you happy once again, to have God heal all the bitterness war had put in your heart."

Nicholas turned to look at Reverend Wakelin, his face ravaged by pain. "How can God heal a heart that is no longer there?"

Reverend Wakelin gazed at Nicholas with compassion. "It is there, my lord; it's just that it has been broken. You must allow God to mend it back together. He loves you, you know. Even after all you've done, God still loves you."

A tiny spark of hope flickered in Nicholas's heart when he heard those words, yet he was afraid to believe them. "I will think on all you have told me, Reverend. Thank you for coming by," he said by way of a dismissal. He didn't want to be rude to Christina's father, but he needed to be alone.

The vicar seemed to understand. He nodded to Nicholas. "I bid you good day, my lord."

Nicholas must have stood looking out his window for an hour after the vicar left. And it might have been longer had he not heard a strange whimpering sound. At first he thought it might be his nephew, but as he listened closer, he realized it was the same strange sound he'd heard before. What in the world was it?

Nicholas moved down the hall, following the sound until he came to the closed door that led to the east wing. He stood close to the door and decided the sound was definitely coming from that particular wing.

Nicholas frowned. That wing hadn't been used since his mother died years before. Had a wild animal somehow gotten into the house?

He was just about to open the door to check it out when Pierce, still holding the baby, swaddled in a blanket, came seemingly out of nowhere. He acted quite nervous as he positioned himself between Nicholas and the door. "Ah, here you are, my lord. I've been looking for you."

Nicholas's black brow rose as he studied his butler curiously. "Well, you have found me. What was it you wanted?"

Pierce tugged at his collar. "Wanted? Yes. . .well, I. . .needed to tell you something!"

Nicholas sighed. "Of course. You want me to take Ty," he surmised as he held out his arms.

Pierce stepped away from him with a quick shake of his head. "Oh no! Master Ty is doing quite all right on my shoulder. We wouldn't want to wake him by moving him about." He gave the infant a gentle pat on his back.

Nicholas waited for more, but when Pierce merely stood there staring at him, he prompted, "If the baby wasn't the reason you wanted to see me, then what was?"

"Oh, of course, my lord! I was to tell you that Cook is preparing rabbit stew for tonight's meal."

Nicholas stared at his butler and wondered if poor old Pierce was working too hard lately. He knew good and well Nicholas couldn't care less about the menu.

Making a mental note to give the man more time off, Nicholas nodded slowly. "That's fine, Pierce. Now if you'll move, I will be able to open this door and enter the east wing."

Pierce didn't budge. "Oh, you don't want to venture into that wing, sir."

Nicholas was fast losing patience. "And why wouldn't I?"

"It's drafty, my lord. Very drafty."

"I think I can handle it, so please move."

"But, my lord. . ."

The butler's words faded as he realized Nicholas was going to get his way no matter what he said. With reluctance, he moved to the side.

As Nicholas opened the door, the musty smell of the unused rooms assaulted his senses. Just as Pierce had predicted, the hall was quite drafty.

The mewling animal sound grew louder. And did he hear the faint sound of voices? Odd.

"My lord, I beg you to rethink—" Pierce attempted one more time to stop him, but Nicholas interrupted.

"I don't know what you're trying to hide from me, Pierce, but I'm going to find out," he stated firmly as he started down the dim hallway.

He heard a nervous "Oh, dear" from his butler, but Nicholas didn't stop as he made his way closer to where the sound was coming from.

When he reached the old ballroom and stuck his head inside, he saw Christina and Helen sitting in the middle of the room, playing with a litter of puppies.

"What are you doing in here?" he asked, his voice sounding harsher than he had intended. But a part of him was irritated she hadn't told him about the puppies. Why did she feel she had to hide them from him? She had evidently even told his butler.

Both young women turned toward him, their eyes wide with surprise at having been caught.

Helen was the first to respond. "Ooh, I knew this would happen! Did I not tell you we would be caught, Christina?" She cast a frightened look toward Nicholas. "Please, have mercy on us, my lord. I pray you will not deal harshly because of our harboring these puppies in your ballroom!" She clasped her hands to her chest in a melodramatic fashion.

Nicholas stood nonplussed for a moment, staring at her as if she'd lost her mind. He turned his gaze to Christina, wondering if she suffered from the same hysterics as her friend.

Apparently not, because the woman was actually grinning at him.

"Please excuse Helen, Lord Kenswick. She's quite convinced, because you've fought two duels, that you are capable of any manner of dastardly behavior." She reached over to pat her friend on the arm. "She also reads the occasional gothic romance, and so her imagination tends toward the spectacular."

Nicholas walked toward the women, ignoring the way Helen shrank back as he drew closer. "And what do you think, Miss Wakelin? Did you think I might have the puppies tossed into the lake if you told me about them?"

Christina frowned at his words. "No," she answered slowly, as if choosing her words carefully. "I merely thought you would refuse to let me keep the puppies here at Kenswick Hall."

"When have I refused you anything that you were not able to contrive in the end?"

The frown disappeared, and her sunny smile was back in place, much to

Nicholas's pleasure. "Excellent point, my lord!" She held up a little black-and-white puppy for him to see. "Now that you know our little secret, why don't you take a look at our babies? Aren't they beautiful?"

Beautiful wasn't the word Nicholas would have used, but he didn't say so. The pups looked to be a mixture of collie and something unidentifiable. But judging by the large paws on the creatures, he had a feeling that the *something* was not a small breed.

He stooped down to where they sat, his gaze drawn to Christina. For one breathless moment, he stared at her, wondering what his life would be like if her father had demanded he marry her. Perhaps she would be able to help him as she wanted to do. Perhaps she could bring light into his dark world.

But then what would her life be like? Would she resent being forced to marry him? Would she become like he was—bitter, lost, even angry? Christina Wakelin did not deserve to be shackled to someone like him. She deserved so much better.

Deliberately he broke eye contact, and in the process his gaze lit on Helen. No longer was her expression fearful; instead, her eyes narrowed with speculation.

What did the little busybody see? Was his attraction for Christina obvious? Surely not. He was always careful to keep his face blank—a trick he'd found useful while leading his troops in the war. Whatever was going through her mind was just as Christina had suggested—the product of an overactive imagination.

"This room is too drafty for the puppies," he stated, seizing on the first thing that came to his mind. "Why don't we take them down to the stables? The hay will keep them nice and warm, and Miles, my head groomsman, can look after them when you are not here."

He saw the wondering look that passed between them as he picked up the box and led them out of the ballroom.

"I missed you at church, my lord," Christina said, her voice sounding nonchalant. "I had high hopes you would be able to see my father. Whenever he speaks of you, there is a fondness in his voice, you know."

Nicholas had trouble believing that statement. "No need to fear, Miss Wakelin. Your father saw fit to bring his 'fond' voice over to Kenswick Hall this afternoon and pay me a visit," he replied dryly, as he reached the door that led outside to the stables. "Would you be so kind as to open the door for me? I seem to have my hands full at the moment."

Christina stared blankly at him for a moment until Helen gave her a nudge. "What? Oh! Yes, let me get that," she mumbled, pushing at the heavy door.

But when they had stepped outside, she said, "I'm sorry, but did I just hear you say my father paid you a visit?"

Nicholas threw her a mocking glance. "Why do you act surprised? Did you not send him yourself?"

She shook her head. "I did ask him to come, but he would not give me an answer. I had no idea he would actually pay you a visit!"

Not quite knowing if he believed her or not, Nicholas stepped around her, resuming his trek to the stable. "Well, he did."

"But. . .wait!"

Nicholas glanced back to find Christina running to catch up to him. He also noticed Helen had not followed them inside the stable.

Recalling the vicar's words of warning, Nicholas said, "You better go back and fetch your friend. One of the promises your father extracted from me was that I would not be in your presence without a chaperone."

Christina stopped just short of running into him, causing them to be no more than a few inches apart.

"Oh no!" she cried, putting a hand to her cheek. "I wanted him to talk to you about God, but he came to warn you to stay away from me, didn't he?"

"Not exactly, but he was concerned for your reputation; and I fully agree, Miss Wakelin. I would not see your good name sullied because of me." He turned and set the box down in the first empty stall he came to.

She followed him. "If I am fodder for the town gossips, then it is no one's fault but my own. It is my choice to come here, and Papa should not have said anything to you. Please don't let yourself feel responsible for my reputation."

Nicholas stared down into her beautiful eyes and wondered about the emotion he saw in them. She looked at him as if she cared a great deal about him. But surely he was mistaken. She had said herself that she came to Kenswick Hall because she'd made it her mission to help him believe in God again. That was all he was to her—just a lost soul in need of guidance.

"What are you doing here, Christina?" he murmured, not realizing he'd used her Christian name. "Why aren't you being courted by some nice farmer who will give you a home and pretty babies of your own?"

She laughed lightly. "Now I know you've been talking to Papa! If he has said that once, he's said it a thousand times!"

Nicholas didn't laugh, nor did he smile. "He's right, you know. There is no reason why you should not leave this place and never return."

He'd hoped his words would drive her away for her own sake. But as usual, she appeared undaunted. "There is every reason, my lord. You need me here, and so does young Ty. For the first time in my life, I feel as though I'm doing something worthwhile, something greater than nursing sick animals or acting as hostess to my father's congregation."

Her words filled him with an emotion he was afraid to name. They were like a healing balm to his heart, yet still he felt so undeserving.

"Do you know that when he started speaking of your reputation, I thought he was here to demand satisfaction?" he asked.

Christina looked puzzled. "You mean a duel?"

He grinned, shaking his head. "No, I mean marriage."

"And you told this to my father?" she said, trying not to laugh.

Nicholas could see nothing funny about it. "Yes," he answered stiffly.

More laughter. "You must give us more credit than that, my lord," she replied.

"Miss Wakelin, I'm at a loss to see what's so funny about me believing your father was demanding that I do right by you. It is a natural summation!"

She managed to stop laughing, but she could not seem to stop grinning at him.

"You are a peer. I am a vicar's daughter. To suppose you would marry so far beneath you, no matter what the reason, would be quite foolish on my father's part," she said. Then, turning away from him, she walked out of the stable. "Fear not, my lord! Your bachelorhood is quite safe where I'm concerned," she called over her shoulder, the laughter still ringing in her voice.

In three long steps, Nicholas had her by the arm, pulling her around to face him. "Do you think I'm such a cad that I would not do right by a woman?"

She smiled up at him, and he wished he could understand the emotion behind her eyes. "Of course not. But I am aware of my place in society, as I am sure you are also."

An odd feeling rushed through Nicholas's mind and heart. It made him want to deny her words and rebel against a society that would make a beautiful girl like Christina think she could not win any man's heart, no matter what her station in life.

It was that feeling that compelled him to say, "If you are aware, Miss Wakelin, I am not exactly in society's favor. And, frankly, even if I were, I would not let them be a factor when I chose the woman I would marry."

"Then you have changed your mind about living the rest of your days in bitter solitude?" she asked.

It struck Nicholas that hiding himself away from society was no longer appealing. He no longer wanted to lick his wounds and live within the bitter darkness he'd enveloped himself in.

No. Not since Christina Wakelin, the vicar's daughter, had dared to climb his tree.

And had dared to tell him she could never be a suitable match for him.

"Perhaps I have changed my mind after all," he murmured with a secretive smile.

Chapter 9

W hat is wrong with the earl?" Helen asked for the fourth time as they strolled along the path that led into town.

Indeed, Christina concurred silently, *what is wrong with the earl?* To Helen, she merely feigned ignorance. "I don't know what you mean."

Helen threw her an incredulous look. "You must know what I'm talking about! For the last week, a transformation has occurred. He is no longer glaring at us or hiding in his study. He has actually been smiling, Christina, and has become a permanent fixture in whatever room we are in." She stepped in front of Christina and put her hands on Christina's arms. "You must see that this behavior is highly unusual and quite disturbing."

Christina sighed. "All right, I do admit he is acting rather strangely; but I wouldn't call it disturbing, nor do I mind the change. Perhaps he is beginning to heal from all that has happened to him. I believe having his nephew in his life has made him see that life is too important to hide from."

Helen shook her head, causing her ringlets to bob like dangled sausages about her head. "I do not believe it is his nephew that has wrought this change, Christina. I believe it is because of you."

Christina studied her friend's grave countenance. "Helen, I don't think. . ."

"I believe the earl has developed affections for you of a most romantic nature!" Helen blurted.

If only it were so, Christina thought. But she knew better. "Perhaps he's beginning to realize he cannot keep himself shut off from the world. I'm sure it is for his nephew's sake that he is coming about."

Helen started to argue the point, when the biggest gossip in Malbury, Mrs. Blaylock, caught sight of them as she stepped out of one of the little shops along the way. She was dressed in her usual colorful, flamboyant style, today wearing a taffeta dress of green and pink stripes. Upon her head she wore an elaborate turban of the same fabric with a bright peacock feather sprouting up in the front.

"Oh, dear," Christina whispered to Helen. "She's headed this way as if she's on a mission."

"Perhaps it's to tell us where in all of England you can actually purchase that particular green and pink striped fabric. Do you think she has it specially made?" Helen whispered back.

"Hmm," was all Christina could reply, for Mrs. Blaylock had already reached them.

"Why, good morning, Mrs. Blaylock! God has surely favored us with a beautiful sunny day, has He not?" Christina sang out with her usual cheery smile, as both she and Helen bobbed a quick curtsy.

"Indeed He has," Mrs. Blaylock returned, although her smile was more calculating than pleasant. "It has also been an informative one."

By the way the woman looked at her, Christina had a sinking feeling that her information had something to do with her going to Kenswick Hall every day. "Well, that's wonderful, Mrs. Blaylock. Now, if you'll excuse us, we really have to be—"

"Yes, indeed. When I saw his lordship, I couldn't understand what he was doing in town, but now that I've run into you, why it all makes perfect sense," she interrupted, her peacock feather bobbing up and down as she talked.

Christina was so shocked at hearing Lord Kenswick was strolling about Malbury that the insinuation flew right past her. "You're joking! Are you sure it was he?" she exclaimed.

"Come, come, Miss Wakelin. There's no need for pretense. We are friends and neighbors after all."

This time there was no misunderstanding.

And this woman was no friend.

"I can assure you, Mrs. Blaylock, I had no idea that Lord Kenswick would be in town, but I'll admit I am happily surprised. Since losing his father and brother, he has let sadness overwhelm him," she said coolly to the busybody. "So I'm sure you'll agree it is indeed a blessing from God to see his heartbreak mending enough for him to be able to face society once again."

Christina should have known her words would not deter her. "Or perhaps it is because you have spent so much time with him, that he is making a fast recovery."

"Indeed, I know that cannot be correct. I've spent time only with his nephew and rarely with Lord Kenswick."

"And then only with me as her chaperone!" Helen interjected in a surprising show of boldness. Usually her friend ran from confrontations.

Mrs. Blaylock, while not looking fully convinced, knew she would not get the information she wanted to hear. "It never entered my mind that you would have been without a chaperone," the gossiper said with mock innocence.

"We really should get that book your father wanted before the noon hour, Christina," Helen broke in, and Christina quickly seized the lifeline her friend had thrown her.

"You are right. Good day, madam. I trust we'll see you at church on Sunday?"

"As always," the woman replied as she swept past them, leaving a wake of oversweet perfume.

As they continued on into town, Helen voiced her concern. "I do not like this, Christina. She could hurt your reputation with her speculations about you and the earl!"

"Nonsense, Helen. Anything that woman says is of no consequence, and everyone in Malbury knows it." Christina didn't know what it mattered anyway. She had never had a single offer for her hand, and there seemed to be no prospects looming over the horizon. If she were doomed to be an old maid, she'd rather be an interesting one!

They spent about ten minutes in the bookstore and purchased the book her father had asked for. Just as they stepped out of the store, Jane Phillips and her mother joined them. While Jane was a sweet, friendly girl, her mother was quite the opposite, especially since her husband had been knighted. This elevated station, in Mrs. Phillips's mind, put them above their country neighbors, and she never let anyone forget about it.

They greeted Jane and Mrs. Phillips, and before they could say another word, Mrs. Phillips said, "I don't suppose you ladies have heard the news?"

"You'll never guess who has been seen riding through town!" Jane blurted.

"Don't gush, dear. It's so unbecoming," her mother scolded.

Jane, standing in front of her mother, rolled her eyes in exasperation, as Christina answered, "Yes, we have heard Lord Kenswick was seen about town this morning."

For a moment Mrs. Phillips just stared at Christina blankly. "My word, I did not know that particular bit of news. No, no, dear. Something much more exciting."

"It was the Duke of Northingshire. Oh, we saw his grand black coach with a stunningly painted ducal crest on either side. And most amazing of all was that it was seen going toward Kenswick Hall!"

"I hear his grace has beautiful estates in both England and Scotland," Helen commented, and Christina had no doubt it was true. Helen was so fascinated with the nobles that she hoarded every word printed or said about them. She probably knew more about these strangers than she did about the members of her own family!

"Of course he has extensive estates, my dear. He is one of the wealthiest dukes in all of England," Mrs. Phillips added, not to be outdone. She then turned her gaze to Christina. "I hear you have become acquainted with Lord Kenswick recently. Perhaps you might know the nature of His Grace's visit."

"I have only assisted with the earl's nephew and his nanny. I would not know anything about a visit from the Duke of Northingshire," Christina replied, silently adding, *and I bet Lord Kenswick doesn't know either!*

Mrs. Phillips smiled haughtily. "Of course you wouldn't know, dear. Though his standing with the ton is not on the best terms at the moment, he is, after all, still the Earl of Kenswick."

Christina exchanged a look with Jane, who mouthed the words "So sorry." She smiled at her friend and looked back at Mrs. Phillips. "On that, you are correct, madam." She held up the package she carried. "Now, if you'll excuse us, we must get this book to my father."

"Yes, and we must find out how long the duke will be in residence at Kenswick so we might issue an invitation to join us for a small dinner party." She smiled fondly at her daughter. "There is so little society here in Malbury and certainly no peers from whom Jane can choose a husband."

Embarrassment lit Jane's face as she said a quick good-bye and hurried her mother on into town.

Christina immediately turned to Helen. "The poor earl! He has no idea the Duke of Northingshire is coming to visit!"

"Never mind that," Helen interjected. "I still cannot get over the fact the duke is here in our little town. Oh, Christina, I have heard he is the most handsome man in all of England! Everyone has been speculating all year that he'll choose a bride soon."

"Helen! We have a much bigger problem!" Christina said. She didn't know of the duke's relationship with Lord Kenswick, but if it were a bad one, she didn't want his visit to undo everything she had managed to accomplish.

Helen's eyes lit up. "Perhaps we should go to Kenswick Hall now. Oh, Christina, to think of being in the same room with such an exciting man just makes my heart all aflutter," she gushed, clutching her hands to her heart.

Christina laughed. "Come, come, Helen. We are talking about a duke who probably thinks too much of himself and wouldn't even notice us if we stood right in front of him. All noblemen are very much alike in that respect."

"Lord Kenswick has surely noticed you, Christina. I will admit he was a little scary at first, but he has proven to be quite the amusing gentleman in the last week."

Christina relented. "Well, perhaps some of them are stuffed shirts," she said with a giggle. "But nearly all the rest are!"

Helen sighed. "And perhaps the Duke of Northingshire is one of the exceptions to the rule as Lord Kenswick is."

It would seem there would be no talking her out of it. Helen was bound and determined to admire the duke, just as she had been bound and determined to like Nicholas Thornton, the Earl of Kenswick. Perhaps a little visit to the hall to make sure all was right would have a double benefit—she could find out if the duke's visit had upset Lord Kenswick, and Helen could see for herself what kind of man the duke was, thus curing all attractions.

"Why don't we stop by Kenswick Hall and find out for ourselves?" she told her friend, making up her mind it was the right thing to do.

Helen squealed with delight. "Oh, I am so excited I feel I might burst with happiness!"

"Just make sure you do your bursting *after* we depart, Helen. I would not have you embarrass yourself in front of the duke," Christina teased.

⌘

"The Duke of Northingshire is here to see you, my lord," Pierce announced from the study doorway. So rattled by the news was Nicholas that he unconsciously crumpled the paper he'd been making sketches on for his next carving.

When he didn't answer, Pierce cleared his throat and offered, "Would you like me to make excuses, my lord?"

"No!" Nicholas burst out without thinking. But as he said it, he knew that he meant it. North, as he called him, had been his best friend since their days at Eton. Months ago, in his bitterness, he shunned his friend's offer to help and, in doing so, thought he'd severed their bond.

Could this mean North had forgiven him?

"Send him in here, Pierce." And then as an afterthought, he said, "Please have a pot of tea brought in also."

Pierce bowed. "Very good, sir."

A minute later, Trevor Kent, the Duke of Northingshire, stepped into the room. North had such a commanding presence about him that even when he walked into a crowded room, a hush would fall and all eyes would turn to him. He was quite a favorite with the ladies, Nicholas knew. With his light blond hair and strong features, he'd heard him likened to Michelangelo's *David*.

Nicholas, however, knew him to be the faithful friend he'd turned his back on when he'd only been trying to help. They'd always been honest with one another, but when North had advised him against breaking his engagement and to curb his wild ways, Nicholas had blown up at him. He told North to stay out of his business and his life, that he didn't need his friendship any longer.

What a fool he'd been. He was so eaten up with self-hatred and bitterness that he'd allowed himself to lose his best friend.

Nicholas stood slowly. Swallowing nervously, not knowing what to say, he finally spoke formally. "It is good to see you, Your Grace."

North grinned. "Well, I must say you are looking better than I imagined. From the accounts of my servants, you've been moping around this empty monstrosity of a house feeling quite sorry for yourself." He drew his gaze to Nicholas's well-cut coat and neatly tied cravat. "I rather expected to see you dressed in sackcloth and ashes, instead of a suit of fine clothes."

All the tension drained out of Nicholas as he smiled and came around his desk to greet his friend. "If you had come a month ago, that is exactly what you would have found." The men clasped hands in a firm, hearty shake. "But I am glad you have come, old friend. I was afraid I had lost your friendship forever."

With his other hand, North gripped his shoulder. "I'll admit to being a little angry at you, but when I had time to think on all you'd been through, I knew you just needed time." He stepped back and looked down at Nicholas's leg. "How's that wound healing, by the way? I'm amazed that you walk with barely a limp, considering the doctors had wanted to cut it off!"

Nicholas smoothed a hand down his thigh where the war wound still gave him trouble. "It is better at some times than others," he explained. "But like all the unpleasant events that have happened to me over the last year and a half, I'm learning to live with it."

Moving to the side, he gestured to a couple of chairs in the room. "Please, have a seat. Our tea should arrive in a moment."

North lifted a brow. "Tea? I must say, it's good to see you are not still drinking yourself silly."

Nicholas grimaced. "I gave that up months ago when I moved into Kenswick. Even in my bitter state, I could see that drinking was only making it worse. So I had decided to shut myself away from the world and wallow in my guilt and grief until. . ." He let his voice drift off.

But North wasn't about to let it go. "Until. . . ?"

"Well, until my nephew was given to my care."

"Ah!" North sat back in the cushioned chair, folding his arms on his chest. "So the Wild Rogue of London has finally been tamed by domesticity! I would have thought you'd have shipped the little fellow off to a relative or something. Certainly not try to raise him yourself."

"Well, that is exactly what I wanted to do, except my only living relative, Aunt Wilhelmina, is abroad at the moment. I had no choice but to hire a nan—" He stopped when he saw the grin that creased the big man's face. "Of course. I had forgotten you had something to do with it."

"Mrs. Sanborne was the nanny for my elder sister's children until they were old enough for a governess and tutor," he explained with a shrug. "I had asked several people about Malbury to keep me informed if you needed anything. When I heard a Miss Wakelin was scouring the shire looking for a nanny, I immediately sent Mrs. Sanborne to her."

Nicholas shook his head in amazement. "You mean you've been looking out for me, even after all I said to you?"

North sat up in his chair, his light blue eyes very serious. "You are my friend, Nicholas. Nothing, not even a few ill-spoken words, will change that."

Swallowing the lump in his throat, Nicholas could only stammer, "I. . . thank you."

North sat back again, his eyes twinkling with mischief. "It's been awhile, old friend, but I can still read you like a book. When you stumbled on your words earlier, you were not going to say your nephew, were you?" He shook a finger at him. "If I didn't know better, I'd say you were about to mention a woman's name."

"And you are grasping at straws!"

"Oh no." North studied his friend's face thoroughly, giving Nicholas the feeling he could read his mind. "There is something about you that's different, and it could only be two things—either religion or a woman."

Nicholas threw back his head and laughed, just as a maid entered with the tea and proceeded to pour them each a cup. He waited until she left the room before he responded. "In my case, those two things go hand in hand." When North gave him a questioning look, he took a sip of his hot tea and said, "She's the vicar's daughter."

Chapter 10

T he what?" he sputtered. Nicholas thought for a moment North was going to choke on his tea.

Suddenly the earl was no longer hesitant of telling his friend about Christina. He needed to talk to somebody about it. "Miss Wakelin, the lady to whom you sent Mrs. Sanborne, is the true reason I have begun living life once again."

North patted his mouth with his napkin. "Nicholas, there was a time when you would not even look a young lady's way unless she was no less than the daughter of a viscount!" He paused a moment, as if measuring his next words. "That is the main reason you became engaged to Katherine."

Nicholas nodded. "I know, but I think differently now. *She* has changed me." He stood and started pacing about the room as he searched for the words to explain. "She is different from any other woman I have ever known. She is funny and kind, yet determined. She doesn't simper and talk about silly things like so many other ladies, and she speaks without guile, in a straightforward manner that I find refreshing." He threw up his hands. "She has won over the whole staff here at Kenswick Hall and practically has them eating out of her hand, yet she isn't manipulative, she's just. . .herself," he said, unable to find the appropriate words.

"This is unbelievable," North said, and Nicholas whirled around, ready to do battle over those words. But when he saw the look of amused yet puzzled incredulity on his friend's face, he came over and sat back down.

"Why is it so hard to believe?" he asked calmly as he picked up his cup again.

"You are in love with her!"

Nicholas balked at the use of the *L* word. "I never said that."

North shook his head. "You didn't have to. It was in your face, your words as you spoke of her." He paused for a moment, his gaze intently on Nicholas. "Love is so rare, Nick, that when you find it, you have to acknowledge it."

Nicholas let North's words penetrate his heart. Did he love Christina? He was certainly fond of her, so much so he seemed to crave her company all the time. But still, with all that had happened to him, he needed to sort through his feelings before he could make such an acknowledgment to himself.

"I know you are right. I just don't want to make any more mistakes," he said after a moment.

An understanding smile curved North's lips. "Indeed, I do understand." He set down his cup and smacked the armrests with his palms. "Now when do I get to meet this paragon?"

Nicholas smiled, stood up, and walked to the window. Peering out to the garden, he motioned for North to join him. "I thought she might be here. There she is."

North joined Nicholas in looking out to where Christina and Helen stood with Mrs. Sanborne. Ty was in Christina's arms, and she was smiling down at him as she lightly swung him back and forth.

"She's lovely," North whispered almost reverently as his gaze took in the sight before him. "Look at all that glorious red hair. What a splash she'd make amongst the ton."

Nicholas shuddered at the thought. "And subject her innocence to the immoral behavior of the upper classes? Never." He stared at her a moment more before looking over at North. "We are from two different worlds, North. I'm not sure either of us would fit into the other's world, even if we wanted to."

"You can do almost anything if you want something badly enough."

"But at what expense?" Nicholas murmured more to himself than to his friend.

"I want to meet her!" North declared, as he turned from the window and started across the study. When he got to the door, he looked imperially at Nicholas. "Well? Are you coming or not?"

Nicholas laughed. "Only if you'll remember I saw her first. Absolutely no flirting!"

North shrugged in an arrogant manner. "Women have always seemed to like me, Nick. There's never been a need to flirt."

"I'm surprised they could fit in the same room with you, with such an inflated ego filling the space!" Nicholas retorted as he slapped him on the shoulders and led the way to the garden.

⟡

"Oh, dear. Oh, dear! They're coming, Christina; they're coming!" Helen smoothed her light blue dress and patted her fat curls. "How do I look? Am I presentable?"

Christina looked at her beautiful friend and knew Helen was much more presentable than she. Already her hair had come loose from the topknot she'd pinned it into this morning, and now it was flying wildly about her face and past her shoulders. Ty had spit up on her dress, and it was wrinkled from holding him.

In short, she was embarrassed at being introduced to a duke looking as she did, but there was nothing for it.

Throwing her misgivings to the wind, she smiled and waved to the men as they came near.

"My lord! You're just in time for our daily walk through the garden," she called out as she placed Ty into his pram.

"Excellent," he called back in reply. After a few moments, they had reached the women.

"Miss Wakelin, Miss Nichols, may I present an old friend of mine, Trevor Kent, the Duke of Northingshire. Mrs. Sanborne, I believe you are already acquainted?"

"Your Grace," the women said in unison as they curtsied.

"It is a stupendous pleasure to see you once again, Your Grace," Mrs. Sanborne added. "Stupendous!"

Christina noticed the handsome duke took great care not to smile as he nodded in her direction. "Indeed, it is my pleasure, Mrs. Sanborne, that you were able to help Lord Kenswick with his nephew."

A few other pleasantries were said before the nanny took control of the pram and went ahead of them on the path.

Nicholas held out his arm to Christina. "Shall we?"

Christina told herself her heart should not be racing madly just because he asked to walk with her. But it did no good. With her heart pounding, she took his arm.

Beside them, she noticed the Duke of Northingshire, or North, as he asked them to call him, had offered the same to Helen.

For one horrific moment, Helen became so pale Christina thought she might faint dead away, right there on the garden path. But her fanciful friend recovered, and a big smile curved her lips as she slipped her hand through the duke's arm.

They had walked a short distance when North remarked, "I have heard it is you I should thank, Miss Wakelin, for this remarkable turnaround in my friend here. I had despaired that he might be lost to us forever."

Christina glanced surprisingly up at Lord Kenswick. Her heart tripped a beat when he smiled down at her. Swallowing hard, she pulled her eyes away from his and looked at the duke. "I would not say that, Your Grace. It is God who led me to his lordship. I just had to let him know he is much too important to God and his friends to shut himself away from everyone."

North smiled but looked puzzled. "If Nick had shut himself away from everyone, how did you meet?"

Wincing a little with embarrassment, Christina opened her mouth to explain, but the earl interjected. "She climbed my tree, then fell out of it and straight into my arms. My life has not been the same since."

Christina stared at Lord Kenswick with amazement. He made the whole encounter seem so. . .*romantic*!

"Surely you jest! I cannot imagine this proper young woman climbing a tree!" North laughed.

"Oh, she climbed it all right. I was there every horrifying moment of it!"

Helen exclaimed. "I tried to talk her out of it, but when Christina gets something in her mind, there is no stopping her."

North laughed again. "A woman with determination! I like that."

Helen quickly changed her tune. "Of course, I would have climbed the tree with her, but I thought someone needed to stand by as a lookout in case the earl came by."

Christina smothered a giggle at Helen's obvious tactics.

"You know, Helen, I didn't know you had been there with Christina. I saw no one until I heard the cry of my poor cat up in the tree."

"When she spotted you coming near us, I told her to leave so that she would not get into trouble also," Christina explained. "She argued, but I insisted!"

They had almost circled the perimeter of the garden, when Lord Kenswick bent down to her ear. "I have something I would like to give you."

His breath at her ear warmed her as she turned to look at him. So close was he that she could see tiny gold flecks in his eyes that she had never noticed before. Staring into those eyes made her feel strange yet wonderful at the same time.

"What is it?" she asked, loving the fact he still had not pulled back from her.

His intense gaze swept her face like a loving caress. "If you can try to get away from the others in an hour from now, I will meet you under the gazebo just on the outskirts of the garden, over there." He nodded toward the ornate white structure standing a few yards from them.

She wanted to say yes, but it did not seem proper. "I don't think. . ."

Nicholas cut her off. "I promise it will only be for a few moments. I have nothing improper in mind. Your reputation will remain safe."

Her heart won out over her head. "All right," she answered.

He covered her hand with his free hand before letting her go. "It's been a pleasure to walk with you this afternoon, ladies. I hate to end our time together, but I must see that North is settled into a suite."

Helen reluctantly let go of North's arm after Christina gave her a pointed look.

"How long will you be at Kenswick Hall, Your Grace?" Helen blurted out.

North seemed unruffled by her too-eager tone. "Only for a few days, I'm afraid. I have business to take care of at my estate near Edinburgh."

When Christina thought her friend might burst into tears at that news, she quickly stepped in front of her to cut off the duke's view. "Well, it's been nice making your acquaintance, Your Grace. I'm sure we'll see you on the morrow."

From the twinkle in the large man's eyes, Christina knew she hadn't fooled him. "Indeed, I shall look forward to it. Good afternoon."

After an hour had passed, Christina convinced Helen to check on the puppies in the stables so she could run over to the gazebo.

Lord Kenswick was already there, standing so tall and handsome as the rays of the sinking sun shone through the latticework and touched his manly features. Taking a deep breath, she stepped into the gazebo, not daring to come too close to him.

Neither of them spoke. Words didn't seem to be required as they stood staring into each other's eyes.

Slowly he brought his hand from behind his back, and within it he held an exquisite glass case about six inches tall. She took the case and brought it closer to peer inside.

And what she saw took her breath away—a carved figurine of a woman holding a puppy in her arms.

The woman was Christina. Every detail of her face, hair, and dress was so true to life.

"Do you like it?" Nicholas asked.

Looking up at him, she could tell he was nervous about giving it to her, unsure of how she would feel.

Without thinking about it, Christina reached up and kissed him on his rough cheek. "It so beautiful, my lord. I cannot express what it means that you have made this for me."

Nicholas took her arms in a soft, caressing grip. Emotions she couldn't understand flashed over his handsome face, and she wondered if he might kiss her.

Oh, she hoped he would. She wished he would take her into his strong arms and tell her he was falling in love with her, just as she was falling for him.

Suddenly he let his hands drop and stepped back from her. Confused, Christina looked searchingly at him, but it was impossible to read his thoughts, for his face was turned away.

"Perhaps you should go before Helen wonders where you are," he told her, his voice gravelly.

Christina wanted to cry. She must have done something wrong. Of course! He must have thought it untoward for her to kiss him like that. Sickened that she'd shamed herself, she mumbled, "Yes, I should go." Clutching the glass case protectively to her, she ran from the gazebo.

⚓

Nicholas banged his hand on the post of the gazebo in frustration and anger. He'd promised not only Christina but also her father that he would not act improperly.

But there he was, all set to take her into his arms and kiss her.

Filled with self-loathing and disgust, he railed at himself for bringing her out to the garden alone. He should have just wrapped the gift up as a parcel and had it delivered to her house.

But he'd been so excited about seeing her face when she realized the figurine was of her. He'd even gone into town just to purchase the case, causing a lot of gossip and speculation in the process, he was sure.

He should have done better. He should not have compromised her honor by getting her alone.

She deserved a gentleman who did not make such foolish mistakes. She deserved someone who did not have an ugly past. She deserved a man of impeccable reputation.

In short, she did not deserve him.

Yet, she had faith in him.

Christina told him God also believed in him and could help him.

So for the first time since he was a young boy, Nicholas Thornton, the sixth Earl of Kenswick, the most notorious rake in all of England, knelt down on the whitewashed boards of the gazebo. . .and prayed.

Chapter 11

The next morning was bright and sunny. Almost everyone in Malbury seemed to be outdoors—walking their dogs, playing with their children, or just strolling about for exercise.

It was a day that should have brightened everyone's mood. But as Christina stared glumly out her window, she could not drum up so much as a smile, her spirits were so low.

She'd already made the decision to stay home today and not go on her daily visit to Kenswick Hall. How could she face him after behaving so boldly? What must he think of her?

She took her eyes from the window and looked down at the figurine in her hand. As her fingers caressed the smoothly carved wood, she marveled again at how much care had gone into the figurine.

Why did he make it? Did she mean something to him? Did he think of her as a cousin or friend?

With a sigh of frustration, she went over to her nightstand and put the figurine back into its glass container. Spending all her time having romantic thoughts about the Earl of Kenswick was not doing her any good.

"Miss Christina!" Mrs. Hopkins called through her door, knocking gently. Glad to have a diversion from her troubles, she called for the housekeeper to come in.

Excitement flushed her plump cheeks, and her hands fluttered around nervously. "Oh, miss! I've never seen the like. Gentlemen such as these, and coming here to your father's cottage!"

Christina went quickly to her. "Take a calming breath, Mrs. Hopkins. I'm afraid I do not follow. What gentlemen are here?"

"I saw Lord Kenswick and another gentleman coming up the drive. A tall man with fancy clothes and almost as handsome as the earl himself. They are something to behold, I'm telling you, miss. Quite takes the breath clear out of me!"

Christina was having trouble breathing herself at the news. "Lord Kenswick? Here?" When Mrs. Hopkins nodded, Christina let go of her hands and whirled to face her large oval mirror. "He must have the Duke of Northingshire with him!"

"A duke, did you say?" the housekeeper gasped. "Oh, dear, and with no warning, too! I still haven't done the dusting!"

Christina tried to tidy her hair, but the curls kept springing out everywhere. Giving up, she grabbed a ribbon and tied it back. "It's all right, Mrs. Hopkins. I'm sure they won't notice," she said, though her thoughts were on other things than the dusting.

What did he want? Was he here to see her?

"Mrs. Hopkins, I believe there's someone at the door!" her father's voice called from downstairs, startling both women.

"Oh, dear! Oh, my! I hope I can remember the proper etiquette for handling one of the ton!" The elder woman fretted as she scurried to the door.

Christina turned back to the mirror and wished, as she had a thousand times before, that she was more sophisticated in appearance, more dainty and elegant. Her gown was a recent style, but with her height and lack of grace, she would never be mistaken for a peer.

Wishing, however, would get her nowhere. She was who she was, and no amount of wishing would make her something she was not. And, besides, she'd always liked who she was. Why should she suddenly want to change everything about herself just because she'd become acquainted with a nobleman?

Maybe because you want him to like you, a voice whispered in her head.

Angry with herself for having such vain thoughts, she turned away from the mirror and waited by her door to see if the earl had, indeed, come to see her.

⁂

"Tell me again why we have come to the vicar's house," North whispered to Nicholas as they sat in the parlor where the housekeeper had sent them. It had been quite an amusing welcome; the woman greeted them both with such a deep curtsy that the men thought they were going to have to help her up.

"Because I want to ask Reverend Wakelin's permission to see his daughter today."

"Hmm," North grunted with a puzzled frown. "And why could you not just wait until she came to Kenswick Hall? Doesn't she visit your nephew every day?"

"Because I felt I needed to make an apology to both Miss Wakelin and her father for my bad behavior yesterday," he explained evenly while keeping an eye on the door, waiting for the vicar to come into the room.

"I'm sorry, but I don't follow," his friend replied.

Nicholas let out a nervous breath. "I asked Miss Wakelin to meet me in the gazebo alone so I might give her a gift." He ran a hand through his hair. "I almost kissed her!" he blurted out in a harsh whisper.

North stared at him as if he were speaking a language he could not understand. "I beg your pardon. You *almost* kissed her? That's what this whole thing is about?"

"Yes."

"Did she protest?"

"No."

"Slap you?"

"Of course not."

"Call you a cad and a rake?"

"Don't be ridiculous."

North scratched his head. "Did she act as though she wanted to kiss you, then?"

"I thought she did, because she kissed me on my cheek, which compelled me to take her arms and bring her closer. That she was only thanking me for the gift I gave her. I realized in the nick of time."

"Sooo, let me understand this," North stated slowly. "You are upset because Miss Wakelin kissed you, and you thought it an invitation to take it a step further and kiss her back. Do I have that right?"

Nicholas threw up his hands. "Yes, except I had promised her father I would stay away from her. Instead, I encouraged her to meet me without her chaperone and all but embraced her! I also promised her that if she'd meet me I would do nothing improper."

North shook his head. "Really, man, you're being too hard on yourself. What is a kiss after all? I daresay it wouldn't be the first lips you've kissed."

"You are thinking about London society, where flirtations are a way of life. This is the country, where even a kiss could cause a scandal."

North was about to comment when they heard the door to the parlor open, and in walked the Reverend Wakelin. "Well, Lord Kenswick, so good to see you again. And I see you've brought a friend."

Nicholas made a quick introduction of North and got right to the matter at hand. "Reverend, I came today because—"

"Because you have decided to join us tomorrow for Sunday service! How lovely of you to come by and let us know," Christina said as she breezed through the doorway, putting herself between the vicar and Nicholas.

Nicholas stared at her with surprise, not understanding the warning look she flashed him with her bright eyes. "Uh. . .I'm not sure. . . ," he stammered.

Christina was mouthing something, but he couldn't quite make it out.

She turned to North with a big smile and said, "And you, Lord Kent, will you be joining us also?"

Nicholas should have known North would find the whole conversation amusing. His friend smiled back at her. "I wouldn't miss it for the world, Miss Wakelin."

"Excellent!" she cried as she whirled around to face her father.

"If you don't mind, Papa, I will walk with the gentlemen back to Kenswick Hall. I need to check on little Ty, as well as feed the pups Lord Kenswick has been boarding for me in his stables."

Nicholas watched as her father gave her a shrewd look that told everyone he wasn't fooled by her act for a moment. His eyes swept past his daughter to give Nicholas a questioning stare.

"We would be happy to escort your daughter, sir," Nicholas told him.

The vicar nodded but glanced back at Christina. "I don't know what you are up to, daughter, but be assured I will find out." He sighed and patted her on the cheek. "And please try to be on your best behavior. I would have Lord Kenswick believe you have matured since the time you were a little girl and pushed his female friend into the lake!"

"Papa!" Christina gasped with embarrassment, as both Nicholas and the duke burst out in laughter.

"Good day, my lord, Your Grace," he told them both with a nod before he exited the room.

On the walk to Kenswick Hall, Nicholas stopped her and demanded, "Can you tell me what that was all about?"

Christina looked up at him. "I heard you!"

"You heard what?"

"I heard you two talking about what you were planning to do! My room is directly above the parlor, and the sound carries." She shook her head. "I can't believe you were going to tell my father about our meeting in the gazebo and about the kiss I gave you!"

"Miss Wakelin, I was just going to apologize for my own bad behavior," Nicholas tried to explain.

"I was the one who kissed you, my lord. I could not sleep all night for wondering what you must think of me."

Nicholas couldn't believe what he was hearing. "Miss Wakelin, you are not to blame, and I was flattered by your kiss. It's just that I promised your father I would not be alone with you. I felt ashamed that I'd gone back on my promise and then almost kissed you."

Christina frowned. "There, you see, it is all my fault. My kiss caused you to get carried away on the wings of romantic emotions."

Nicholas stared at her blankly. "On the wings of what?"

She sighed with forbearance as if she were dealing with a child. "On the wings of romantic emotion. Helen told me that in her gothic romance books, this often happens to men when a woman gets too close."

A loud blast of laughter startled them both. They turned to see North shaking his head as he tried to curb his mirth. "I'm sorry, but you two are more entertaining than the comedy I saw last month in a London theatre."

Christina covered her mouth in horror. "Oh, dear. I forgot you were there, Your Grace."

This time it was Nicholas who laughed, especially at the bemused expression on North's face. "I daresay he hasn't heard that many times in his life."

North grinned. "Indeed. I believe I've changed my mind about going back to the hall and favor a walk in the country instead. Miss Wakelin, would you please excuse me if I cannot help Nick escort you the rest of the way?"

She smiled back at him. "Of course."

North had the audacity to wink at them both before walking away. Subtlety was not one of his virtues.

Taking Christina by the arm, Nicholas turned her toward him. "Miss Wakelin, before we come to Kenswick, I want to be sure everything is all right between us—that you are not upset at me."

Her smile was so breathtaking that he wished he could kiss her. Perhaps Helen's books were not too far from the truth where "romantic emotions" were concerned. But a kiss was not the most important thing he desired. No, he wanted to put his arms around her and just hold her—to claim to the world that she was his.

He wanted her to return those romantic feelings.

She liked him; he could tell. But he could not tell if that liking ended at friendship or not. Perhaps she was after her first objective where he was concerned, to help him find God again.

If he told her he had begun to pray again, would she feel her duty was done and stop coming to his home?

He wasn't going to take that chance. Not yet.

"Of course I am not upset! The figurine you made me was the most beautiful gift anyone has ever given me. I shall treasure it always. But you must forgive me for being so bold, my lord. I reacted before I thought about it."

Her words filled him with hope. "If you were not so bold, you would not be the Christina Wakelin I have come to know since childhood. You are the most unique woman I have ever met, and you constantly keep me on my toes!"

"I can't tell if that was a complaint or a compliment," Christina said.

He laughed. "Most definitely a compliment."

Nicholas held out his arm. "Now that we've cleared the air, shall we continue on to Kenswick Hall?"

She placed her hand in the crook of his arm, and it felt so right to be by his side—like she truly belonged there.

As they walked, Nicholas dared to ask one more thing. "Do you suppose now that we've become such good friends you can call me Nicholas?"

"Thank you!" she cried out with relief. "We have so few neighbors with titles that it has been hard to remember to refer to you as 'my lord.' "

"I've been acknowledged by some sort of title or other since birth. I suppose I don't even notice it."

"I think it would be very hard to get used to, all that bowing and scraping people do just because of some exalted title you had nothing to do with!"

An enigmatic smile crept over his face. "I think you could get used to almost anything, Christina. Even an exalted title."

She shrugged. "There's no point in arguing, since I shall never be in such a position anyway."

Never say never, dear Christina, Nicholas thought to himself, determination strengthening his resolve to be the kind of man she could love.

Never say never.

Chapter 12

I'm in love; I just know it. I've got this nervous feeling in my chest, and I feel quite dizzy when I look at him, so it must be love."

"Either that or you're coming down with a bad cold," Christina said to Helen in a wry voice. She really wished the duke would leave Kenswick so her friend would cease making a fool of herself over the man.

"No, no. I'm quite sure of my feeling." Helen continued with firm resolve. "We shall have a large wedding, since he is quite known in England, and a long wedding trip to Paris, Rome, and possibly Milan."

Christina rolled her eyes in exasperation. "Dear Helen, it is good to dream big dreams, as long as you can separate fancy from truth." She gave her friend a gentle look. "You know as well as I the Duke of Northingshire must marry within his social class. It would never be accepted by his family if he decided to marry a commoner."

Helen sighed. "Yes, but miracles have been known to happen. Just look at you and Lord Kenswick."

Christina frowned. "For the last time, Helen, Nicholas and I are just friends. Anything more is impossible!"

Helen leveled a gaze at Christina. "I know when a man's smitten with a woman, and Nicholas Thornton is that man! Lord Kent does not yet display his feelings when he looks at me, but given a little time, I'm sure he'll come around."

Poor North had been wearing more the look of a hunted man these last three days. More often than not, when he walked into a room and saw Helen there, he quickly walked right back out.

Christina had tried to warn Helen that ladies do not pursue gentlemen so blatantly, but she merely replied that she was going to be twenty-two in a month and was not getting any younger.

Christina could have told Helen that Archie McGregor, a young Scot who'd just inherited a farm in Malbury, had tried in vain to speak with her several times in church lately. But Christina doubted Helen would even hear her.

Soon North would leave, and Helen would be able to come to her senses again.

Christina stood up from the bench they were sitting on, located within the church courtyard, and tightened the ties to her bonnet. It was Sunday, and the two had been enjoying the sunlight while they waited for the service to start.

"Well, I suppose we must go inside," she told Helen with a sigh. She tried to sound more cheerful, but it was difficult.

Nicholas had not come.

Knowing her thoughts, Helen stood and linked her arm with Christina's. "I'm sure he's just delayed."

Christina nodded. "I'm sure you're right. Yet I can't help feeling I bullied him into this."

"Well, come along. Waiting out here is just making you worry."

The choir had begun to sing the first few measures of a hymn, when a low hum of whispers started at the back and quickly filtered its way forward in the church. The more indiscreet of the parishioners craned their necks to see who had come through the door, while others made a subtle show of taking peeks behind their fans.

Christina, however, had no need to look back, for she knew exactly who it was.

The Earl of Kenswick had come to church.

From her pew, Christina had an excellent view of the two gentlemen, but her eyes studied only one of them. He was so handsome in his black coat and gray britches. He'd even trimmed his hair. He looked every bit the nobleman he was, and it was a heavy reminder that his station was so far above her own. All her feelings for him were going to cause her nothing but pain. They were from two completely different worlds.

Why couldn't she remember that?

"Oh, here they come!" Helen whispered excitedly as they stood outside the church after the service ended.

All the love she felt in her heart came bubbling to the forefront the moment she, too, spotted the men coming their direction.

Nicholas gave Christina a teasing grin. "Were you worried I wouldn't show?"

She suppressed a smile and gave him a mock glare. "Were you late just to make me worried?"

North threw back his head with a booming laugh that drew everyone's attention. "I really like this girl, Nick," he declared as he slapped his friend on the back. Then to Christina, he said, "It's too bad you were never presented at court. With your wit and spunk, you'd be declared an original!"

Nicholas shook his head, laughing. "It would never work. In town there are too few trees to climb and animals to doctor. Christina would be like a fish out of water.

"Well, ladies, we'll bid you a good day," he told them after his laughter subsided. "But before we go, I would like to invite you to tea, along with Mrs. Sanborne and Ty, of course, this afternoon."

Annoyed that he thought her so unsophisticated, it was on the tip of

Christina's tongue to refuse when Helen broke in with "We'll be there!"

"Splendid!" Nicholas declared, while giving Christina a curious look.

After the men walked away, Christina noticed that almost the entire congregation was still standing in the church courtyard, staring at her with speculation.

Straightening her backbone, she forced herself to smile and mingle among the crowd, speaking pointedly to each one, inquiring about children and health and anything her mind could think of. If she pretended all was normal, then perhaps they'd believe it.

But everything wasn't normal. She was in love with a man who was far beyond her reach. That fact was made even more clear that afternoon when she and Helen went for tea at Kenswick Hall.

❧

Christina held Ty on her lap, and Mrs. Sanborne was making everyone laugh with a story of how the baby had rolled off his mat and under the decorative skirt of his baby bed. She'd ransacked the room in a panic before he came rolling right back out.

Christina was looking down at the baby with a smile, when the laughter came to a strange, abrupt halt. She looked up to find out the reason for the sudden silence and noticed every eye was turned toward the parlor door.

"Well, nephew, have you lost all your manners, or will you give your aunt a proper greeting?"

Christina's eyes flew to the door, where she found a short, trim woman, her nose and chin thrust upward. As her cold blue eyes scanned the room, they soon came to rest on Christina.

A look of horror crossed her aging features as she fastened her dagger gaze back on Nicholas.

Nicholas, as well as North, had stood up the moment she spoke, and both men bowed in her direction. "Aunt Willie. So good of you to visit. I had heard you were abroad," Nicholas greeted smoothly, his face unreadable.

His aunt's chin rose even higher as she frowned and made a sniffing noise. "Do not call me that atrocious name! Now, I would like to know if the baby being held by that unfamiliar young woman over there is my great-nephew."

Nicholas glanced at Christina and then turned back to his aunt. "Yes, it is. Now let me make introductions," he began, as he motioned toward the duke first. "You know North, of course."

"Of course," she answered with an imperial nod. "I've known His Grace's family for many years."

"Always a pleasure, my lady," North greeted with another bow.

He motioned to Mrs. Sanborne. "This is my nephew's nanny, Mrs. Sanborne." He turned to his employee. "Mrs. Sanborne, this is my aunt, Lady Wilhelmina Stanhope."

Christina watched as the nanny rose to greet the lady but was cut short when the haughty woman didn't even acknowledge her presence. Instead she glared at Christina and Helen.

"And who are they?" she demanded.

"These dear ladies have been a great help to me since my nephew came to Kenswick. May I present Miss Christina Wakelin and Miss Helen Nichols," Nicholas replied, his voice filled with warmth as he spoke.

Lady Wilhelmina's sharp gaze focused on Christina. "Wakelin? Where do I know that name from? Who is her father?"

Christina answered before Nicholas could. "My father is Reverend Wakelin, the vicar of Malbury."

"I see," the woman said, her tone suggesting the information was of no importance. "Well, it appears I have come none too soon. Nicholas, have my rooms readied. I shall need to rest before I rectify this dreadful situation you have gotten yourself into. And do not doubt that I have heard of your abhorrent behavior in London and your withdrawal from society. That is another matter that needs my immediate attention. Now ring your man, and let's get on with it!"

Christina glanced at Nicholas and noticed the muscle in his jaw clenched with tension. "Pierce!" he bellowed. The butler appeared right away.

"Yes, my lord?"

"Have the upstairs maids prepare my aunt's rooms right away."

Pierce bowed. "Very good, my lord." He bowed to Lady Stanhope. "My lady? This way, if you please."

Without a second glance at anyone, she marched out of the room behind Pierce.

For a moment, no one spoke. "What do you think she meant by rectifying a dreadful situation?" North finally asked.

Nicholas shook his head while raking a hand through his curls. "I was afraid to ask."

Christina had the feeling the "dreadful situation" had something to do with her. Standing up, she carried Ty over to Mrs. Sanborne. "I think it best we leave," she said, looking toward the earl.

North nodded. "I believe my time here has come to an end also. I need to get up to my estate in Scotland."

"What you both are saying is that you are abandoning me, am I right?"

Christina grinned as she and North exchanged a glance. "Yes," they replied together.

"But. . .but you cannot leave!" Helen cried as she stood up and looked wildly in North's direction.

"Now, now, Helen," Christina said. "I realize we'll both miss our newly acquired friend, but I'm sure he'll visit Kenswick Hall again." She maintained a death grip on her friend's arm.

" 'Tis so!" North concurred. "But it shall not be until the new year. I will be journeying to America from Scotland and will not be back for some months."

Helen started to protest, but Christina whispered in her ear, "Perhaps distance will make his heart grow fonder!" She felt guilty for giving Helen false hope, but at least it worked, for her friend stifled whatever she was going to say.

Nicholas grimaced. "So I will have to deal with my new visitor alone, I see."

"She is, after all, your aunt," Christina teased. "Surely she can't be all that terrifying."

"You'd be surprised," Nicholas replied.

Chapter 13

I t didn't take long for Nicholas to realize his aunt's sole purpose for being at Kenswick Hall. She intended to ruin his life.

Or so it seemed.

"Now, I have already sent out invitations." She stopped and glared at her nephew. "Nicholas, do pay attention, dear. I'm doing all this for your benefit!"

From behind his desk, Nicholas stifled a sigh and drew his tired gaze to the settee his aunt was perched on. "Aunt Willie, I know you mean well, but I do not feel like entertaining members of the ton here at Kenswick. If I can refresh your memory, I'm not exactly in the ton's favor at the moment, and I've grown quite provincial in the last few months. I relish the peace and quiet the country provides. If you bring strangers here, it will no longer be so."

"It's *Aunt Wilhelmina*, and these are not strangers we are talking about. These are your peers. Peers who are all set to forgive your lapse in decorum, especially since I explained the reason you behaved that way."

Nicholas found it hard to clamp down his anger. His life was finally getting to the point where he enjoyed it again. He liked the person he was becoming, and he enjoyed being with the lady who had helped him get there.

His aunt's interference in his life could ruin everything.

"Let's be honest, shall we, Aunt? Every family on your list has a daughter of marital age. It is your plan, is it not? To get me married?"

She seemed unconcerned that he was upset. With a shrug of her shoulders, she told him, "Yes, I will not deny it. You have a child to raise, and every child deserves a mother." She held out her hand to examine one of the diamond rings on her fingers. "And I would not have enlisted the help of the local riffraff to help with the baby. Really, Nicholas! The vicar's daughter?"

"For your information, Christina Wakelin helped me at a time when no one else would, and I would not have her spoken of in such uncomplimentary terms!" he said as he stood and glared down at his aunt.

"You seem to be quite fond of this woman, Nicholas, and though she has come to your aid, it is simply not done!" his aunt snapped back, she, too, rising from her seat.

"She is none of your business," he stated slowly through gritted teeth.

"No, but you are, and I will see that you are taken care of."

"I am thirty years old, Aunt, and long past needing your care!"

She gasped. "You impertinent boy! I will have—"

"Excuse me, my lord," Pierce spoke from the doorway, interrupting the tense exchange.

"Yes, what is it, Pierce?"

"Miss Wakelin has asked to see you in the garden. It concerns the young master."

Without a glance at his aunt, Nicholas sprinted toward the door, ignoring her as she called out his name.

He was out of breath from running by the time he reached the garden. When he saw Christina and Ty, it took him a few seconds to realize they both seemed fine. They were sitting alone in the center of the garden on a blanket, the baby in Christina's arms.

"What is wrong?" he asked.

Christina turned her radiant smile to him. "There is nothing wrong. Ty has just done something remarkable, and I thought you'd like to see it." She laid the baby facedown on the blanket. "Now watch this!"

He watched as the wiggly little creature waved his arms and legs about, then braced his arms on either side of him and sat upright.

Christina began to clap and coo all sorts of praise to Ty, who responded by plopping back down on the blanket. She patted his back. "See!" she exclaimed to Nicholas. "Isn't that amazing?"

The only thing Nicholas found amazing was how the sunlight shone on her lovely face. But, of course, he had the sense not to say that.

She, however, was expecting some sort of reaction, so he did the best he could. "Umm, yes, quite amazing," he said.

Christina was not so easily fooled. "You weren't even paying attention," she countered with a frown.

"Of course I was."

Taking the baby in her arms, she patted the space beside them. "Have a seat. Ty, I'm sure, would love to visit with you this morning."

Did she also want to spend time with him, or was it only one-sided? Was he the only one who felt this warmth and kinship between them? Nicholas wasted no time in doing as she asked, and when she placed Ty in his arms, he realized holding the baby was becoming more comfortable.

"You are getting quite good at that, my lord!" Christina said.

Nicholas smiled proudly as he cradled the baby close and kissed him on the forehead. "Yes, I am!" he admitted immodestly, making her laugh.

For a few moments they sat together talking about the baby in contented companionship. *This is what it must feel like to have a family,* Nicholas thought. A sense of completeness, of warmth and love, enveloped them like a cocoon.

And he did love her. With every fiber of his being, he wanted this woman to be his wife and to live with him forever.

But he could not. So much stood between them. Yet, if only he knew that she loved him in return, none of the obstacles would stop him from making her his own.

"Are you enjoying your visit with Lady Stanhope?" Christina asked, breaking through his heavy thoughts.

"Unfortunately, the word *enjoy* is usually absent when dealing with Aunt Willie. She is determined to insert herself into my life and wreak havoc on it."

"Perhaps if you spoke to her and made her understand. . ."

"I've talked until I am weary of it, and yet it will not stop her. My aunt has already invited half the ton to Kenswick Hall beginning tomorrow afternoon," he confessed.

Her eyes filled with compassion. "Oh, Nicholas! Does she not know all you've been through in the last few months?"

Nicholas gazed at her with wonderment. This beautiful woman actually cared about his welfare. Wasn't that a beginning to love?

He prayed it was so.

"My aunt knows some of it, at least what gossip has come her way, but she believes this is the best solution for my situation." He took a fortifying breath and gave her a searching look. "She is trying to make a good match for me. These families she has invited all have daughters. She intends that I choose one to marry."

Nicholas saw surprise and dismay fill Christina's eyes. It was a reaction that gave him hope. "Oh," she murmured. She tried to smile at him.

She failed wonderfully.

"Of course, I have no intention of going along with her plan," he said carefully, gauging her reaction.

Her eyes widened. "You don't?"

He shook his head slowly, never taking his gaze off her. "No."

He wished he could read her thoughts, but her expression became shuttered as she looked away. "But I thought you had changed your mind about living a life of solitude."

"Oh, I have. I do not know what I must have been thinking to believe I would be happy without a wife and family." He took a chance and reached out to lift her chin so that she was staring back at him. "And my change of heart is all because of you."

"I hope I have been of some help. But above all, I wanted you to realize God still loves you and never gave up on you."

Nicholas smiled as his thumb caressed her jawline. "How could I not know God loves me, Christina? After all, He sent me you, didn't He?"

She visibly swallowed as she looked at him with hope and wariness all at once. Did he dare hope that she understood he had strong feelings for her?

For a moment, her eyes grew luminous with emotion, but then she pulled away from his touch and started fiddling with the baby's toys scattered on the blanket. "I was just doing what I felt God was asking me to do," she said, her eyes refusing to look at him.

"Christina!" he whispered roughly, stopping one of her hands by covering it with his own. "What I'm trying to tell you is that I—"

"Whatever are you doing there on that filthy ground—and holding the baby no less?" Aunt Wilhelmina's voice boomed as she marched over to where they sat. "And where is the nanny? Shouldn't she be looking after the child?"

Nicholas quickly let go of Christina's hand when his aunt appeared, but he knew she had witnessed it. Her eyes were narrowed with suspicion, her nostrils flared with indignation.

"Aunt Willie, will you please give us a moment? There are some things I need to discuss with Christina," Nicholas tried to explain.

"I most certainly will not!" She looked scathingly at Christina. "Young lady, have you no manners or decency? Where is your chaperone? Why have you been left with my grandnephew when you are not trained?"

"My chaperone got a splinter in her hand, and Mrs. Sanborne took her to her room to extract it," Christina said evenly. "I have looked after not only this child but also many children before. I can assure you I am well capable of dealing with a baby."

He admired the calm way Christina spoke but knew his aunt was going to ruin everything.

"Aunt Wilhelmina, please give me a moment. I shall meet with you directly," he stated again.

"There is no time," she snapped. "Our first guests, the Birkenstocks, have arrived earlier than expected. They are awaiting you in the drawing room."

Nicholas closed his eyes a moment to get hold of his flaring temper. "I cannot believe you are interfering in my life this way!" he said, his voice gritty with aggravation.

"Believe it and accept it." She took a deep breath, causing the sapphires at her throat to glimmer in the sunlight. "Now do come along. Let's hope you have not wrinkled your clothes too badly by frolicking on the ground like a petty commoner."

Beside him, Nicholas saw Christina stiffen at her cruel words. She reached over and took the baby from his arms, her eyes downcast and her expression stony. "I'll take the baby to Mrs. Sanborne," she murmured.

"No!" he bellowed, startling both women and making the baby cry. Turning to his aunt, he lowered his tone. "Tell the Birkenstocks I will see them in a moment, Aunt. There will be no discussions on this point!"

Wisely, his aunt relented, albeit with disdain. She spun about and marched away from them, her displeasure sounding in every step she took.

"I think it best I go in," Christina said.

Nicholas put his hand on her shoulder. "Christina, I apologize for my aunt's behavior. Her opinions are not my own." When he saw that she was not going to flee, he let go of her shoulder. "Now, there is something I would like to ask you before I go in."

"What is it?"

"Well. . ." He hesitated. "I don't quite know how to say this. . . ."

"You don't need me to come here anymore," she surmised wrongly. "It's all right, really. I—"

"Christina!" he interrupted. "Of course I don't want you to stop coming to Kenswick. In fact, your presence here means a great deal to me, and that's what I need to talk to you about."

She looked at him a little warily. "I don't understand."

"Christina. . .I need to know just. . .how you. . ." He stumbled. Then, taking a deep breath, he blurted out what he needed to say. "I need to know what your feelings are toward me."

She could do nothing for a moment but gape at him. As his words finally sank in, she seemed embarrassed, her face turning a deep shade of pink.

Yanking a hand through his hair, he apologized. "Forgive my impertinence, Christina. I should not have presumed that you would feel free to discuss so intimate a subject with me."

"Oh no! Please don't apologize, Nicholas. I'm just taken aback that you would want to know about my feelings. I haven't been so obvious with my feelings, have I? Have I embarrassed you, as Helen has done with the duke? I was not aware I wore my emotions so—"

"Then you do!" he exclaimed, grinning broadly. "You do have feelings for me."

She looked down at Ty. "You must know I do."

He threw back his head and laughed. "That's marvelous!" he cried, then leaned over and kissed her on the cheek, surprising them both with his impulsiveness.

"Nicholas!" she gasped, but still wearing a hesitant smile.

"I need to see to my guests, but may we talk again tomorrow?"

She nodded, looking a little dazed.

He threw her another happy grin. "Tomorrow. Here in the garden."

With that, he got up and walked back into the house.

And the moment he closed the door, he realized he hadn't told her about his own feelings.

But no matter, he thought. He would see her tomorrow, and then everything in his life would be just the way he wanted it.

Chapter 14

H e asked you what?" Helen blurted out and quickly put a hand over her mouth when Christina hushed her for speaking too loudly.

Conflicting emotions had swirled in Christina's heart all night, allowing her only a few moments of sleep. Over and over she had gone through the conversation she and Nicholas shared. Over and over she tried to find a reasonable explanation for his asking her to reveal such personal feelings.

The only conclusion she could reach was he, too, had strong feelings for her. Oh, if only he had voiced them!

So, unable to think objectively, she thought it wise to get Helen's opinion.

"He said he needed to know what my feelings were for him," she repeated, chewing her lip as she waited for Helen's reply.

"And you told him you cared very much for him," Helen surmised correctly.

"How did you know?"

Helen smiled. While it was true she wasn't good at dealing with her own love life, she was incredibly perceptive where others were concerned. "You are my oldest and dearest friend, Christina. How could I not see the love you have for him shining in your eyes when you thought no one was looking?"

Christina sighed, feeling tired and confused. "I tried so to fight my caring for him, Helen, truly I did. But the more he came out of his depressed state and opened up to us as a friend, the more I realized I was falling in love with him. But does his asking me about my feelings mean he has feelings for me, too?"

Helen reached out and grasped her friend's hand. "Of course it does. I have believed for some time the earl cared for you. I am sure it is the reason why he has changed his mind about shutting himself off from the world."

Hope sprang up in her chest at hearing Helen's words, but something else worried her. "But my goal was to allow God to change him."

Helen gave Christina an exasperated look. "Have you not heard your father say over and over that God uses us to help Him do His work on earth? You were willing to face his bad manners and ill humor just because you believed God wanted you to help him. And you have, Christina! God has used you to help him!"

Christina smiled tentatively. "I suppose you're right. He has come to church and promises to attend every Sunday."

"Well, there you are!"

They were silent for a moment as they sat in the small garden of Christina's home. She allowed herself to begin to hope there might be a future for them. Perhaps what she thought was impossible might be possible after all.

With that in mind, Christina decided to go with Helen to Kenswick Hall and see how Mrs. Sanborne was coping with the new visitors at the estate.

They found her in the nursery folding Ty's diapers, but the nanny was not in her usual chipper mood. In fact, she was very upset.

"I'm awfully glad you ladies have come. Awfully, awfully glad," she told them, tears swimming in her downcast eyes.

"Whatever is the matter, Mrs. Sanborne?" Christina asked. "Has something happened?"

The older woman shook her head. "I'm awfully afraid that I shall be dismissed," she told them, her voice wobbly with worry. "I'm in an awfully dreadful state over this. You see, I overheard Lady Stanhope say that she wanted to bring someone she already knew into the home to be Ty's nanny, that she was awfully displeased with my work so far."

Christina patted her back. "But that is only her opinion, Mrs. Sanborne. It is not how Lord Kenswick feels! He is awfully. . .I mean, he is very pleased with how you have taken care of Ty. Never would he fire you!"

"The woman is a busybody!" Helen cried.

Christina, no matter how much she agreed, did not want to speak unkindly about someone behind their back. "Helen, I'm sure this can all be worked out. I will go and speak to Nicholas about it. I'm sure all will be well."

Mrs. Sanborne gave her an encouraged smile. "Oh, thank you, dear. What would I do without you?"

"You would do fine, I'm sure." She dismissed her praise with a wave of her hand. "I'll be back directly."

Christina made her way to the stairs and down to the main hall of the house. She had not seen any of Nicholas's guests since she and Helen had entered, as they always did, through the servants' entrance.

She heard them, however, as she stepped off the bottom step. Their laughter drifted to her from the sitting room to her left. She paused, unsure if she should interrupt or not. But then she thought of Nicholas and knew he would not mind if she went in to talk to him.

The door was already slightly ajar, so she pushed it enough so that she could slip inside.

For a moment, no one noticed her, so Christina had a chance to study the room. Nicholas caught her attention right away, sitting on the settee with a beautiful young woman with dark hair so artfully arranged it must have taken her maid hours to accomplish it. Her exquisite dress was stunning, as well, the deep blue silk complementing the creamy paleness of her skin.

Her first thought was that they looked so perfect sitting together. Nicholas grinned at something she was saying. Just the kind of woman an earl should marry—poised, self-assured, and a member of the ton.

She silently chastised herself for thinking so negatively and looked around to the others in the room.

Not surprisingly, Lady Stanhope was smiling charmingly at the distinguished couple sitting directly in front of her. Wealth and prestige emanated from the couple, so different were they from the simple ladies and gentlemen of Malbury.

And so different from Christina.

"Christina!" Nicholas called. She turned to see him stand and smile her way.

Relieved he was glad to see her, she stepped farther into the room, pretending not to see the familiar frown appearing on Lady Stanhope's face. "I'm sorry if I've intruded," she began hesitantly.

Perhaps, she thought, *I should not have been so bold!*

"Nonsense!" Nicholas assured her. "Please let me introduce you to my guests. May I introduce Lord and Lady Delacourt? And this is their daughter, Lady Serena Delacourt." He then motioned toward Christina. "My lord and ladies, this is my neighbor and good friend, Miss Christina Wakelin."

Christina curtsied, smiling a greeting at the three of them. They barely nodded in return, eyeing her with a great deal of curious speculation.

Especially the younger Lady Delacourt.

Thanks to her father, Christina grew up confident in the person that she was. God was no respecter of persons, he'd often quoted. He loved everybody the same, no matter their class or how much money they had.

But now she did not feel so confident. She felt way out of her element, and all she wanted to do was run from Kenswick Hall and surround herself with people she knew and loved.

She was about to do just that when Nicholas asked, "You are here to remind me of my daily meeting, are you not?"

Taken off guard, Christina paused, then stammered, "Uh, meeting?" Then she realized he was trying to give them both an excuse to leave the room. "Oh! Yes. I thought. . .perhaps. . .I should come down and. . .uh. . .remind you. Of the meeting."

Christina refused to look at anyone but Nicholas, but she could feel their eyes on her and knew they were thinking the same thing she was—she had sounded like a complete idiot!

"I'm afraid I'll have to leave you to my aunt," he told everyone in the room. "I always meet with my nephew every day at this time, so I know you will understand if I hesitate to break our regular schedule."

"Nicholas!" his aunt spoke up. "Surely you can postpone for one day."

"Oh, no, please keep your schedule with your nephew," the elder Lady Delacourt chimed in. "Bonding with one's parent is so important at this age. I myself met with my daughter for one hour a day when she was a babe, and now we enjoy the closest of relationships."

Christina glanced at Serena Delacourt just in time to see the bored look she gave her mother at that comment. She didn't blame her. Christina couldn't imagine one hour a day being enough time for a parent to spend with their child.

"You are correct, Lady Delacourt," he responded with a nod.

After assuring them he would see them at dinner, Nicholas motioned for Christina to precede him out the door, which he shut firmly behind them.

"If you had shown up a minute later, I fear I might have gone mad!" he whispered, then grinned at her. "Listening to how many ladies were wearing pink at the last ball Lady Serena attended was not what I call stimulating conversation!"

"But she is quite beautiful, don't you think?" Christina said. "Very poised and, I'm sure, extremely accomplished."

"Accomplished in what, pray? Boring a man to tears?" He shook his head. "No, dear Christina. I know what you are saying, and I'm telling you to put your mind at ease." They were walking out to the garden when Nicholas suddenly pulled her off the path and into a secluded nook.

He cupped her face with his large, strong hands and gazed at her as if she were the most important person in the world to him.

"Christina, I asked you yesterday what your feelings were concerning me, but in my excitement I neglected to tell you just what my feelings are for you."

Her heart felt as though it might pound right out of her chest. "And?" she prompted.

"My feelings are so great that I cannot envision a life without you," he stated fervently. "But I am afraid I am not worthy of you, Christina. You deserve so much better a man than I have been."

Christina's eyes filled with tears of wonderment and complete happiness. "It is the past, Nicholas. You are that man no more. You've allowed God to change you; you must realize that."

He caressed the sides of her face with his thumbs. "I know He is changing me. I've been studying the scriptures and want the kind of relationship with God that you and your father have. I just feel as though I need to make restitution for some of my past misdeeds. That is why I have agreed to let my aunt invite half the ton to Kenswick Hall. When I ask your father for your hand, I want to be able to present to you a name of good standing—not one that has been sullied. Perhaps these visits will let me once again be in their favor."

"But, Nicholas, my father will see that you have changed. And, besides, you know I care nothing for London society. Why should I be bothered if they accept us or not?"

"But you must, Christina, for our sake, for Ty's sake, and for any other children we will have. We don't have to be in their inner circle, but it is always better to be on good terms with them."

Christina had to voice her most important concern. "But will not your marrying a commoner such as I ostracize you anyway?"

"The ton is a fickle and hypocritical lot! As charming and beautiful as you are, my dear, I daresay you would win over the most ardent critic," he assured her.

Christina was about to ask him how long they would have to wait before he spoke to her father, but Mrs. Sanborne called her name from the other side of the garden. Sighing, she said, "As much as I hate it, I should probably let you go back to your guests." Then she remembered something. "Oh! Please reassure Mrs. Sanborne that you do not intend to let her go from her position. She overheard your aunt berating her competence as Ty's nanny."

Nicholas groaned. "She must have berated my new valet, Smith, in the same conversation, for he kept asking me this morning if his work was sufficient to my needs. I didn't understand why he was suddenly insecure when he'd been nothing less than swaggering before. Now, however, it all falls into place."

"I shall be glad when all your visits from London society are over with and your aunt has gone from Kenswick!" she confessed, unable to hide her frustration with the whole matter.

Nicholas laughed softly as he bent down to kiss her on the nose. "No more so than I," he agreed before kissing her again. This time on the lips.

"Now I shall go and say hello to my nephew before returning inside. I don't want to become a liar on top of everything else I have done," he teased, then left her standing alone.

Christina could not even remember telling him good-bye, so stunned was she at the warm touch of his lips. In fact, she might have stayed there all day had not Mrs. Sanborne called her name again, urging her to join them.

She and Nicholas exchanged a secret look when she approached. It was as if they both wanted to keep their news to themselves for a while. After a moment he went back inside, and Christina stayed in the garden.

It took great effort to concentrate on the conversation as the women chattered about the guests and wondered what styles they wore. Nicholas's lovely words kept swimming around her mind, thrilling her every time she recalled them. She wanted to remember them, dream of them for a few days, until Nicholas's promise came to fruition.

Until he asked her father for her hand.

Chapter 15

I have paraded four exquisite young women in front of you in the last week, and yet you show no inclination to make an offer to any of them!" Nicholas's aunt declared as she entered his suite of rooms unannounced. He was busy putting the finishing touches on one of his small figurines.

She stopped abruptly. "Whatever are you doing?"

Blowing away the remaining wood shavings, he set the figurine of his cat, licking one of its front paws, on the edge of his worktable.

Still somewhat bemused, Aunt Wilhelmina picked it up and studied the intricate detail. "You have the gift," she whispered with awe, her eyes still on the figurine.

He raised an eyebrow. "I beg your pardon?"

"My father—your grandfather—used to carve the most wonderful little statuettes and give them to the children of the village. I have five of them in my home in Stafford."

Stunned, Nicholas shook his head. "I don't remember him. I was only two or three when he died, and Father never mentioned it."

"Of course he wouldn't have. If memory serves me correctly, William used them as his targets when practicing his archery."

Nicholas chuckled. His father had been the consummate hunter and fisherman. He wouldn't have cared about a few chunks of decorative wood—not when they served his purpose better honing his own hobby!

"Now, back to your marriage," Aunt Wilhelmina began.

"What marriage?"

His aunt placed the carving back on his desk and folded her arms across her chest in a no-nonsense manner. "My point exactly. You must try to make a worthwhile effort if there is going to *be* a marriage! Really, Nicholas. You cannot shirk your responsibility to your nephew or your title. You must make a match, and the sooner the better."

Nicholas was so tired of playing his aunt's game. Because of the many guests she'd paraded in and out of his home, he had not spoken to Christina but a few minutes each day. And the day before, when he spoke to her, she'd said she would be too busy to come by for the next few days. She'd seemed preoccupied, even a little distant.

What in the world was she doing? Had she decided to move on with her life without him? Perhaps she'd decided to marry a farmer the vicar had picked out for her. . . .

"Nicholas, are you daydreaming?" his aunt scolded as she tapped on his table with her blue silk fan. "Will you stop dillydallying and start taking this seriously?"

"I already have," he stated firmly, deciding it was time to tell her of his true plans.

"I beg your pardon? What does this mean?"

"I have already chosen a bride."

When his aunt broke into a triumphant smile, Nicholas knew she had taken his words the wrong way. "Which one? The Delacourt girl? No! I know it's the beautiful blond one. . . . Constance, I believe her name was."

"You misunderstand me, Aunt," he interrupted before she became too excited. "I intend to marry Christina Wakelin."

"That little vicar's daughter?" she cried with unbelief. For a moment, Nicholas was afraid she might faint from the shock, but she seemed to pull herself together. Taking a breath and clearing her throat, she told him, "Nicholas dear, girls such as that are for mild flirtations and amusement to a nobleman of your station. You do not, however, *marry* them."

"I'm in love with her," he stated bluntly.

She gave a trilling little laugh at those words. "Is that all? What has love to do with anything? Once you are married to a girl of good breeding, you'll soon forget about this lapse in judgment."

Nicholas grew irritated by her flippant attitude for all that he considered precious. He stood to his feet. "She is not a lapse, Aunt. She is the woman I intend to marry, the woman who will bear the next Earl of Kenswick."

Aunt Wilhelmina grabbed her fan and cooled her face in a rapid, erratic manner. "Do not say that, I beg you. You mustn't even joke about such a travesty!"

Nicholas replied calmly. "My mind is made up. There shall be no more discussion on this subject."

She did not speak for a moment, and Nicholas could not read her face. She made a show of smoothing the lace at her wrist. "And have you asked her father for her hand?" she questioned, a strange calmness to her voice.

Nicholas did not trust it. "No."

"Ah," she said and stood. "And what of the other guests I have invited? Would you have me cancel their invitations when some of them might already be on their way?"

Of course he could not do that. It would further cast a stain against his name to make such a social faux pas. "No, but issue no more invitations. At the week's end, I shall speak to Reverend Wakelin and make the announcement to the newspapers."

"Of course, dear," she answered with a submissiveness that rang false in Nicholas's ears. "No more invitations." He noticed she completely ignored his latter statement.

After she left, Nicholas did not dwell on his aunt's strange behavior. Instead, he stood and closed his eyes in a prayer to God.

"Let this week pass quickly, Lord," he prayed. "And prepare the vicar's heart so I might find favor with him at the week's end."

The latter request was the one thing Nicholas feared would foil his plans with Christina. The last time marriage was mentioned concerning his daughter, the vicar's feelings on the subject had been clear—he was not in favor of any connection between Christina and Nicholas.

☙

Christina had worked tirelessly for two days as she helped Mrs. Ledbetter, a young mother in the village, care for her one-year-old twins as she delivered yet another baby. Her husband, a soldier, had recently left with his regiment for three months. The woman had no one to help her.

How fortunate for him, Christina thought in a rare moment of feeling sorry for herself. Although other women from the village had taken turns helping Christina, she had been there the entire time, with little sleep.

In the late afternoon, she was relieved by an older woman from the church who had reared eight children of her own. She told Christina to go home and rest.

Back at home, Christina was even too tired to eat. All she wanted to do was fall into bed and sleep for the rest of the day and night.

Her father came out of his study as she reached the stairs and looked up from the book he'd been reading. He stepped forward to pat her on the head as if she were a little girl, then mumbled something about God rewarding her for her hard work. Since this was not unusual behavior, she smiled at him and started up the stairs.

She got no farther than the fourth step when a knock sounded at the door.

Mrs. Hopkins looked up at Christina as she hurried to answer it. "Were you expecting someone, Miss Christina?"

"No," she answered, wishing she could just ignore the knock. "I suppose you better answer it. I am not dressed to receive visitors, but with Father busy reading, I suppose I'd better." She looked down at her soiled brown dress. "Perhaps it is someone in need."

But it wasn't, much to Christina's horror and dismay. There on the vicarage doorstep stood Lady Wilhelmina Stanhope, looking as out of place in the humble home as a fish in the desert. Draped in a mint green silk gown of the latest London fashion, she had the accessories to match, including a perfectly dyed umbrella she used as a cane.

"Lady Stanhope!" Christina greeted with a pleasantness she did not feel as she came back down the stairs. "To what do we owe this pleasure?"

Her ladyship's eyes widened as she perused Christina's dress. "I seem to have come at a bad time," she said. "I don't believe I've ever seen you look so dreadfully ill in all the time I've been at Kenswick."

It was all Christina could do to remain calm. What she really wanted to do was demand that the horrible woman leave her home and take her critical words with her.

But, of course, she did not. If Nicholas could change his life, surely Lady Stanhope could, also—with some time and a lot of effort.

"I've just come from the home of a young mother who has delivered a baby. I've been there for two days, helping her with her young twins," she explained, hoping the woman would take the hint that she was quite tired.

She did not. "I see," she said, although it was clear from her tone that she did not see and certainly did not understand. "I've come to have a word with you, Miss Wakelin. It is a matter of great importance."

Christina could not decline. "Why don't we go into the front parlor?" To her housekeeper, she asked, "Could you bring us some tea, Mrs. Hopkins?"

"I'll not be here that long," Lady Stanhope declared before the housekeeper could even nod her head.

Christina sighed and shook her head toward Mrs. Hopkins to let her know tea, apparently, would not be needed.

She led Lady Stanhope into the bright, cheerful room that was a favorite of Christina's with its yellow floral wallpaper and her mother's colorful paintings on the walls. She motioned for Lady Stanhope to take the sofa, and she did so, but not before casting a disapproving glance around the room.

"Your living arrangements are very small, Miss Wakelin," she observed, keeping a hand on the handle of her upright umbrella. "Have you but one servant?"

"No, we also have a cook," Christina replied a little defensively. "My father and I have always found our home quite sufficient for our needs."

"Ah. And your mother?"

"She died when I was a small child. Lady Stanhope, did you not say you had a matter of great importance to discuss with me?"

The woman's back stiffened at Christina's blunt remark. "Let me get right to the point. I know you have been a great assistance to my nephew these last few months and helped him to overcome the troubled state that prevailed upon him after he left the war."

"Well, I was simply doing what I felt God led me to do," Christina replied. "I knew he could overcome his bitterness and pain once he—"

"Yes, yes, dear. There's no need to go on about it," Lady Stanhope interrupted. "The point I am trying to make is, that because he was weak, and I might say *vulnerable*, during this time, he has allowed his emotions, it seems, to replace his good judgment." She leaned forward, giving Christina a hard look. "You understand what I am saying, don't you?"

"Nicholas told you about his feelings toward me," Christina whispered in wonderment.

Lady Stanhope gripped her umbrella, tapping it on the floor for emphasis. "He says he intends to marry you!"

Christina smiled widely.

"Do not look so happy about it, young lady. I'll have you know that by marrying you he is jeopardizing his entire future and bringing shame upon a family title that has flourished for six generations!"

Christina tried valiantly to hold her temper. "How? How am I jeopardizing his future and bringing shame to him?"

The elder woman tapped hard on the floor again. "Who is your family? What are their connections other than some minor baronet in your family tree? What do you bring to this marriage if not position? A large dowry perhaps?" she said snidely, peering down her nose at Christina.

"I bring him love and happiness!"

"Humph!" the woman sniffed.

Christina stood with hands on hips. "I also bring to him a relationship that is grounded in God's love, stable and unwavering."

Lady Stanhope stood, as well. "What good is love if all of society snubs him and his offspring? How happy will you be watching his peers laugh behind his back or, worse, feel sorry that at a moment of weakness he allowed himself to settle so far beneath him! How stable will your marriage be when he wakes up one morning realizing he made the worst mistake of his life by marrying a vicar's daughter?"

Tears prickled behind Christina's eyes as the woman's words drove like daggers into her heart. "Is that what you think?" she asked hoarsely. "Do you believe he only thinks he loves me because he is grateful for my help?"

"Think about it, dear," she soothed. "Nicholas was once the most sought-after nobleman in England. He knew of you even then, did he not?"

Christina nodded slowly, not wanting to hear any more.

"Had he ever sought you out before?"

"No, but I was young when he left."

Lady Stanhope smiled. "But let us be honest with ourselves, shall we? If nothing had happened to Nicholas, do you think he still would have chosen you for his bride?"

Christina's mind flew back to Nicholas as a young man and how annoyed he always seemed to be with her. She replayed the scene at the tree and his reaction to finding out who she was.

He had been appalled at the revelation!

Perhaps Lady Stanhope was right. Perhaps he cared for her out of a sense of gratefulness or, worse, because she had practically thrown herself into his life, giving him no choice but to think he needed her around him permanently.

Weary from the last two days and now with the realization that she was about to lose her true love, Christina sat back down on her chair, clasping her hands tightly in her lap. "I do not want him to ever feel shame or regret for marrying me," she stated, her tone listless.

"Of course you don't, dear," the woman mollified, taking the seat next to her. "I have a lovely estate in Stafford. Why don't you use my carriage to go there for a fortnight? It will allow you an occasion to sort through your feelings and permit your heart to heal." She reached out to pat Christina's hand. "It will also give Nicholas a chance to sort through his emotions. With you being there, perhaps he'll be able to see his way more clearly and make decisions that are right, not only for him, but for his family, as well."

Christina didn't want to go to Stafford or anywhere else. All she wanted to do was run up to her room and cry her heart out.

But neither did she want Nicholas to regret marrying her. Only with her gone would he be able to understand what was best for him.

"I will go," she said at last.

"Excellent!" Lady Stanhope exclaimed as she used her umbrella to stand. "No, please do not stand. I will show myself out. If you'll have your things packed and ready by morning, my driver will be by with the carriage."

Christina did not remember saying good-bye. All she could do was cover her face as her tears finally came forth. "Why, dear God? Why do I have to let him go, when it was You who seemed to bring us together? How could I have been so wrong?"

But she had known all along that a match between them was impossible. She had told herself, even warned herself, it could not be—but allowed hope to flourish anyway.

Now she loved him.

And now she must let him go.

Chapter 16

I think it's quite noble how you spend time with your nephew, my lord," Lady Judith Grisham told Nicholas with what he considered an excessively high and irritating tone as they strolled in his garden. Ty was sound asleep on his shoulder, since he'd learned that having the baby with him stopped any ideas of romance from whatever lady was visiting him.

"I believe that time spent with your child can only improve their chances of growing up to be an adult of extreme confidence and abilities," he told her, trying not to wince over having sounded so stuffy.

"Uh, yes, I suppose so. But do you think that some time apart from him would benefit the child, as well?" she asked hopefully.

"No."

"Oh." Nicholas heard her sigh as they completed their lap around the garden.

The Grishams were the last guests, and he was grateful for that. They'd be leaving today, and that meant he could finally get on with his life.

If she were still willing to marry him, that is. Nicholas had not seen Christina in five days, and he was beginning to worry. Every time he questioned Helen about it, she would only tell him Christina had been very busy and could not come. It was clear she didn't want to talk about it.

To make matters worse, thanks to his aunt, he'd had no time to ride out to the vicarage himself.

And he was becoming worried.

Ty chose that moment to wake up and cry, giving Nicholas an excuse to leave Lady Grisham's company. "I do beg your pardon, but I believe he must be ready for his nap."

"Must you be the one to take him to the nursery?" she asked, allowing her exasperation to show.

"I fear I must." He started to walk away from her toward the side entrance.

"But. . .but will I see you again before my family departs?" she called out.

"Certainly."

She began to look hopeful again, a smile blooming on her attractive face.

"I shall meet you in the front hall to say my good-byes before you embark on your journey home."

She stopped smiling.

As Nicholas bolted up the stairs, he felt a sense of relief. All the tedious

101

entertaining was almost at an end, and now he could get back to his life and to Christina.

But first he must go and speak with her father.

Three hours later, Nicholas rode on horseback to the vicarage. Excitement mixed with nervousness coursed through his veins as he thought about speaking to her father.

He couldn't wait until Christina was his wife. The time spent apart from her these last days only confirmed to him that he could not live without her.

She was everything he could ever imagine in a mate. She'd even seen him at his worst and did not give up on him.

Though he'd committed a social faux pas by ending his engagement to his former fiancée, he could now only thank God he'd done it. He could not imagine spending his life with any woman other than the redheaded, outspoken girl who had climbed his tree and fallen right into his arms and life, changing him forever.

He tied his horse to a post in front of the house and made his way to the door. He did not understand the frightened look that came upon the house-keeper's face when she saw who it was at the door.

"My. . .my lord!" she stammered. "What can I do for you?"

Nicholas smiled at her. Perhaps it was his title that made her so nervous. "You could call your mistress, for starters. I would very much like to speak with her."

Her eyes darted to a space behind the door and then back to him. "I'm afraid you can't."

He blinked. "I beg your pardon? Is she ill?"

"No, it's just that she is not here, my lord."

"Oh, I see," Nicholas replied. He had not seen Helen today, so perhaps Christina was visiting her. "Well, could I possibly speak to the vicar then?"

The woman seemed relieved he'd dropped the questions about Christina. She stepped back and motioned for him to go to a side parlor. "Wait here, my lord, and I will get him for you."

Nicholas nodded and went into the room. As he waited, he admired the paintings that hung on all four walls.

"Those were my wife's paintings." Nicholas spun around to find the vicar standing in the doorway. The man nodded toward the painting Nicholas had been studying. "She painted that one when she found out she was with child." It was a portrait of a young woman sitting in a meadow, cradling a baby in her arms.

"They are all quite amazing," Nicholas complimented honestly.

"She was quite an amazing woman. Not a day passes that I don't miss her." His thoughts seemed to drift to the past as he gazed at the portrait. Finally he looked back at Nicholas. "I'm sorry; I've drifted off a bit. Mrs. Hopkins said you wanted to see me?"

"Yes, sir. I was hoping to speak to Christina before I had this talk with you, but she seems to be out and about this afternoon," he began. The vicar interrupted with a concerned frown.

"I'm sorry, but I thought you knew," Reverend Wakelin said.

"Knew what, sir?"

"Christina has left Malbury for a brief holiday at your aunt's estate in Stafford. I thought perhaps your aunt or even my daughter would have mentioned it."

Nicholas reached out to grip the back of a chair nearby. "No one told me. When I asked Helen about her, she told me only that Miss Wakelin was very busy."

The vicar studied Nicholas for a moment, his keen eyes missing nothing. "Perhaps we should sit down."

"No! I must know, sir, how this trip came about. When did my aunt speak to her?"

Reverend Wakelin scratched his head as he thought about it. "I suppose it was three days ago. I did not see her, but Christina told me about the visit and about your aunt's invitation." He shook his head, his face showing his concern. "I did not like the look of her, my lord. She'd been up for nearly forty-eight hours, helping one of our young mothers who'd delivered a child. I could not deny her the trip when she seemed so determined to leave."

Confused and a little hurt by this news, Nicholas began to pace about the small room. "She mentioned nothing else about the conversation with my aunt? Did she seem upset or angry?"

"No to both questions, my lord." After a hesitant pause, he said, "You mentioned before that you came to speak with me. To what does it pertain?"

Nicholas stopped and looked directly at the vicar. "I came to ask for your daughter's hand in marriage," he told him bluntly. "I spoke to Christina a week ago and told her how I felt, but I have not seen her since."

The vicar did not seem very surprised. "I see," he said. "And does she return your feelings, my lord?"

"Yes!" he declared. "She knew I would be coming to speak to you after my guests left. I thought it was understood she would be waiting for me."

"Do you love her?"

"With all my heart, sir," Nicholas answered with great feeling as the two men shared an understanding look. "I must go and see her!"

Nicholas started to leave, when the vicar stopped him. "One moment, my lord. I believe I have more to speak to you about before you go to her."

Nicholas bit back his irritation at being delayed, reminding himself he needed this man's approval if Christina was to be his wife. But it was late in the day, and traveling would not be easy. "Yes, of course," he relented and sat in the chair the vicar motioned him toward.

Sitting across from him, the vicar began. "Christina tells me you have changed a great deal from when she first met you again on your estate." Nicholas nodded. "The fact you are titled and considered a good catch by all of society, despite your past reputation, does not matter to me in the least. What I am most concerned about is your spiritual condition. Are you a follower of Christ, my lord?"

Nicholas answered sincerely. "Yes, sir. At times I have blamed God for my circumstances, but not anymore. Christina has shown me what it means to be a Christian, what it means to put my faith in the One who created me."

"Have you changed your mind only because of Christina?"

"No. I've started to believe in God again because I need Him in my life, sir."

"Then you indeed have my blessing," the vicar replied with a smile, his gaze going to the clock on the mantel. "But if you want to reach Stafford before midnight, I would say you should be on your way."

Nicholas stood up and shook his future father-in-law's hand enthusiastically. "That is just what I intend, sir, and thank you. You shall not regret giving your blessing!"

"Please see that I don't!" the vicar said with a teasing light in his eyes.

Nicholas wasted no time in riding back to Kenswick and ordering one of the stable boys to ready his horse for the long journey.

"You're not going to take the carriage, sir?" the young man asked, aghast.

"No, it will be quicker on horseback. I'll just need to go inside the house for a few things. See that the horse is ready."

It didn't take long for Nicholas to get what money he might need and the betrothal ring that had belonged to his family for six generations. He retrieved both from the safe in his study. It was there he encountered his aunt.

"What are you doing?" she demanded from the doorway.

"I am going to undo whatever damage you have wrought concerning Christina," he answered coldly.

She grabbed his arm as he passed, looking down at the tiny box in his hand. "What are you intending to do with that?"

He jerked his arm free. "Just what you think I am going to do with it, Aunt. I don't know what lies you told her, but I intend to convince her to be my bride. When I return, I will expect you to be gone!"

"How dare you speak to me in that manner!"

He stepped close to her, staring her straight in the eyes. "And how dare you try to interfere with my life. You had no right to speak to her."

His aunt took a wary step back. "I only told her the truth, Nicholas. Marrying the girl will only bring more shame to your name and title. The ton will never accept her!"

"I don't care what the ton thinks!" he growled.

"You will regret this! Mark my words!"

"I will regret it if I don't leave right now and bring her back!" With that he left the room, stopping to speak with Pierce before he got to the front door.

"Inform Mrs. Sanborne I will be gone for tonight, but I will return by tomorrow."

Pierce's face wore a proud smile. "I will, my lord. And might I say Miss Christina will be a welcome addition to this household."

Nicholas shook his head with a chuckle. "One of these days, Pierce, your eavesdropping will get you into trouble."

"You are probably right, my lord." He opened the door with a bow. "Bring her home safely."

❧

Hartshorne Castle was a truly amazing place. Having been refurbished over the centuries, the castle was surprisingly lavish and comfortable. But for Christina, it was hard to enjoy any of the beauty or history about the place. For three long days she'd walked up to the tower near her bedroom and sat staring out over the vast countryside. She'd cried, felt sorry for herself at times, but mainly wondered how Nicholas was doing and if he missed her as much as she missed him.

She even imagined he might come and get her, but as the days passed, it became unlikely he would do so. If he loved her, surely he would have come the day she left.

"Can I fix you a spot of tea, ma'am?" one of the young maids asked from the open door. Christina saw that she was staring at her with worry, much like all the other staff had done since she'd arrived. She'd tried to pretend everything was all right but had been unable to carry off the charade.

"No, thank you," Christina answered. "I'm just going to sit here for a few moments before I turn in."

"Yes, ma'am," the maid replied, but as she went back down the stairs, Christina heard her murmur "Poor dear."

Sighing, Christina looked back out into the dark night from her seat by the window. There was no moon out, but the stars were shining brightly, twinkling like tiny jewels all around her.

She closed her eyes, letting the cool night breeze blow over her features, and she prayed like she had so often in the past few days. She prayed that God would allow her pain to cease, that He would help her to move on with her life.

A life without the Earl of Kenswick.

Weary, she folded her arms on the window seat and laid her head on them.

And dreamed of Nicholas.

Chapter 17

Nicholas tried not to think of the pain shooting through his wounded leg as he climbed the tower steps of Hartshorne Castle. Riding a horse was probably not the smartest thing for his health, but he knew the pain would be worth it all once he got to Christina.

When he reached the top of the stairs, he found her right where the young servant said she'd be.

His heart had broken when she told him how unhappy Christina had been—how the servants had heard her cry when she thought no one was around.

What had his aunt done to the woman who had been so full of life and joy? Could the thought of losing him have brought so much pain?

If so, he knew she truly did love him, just as much as he loved her.

Gently he reached out to tuck an errant curl behind her ear, then allowed himself to caress her pale cheek. Her eyes fluttered, but still she did not awaken.

"Christina," he said softly as he knelt down beside her. "Wake up, my love. Wake up so I might talk with you."

She slowly opened her eyes. "Nicholas?" she murmured groggily, as she lifted her head and tried to focus. "Nicholas!" she cried aloud once she realized it was really he.

She held out her hands to him, and he took them, kissing each one. "My love, are you really so surprised to see me?" he chided with a smile. "Surely you knew I would come."

Christina shook her head, and Nicholas could tell that the fog of sleep was clearing. "But it's been three days. I thought. . ."

"I just found out this afternoon. Helen had been telling me only that you were busy. I didn't know anything about you leaving Malbury."

"I felt I had to leave. After your aunt's visit, I—"

"Yes, my aunt," he said, letting his frustration show. "What exactly did she say that caused you to leave?"

Christina stood and walked to the other side of the room. "She told me the truth, Nicholas."

He stood also but stayed where he was. "And what truth was that?"

"That what you feel toward me is only gratitude. I came into your life when you were vulnerable and helped you get through it. In time you'll come to regret your decision to marry me, perhaps even feel embarrassed you married so far beneath you."

"Do you really think me so shallow or perhaps so unconnected with my feelings that I would confuse love with gratitude?" he roared, throwing his hands up to emphasize his words. "What about *your* feelings? Are they so weak that the first person who comes and tries to destroy what we have is actually successful?"

She gasped. "That is quite unfair! I left because I wanted to do what was best for you. If being married to me was going to cause your peers to snub you or, worse, to feel sorry for you, then I was going to spare you that."

Shaking his head, he stared at her for a long moment, reading the sincerity and love in her eyes. Slowly he began to walk toward her. "What's best for me is you, Christina. You must know that."

She blinked as if she were trying not to cry. "You must be sure, Nicholas. I could not bear to see you unhappy. I would. . ."

"Shh!" He pulled her into his arms and kissed her on the lips. After a moment, he leaned back and smiled lovingly into her shining eyes. "I love you, Christina, and that love will never go away, no matter who disapproves of us. Will you marry me and take away this misery I've been feeling for the last five days without you?"

"Oh, Nicholas. That was so beautifully spoken, I think I might cry," she said, sniffing.

"Do you think perhaps you could answer my question before you cry? I do feel a bit at loose ends here!"

She laughed as she threw her arms around his neck. "I love you with all my heart, Nicholas. Of course I'll marry you!"

He hugged her to him and closed his eyes, soaking in how wonderful it felt to hold her in his arms.

"I have something for you." He stepped back and reached into his coat pocket for the small velvet box. When he opened it, her eyes grew round at the size of the ruby within. The stone was centered in an ornate setting of gold, surrounded by small diamonds.

"Nicholas," she whispered, as he took the ring and reached for her hand, placing it on her finger.

"There! It fits you perfectly. Just as you fit me perfectly," he whispered back. "God brought you to me, Christina, and I'll thank Him every day of my life."

She smiled, turning her hand so that she could lace her fingers with his. "I knew He led me to you. I just didn't realize the full purpose. Actually, I couldn't imagine an earl ever being interested in an ordinary vicar's daughter."

"Ah, but there is nothing ordinary about you, my love. Ordinary girls do not climb trees to save cats or nurse half the animals in the shire back to health. Nor do they hide puppies in ballrooms or badger a bad-tempered man into realizing that life is too precious to waste feeling sorry for oneself."

Christina winced. "Could we just forget about the tree incident? I'm not really proud of that particular escapade."

Nicholas laughed. "Oh no! It shall be a tale that will be told to our children and to their children. Not everyone can say their true love fell from above and directly into their arms."

She suddenly remembered something. "Oh no! What about my father? Suppose he does not give us his blessing? He's always been a little wary where you are concerned."

Nicholas put a finger to her lips and smiled reassuringly. "I've already asked him. That's how I found out about you being gone from Malbury. Though he didn't know the details, he explained about my aunt's visit and where you had gone afterward."

"And his answer was. . . ?"

"His answer was yes. But only after he was sure I was the kind of man you needed—the Christian man I needed to become."

He cradled her face with both hands. "In a very short time, Christina, you are going to be the Countess of Kenswick. Do you suppose you could get used to all the bowing and scraping that goes with the title?"

"Oh my," she cried after a quick intake of breath. "I have no idea what is required of a countess." She looked worried for a moment. "I do not have to give up all my animals, do I?"

Nicholas laughed, then leaned down and gave her another kiss. "You may have as many animals as you please, as long as you keep them out of the ballroom."

She smiled. "I think I can manage that!"

Two months later, Reverend Wakelin married Christina and Nicholas in the parish church. After the ceremony, Christina stood with her husband on the lawn of Kenswick Hall as their guests mingled about.

She sighed happily as she felt Nicholas's hand on her back, drawing her close to him. "Happy?" he asked.

"Very." And she was. So very happy that, at last, he was her husband.

What made this occasion even more joyous was the support he'd received from high-ranking members of the ton. She'd met so many noble families in the last two months, and though they were hesitant at first, they all seemed to accept her into their elite group.

Christina was glad, not because being a part of them was important to her, but because she knew it was important to Nicholas to restore his family's good name.

"Did you see Ty when Mrs. Sanborne brought him down earlier? Fine-looking little man, don't you think?"

"Just like his handsome uncle," she acknowledged, as someone walking from the courtyard into the side lawn caught her attention. The man looked so much like Nicholas that Christina thought he might be a cousin.

"Nicholas, who is that man over there?"

Nicholas looked to where Christina pointed, and she felt him tense as if shocked at what he saw. "I cannot believe my eyes," he whispered hoarsely, shaking his head. "This cannot be. . . ."

"Who is it, Nicholas? Why does this man upset you?"

"It's my brother!" he gasped.

"What?"

"My brother. Christina, that is my brother, alive and breathing, walking across my lawn!"

⤜⤐

Watching his brother stride toward them was the most surreal occurrence Nicholas had ever experienced. As if in a trance, he walked out to meet him.

Thomas Thornton saw him, also, and with a smile Nicholas knew so well, he waved at him.

The two men embraced before speaking a word, slapping each other heartily on the back. Finally Nicholas drew back, holding his brother by the shoulders as he studied him.

"You look quite healthy for a dead man," he said, his voice quavering with emotion.

Thomas chuckled. "I'm not dead yet, brother. Almost, but God saw fit to save me."

Nicholas's eyes moved over his brother once again. "What happened, Thom? Why were you reported dead?"

Thom shook his head. "Our ship capsized in a bad storm, and a small group of sailors and I were able to cut loose one of the lifeboats and hold on until the storm passed. We were rescued by a merchant ship two days later; unfortunately, they were sailing to Canada to drop off a load of goods, so it took awhile to get back and notify my superiors in the Royal Navy that I had survived." He spread his arms out to indicate his lack of uniform. "And as you can see, I've also resigned my commission. I've had quite enough of the sea."

"How long have you been back?" Nicholas asked with a frown.

"About a fortnight. You see, after speaking to the navy, I went straight to Rosehaven to see. . .Anne." Thom's voice broke.

"Then you know."

He nodded. "I hate that I was not there for her, Nicholas. Even though our marriage was arranged by our fathers, I was truly fond of her. I might have grown to love her if given the proper time."

"Well, you must also be aware you are the father of a very bright and handsome little boy!"

"Indeed, I am! Can you take me to him?" he asked eagerly.

"Of course."

"Nicholas!" Christina called. He turned to see her walking toward him. She'd obviously given him time to speak to his brother, but curiosity had gotten the better of her. He smiled as he noticed her eyes darting back and forth between his brother and himself.

"Isn't this the vicar's daughter?" Thomas asked. "The mischievous scamp who used to play tricks on you as a child?"

Nicholas chuckled. "It is indeed." Smiling teasingly, he put an arm around Christina as she came up beside him. "Thomas, meet my wife. I believe you two already know each other."

Thomas's eyes widened as he stared at them. "But I thought you. . .uh. . ." He let his voice drift, unsure of how to say what he wanted to say.

"Were to marry someone else? Yes, I was, but it's a long story for another day. Suffice it to say God sent this special woman into my life again, and I knew I would be a fool to let her get away."

"It's so wonderful to see you are alive, Lord Kenswick. This is truly the best wedding present we could have asked for," Christina told him.

Still dazed at the news, Thomas shook his head as he smiled at her. "Little Christina, the vicar's daughter," he mused. "I have kept many a sailor entertained on long journeys across the ocean with tales of your antics as a child."

"Not you, too!" she groaned as Nicholas laughed.

"Wait until you hear what she's done lately!" he trumpeted, ignoring the small fist pounding him on the arm at the suggestion.

"I can't wait!" Thomas replied eagerly. "But before you ruin your wedding day, why don't we go and see my son."

Once they had gone back to the house, both Christina and Nicholas watched from the nursery doorway as Thomas reverently picked up his small son and held him close to his chest. A tear ran down his cheek as he bent to kiss the whisper-fine hair on his soft head.

"I know this means Ty will no longer be ours to raise, but I cannot be too disappointed when I see how much Thomas loves him," Christina whispered to her new husband. "I shall miss him, but I know he will be well taken care of."

Nicholas bent and placed a kiss on her head. "Rosehaven is not very far from here. We'll see them often. And once our children are born, perhaps it will make the pain of losing Ty easier to bear."

She sighed. "Our children. I like the sound of that."

"I suppose one consolation will be that he'll have to take Mrs. Sanborne with him."

Christina put her hand over her mouth to hide her smile. "But I was planning on hiring her back once our first child was born!" she teased.

"Then I shall begin now to search the countryside for a replacement, just to ensure you don't!"

She laughed softly, turning her face upward to look at him. "Even though you can be a bit boorish at times, I love you very much, Lord Kenswick." Her tone matched her mischievous grin.

"Although you nearly broke my back falling on me from out of that tree and you want to turn my home into a menagerie, I love you very much, too, Lady Thornton."

Nicholas nodded toward his brother. "I hope he finds the same happiness in life I have. He truly deserves it after all he's been through."

"Do you think he'll ever remarry?"

"I hope so," he answered softly. "Perhaps a young lady will fall out of *his* tree."

"It would take a miracle!" she declared, shaking her head.

Nicholas looked down at her with love in his eyes. "It just so happens I believe in them."

The Engagement

Chapter 1

London, England—Spring 1814

Is it just I, or do you find these dinner parties dreadfully dull?"

"I, too, share the sentiment, but then again, I find many things dull. You, on the other hand, have a better excuse than I," Trevor Kent, the Duke of Northingshire, answered his friend as they watched the guests who were in attendance at the Beckinghams' party. "I don't imagine you can compare adventure on the high seas and your escapade with pirates with our monotonous English society and their dreary little efforts at entertainment."

Lord Thomas Thornton gave North, as the duke was known to his friends, a sardonic grin. "You could not be further from the truth. I didn't like dinner parties before my 'adventure,' as you call it, and I will die a happy man if I never get on another boat," he informed him. "And it was a merchant ship that rescued me, by the by."

"Yes, but let's keep that between us, eh? The story sounds so much more thrilling to add the pirates."

Thomas chuckled. "If it had been pirates, I might have been the dead man everyone thought I was!"

Thomas and North shared a sobering glance. "Indeed. God must surely smile on all the Thorntons, since both you and your brother have truly been blessed this past year."

While Thomas could now make light of his harrowing scrape with death, it had been the blackest time of his life. When he was a lieutenant in the Royal Navy, his ship had been destroyed during a horrendous storm at sea. He and only a handful of others managed to survive by holding on to pieces of the hull until a merchant ship heading to Canada picked them up. Because of the war between the Britons of Canada and the United States, he was not able to return home until nearly a year later. Unfortunately, during this time, all aboard the ship had been declared dead. And that is what his family and friends had been told.

His surprising homecoming was made bittersweet when he learned his young wife, with whom he'd had an arranged marriage, had died giving birth to their son, Tyler. His brother, Nicholas, had looked after the baby until Thomas could return.

"If only He would also bless me with a wife as He bestowed upon my dear brother." Thomas smiled as he referred to his new sister-in-law, Christina, who was also the vicar's daughter in his hometown of Malbury. That smile dimmed a little as he recalled his past. "Dear Anne, my late wife, was a good woman and gave me a wonderful son. Perhaps I have no right to want more."

"Of course you have a right. Which is why you have dragged me to this 'dreadfully dull' affair, or have you forgotten? We must endure such events to find you a wife and a mother for young Tyler," North stated matter-of-factly. "Now tell me which young miss has caught your eye, and I'll see to the introduction."

Thomas made a show of scanning the room. "Therein, unfortunately, lies my problem. They are all very nice and most comely to admire, but. . ." His voice drifted off, as he was unable to put his feelings to words.

"Mmm." North nodded. "I know what you mean. You are searching for what I've sought after for quite some time—someone who is original."

"Exactly!"

"Someone who is pretty yet doesn't give the impression of being like all the rest."

"Yes!"

"She must be easy to talk to and not bore you with relentless chattering about fashions or gossip about the neighbors." North added to the list.

"Absolutely!"

"And above all, she must be loyal, loving, and kind!"

"Here, here!"

They held a moment of silence as they both paused to think about what they had just said. Suddenly they glanced at each other and began to laugh.

"I believe I just described my dog," North sputtered between laughs.

Thomas wiped the moisture from his eyes. "I was thinking of my horse!"

It took a few moments for both men to regain control. By then the whole room was staring at them with curiosity and censure, the latter, of course, from the older set.

"I believe we have drawn enough attention to ourselves this evening. Perhaps we should say our good-byes to our host."

Thomas nodded. "Indeed. I do not think I shall find my bride among this crowd anyway. Perhaps I should take a page from my brother and start attending services in various churches across the shire. There could be another vicar's daughter like my brother's wife, out there—somewhere."

North grinned. "Or you could forgo your loathing of sea travel and go with me back to America. My cousin and I have established a sugar plantation near the city of New Orleans. I was supposed to go and see how he was faring this last year, but a war was still going on. Now that it seems to be over, I shall leave in just a few months."

"I think I've seen enough of North America. We were docked in some little Canadian harbor for two months, and I was glad to leave," Thomas answered with a shudder. "If I cannot find a bride on English soil, then I shall remain a single man."

"Well, if you. . ." North's sentence drifted to a halt when they both noticed the room had become quiet. They glimpsed around to see that all eyes had turned toward the door.

The woman who stood at the entrance to the hall was even more beautiful than the last time Thomas had seen her. Her light blond hair curled artfully about her face while the length of it was pinned atop her head and cascaded in tiny curls down the back. Even from where he stood, he could see the smoothness of her cheeks, the arch of her light brows, and the glow from her incredible golden eyes. Her dress was the color of bright copper, with delicate beaded lace at her neck and high waistline.

But something was different about her from the last time they'd met. No longer was there an enchanting smile on her face or a confidence in her stance as once had been. Instead, he saw a wariness in her eyes, a brave tilt to her proud chin, and a challenged air to the way she stood, as if she were readying herself for an assault.

Even so, she was magnificent to fix one's eyes upon. Her presence seemed to outshine all other ladies around her. Under any other circumstances, Thomas would have had no reluctance about rushing up to reacquaint himself with her, perhaps even pursue her, for she was exactly what he wished for in a wife, and more.

But Lady Katherine Montbatten could not be his—would probably laugh in his face if he even suggested a match between them. No. She probably hated the very mention of the Thornton name. And he didn't blame her.

Katherine had almost been his sister-in-law.

When his brother, Nicholas, the Earl of Kenswick, returned from the war, he'd been wounded and bitter from all he'd seen and done during the battles. In his confused and anxious state, he'd broken his betrothal with Katherine just months before the wedding and conducted himself in a manner in which no gentleman of his station should behave. During this time, their father had died; then Nicholas had thought Thomas was lost to him, also. With the help of Christina, the vicar's daughter, he'd come to realize he needed God's help and forgiveness. Since then, he'd completely changed and settled down to family life at Kenswick Hall with his new bride.

But that didn't change the fact that Katherine had been hurt by the whole affair.

As the crowd around them started to move about and resume their chatter, he watched her trying to smile while greeting their hosts for the party, Lord and Lady Beckingham. She tried to pretend nothing was wrong, but clearly something was.

And Thomas had a horrible feeling he knew the reason. "She has been ostracized by the ton," he murmured, hoping he was not correct in his summation, for the ton represented England's noble families and was known to judge harshly, even among their own relations.

"Not entirely," North corrected. "Only by the marriageable bachelors of the ton. Of course, there are always those who would have other propositions for her, but it is good she has her family to support her."

Thomas grimaced. "Does Nicholas know?"

North nodded. "He does and has repeatedly offered to make amends by providing her father money to add to her dowry, but he was refused." He sighed. "The Montbattens are nearly as rich as your family, so, of course, money is not the problem."

Thomas once again studied her brave features as she pasted on a smile and greeted those around her. "Why the censure? Others have suffered a broken engagement with little repercussions."

"Apparently some idiot started a rumor after Katherine declined his offer to dance at a ball. From there, the lie grew bigger, and before it was all done, it sounded as if your brother had engaged in a duel because he'd found Katherine in a compromising situation with another man—though far from the truth." He shook his head distastefully as he referred to the duels Thomas's brother had fought after he returned from the war; they'd actually had nothing to do with Katherine.

They were quiet for a moment, both watching her from where they stood at the back of the room. "She is beautiful," Thomas murmured, voicing his thoughts.

"Beautiful but cold," the duke stated bluntly. "She was always aware of her beauty, Thomas, and, in my opinion, overconfident in the fact that many adored her. I always knew she wasn't the one for your brother. I'm just sorry he ended it so badly."

Thomas knew all this, since he'd been acquainted with her before he was married. But he'd always felt that her coolness was a facade, almost as if she were afraid to show who she really was. He would see flashes of wit and intelligence before they were quickly banked beneath a serene smile and cultured conversation.

"It would seem her confidence has taken quite a blow," he finally commented.

North shrugged. "I would not doubt it." He tugged at his lapel. "Well, I've had enough of this scene. Would you like to leave now?"

"I believe I have changed my mind after all," he answered, his eyes still on Katherine.

His friend was silent for a moment, and when Thomas looked at him, he saw speculation and a little worry in his eyes. Thomas knew North wanted to say something more, but he only nodded and responded, "I will fetch us more punch then."

He barely noticed North's departure, for he was already scanning the crowd once more for the beautiful blond.

He was stunned to find her golden eyes had found him first. Several unreadable emotions passed over her face as she gazed at him. Thomas was sure her next movement would be to jerk her eyes away from him in disgust once she realized who he was.

But she didn't.

Suddenly she smiled at him, and the confusing emotions that had been swirling in her eyes were gone. Thomas felt the smile all the way down to the pit of his stomach and did not take one breath, so stunned was he by her reaction.

Thomas was afraid to think of how he felt as she began to make her way to him. He didn't dare speculate on what this could mean. He refused to have expectations.

Yet. . .he could not help but hope.

❧

All afternoon, Lady Katherine Montbatten, the elder daughter of the Duke of Ravenhurst, had meticulously plotted her revenge. With help and much coaching from her cousin Theodora, they derived the perfect way to execute their plan—the plan that would vindicate both her and her family and teach the Thorntons a much-needed lesson.

Of course, Katherine had initial doubts about using Nicholas Thornton's brother, Thomas, to do the deed, but Theodora convinced her Thomas must have had a hand in persuading Nicholas to break their engagement. And, besides, what was done to her reputation hurt not only her but also her parents and her siblings. It was only fair the whole Thornton clan suffer, as well.

For over a year, Katherine had had to endure humiliation after humiliation as more rumors and speculation spread about her. Slowly she noticed the offers for her hand had been rescinded and her admirers had fallen away. Even her brother, Cameron, had striven to correct the false assumptions about her character, but he'd been unable to do much good.

The horrible rumors would not die, and she was ruined for it.

And then Theodora had told her about Thomas Thornton returning to society and finding out his wife had died in childbirth. As a widower, she pointed out, he would soon be in need of a wife.

From there they plotted and schemed on the steps they should take. Even though Katherine doubted and wanted to give up the whole plan, Theodora was there, cheering her on, telling her she would feel so much better once revenge was theirs.

Now as they stood on the threshold of Beckingham Hall, she once again was plagued with doubts. A part of her still knew what she was about to do was wrong. It was the same part that spoke to her through Sunday sermons from the vicar and nagged at her when she tried to read her Bible. The last time she'd opened her Bible, the scripture in Romans leaped out at her: "Vengeance is mine; I will repay, saith the Lord." But Theodora had convinced her that, in this instance, God surely understood.

And to make sure she had no more doubts on that score, Katherine had put away her Bible and refused to bring it out until all of this was over.

She wasn't sure God understood at all; otherwise, why would she be plagued with so much guilt?

But tonight there was no going back. They had arrived, and already she had noticed that, indeed, Thomas was in attendance at the party.

She was just not prepared for the effect his presence would have on her. She was certainly not prepared for the memories of how fond she had been of him or how truly nice he'd been during her engagement to flood her mind and heart. She'd forgotten how nice his dark brown hair complemented those Thornton blue eyes or how his manly features could melt the strongest of female hearts.

He did favor his brother, but in many ways, he was nothing like Nicholas. Unfortunately she had hoped he would be.

How could she forget he'd always been so nice and kind to her? His ready smile could lift her spirits, and his low, smooth voice would make her feel warm and welcome.

I can't do this, she thought in a panic. *He doesn't deserve what I'm going to do to him!*

Alarmed, she grabbed Theodora's arm. "This will not work!" she whispered harshly in her cousin's ear. "We have to leave. Now!"

"No!" Theodora answered, while she continued to walk toward their hosts. "It is all planned. There is no backing away from it!"

"Lady Montbatten! We are delighted you could come." Lady Beckingham greeted her warmly, forcing Katherine to walk forward into the room.

She swallowed hard and pasted on a smile. Nodding to her hosts, she answered, "Lord and Lady Beckingham, may I introduce you to my cousin, Miss Theodora Vine."

Introductions and greetings were made, and finally she and Theodora were once again alone. "Theodora, please. I remember Thomas now that I have seen him. He is too nice—too good of a man to have this done to him!" Katherine pleaded.

Theodora turned and gave her a stern look—a look she did well since she stood so tall and had a long, hawkish nose from which to gaze down. "Think, Katherine! Think of how humiliated you have felt all these months. Think of how Nicholas Thornton has been happy in his grand estate with his new wife, while you've been alone with no prospects. Just think, dear, of how the men in the room stared at you when you walked in tonight." She smiled cunningly. "Why, they were almost sneering at you, Kate. You, who were once declared the 'original' of the entire ton! You cannot let this humiliation go unpunished. Can you?"

The hurt and bitter feelings flooded her mind. Indeed, she had noticed how they gawked at her tonight, but she tried not to dwell on it. As she glanced around the room, however, she could not let go of the truth of her circumstances.

She was ruined, and never would her reputation be spotless again.

It was all thanks to Nicholas Thornton. And if Theodora was correct, his brother was not completely innocent, either.

Somebody had to pay. Vengeance had to be taken on some level.

She looked to the back of the room, and her gaze lit on the handsome man standing beside the Duke of Northingshire.

"See how he does not seem to have a care in the world?" Theodora whispered softly in her ear. "He does not have to worry about what people are saying when he enters a room. He does not lie awake at night crying over his fate and how unfair his life has become."

"You're right," she said resolutely, studying his impeccable black suit with his snow white cravat tied neatly at his throat. He and his brother were surely cut from the same cloth! Of course, Thomas would have known about Nicholas breaking their engagement. He did nothing to stop his brother and perhaps even had a hand in the decision. "Tonight our plan shall begin," she murmured more to herself.

Suddenly he turned and caught her staring at him. Her doubts resurfaced, and she nearly turned around and ran out of the room. But the hurt and anger stirring in her heart made her stay where she was.

She refused to wonder why her heart seemed to pound so as his beautiful eyes met her own. She did not dare contemplate how handsome he was and how stately he appeared standing there against the dark blue wall of the room. She would not dare let herself believe she was attracted to the very man she had vowed to ruin by securing his affections, making him think she wanted to be his wife, then leaving him at the altar.

Tonight she would begin to avenge her honor.

Tonight Thomas Thornton would regret the day he ever met her.

With a slow curve of her lips, she smiled at him and began to walk his direction.

The plan was in motion. There was no backing out now.

Chapter 2

Katherine had almost reached Thomas when suddenly Lord Malcolm Paisley, a tall, meticulously dressed man whose snobbery and condescension were only surpassed by his waspish tongue, blocked her path. A calculating smile curved his thin lips as he made a sweep of her figure while tugging on the delicate lace of his sleeve.

His eyes made her skin crawl.

"Dear Lady Katherine," he purred with sarcasm. "You appear quite a bit older since last we met. I should not have known you had I not heard your name announced."

Katherine felt the barb as she was meant to, since she'd seen him only two months ago, but was far too sophisticated to let Paisley know he'd hurt her. "Hmm." She gave him equal measure, letting her eyes scan his flashy attire. "I don't believe I shall take the opinion of a man who mixes pink with yellow."

He smiled, but Katherine could tell her words had irritated him. "Perhaps you should dull your tongue, my lady; otherwise, not even a poor farmer will want you for a wife." He made a snorting laugh that was not at all attractive. "Of course, after they hear of your scandalous past, they'll be likely to turn and run anyway."

"Tsk-tsk, Paisley." A deep voice sounded behind Katherine, and she knew right away it was Thomas Thornton. "I believe you've forgotten the correct manner in which to speak to a lady."

The sneer fell from Paisley's face as if someone had taken a big swipe and wiped it away. In its place was a simpering smile, typical behavior for him when he was confronted by a "favorite" of the ton. Paisley knew exactly whom he could sharpen his claws on and who would destroy him socially—and, in all probability, physically.

Thomas Thornton, former navy lieutenant and brother of the Earl of Kenswick, was one such man.

"Thornton! Can't tell you how glad we all were to know you were alive and well. Why, I was telling Crowler the other day—"

"I believe you owe Lady Katherine an apology, Paisley," he bluntly interrupted, causing the smaller man's neck to burn fiery red with anger.

Paisley tugged at his cuffs again. "I see you don't quite know the way of things, Thornton but that is understandable since you have been away for quite some time."

"I *understand* if an apology is not offered in the next minute that I shall be forced to—"

"Don't you dare say it!" Katherine hissed, cutting off what she knew was a threat of a duel between the two men. She glanced around and was somewhat relieved they had not drawn too much attention. "My reputation, as tattered as it is, cannot survive another scene between gentlemen. I beg you, please, Lord Thornton—let this go!" she implored Thomas.

A moment of strained silence passed as the two men contemplated one another; then Paisley backed down, grudgingly nodding to them both before turning away. They watched Paisley slink back to his circle of friends. As for Katherine, she was trying not to be moved by the way Thomas defended her.

"I thank you, my lord, for desisting in your argument with him. I have to be careful since—" She faltered as the bitterness rose up and threatened to make her cry. How could she go through with this charade when he was a constant reminder of what she'd lost?

"Since my brother broke your engagement," he finished for her with a weary sigh. "Would you like to take a turn about the terrace? I believe the fresh air would do us both good."

Katherine nodded, grateful for the chance to compose herself. But when they began to walk together toward the terrace doors, she realized they had become the object of everyone's attention.

He must have sensed her panic, for he put a steadying hand under her arm and guided her to their destination. "Relax," he whispered. "They shall soon lose interest."

He guided her to a stone bench, and when she had sat down, he stood beside her, leaning against the smooth railing. "Shall I get you something to drink?"

"No," she answered quickly. "I am fine, thank you."

He raised a brow as if he didn't believe her but refrained from saying so. "How long has this been going on?" he asked bluntly, forgoing any of the meaningless talk she'd expected.

She didn't pretend to misunderstand. "For quite a few months now, just before your brother married," she said, wincing that her words had sounded so bitter. Would the hurt of the situation ever go away?

"I wish I could help, Katherine. You know I have always held you in the highest esteem."

She turned her face away from him with a brittle smile. "That is what Nicholas wrote in a letter to me, right before he married that little vicar's daughter!" She stood and paced around the bench. "Of course, he also said he was sorry and wanted to make restitution. Well, if he truly wanted to do that, he could have reinstated the engagement and married me instead of that commoner!" she cried softly with her arms held out to her sides.

But as soon as those words left her mouth and she saw the dismay on Thomas's face, she regretted her outburst. What was she doing? She was supposed to be cozying up to him and drawing him into her life—getting him to like her.

Dropping back down to the bench, she covered her face with her hands, wishing she could leave. She knew, deep in her soul, she was not cut out for this revenge business. "I'm sorry. I should not have said—"

"Shh," Thomas whispered as he sat beside her, taking one of her gloved hands. "I know it has been a trying time, and I am truly sorry for it." She looked up at him, breathing in the light fragrance of his cologne and feeling the warmth of his closeness. Thomas was different from Nicholas in the way most second sons usually were. He did not have the seriousness or regal bearing the earl did; instead, he seemed more friendly, a man who didn't dwell too heavily on the problems around him. He was kind and had a ready smile, even after all he'd been through.

And this revelation again made her want to abandon the crazy plan to ruin him.

Suddenly Theodora was there, as if she'd sensed Katherine wavering. It was uncanny, really.

"Ah! There you are." Theodora spoke up in her nasal tone, though she was staring at Thomas and none too friendly.

Seeing Thomas's reaction to her was something like watching a cat's back bow up when a stranger approaches—only he never moved a muscle, except for the tightening of his jaw. He didn't like either her cousin or her interruption.

Thomas came instantly to his feet. "I don't believe we've been introduced," he announced imperially while peering down his nose at Theodora.

Katherine almost smiled when she realized Thomas *could* act like his brother when he wanted to.

She was musing over his extremely good looks when Theodora snapped her back to reality. "I am Theodora Vine, my lord."

Katherine's cheeks grew hot as she realized she'd been staring at Thomas and totally ignored his question. "Uh—yes! This is my cousin, my lord. She has been staying with us in town and will be going back with us to Ravenhurst Castle."

Thomas gave her a knowing expression and a grin. *The scoundrel!* He'd known she was admiring him! He looked back to Theodora, and all manner of pleasantness was gone from his face as he gave a short and snappy bow. "Miss Vine."

"I believe you, too, will be retiring to your country home, is that not right, my lord?" Theodora asked, and Katherine could tell he did not appreciate the prying question from one he knew so little. But after a pause, he answered, though not to Theodora.

He gazed directly into Katherine's eyes. "Indeed, I shall be there late tomorrow.

I find it a most fortunate circumstance that you shall also be returning to your home, since they are but a stone's throw from each other." He glanced at her cousin as if annoyed she was there and listening so intently but then brought his attention back to Katherine.

Thomas paused a moment as if he wanted to say more, then decided against it. Instead, he picked up Katherine's hand and kissed the satin-covered knuckles. "It has been a pleasure, my lady."

To her cousin, he barely nodded his head. "Miss Vine," he murmured, then walked away.

Theodora waited until Thomas had entered the ballroom before she began her tirade. "What do you think you were doing out here alone with that man?"

Katherine was confused. "Dora, is not that the whole point of the evening—becoming reacquainted with him so he will begin courting me?"

Theodora's lips tightened, and her nose flared with displeasure. "Reacquainted, yes—but it seemed as though you two were almost in an embrace when I walked out here! Is your reputation not black enough?"

"What do you care of my reputation? It will be in tatters anyway after our plan is finished."

"But you will have the satisfaction of knowing vengeance has been served upon the Thornton family! Remember why we are doing this!" Theodora took a deep breath as if calming herself. "You want to appear interested in Lord Thornton so he will want to call on you once he has settled into Rosehaven. He all but implied that was his intention anyway! If you persist in coming on too strong, he will believe the rumors that have been spread about you!"

Theodora's words cut her deeply, as her cousin knew they would. She didn't deserve what had been done to her. She didn't deserve to have her hopes and dreams dashed.

But does Thomas deserve to have his own life trampled upon, either? a voice whispered in her head.

"Perhaps he already does believe them," Theodora said softly. Katherine looked up, her gaze going to the window through which her cousin was staring.

There she saw Thomas standing with Miss Claudia Baumgartner, an American girl who had just come to England to live with her grandfather, the Marquis of Moreland. At first she had been considered an oddity—a rustic. But, according to local gossip, she had charmed her critics and won over more than one heart of the elite ton.

Lord Thomas Thornton appeared completely captivated by her.

Katherine swallowed and refused to examine the strange feeling coursing through her as she watched Thomas smile at the girl.

It felt a lot like. . .jealousy.

"Don't just stand there, Kate!" Theodora charged, giving her a stern look.

"Go in there! Charm the man!"

Exasperated, Katherine shook her head. "First I'm coming on too strong, and now you are throwing me at him! He will think I am a lunatic if I seek him out now. It has been only a couple of minutes since we met."

Theodora shrugged her bony shoulders and tilted up her chin. "Do you want to have your revenge or not?"

Katherine sighed. "Of course I do."

"You're correct, though, in saying you cannot just walk up to him." Theodora tapped a long, thin finger on her pointy chin, then smiled.

Katherine was disturbed at the coldness radiating from that smile.

"Give me your gloves!" she demanded, holding out her hands expectantly.

"What?"

Theodora all but growled. "Give me your gloves! I have a plan!"

Katherine reluctantly did as she bade. "I don't understand why—"

"Because you are going to walk past Thornton and 'accidentally' drop your glove. He'll pick it up, drawing attention away from the little American and onto you," she explained while straightening Katherine's gloves, then handing them back to her.

"That's the oldest trick in the book, Dora! He'll know right away it was no accident!"

"It's the oldest trick because it works, Kate," she explained as if she were talking to a child. "And it doesn't matter if he knows the truth or not. He will still be flattered you attempted such a ploy to grab his attention."

Katherine felt as though every eye in the room were watching her walk toward Thomas and waiting for her to make a fool of herself. She was mortified she was reduced to performing such tactics to draw a man's attention. Two years ago, she had only to walk into a room and the gentlemen would be instantly at her side, competing for even a moment of her time.

How she longed for that life again.

Miss Baumgartner was staring up into Thomas's face, laughing at something he had just said, when Katherine reached them. She had been hoping the glove trick would not be needed, that he would acknowledge her presence and be drawn to her side.

It was clearly not going to happen.

So, with a fortified breath and a glance about the room to make sure no one was looking, Katherine opened her hand, letting one of her long, satin gloves drift to the ground at Thomas's feet.

She took one step, then two, and by the time she took the third, it dawned on her that he was not coming after her or calling out that she'd dropped her glove.

Nonchalantly she stopped, and pretending to study the arrangement of flowers beside her, she carefully took a peek at where Thomas was standing.

There he was—still standing by Miss Baumgartner—still talking and smiling at the woman—completely ignorant of the fact her glove was lying at his feet.

Then it was under his feet as he moved a bit to take a glass of punch from a servant passing by.

Katherine wanted to cry. She peered past Thomas and saw Theodora glaring at her; then she truly wanted to cry.

With a resolve to go home no matter what her cousin said about it, Katherine turned quickly and took only one step before she crashed into the flower arrangement and the ceramic pedestal it sat upon.

The sound it made crashing onto the marble floor was akin to the blast of a cannon. Now she had not only Thomas's attention, but everyone else's, as well.

"Are you all right?" Thomas asked as he put a steadying hand upon her back, his voice filled with concern.

Katherine glanced at him, then uneasily scanned the room at the curious and scandalized faces staring at her in fascination. *Is this what happens to those whose reputation is destroyed? Does their dignity leave them, as well?* she thought wildly.

"I believe I feel faint," she lied and for the first time in her life fell into a pretend swoon.

Thomas, just as she knew he would, caught her perfectly, swept her into his arms and out of the Beckinghams' ballroom.

❧

"You can open your eyes now. We are quite alone," Thomas whispered into Katherine's ear, as he stood in an empty corridor of Beckingham Hall, still holding the beautiful lady in his arms.

Her eyes came instantly open and gazed at him with disbelief. "You knew?"

Thomas grinned as he reluctantly lowered her to the ground. "I deduced you considered it the best possible action to take. And it worked. It got you out of the room and away from the curious stares of the ton," he said with a shrug.

Katherine laughed. "Am I that transparent?"

Thomas grinned. "Not a bit. I would never have imagined you would drop a glove at my feet, or I would have noticed it when it happened!"

He saw Katherine's face turn red; she opened her mouth as if to speak, but nothing came out. He continued. "I found it after your dance with the flower arrangement."

Katherine covered her face with her hands. "That was possibly the stupidest thing I have ever done!"

Thomas stood staring at her for a moment, trying to sort out the feelings that were swirling around in his mind where this enchanting woman was concerned.

Never could he remember being so captivated.

He put his hand in his pocket and closed it around the smooth silk of the glove he'd scooped off the floor after her fall. He started to give it back to her, but for some reason unknown to him, he let the glove go.

"I would never call you stupid, my lady. Clever, smart, beautiful, and even enchanting maybe," he teased, as he pulled her hands away from her face.

Katherine glanced up at him, then quickly turned away with embarrassment. "I suppose you are wondering why I would do such a thing."

"No," Thomas stated firmly, causing her to bring her gaze back to his. "I prefer to find that answer when we return to Derbyshire."

A myriad of emotions passed over her face, most of which Thomas could not decipher.

"What. . .are you saying, my lord?" she asked carefully.

"I am asking if I might call on you the day after tomorrow. Shall we say ten in the morning?"

The dread he saw in her eyes when that question left his lips had him truly baffled. But it disappeared as quickly as it had arisen. "Indeed, my lord. My family and I shall eagerly anticipate it," she told him formally. "Now if you'll excuse me, I must go find my cousin so we may leave."

"Yes, of course," he murmured, as he watched her hasten away.

Thomas stood there for a moment, puzzled as to her quick change of mood. One moment she appeared to show genuine interest in him; the next, she became cold and proper.

It was a mystery he was determined to solve! He'd have ample time at Rosehaven to get to know Katherine a little better and find out if possibly she was the right woman for him.

He then thought of his son, Ty, and wondered how she would respond to the toddler. That was also an important consideration in his quest for a wife.

A quest he now hoped and prayed would end with Lady Katherine Montbatten as his wife.

Chapter 3

I think perhaps I should tell you something I'm not sure you are going to like," Katherine began as she stood before her parents in their elegantly furnished drawing room two days after the ball. The gentle candlelight shining through the crystal lamps about the room should have been soothing to her nerves, but until she finished this meeting, nothing would help. She had wanted to avoid telling them of Thomas's visit, but knowing he would probably want to speak to them, she had to prepare them.

"Do sit down, dear, while you tell us. It is giving my poor neck an ache having to look up at you," her mother, Lady Montbatten, complained as she waved about a lace handkerchief she was rarely without.

Stifling a sigh because of her mother's frequent complaining, Katherine sat down on the blue velvet settee across from her parents. Still dreading to tell her parents the news, she took a moment to smooth the cream taffeta of her day dress.

"Well, spit it out, girl!" her father's loud voice boomed, causing her, her mother, and her sister, who was pretending to read a book, to jerk. His tall, large stature frightened those who didn't know him, but all his friends and family knew that underneath his austere gruffness he was quite a marshmallow.

"Yes, well, I need to tell you someone will be coming to call here this morning," Katherine started again, unable to blurt out the news as she wanted.

"Who, dear?" her mother asked when Katherine did not finish.

"A man, Mama. A man who will come to call on—me."

A loud, thoroughly irate sigh came from the duke as he slapped his large hands on the delicate wooden arms of the chair, making her mother frown with disapproval. "Is this to be a game of charades or question-and-answer? Say what you must and cease shilly-shallying!"

"Lord-Thomas-Thornton-is-the-man!" she all but yelled in one quick breath. "There! It is said!"

"Dear, a proper lady does not raise her voice so—"

"Margaret, please! Did you not hear what she just told us?" her father interrupted, his voice sounding stunned.

Her mother's eyes widened. "Lord Thomas Thornton, did you say?" She fell back in her chair, waving her hand in front of her face in a frantic motion. "I do believe I might need my smelling salts. Lucinda, please ring for Amelia to bring

129

them," she ordered Katherine's little sister.

Lucinda, or "Lucy" as most everyone called her, showed her displeasure at having to leave the room by loudly plopping her book down on an end table and making a huffing noise. "I do not understand why I am always sent on one errand or another to do everyone's bidding!" She whirled dramatically after opening the door, then paused. "Isn't that what we have servants for?" she cried and, without waiting for an answer, flounced out of the room in typical twelve-year-old fashion.

"That girl must be taken in hand! She has grown so very wild in the last year." Her mother groaned, still in her semireclined condition. "We must see to finding her a new governess."

"Yes, yes, all that can be dealt with later, but let's get back to the subject at hand," Lord Montbatten complained impatiently, still staring at his daughter. "How is it you've become acquainted with the Thorntons again, daughter? I would have thought you would find any connection with that family distasteful and even hurtful."

If her father only knew the truth of how she had deliberately sought out Thomas Thornton, of how she planned to ruin his family's name. "We met at the Beckingham ball, Papa, two nights ago. We were always friends, you know, before"—she faltered, then continued—"before the incident."

The duke continued to frown, and Katherine became distinctly uncomfortable under his penetrating gaze. "Are you saying you would welcome his suit if he should choose to pursue you?"

No! she wanted to cry. She wanted nothing to do with anyone from the Thornton family. But she could not say that. Minutes before she'd met with her parents, Theodora had reminded her—strongly—of her purpose, her mission.

"What would you say, Papa, if I said yes?" she asked instead.

Katherine had expected her father to vehemently oppose any sort of match between Thomas and her. In fact, part of her secretly wished he would, so she wouldn't have to go through with the plan.

"Why, I think it is a marvelous turn of events!" Lord Montbatten crowed, lifting his arms in a triumphal gesture. "I had despaired of your ever receiving another offer for your hand, and the fact it is Lord Thornton's brother makes the whole affair work to our advantage!"

Katherine frowned. "Papa, he is just coming to call, not pledging his troth, and how would his pursuing me work to our advantage?"

"It will speak loudly to all the ton if the Earl of Kenswick's brother shows his favor to you; then all those rumors about you and the duel will be unfounded. Don't you see—if they were true and Kenswick did throw you over because of something you did, then his brother wouldn't speak to you, much less come to call!"

THE ENGAGEMENT

Katherine sat there stunned as her father's words sank into her brain. To think her reputation could be restored simply by being seen with Lord Thomas Thornton. The need to ruin him and his family would no longer be necessary. All she would have to do was be seen with Thomas, making it clear she was not interested in marriage, and in a month or two, they could go their separate ways.

Her reputation would be restored, and there would no longer be a need for the plan.

"You are right, Papa, even though I had not thought of it that way," she murmured, as the excitement of her new idea took root.

"But you must, darling!" her mother chimed in, apparently fully recovered from her swoon without the aid of smelling salts. "Since the breakup of your engagement, it has been hard on all of us, especially me." She fell back in her chair again, laying her hand over her forehead. "Being snubbed at every gathering can be quite vexing on my fragile health!"

Shaking her head and stopping short of rolling her eyes, Katherine retorted, "It is my aim in life, Mama, to put right every wrong in my life so that it might benefit your own."

The sarcasm breezed right over her mother's flighty head. "I appreciate that, dear. Truly I do."

Katherine and her father shared a wry glance; then Katherine stood. "If you both will excuse me, I had better freshen up before Lord Thornton arrives."

"Yes, do make yourself extra presentable, dear. We can't lose this one, you know. It might be quite some time before another comes to call!" her mother said, her voice shaky with false bravado. "If you happen to pass Lucinda in the hall, can you please tell her to rush with those salts, dear?"

"Yes, Mama," she said in a singsong voice as she hurried from the room.

It was Theodora's room she ran to, however, instead of her own. "Dora! I have just met with my parents, and Papa made the most excellent point!" Excitedly, she told her cousin what her father had said. "So you see, Dora, we do not have to carry out this plan to the bitter end! Just being seen with Lord Thornton will boost my reputation."

"No!" Theodora practically screamed at her as she stood and took Katherine by the arm. "You must see this plan through—you must! It's the only way we—I mean, you—can be fully vindicated!"

Katherine became alarmed at Theodora's anxiety. She had not expected such a response. "But we do not have to ruin Thomas to be vindicated. Just getting my good name back would be—"

"Enough? Is that what you were going to say?" Theodora spat. "Enough for all the turmoil you have been through? Enough for having your heart broken into a million pieces?"

Katherine knew the breakup of the engagement was more of a humiliation than a heartbreak, but her cousin seemed in no mood to hear that. She seemed quite—vexed!

"Dora, I just think this would be so much simpler—"

"We will stick with the plan, Kate. We must if we are to see all made right! We must!"

Katherine backed away from her, pulling her arm out of her painful grasp, and walked to the window. Confusion crowded her mind and heart as she wrestled with the dilemma.

Two riders on horses appeared in her line of vision, and she focused to reveal their identity. The two handsome men were dressed for riding in their fine suits, both expertly handling their mounts as they rode up the path.

It was Thomas and North, the Duke of Northingshire.

❦

"Are you absolutely sure you want to pursue this?" North asked Thomas again for the third time as they rode toward Ravenhurst Castle. "Many other women would be glad to be your wife and the mother to your son."

"Yes, but there is something about Katherine I must follow up on. There was such a strong connection between us that I cannot help but think God had something to do with our meeting again."

And he was yearning to see her again.

Chapter 4

Three days, Dora! Three days have passed since I last saw Lord Thornton! Not that his visit to Ravenhurst was very memorable, since he stayed for only a few moments!" Katherine complained as she paced before Theodora. The cousins had been strolling in the park and had stopped to rest—at least one of them was resting. Katherine found she could not. "We have ridden or walked to this park not once but two times a day, and nothing!" She threw her arms up in exasperation. "I must have said something to put him off. Did I not make it clear I was interested in meeting him again?"

Theodora scanned the area around them and frowned with disapproval toward Katherine. "The whole village will know you are interested if you speak any louder."

Katherine stopped and returned the glare with one of her own. "Do not scold me as if I'm a child, Dora. My nerves have been so on edge this week that I fear turning into my mother!" She flounced herself down in a most unladylike manner, not caring one whit whether Dora disapproved or not. "And, speaking of my parents, have you not heard for yourself their conversations of a wedding between Thomas and me that will never take place? It's a terrible prospect to bear, cousin, knowing I shall break their hearts when I refuse to marry him."

Dora reached over and gave her hand a brief pat. Katherine knew even this little show of affection was a stretch for her rather cool cousin. "We'll cross that bridge when we arrive at it, Kate. We need to focus our concern now on Lord Thornton and how we can get his attention."

Katherine stood again, too jittery to sit still. "Oh, why can we not forget about this stupid plan? I know I was all for it when we first spoke of it, but I did not realize how taxing it would be on all concerned."

Katherine was watching a lady enter the park pushing a baby carriage, when she heard Theodora's sigh. "When it is over and you have been vindicated, you will thank me," she claimed, just as she always did when Katherine began to have doubts.

Katherine thought of something else. "But what of my parents? They are ecstatic I am being sought by Thomas! They will disown me when I deliberately do not show for my own wedding!"

"Then you must plant doubts about his character in their minds," Theodora reasoned.

"What about his character could I say? He has shown to be a gentleman in all things."

"He has not called on you in three days, Katherine. Start with that. Say he often neglects you and, if nothing else, lie."

Katherine got a sick feeling in her stomach. "I'm not very good at lying," she said quietly as she turned and looked back across the park.

"Then learn" was Theodora's harsh reply. "You can do this, Kate. You *must* do this."

"I don't know," she murmured, her attention becoming more drawn to the woman who had stopped the carriage and was taking the toddler into her arms.

"What don't you know?" Theodora demanded, as she got up from her seat and came to stand by her.

"Dora, who is that lady?"

Theodora barely glanced over, clearly disinterested. "I have no idea, Katherine, but can we—"

"He's such a beautiful child, isn't he? And those dark brown curls are precious! I must go and have a closer look!" She started across the park, but her cousin grabbed her arm.

"What can you be thinking, Katherine? We don't even know who she is! What if she is from a family who is beneath our attention?"

Katherine pulled her arm away from Theodora's grasp and shot her a pointed expression. "I did not realize you had become such a snob, Dora. I will only be a minute. You do not have to accompany me."

"And I shan't!" her cousin called after her.

Katherine walked across the small park to where the lady was now watching the child play with a ball while sitting on the grass.

"Hello," Katherine greeted her. Now that she was closer, she saw the lady was dressed in conservative black like that of a nanny or governess. "I couldn't help but admire the child and had to come over for a closer look."

The woman peered up at Katherine, and her eyes grew big with recognition. She stood at once and bobbed a curtsy. "My lady! It is a stupendous honor to make your stupendous acquaintance. Just stupendous!"

Katherine was momentarily nonplussed, but she recovered. "Well—I see you know who I am. May I have the honor of knowing your name?"

She was presented with another of the woman's incredibly big smiles. "Indeed, my lady. I am Mrs. Sanborne, employed as a nanny for the young master Tyler Thornton."

Katherine was glad the woman chose that moment to bend down and pick up the child, because, for an instant, she could not speak—so shocked was she from that bit of news. "Would his father perchance be Lord Thomas Thornton, ma'am?" she asked breathlessly.

"Yes, he is, my lady." She hugged the smiling child to her, and for the first time, Katherine got a good look at the boy. Of course, he was Thomas's child. There was no mistaking his "Thornton" blue eyes.

"I know Lord Thornton, but this is the first time I've met his son," she told the lady, still gazing upon the sweet child. Every maternal feeling in her body reached out to the boy, who was now motherless in this world with only his father and nanny to care for him.

You could be his mother, a voice whispered in her head, and for a moment, she let herself think about how it would be. How lovely it would be.

"May I hold him, do you think?" she asked impulsively.

Mrs. Sanborne was taken aback briefly. "Of course, my lady. But watch those pretty pearls you are wearing. He's broken a necklace or two of my own!"

"You wouldn't break my necklace, would you, dear boy? Oh my, you are a handsome young man!" she crooned and was startled when Ty did reach out to grab her necklace. She caught him just in time. "Why, you are a little scamp!" She kissed his soft curls. "And you are so much like your father," she added.

"Are you saying I am a scamp also, my lady?" A deep, teasing voice sounded behind them, and she turned to find Thomas standing there, dressed handsomely in brown and light beige, his feet shod with his shining black Hessians.

With both the piercing eyes and his brilliant smile focused solely on Katherine, she found it very hard to answer without stumbling over her words. "I think you can be a scamp on occasion, my lord," she said slowly, thankful she was holding on to her composure.

Thomas threw his head back and laughed. "If you ask my brother, he will agree with you!"

His words were like a shower of cold water suddenly thrown on them. Only young Ty seemed not to be disturbed by it as he laughed at his father, clapping his little chubby hands together.

Thomas reached out and fluffed his son's hair affectionately. "I did not mean—" he began.

"No, please," she interrupted. "I do not want you to feel as if you cannot mention him when we are together. I am quite over our breakup, I assure you," she lied, all the while wishing her words were the truth.

He smiled, but his eyes told her he wasn't quite convinced. "Well, I see you have become acquainted with my son," he said, changing the subject. "What do you think of him?"

Katherine smiled down at the little boy, who was once again trying to reach the pearls around her neck. "I think he's quite the little gentleman." She paused for effect while glancing up at Thomas. "Despite having a father who loves to tease defenseless women!"

Thomas put a finger to his lips. "Shh—he thinks I'm the perfect father.

Wouldn't want to spoil the illusion, you know," he added with a wink.

Ty suddenly wanted his father and, giving a disgruntled cry, held out his chubby arms to Thomas. Katherine was startled when Thomas plucked the toddler out of her arms and swung him up in the air making "da-da" noises, causing his son to laugh with glee.

She had never seen a gentleman carry on like that with a baby. Not even her own father. Most left the rearing to the mother or nannies until the child was of age to learn, and then it meant hunting or schooling.

She was. . .enchanted.

❧

Thomas found himself intrigued with the elusive Katherine. When he'd come up and seen her holding his son with that much affection, he'd hardly been able to bear it.

It had been his main worry—whether Katherine would accept his son. He'd even worried she might not care for children. But all those fears had dissipated the moment he'd walked up and found her holding Ty as if he were her own.

Thomas had missed her in the three days they had been apart, but he'd been so confused at her odd behavior. He wanted to pursue her but sensed a strong pull inside him urging him to be careful.

He'd been praying lately about the course he should take and where God was leading him. It was the reason he'd stayed home at Rosehaven. Until he knew what God wanted him to do, he did not want to chance meeting Katherine, letting his attraction to her override God's will.

The more he sought God's counsel, however, the more he felt God had brought Katherine into his life and that he should try to discern her true feelings for him.

So, with the latter thought in mind, he'd finally ventured out and journeyed into town on the sincere hope of seeing Katherine there.

His hopes had soon become a reality.

There, under the cover of the large elms, she stood out like a glistening gem in her pale green dress and her hair swirled up in curls with some falling about her face. He knew the moment she looked up at him with her mysterious golden eyes that he'd fallen in love with her.

It stunned and humbled him all at once.

He hardly knew her. He'd known her only as his brother's fiancée, then the few moments he'd spent with her at the ball and at her parents' home.

But he so much wanted to know her better.

If only she weren't so. . .elusive! If only she were consistent with her actions and outward emotions, then he might not hesitate to ask for her hand, even at this early stage.

It wasn't uncommon, even for those couples who had met only once, to enter into an agreement of marriage. He'd done it himself with his first wife.

But he wanted this marriage to be different. He knew he loved Katherine and would do all he could to show his love to her, but he couldn't be sure of her feelings. He wouldn't enter another marriage where love was only one-sided, as his first marriage had been. It wouldn't be fair to either of them.

After Thomas had taken Ty from Katherine's arms and had him settled onto his side, he noticed she was smiling at him in wonder.

"What?" he asked curiously.

She shook her head. "I'm just amazed at your freedom of expression with your son, my lord."

"You don't like it?"

She smiled a smile that made his heart ache. "I think it's quite wonderful. I'd love to know the father of my children would treat our children the way you do yours," she explained, her voice wistful.

Thomas took a chance. "Perhaps you will have what you desire after all."

A strange moment passed between them when he spoke those words. A million emotions seemed to play across her expressive, dainty features. Thomas thought among them were happiness, wonderment, and—uneasiness? But that made no sense. What would cause her to feel uneasy with him?

"Perhaps," she finally answered, her eyes no longer focused on him but on his son, instead.

Thomas wanted to shake her as he realized she'd once again distanced herself from him.

"It has been good seeing you this morning, my lord, and meeting your son." She backed away. "I believe Dora must be wondering what has happened to me."

Thomas didn't want her to leave, not before he could figure out why she behaved the way she did. "Tea!" he blurted out, then winced when he realized how silly that sounded.

"I beg your pardon?"

"Have tea with me—at Rosehaven—this afternoon," he stammered. "You may bring your sister and your mother, also." Then as an afterthought, he added, "Oh, and your cousin may come along, too."

She paused, then shook her head with regret. "I fear I will have to decline your kind offer, my lord. My brother is coming home for a small holiday from Cambridge and will arrive at Ravenhurst today. I must be there to greet him."

"Ah, I understand. Perhaps another day," he told her, disappointed he would not see her later on.

Indecision played across her pretty features, and Thomas could tell she was trying to decide something. "My lord—" she began.

"Please, call me Thomas."

She sighed. "Thomas," she repeated. "I would extend to you an invitation to our small gathering tonight, but—"

Thomas held out his free hand, palm toward her. "Please, do not explain. Your family will want to be alone with your brother."

She shook her head and reached out and took hold of his hand, surprising him to his core. "It is not that, Thomas. I fear what Cameron might do if he sees you. He's been very upset about the whole scandal, you see. We've always been close, and he blames your brother and your family for what has befallen me."

Thomas lowered his hand, turning it slightly so he could hold on to hers. "Might I try to talk to him? Perhaps I could ease some of his anger."

"I don't know, Thomas. He grows furious every time your family's name is mentioned." It was then she realized she was holding his hand. Her eyes widened as she viewed their hands, and her cheeks were burning when she finally looked up at him.

Hastily she pulled her hand away and backed up a few steps. "I—I think per—perhaps I'd better go," she stammered, clearly out of sorts from the encounter.

Thomas felt oddly elated by her reaction to him—first the spontaneity of holding his hand, and now the embarrassment of being caught.

"Of course. Give my regards to your family," he replied smoothly, holding back a grin.

She kept backing up until she bumped into a tree. She was quick to regain her composure as befitted a duke's daughter. "Yes, uh—good-bye."

"My, she is quite a stupendous young lady, my lord." Mrs. Sanborne spoke as they both watched Katherine dash back to where her cousin was waiting for her. Thomas had completely forgotten about his son's nanny and wondered if she'd overheard their conversation.

"Indeed, she is, Mrs. Sanborne. Indeed, she is."

"It is a pity you will not be able to take tea with her this stupendous afternoon. Perhaps you should call on her tomorrow. I would be stupendously surprised if she is not hoping for such a visit."

Thomas hid a smile as he continued to look in Katherine's direction. Mrs. Sanborne didn't seem to realize servants were not supposed to converse with their employers as if they were good friends. He rather liked it, though.

"I think I shall not visit tomorrow, Mrs. Sanborne, but wait until church on Sunday," Thomas replied. Perhaps seeing her family in a safe haven like the church would put the future Duke of Ravenhurst in a better frame of mind for their first meeting.

"Oh, indeed, sir!" Mrs. Sanborne cried. "Absence does make the heart grow fonder, my mother often said."

This time Thomas laughed aloud, unable to hide his mirth at his governess's unusual way of looking at things. "Perhaps your dear mother was correct,

Mrs. Sanborne. We shall see, won't we?"

He took one last glance at Katherine before leaving the park. At that moment, she, too, looked back at him. One second passed, then two. Thomas caught his breath for the brief span that she gazed at him, and his heart felt as though it were racing away.

It was soon over when she turned and followed her cousin deeper into the wooded area of the park. Thomas turned, also—his heart filled with hope she would soon be his bride.

Chapter 5

G od must surely be vexed with me," Katherine whispered to Theodora as they sat in the small village abbey on Sunday morning.

Theodora's patience was clearly reaching the straining point as her thin nostrils flared. "It is only a sermon," she stressed.

Katherine shook her head, a panicked feeling building in her chest. "It is a sign, Dora! It must be!"

"Shh!" Lady Montbatten admonished, causing both ladies to face immediately toward the vicar.

As the vicar spoke on how Joseph forgave his brothers for their betrayal and how it paralleled the betrayal of Jesus, and yet He also forgave, Katherine leaned again toward Theodora.

"It is a sign from God!" she repeated in a whisper.

"Angels appearing out of nowhere are a sign. Dreams as Joseph had are a sign. Sermons are not!" She shook her head. "Now hush and peek around to see if Lord Thomas has arrived."

Though not convinced by Theodora's words, Katherine pretended to adjust her bonnet, giving her the chance to glance about. Upon meeting Thomas's gaze, Katherine turned back so quickly, she earned another disapproving look from her mother.

Thomas, as usual, appeared very handsome sitting beside North. She had noticed he wore a dark green coat and his hair was slightly disheveled, possibly done so by the morning breeze she'd also experienced when riding in their open carriage to the abbey.

"He's here," she told her cousin under her breath.

"Excellent," Theodora answered, still giving the impression of listening to the vicar, her lips curved in a satisfied grin.

Katherine, too, looked back at the vicar, but unlike her cousin, she could not sit there calmly and not feel the meaning of his sermon and the guilt it rained down on her soul. And now that she knew Thomas was only a few feet from her, the feelings were compounded. She tried to take calming breaths but found it did not help. Suddenly she could take it no more. Jumping up from her seat, Katherine all but stumbled past her family to the aisle, then hurried out the door, not daring to acknowledge Thomas as she passed him.

Katherine ran until she reached a small grove of trees, then with a heartfelt groan fell to the fresh green grass. Covering her face with her hands, she wished she could cry and release all the pent-up feelings that had been building in her heart—the bitterness, anger, betrayal, and, lately, guilt.

But she couldn't, and she thought maybe she didn't deserve the luxury of a good cry—not when she was set on a course that was so contrary to her character.

"Are you all right?" a voice asked from up above her. A voice she knew was Thomas's.

And for some reason, Katherine became highly irritated at his presence. Lowering her hands, she peered up to find his handsome face swathed with worry and concern. "Are you always like this?" she blurted out, her tone none too friendly.

He froze for a moment, seemingly stunned by her abruptness. "I beg your pardon?"

She stood up, ignoring his outstretched hand. "Do you always do the right things?" When he continued to appear puzzled, she let out a breath of frustration. "Are you always such a gentleman? Do you ever do anything—well—*wrong*?"

He studied her, then asked carefully, "Katherine, are you feeling all right? Perhaps I could see you home so you might lie down for a—"

"I am not sick!" she interrupted, childishly stomping one foot. "What I am trying to ask is if you are always this nice? Do you ever say the wrong thing or do something you are not proud of—"

"Are you saying you want me to act ungentlemanly?" he interrupted this time.

Katherine rolled her eyes as she threw her arms up in frustration. "Are you mad? Why would I want that?"

Thomas opened and closed his mouth twice before any words came out. "I don't think *I* am the mad one!" he finally answered, his deep voice calm though highly strained.

Katherine knew she was sounding like a lunatic, but like a cart rolling down a hill, she could not seem to stop. "Ha! There, you see! You have insulted me!" She folded her arms and smiled smugly, glad finally to find some nibble of ammunition she could use against him. "You do not always do or say the right thing after all!"

Thomas surprised her by letting out a wry chuckle. "My lady, are you always this conflicting? First you are dropping gloves at my feet and crashing into vases; next you are cuddling my son as if he were your own." He paused. "A sight, I might add, that took my breath away and gave me great hopes for the future." He smiled and reached for her gloved hand. "Then finally you are berating me for being a gentleman and smile when you think I am not one. All this makes no sense to me, but I must say I find it quite enjoyable!"

Katherine took a swift breath as he bent his head over her hand, kissing her knuckles gently, sending a wave of excitement to her heart.

Then a loud voice, which could only belong to her bratty sister, broke their moment. "I see Mama's fears are to be realized!" Lucy declared as she stood there with her arms folded and her eyes narrowed suspiciously upon their clasped hands.

Katherine quickly stepped back, snatching her hand away and holding it behind her as if she were hiding it. "Lucy! Why aren't you in church?" she demanded, chagrined to find her voice slightly breathy. She could only hope she wasn't visibly blushing!

"Why aren't you?" her sister shot back.

"I had to, well, I"—she stumbled for an excuse—"I had to get a bit of fresh air!" She lifted her chin and gave her sister equal measure on her stare.

She should have known better than to get into a verbal challenge with her sister. Lucy, though only twelve, could outsmart and outtalk most of the Montbatten family when she chose to.

"And I suppose you needed Lord Thornton to help you find the fresh air?" she questioned smoothly while shifting her sharp gaze to Thomas.

Katherine now knew she was blushing. Her cheeks were practically on fire! "Lucy! Can you please go back to the abbey—"

"If I go, you must go with me," she interrupted. "Mama and Papa sent me to be your chaperone."

Katherine groaned and looked over at Thomas, who grinned. "There is a very fine incline over there that is shaded and grassy. Why don't we wait over there until your parents can join us?" Thomas suggested.

Katherine was surprised when he extended his arm not only to her but to Lucy, as well. For the first time, Katherine saw Lucy blush as she took his arm, gazing up at him with adoring eyes. Even Lucy, apparently, was not immune to Thomas's charm.

Fine, Katherine thought. Not only would she have to deal with her parents after the whole ordeal was over with, but she'd also have to contend with her sister's feelings.

Once they were seated, Lucy stated, "You do know our parents are all quite giddy about your interest in my sister."

"Indeed!" Thomas sputtered with a shocked laugh.

Katherine was behind him, dismayed, as well, but she was not laughing! "Lucinda Ann Montbatten! Ladies do not say such—"

"We'd all thought her as 'on the shelf,' an old maid, forever without a hus—"

"I think he understands your meaning, Lucy. Now, please—" Katherine tried to silence her again, even attempting to reach across Thomas to give her a pinch of warning, but it did no good. Thomas merely plucked her hand and folded it into his own and encouraged Lucy to continue.

Ignoring Katherine's outraged gasp, Lucy did as he asked. "As I was saying, we thought her doomed to a life alone until, of course, you came along, my lord." She gave him another smile, and Katherine thought she might have even winked at him, but she could not be sure.

"Ah! Just like a fairy tale, wouldn't you say, Katherine?" Thomas teased, smiling into her perturbed stare, holding fast to her hand when she tried to pull away.

"Yes, that is exactly what Mama said. She also said she hoped you wouldn't wait long to propose, since you were Kate's only chance for matrimony and she did not want anything to happen to run you off."

This time Katherine managed to pull free of Thomas's hold. Leaping to her feet, she shook her finger at Lucy, who was now trying to scoot behind Thomas for protection. "You will end up in the same situation, sister dear, if you don't act in a more ladylike manner!" Katherine shrieked.

By now Katherine was so angry she forgot to mind her own behavior. All she could think of was getting her hands on her big-mouthed sibling. Twice she circled around the man as her sister kept scrambling away from her.

Then, in a moment of triumph, Katherine caught her. "Ha! I've got you. Now what are you going to do?" she growled as she tugged her sister by the arm and glared down into her panicked face.

But then the panic turned to glee as Lucy focused on something beyond Katherine. "Mama! Papa! Help me!" she yelled in a pitiful voice. "Katherine was angry because I caught the two of them in a kiss, and now she is trying to harm me!"

Katherine knew she'd been bested. But it wasn't the fact that her parents were there to witness her unladylike behavior—they'd seen her and Lucy get into tussles before. No, it was because she suddenly noticed Thomas watching her, doing all he could to hold back his laughter!

"Katherine! I say, daughter, your behavior is not at all befitting your station!" her father scolded in his booming voice, as he kept glancing with apprehension to Thomas.

"Uh, yes, dear! We don't want to give anyone the wrong impression, do we?" her mother seconded, emphasizing each word in her last sentence while motioning toward Thomas with a nonsubtle movement of her head.

Thomas chose to rise at that moment, giving her parents a brief bow. "Your Graces," he greeted them with a dashing smile. "Trust me when I say there is nothing Katherine could do to change my good opinion of her." Thomas turned his gaze to her, and she felt the power of his tender smile all the way to her toes. "I think she is the most beautiful, most fascinating woman I have ever met."

Katherine was barely aware of her parents crowing with approval and flattery aimed at Thomas, for she was momentarily struck blind and deaf from all else in the world except Lord Thomas Thornton—a man Katherine was beginning to realize was a most extraordinary man, indeed. A fact she wished with all her heart she'd known before making her ill-fated plans.

What would it be like, she wondered, if he were to be her fiancé in truth? What would it be like to make plans for the future with this man in it?

"Did anyone hear me when I said I caught them kissing?" Lucy called out, breaking the connection that had been flowing between them.

Katherine opened her mouth to defend herself when Thomas spoke. "I beg your pardon, Your Graces, but I was only kissing Katherine's hand." He smiled a charming smile at her mother. "Her *gloved* hand, at that."

Katherine watched her mother gush with glee. "Of course, we suspected nothing else," Lady Montbatten assured him, waving her lacy handkerchief in his direction. "But I was young once, my lord, and I do know what it's like when you are"—she paused for effect—"in love?"

Katherine watched in wonder as Thomas handled her prying with cunning. "Your Grace, one would only have to gaze upon your fair skin to suppose those memories were not so long ago," he told her smoothly.

Lady Montbatten giggled into her handkerchief like a schoolgirl, and Katherine realized she was actually feeling jealous of her mother!

It was at that moment Theodora arrived, followed by North.

"Cousin." Theodora spoke first. "We've been all over the church grounds trying to locate you," she told Katherine. "Is everything all right?"

Katherine resented Theodora's prying question and curious expression. In fact, Katherine was beginning to wonder how she could convince Theodora they should not go through with their plan.

But even if she did achieve that difficult task, how would she ever convince her cousin she might just *want* Thomas to ask her to marry him? She might just want everything about their relationship to be—real.

Katherine sighed. That line of thought would require more reflection, however. Now she would just pretend to go along with Theodora.

"Of course, everything is all right," Katherine answered. "We were just about to come and find you."

"Actually," Thomas inserted, causing all eyes to turn toward him, "I thought perhaps you'd like to join me for a picnic in my garden. It is so beautiful this time of year, and the roses are beginning to bloom." He nodded toward her parents to make sure they knew they were to be included.

"What a delightful suggestion, my lord!" Lady Montbatten crooned, clapping her hands together. "We would be honored, wouldn't we, Raven?" She spoke to her husband, using his nickname from his title of Duke of Ravenhurst.

"Capital idea!" the duke seconded with a satisfied smile. "I'll send a servant to inform Cameron of our plans, and we will meet you at the noon hour."

Thomas nodded. "Cameron is, of course, invited, also."

The Montbattens all exchanged uneasy glances. "I think we shall wait until another day to include our son," Lord Montbatten finally answered.

"If you think it best."

The duke frowned. "Trust me—it is best."

"On second thought, my dear, why don't we send Theodora to give Rogers the message?" Lady Montbatten chimed in, referring to their footman waiting for them at the abbey. "Rosehaven is not too far, and it will give us a chance to talk more, don't you agree?"

Katherine saw her mother send her father a significant look, and he was a little slow at catching its meaning but soon did. "Well, I had not wanted to walk— uh—but, of course—I think the walk would be a wonderful idea," he answered slowly and carefully. "Run along, Theodora, and see to Rogers, will you?"

Katherine knew Theodora did not like being treated like the poor relative she was. Though she was treated better and more equal than most, she was still Katherine's companion, totally dependent on the generosity of the duke and duchess.

With her pinched lips and pointy chin thrust high in the air, Theodora stalked away, but her displeasure had not gone unnoticed. Katherine saw her father frowning after her, so she turned his attention elsewhere.

"What about your son?" she asked Thomas brightly.

It was North who answered. "I sent them along in the carriage. They should be waiting for us at Rosehaven."

Thomas nodded, motioning ahead on the path. "Then let's meet them, shall we?"

As they began to walk, Katherine found herself walking in front with Thomas, Lucy was paired with North, and her mother and father brought up the rear. The silence between them all was quite comfortable as they strolled along the tree-lined path, with the sweet smell of the spring flowers drifting upon the light breeze.

Lucy apparently didn't think so, though. As usual, she spoke exactly what was on her mind. "It is really quite odd to be walking with you, my lord, when just last year we were attending your funeral," she commented, referring to the time when Thomas's ship had gone down during the war and he'd been declared dead.

Both Katherine and her parents scolded the girl at one time. "Lucinda! Do not say another word!" "Please be quiet!" "Hush—"

"It is quite all right," Thomas interrupted, turning slightly to smile at the precocious girl. "Of course, it must seem odd to her."

Katherine turned to see her mother dabbing frantically at her forehead with her handkerchief. "Yes, but she should not say so aloud. It is quite unbecoming!

Quite!" her mother emphasized, her voice shaking with embarrassment.

"Why shouldn't I say so aloud? He is alive, isn't he? I should think he would be glad to talk about it," Lucy insisted. "What do you think about it, North?" She directed her question to her walking companion.

" 'Your Grace,' Lucy. You must address him as 'Your Grace'!" Lady Montbatten admonished.

Lucy let out a sound of disgust and rolled her eyes. "What do you think about it—*Your Grace*?"

North chuckled. "I think we are blessed to have Thomas among us. Our sorrow was turned to great gladness when he came home to us."

"I know my parents are glad about it. At least they are now since he's been courting my sister!"

More instantaneous scolding came from Katherine and her parents. But Thomas's laugh interrupted them all in surprise. "Was there much crying at the memorial service, Lucy? Were pretty words spoken on my behalf?" he asked in a teasing voice.

Lucy nodded seriously. "Oh yes. And I'm sure I would have cried over you, too, had I known you better then."

Thomas's laughter again stopped Lucy from being scolded too much, but Katherine knew she must have a talk with her sister as soon as possible on proper conversation etiquette.

Katherine felt compelled to put an end to their talk of death and funerals. "I am sure you will not have to worry about crying over Thomas for a great many years. I am sure God will see fit to give him a long life after all he has been through."

She peered up at Thomas to give him a quick smile, but when she found him looking back at her with such a tender expression, she nearly stumbled with its impact.

"Indeed, I pray you are correct. I have a whole life I want to experience before I enter heaven—one that includes my son and a very beautiful, very special lady," he told her in a low, intense voice.

He took her hand and tucked it into his arm as they continued on their path to his estate.

Katherine had not been sure his words were loud enough to reach her parents behind them, but obviously they had. "Did you hear that, Raven? I believe he was referring to our daughter," her mother whispered to the duke but not low enough to keep everyone from hearing.

Katherine wondered if she'd spend the entire courtship in a constant state of humiliation.

Then again, perhaps it was the least she would deserve.

Chapter 6

While his servants were preparing the garden for their picnic, Thomas took the opportunity to show the Montbattens around the manor. He was proud of the large estate that had been in his mother's family for three hundred years. His late wife, Anne, had started renovations on it, but he had not done anything else to it since his return. He was now glad he had not, since he had an idea of letting Katherine do the honors. But, as it was, Rosehaven was beautiful with its old family paintings and crystal chandeliers.

His pride and joy, however, were the sixteenth-century tapestries that hung in what used to be the great hall of the manor and was now his drawing room. When the workers had begun cleaning the attics, they'd found the pieces of art still intact and well preserved.

"It is wonderful how they could depict the various aspects of their lives with only a needle and thread," Katherine commented, as she studied one of the larger tapestries about the large room. He'd been thrilled to learn she was interested in history as much as he.

"I don't see what all this fuss is about. They're just musty old cloths with funny-looking pictures nobody cares about. Didn't they have anything else to do with their time?" Lucy plopped down on one of the cushioned chairs in the center of the room, a bored expression clearly marked on her pert features.

"Lucy, if you'd turn your attention to acting more like a lady, you'd know all accomplished ladies do needlework, play the pianoforte, and follow all manner of other pursuits," Lady Montbatten said. "Take your sister for an example. She does some of the finest needlework I've ever seen."

Upon hearing more praise about her older sibling, Lucy threw back her head and groaned. It was all Thomas could do not to laugh at her antics, but he contained himself when he saw the frown of disapproval Katherine shot her sister.

"Mother, you cannot compare my little needlework to these great works of art. It is like comparing apples to oranges."

"Speaking of fruit," Thomas said when he saw his butler, McInnes, nod at him from the doorway, "I believe our luncheon is ready for us in the garden. Shall we?"

Thomas offered his arm to Katherine, and with Lucy trailing behind them, they followed the duke and duchess out into the garden. Before they reached their table, Thomas took the opportunity to whisper to Katherine, "After we dine, perhaps you'd like to see my stables. I have been told you are a great admirer of Arabians, and I've just purchased two."

Katherine's eyes lit up, causing Thomas's insides to do a strange little flip-flop. "I would, indeed, like to see them!"

"Me, too!" Lucy broke in. "I absolutely love horses!"

Katherine and Thomas glanced back to find the girl imploring them with hopeful eyes. Thomas then shared a helpless look with Katherine. "Of course, you may come, too."

"She is quite the clever girl, isn't she?" Thomas whispered with a chuckle once they'd continued to walk in the garden.

"If you want to call being a troublemaker and eavesdropper clever," Katherine returned with a sigh. "I keep waiting for her to grow up and out of her direct-ness and become more ladylike. I fear I shall not survive it if she does not do it soon!"

Thomas shrugged. "When you are living apart from her, you will be able to appreciate her more."

"When would I—?" Katherine froze in midsentence.

Thomas smiled, thinking she must have contented herself with the notion she would probably never leave her parents before he came along. "When you marry, of course," he finished smoothly, giving her a significant glance.

He watched her blush and look away.

North was already waiting for them, as well as Mrs. Sanborne with Ty. Theodora, Thomas noticed with dissatisfaction, had also returned. An uneasiness stirred inside him. He still had not figured out how much influence the woman, who appeared to be in her midthirties, had on Katherine. But something was there, for Katherine was constantly looking to her cousin when she was around.

As she was doing now, he observed. The minute she realized Theodora was present, she left his side and went to greet her. They shared a few whispers between them, and Theodora seemed to be arguing with Katherine about some-thing. She was frowning at first, but when he started toward her to direct her to her seat, she was all smiles.

"Is everything all right?" he asked in a low voice as he held out her chair.

"Of course!" she exclaimed, her expression questioning.

He stared at her a moment, trying to see behind the facade she'd suddenly put on, but he could decipher nothing. With a silent sigh, he gave her a small smile and went to his seat at the head of the table, where she sat on his right and her mother on his left. Theodora was seated well away from them—he made sure of it.

As they partook of the delicious chicken his cook had prepared, conversation flowed easily between Thomas, North, and the elder Montbattens. Katherine was noticeably quiet during the meal, a problem Thomas hoped to question her about once they were at the stables later.

At one point, his son became cranky as he usually did around his noon naptime, but when Mrs. Sanborne got up to take him inside the manor, Katherine surprised him by stopping her and asking if she could hold him for a while.

Thomas tried to pay attention to the conversations around him after that, but his gaze was drawn to the interaction between Katherine and Ty. He'd immediately quieted when she took him, and as she carried him about the garden, singing softly to him, he'd slowly begun to nod off. Thomas was surprised she could handle carrying Ty about like that, since he was over a year now and getting fairly heavy. After that, she'd settled on one of the iron benches and leaned back so the toddler was straddling her waist with his chubby legs and resting his head under her chin.

The sight of them made his heart yearn for her to be his wife and mother to his son. This would be a familiar sight, one that would extend to other children they would have.

And she would be his. He would be able to reach out to her as he wanted to, wrapping his arms around her, holding her to his heart, knowing she would be his wife and love forever.

God knew he wanted that more than anything.

"Isn't that right, Lord Thomas?" Lucy's voice jarred Thomas out of his reverie. He glanced around to find everyone at the table staring at him.

"Isn't what right, Lucy?"

Thomas had the eerie feeling the young girl knew exactly what had been on his mind. "The horses. Were not you going to show me your prized Arabians?" she asked, apparently for the second time.

"Oh! Yes, of course." He glanced about the table. "I promised Lucy and Katherine I would show them my horses I have just recently acquired. Would anyone else like to join us?"

The duke shook his head. "Not I. I fancy sitting here in the shade a bit and resting after such a fine meal." He nodded toward his wife. "You may go, my dear, if you would like."

Lady Montbatten smiled. "Oh no. I'll join my husband in his rest." She turned to her younger daughter. "You should rest also, Lucy. Why not let Theodora go in your place?"

Before Lucy could voice her protest, Thomas intervened. "Both ladies are welcome to join me." He sent his friend a pointed look. "You will come also, North?"

North must have understood he needed him along for distraction. "Indeed. But I warn you, if I spend too much time admiring them, you might find some of them missing when I am gone!" he teased.

Everyone laughed, and Thomas took the opportunity to walk to where Katherine was holding Ty. "Why don't you let Mrs. Sanborne take him now and put him to bed? I would imagine he is growing quite heavy for you."

Katherine nodded and slowly stood up with the sleeping child. Mrs. Sanborne took him from her, and Thomas noticed a bittersweet smile on Katherine's lips as she watched them go into the manor. "I believe my son is quite enamored of you," Thomas told her, bringing her gaze back to him.

She grinned up at him. "As I am with him. Tyler is a fine little boy, Thomas. You seem to be doing well with him."

Thomas nodded thoughtfully, debating whether to say his next words. He decided it would not hurt to start hinting around at his feelings. "I suppose I do well enough, but it doesn't follow we are content in our situation." She merely seemed curious, so he continued. "Every little boy should have a mother."

At those words, Katherine turned away, and he was unable to read her reaction.

"May we go now?" Lucy asked impatiently then.

Thomas sighed inwardly and watched Katherine use the interruption as an excuse to walk away from him. "Yes, of course." He walked toward the group and noticed Theodora was now talking to Katherine. Confused again at her odd behavior, he held out his hand to Lucy, then motioned his head to North to join him.

As the men and Lucy took the lead down the path that led to the stables, Katherine and Theodora hung back a ways, still whispering in what sounded like an argument.

"Lucy," Thomas said in a low voice, "I was wondering if you might help me in a plan that involves your sister and Miss Vine."

Lucy, just as Thomas had supposed, grew excited by the idea of conspiring against her sister. "Oh, I would! What did you have in mind?" she whispered back, her voice full of excitement.

Thomas exchanged a glance with North. "I need you and North to distract Theodora so I might speak with your sister alone. It would be only for a few minutes."

Lucy's eyes narrowed on Thomas, and a conspiratorial smile curved her lips. "You like my sister, do you not?"

Thomas smothered his chuckle with a choked cough. "Uh—yes, I do."

She nodded with wisdom beyond her years. "And I suppose you want to be alone with her to recite sonnets or some other such romantic gesture."

North was the one choking back a laugh this time. "Do you have your sonnets on hand, Thom?"

Thomas chuckled. "Perhaps I shall save the sonnets for another day. Today I only want to talk to her."

"All right," she said with resignation; though by her tone, Thomas understood the girl thought her idea of sonnets a better plan than his.

They had arrived at the stables, so Thomas ushered them inside. As usual, the large building appeared clean and tidy.

"It smells in here," Theodora was quick to comment.

"It *is* a stable, Theo," Lucy retorted.

"Do not call me that, Lucinda!" her cousin snapped back in a low, menacing voice.

Thomas saw Lucy was about to say something back, and he jumped in hastily. "North, why don't you escort Theodora and Lucy outside where the air is fresher."

North nodded, giving Theodora one of his charming smiles. "Excellent idea!" He held out his arm to the woman. "Shall we?"

Thomas was interested to see the older woman actually start to blush and preen a bit. "I would love to," she said softly, but then she suddenly remembered her duty. "But Kate will be without a chaperone."

"We will only be right outside. I am sure her reputation will be safe with that and all the groomsmen about," North countered smoothly.

That was all the convincing it took. North had so enthralled the woman with his appeal she would have probably followed the handsome duke anywhere. So with Lucy on his other arm, they left Thomas alone with Katherine.

Finally.

◈

Katherine watched her cousin with astonishment as she walked out of the stables hanging on to the Duke of Northingshire's arm and gazing at him with adoring eyes.

Where has the spinsterish woman gone who is always quoting platitudes on why women are better off without men? she wondered.

"Ah! Here we are." Thomas brought her attention to the horse he was standing beside. "This beauty is named Sultan, and though he is a lot to handle, he can run like the wind. Come—you can pet him. He's like most males who become big babies when a lovely lady is around."

The sleek black horse was, indeed, beautiful, and with a little reverence, Katherine reached out and ran her hand down his forehead and nose. The horse, just as Thomas had predicted, moved to snuggle his head more into her hand. "Oh! You are a big baby, are you not?" she crooned.

Katherine looked up to find Thomas studying her. She became disconcerted, because it seemed he could see so deeply into her heart and mind, discerning her secrets. She lowered her eyes. "Why do you stare at me so?"

Thomas turned away, and he, too, began stroking the horse's mane. "I suppose I am trying to understand you," he commented evenly, but Katherine could tell it was a subject that was serious to him.

She did not want to speak of serious things with Thomas. Serious talk would lead to serious questions such as those concerning marriage. And as much as Theodora was urging her to hint around about the subject, she was experiencing much anxiety about doing so.

"There is nothing to understand," she countered with a shrug, walking over to the horse in the next stall.

"Sometimes you seem very comfortable in my presence; then in an instant, you become uncomfortable." His voice was low and full of confusion and concern as he came up behind her.

Katherine closed her eyes, fighting off feelings that would only complicate the already horrible situation. "I—I don't know what you're talking about. I—"

"Is it because of my brother? Do I remind you of him, and that is what makes you become distant?" he interrupted her, then placed his hands on her shoulders and gently turned her to face him. "Do you love him still?"

Katherine felt the warmth of his hands linger on her shoulders, and part of her wished she could step a few inches more into his arms. Somehow she knew his strong arms would make her feel safe—that everything would make sense.

She looked fully into those deep blue eyes that were so much like his brother's yet filled with a love and respect she had never seen in Nicholas's, and she knew she'd never been in love with his elder sibling. Neither had he been in love with her. They'd had an arrangement, one that benefited them, their families, and their station. She wanted revenge against him, not because she'd been scorned by love but because she had been so humiliated over the aftermath of the breakup.

And she was going to make Thomas pay for a humiliation he had nothing to do with? It made no sense now. Not when she was staring into the eyes of a man whose honor and integrity showed so clearly there.

What a wicked person she was. Would God ever forgive her for what she had planned to do?

"I am not in love with Nicholas, Thomas," she told him honestly, and it hurt her physically to see his eyes light up with relief. "And though you resemble each other, there is not much about you that reminds me of him. To be honest, we never really talked much, and I saw him as rather arrogant and self-seeking, whereas you are unpretentious and very giving."

His smile grew at her words, and Katherine knew he was pleased. "I am glad you do not compare us and that your heart is not tied to him." He stopped for a moment, then continued hesitantly. "But I do want you to know he is not the same man he was. I can honestly say God has wrought a great change in his life. I do not think you would recognize him as he is today." He smiled teasingly. "Although he can still be a little arrogant. But I believe being the Earl of

Kenswick brings that on ever so often."

A wave of resentment shot through her as Thomas spoke of the changes in his brother. It seemed unfair for Nicholas to be so much in God's favor when she felt as though God had forgotten her. And with the terrible thoughts she'd had and the dastardly plans she had made, she would probably never feel His favor again. "I have also changed, but I sometimes think it is not for the better and that God has had little to do with it," she found herself admitting, surprising them both.

Thomas frowned and moved to take her hands into his own. "You are wrong, Katherine. God can take any bad situation and turn it around for good. Of course, you know what He did for me! Coming that close to death made me realize how much I needed God and how much I should cherish the people in my life. I hated going through it, but now that I am on the other side, I can see God's plan." He caressed the backs of her bare hands. "Now that we have met, can you not see how everything can turn out to be better than either of us ever dreamed?"

Katherine wanted to turn and run away from him and his eyes full of adoration. His words were like someone putting bricks upon her shoulders, weighing her down with even more guilt and shame. Why didn't she turn to God when the rumors had started? Why had she allowed bitterness to choke out her happiness and peace?

But she couldn't run. She was caught in a web of her own making—one she didn't know how to get out of.

"Yes, of course I can," she murmured, hating herself for being such a coward and not confessing the whole truth to him.

"Look—why don't you come to the manor tomorrow? Nicholas and his wife, Christina, should be arriving at noon. I think it would help you to talk to him after all this time. I know he has some apologies he would like to make to you personally."

"Oh no," she answered quickly, knowing she was not ready to face Nicholas. Not yet. Maybe not ever, if she could not find a way of backing out of the plan. "I'm sorry, Thomas, but I just can't."

Thomas seemed disappointed, but he tried to hide it. "It is all right, Katherine," he said. "There will be other times. And when the time is right, I will be with you."

Katherine squeezed his hand and smiled at him, although she felt like crying.

Chapter 7

Thomas waited until his brother and sister-in-law had reunited with Ty before he told them of his involvement with Katherine. Because they had both raised his son the first few months of his life, when everyone had presumed he was dead, Thomas did not want his news to upset them right away.

As Christina and Nicholas played with the toddler and chatted with him, Thomas could see they were very happy in their marriage. Nicholas, though always retaining his regal bearing, was a more considerate person now, friendlier, with a ready smile, than he had been after their father died.

The more Thomas talked with them, the more he began to think that maybe his news would not bother his brother at all. Perhaps he would even be happy for him!

"By the way"—he decided to go for the nonchalant approach—"Katherine and her family are at their castle for the season."

Thomas saw Nicholas turn to gauge Christina's expression as if to see her reaction to his old fiancée's name. When she merely smiled at him and continued to play with her nephew, Nicholas responded. "Indeed? I am surprised they are not in London this time of year. The London season was always an event of great importance to the duke and duchess." His voice was calm, and in fact, he didn't seem interested in pursuing the subject, giving Thomas even more confidence in what he needed to say.

"Yes, well, I believe the Montbattens felt their stay in the country was more beneficial than attending the season." When he received no response from his brother, who had reached for the baby and was now holding him up in the air, he became more specific. "More beneficial to Katherine."

Nicholas froze, then slowly lowered the baby, keeping his razor-sharp gaze trained on his nervous brother. "Are you trying to tell me Katherine has a suitor?" Then to Thomas's amazement, he laughed. "And you thought this would bother me?"

Thomas cleared his throat. "Well, yes, but—"

"Thom, this is the best news I've heard all day! Do you know how guilty I've felt knowing Katherine's name was so blackened over our engagement that she's had no offers? This brings a sort of closure to that whole dreadful episode in our lives!"

"Tell us, Thomas! Who is he?" Christina piped up as she ran to sit on the sofa next to him. It amazed him to think this beautiful redhead had been the vicar's little daughter who gave them so much grief when they were younger. She still had that unchanging spark shining in her eyes and the impish grin he remembered so well. It was her hope and faith that had refused to give up on his brother, even when Nicholas tried to shut her and everyone else out of his life after the war.

"Yes, tell us! Do you know him?" Nicholas seconded.

Thomas took a deep breath. "Yes, and you know him, too. I am Katherine's suitor."

There was a moment of stunned silence as both Nicholas and Christina stared at him, but then his brother leaned his head back and roared with laughter. "You?" He laughed some more. "That is good, Thom. You have developed quite a keen wit since your return from sea."

Thomas looked helplessly from Nicholas to Christina; then he noticed she did not share her husband's laughter. "I do not think it is a joke, Nicholas," she said to him, but her eyes were studying her brother-in-law.

Nicholas wiped the tears of laughter from his eyes with one arm as the other rolled a ball to Ty, who was sitting in front of him. "Of course he is, Christina. If you knew Katherine, you would understand the two of them would be a mismatch if ever there were one! Tell her, Thom. Tell her you are only joking!"

Thomas pulled his gaze from Christina and settled on his brother. It didn't take long for the mirth to fade from Nicholas's face. "You can't be serious!" he charged, his low voice incredulous.

"I have never been more serious, Nick. I am soon going to ask for her hand, and I believe she will accept."

Nicholas picked up the baby, stood, and placed him in Christina's arms. He then turned and grabbed Thomas by his lapels and yanked him up to stand in front of him. "Have you gone completely mad? You cannot marry that woman. She is all wrong for you!" He gave him a hard shake. "You deserve someone better than a society girl for you and for Ty!" At those derogatory words toward Katherine, Thomas got angry and pushed his brother away. "Katherine has changed as much as you have, Nick. How could she not after all she has been through?" he roared at him. "And I do not believe Tyler could have a better mother than Katherine, either, so I will not have you malign her character when you do not know the truth."

Nicholas was not stirred by his loyal speech. He stepped closer to his brother and ignored his wife's plea to calm down. "I was engaged to the woman, you idiot! I probably know her better than you do, so don't paint a pretty picture of a matronly paragon when I know her for who she is!"

The brothers were practically nose to nose now and breathing heavily. Thomas thought if he could just get in one good punch that it certainly would make him feel better.

"What does that say about you if you think of her as unmarriageable? You were only weeks away from marrying her yourself!"

Nicholas snarled. "I was marrying her because of her position, brother, the exact reason she was marrying me! We were a social match, nothing more!" He poked Thomas in the chest, causing Thomas to ball his fist. "She's using you, Thom, because no one else will have her!"

"You are wrong!" Thomas stated emphatically.

"I wish I were, but I fear I am not!"

"Would you look at yourselves?" All sweetness was gone from Christina's voice, and a steeliness was in its place. "What a fine example you are setting for Tyler!"

The brothers did not back away from each other, but they did glance in her direction—both of their faces swathed in hostility.

Christina shook her head with a snort of disgust. "Just try not to kill him, will you, Thom?" she snapped as she started toward the door with Tyler sitting on her hip. "His baby will need a father, too!"

Both men started as she slammed the large door behind her, but Thomas wasn't sure it was from the sound or the news she'd dropped at their feet.

"Did she say 'baby'?" Nicholas asked, staring back at his brother.

Thomas nodded. "I think she did."

Suddenly Thomas was swallowed in his brother's joyful embrace. "I'm going to be a father! Did you hear that, Thom? We're having a baby!"

"I heard it—I heard. Now can you please—cease—pounding my back!" Thomas gasped and took a deep breath when he was finally released.

Nicholas shook his finger at his brother. "This conversation is not over with, Thom. I will not stand for you throwing your life away on someone who doesn't truly love you!"

Thomas was quickly regaining his anger. "She does care for me, and I will find a way to prove it to you!" he shot back, knocking Nicholas's hand away. "As a matter of fact, I'm going to Ravenhurst to propose right now!"

He stomped to the door, determined to see it through.

"You are making a mistake, Thom! Just wait until—" Nicholas tried to reason, following him to the door.

"Go to your wife, Nick. You know—the wife that all society thought you should not marry because she was not of our class!" he countered.

"You will regret—" Nicholas began to threaten. Thom walked out of the room, however, ignoring his brother's roar of anger, and slammed the door of the manor behind him.

⤙⤚

"I have been searching for you all morning!" Theodora announced in a peeved tone as she stepped carefully down the steep incline to where Katherine sat on the ground with her book. Usually no one thought to seek her out in the grassy ditch that had once been the castle's moat long years ago. That could only mean her cousin was determined to converse with her.

Not bothering to hide her sigh, she lowered her book of poetry and waited for Theodora to reach her. "Was there something important you wanted?" she asked, though she knew what the answer was.

"Of course I have something important I need to discuss with you, and you are quite aware of it!" Theodora snapped. She sat opposite Katherine, clearly uncomfortable on the uneven surface. "I want to know why you did not accept Thomas's invitation to meet his brother today. Proving to him his brother matters little to you would be all he'd need to ask for your hand!"

"How did you know about that? Were you eavesdropping?"

Theodora stuck up her chin with a defiant air. "No, but Lucy was; then she told me."

Katherine closed her eyes and shook her head tiredly. "I cannot face Nicholas. Not yet."

"You do not want to face him because then you will remember the reason you need to take revenge." She shook her finger at the younger woman. "You are beginning to like him, aren't you? You are allowing yourself to be taken in by yet another Thornton!"

Katherine licked her bottom lip as she gathered up courage for what she needed to say. "There may be truth in what you are saying, Dora," she admitted. "I just know he is too good a person to hurt the way we had planned."

"Not this again!" Theodora threw her arms up in disgust. "I never realized you were such a coward, Kate!"

"It is not cowardly to want to avoid hurting someone, Dora. Thomas is not his brother. He would never break an engagement and leave me to suffer society's rumors for it! He is more honorable than that!"

Katherine could tell Theodora was not at all happy with what she was saying. "What if he knew all along what his brother had planned?" she asked finally, her eyes becoming shrewd as she pinned them on Katherine. "He left for sea right after Nicholas broke your engagement. How do you know Thomas did not encourage his brother in this pursuit because he wanted you for himself!"

Katherine gasped. "You are mad to think such a thing! I will not hear such awful allegations—"

"Don't you think it a coincidence that the first woman he decides to court after his time of mourning is you, when there are many other women he could have pursued."

Katherine covered her ears. "I will not listen. He was a married man then!"

Theodora pushed herself closer to her cousin and pulled her hands away.

"I am simply trying to open your mind to the reality of who the Thorntons are! They are brothers, Katherine, cut from the same cloth!"

Theodora's words did not achieve what she had hoped. Katherine knew in her heart Thomas was a good man; she could see it in his eyes, feel it in his words. "Thomas has told me his brother had a difficult time following the war, and that is why—"

"Do you hear yourself? Now you are defending the man who made you the scourge of all society!" Theodora all but screeched as she jumped up, waving her arm about to emphasize her words.

"I'm not. I—"

"Yes, you are!" Theodora interrupted. "Are you going to let Lord Nicholas Thornton get away with what he did to you? Are you going to let him live an unscathed life with his wife and future children while you wither away as an old maid? Must he live a happy life while you suffer?"

It occurred to Katherine she would still live as an old maid even if she did go along with the plan.

But you could be happily wed if you forget the plan and decide to marry Thomas instead, a little voice sounded in her head. A voice Katherine wanted so much to follow but was afraid to.

"I need time to think," she cried softly, as she arose from the ground and dusted the grass from her cream-colored morning dress.

"My lady!" a voice called from atop the ditch by the castle wall, and Katherine squinted up through the bright sunlight to see her maid looking down at her.

"Yes, Stevens, what is it?" she inquired, glad for the interruption.

"His grace has asked to see you in his study," she explained, but then added, "Lord Thornton is with him, also."

"He has done it! He has come to ask for your hand!" Theodora crowed with delight, not caring that the servant was hearing every word.

Katherine hastily dismissed the girl. "Tell my father I will be right up."

When she'd gone, Katherine glared at Theodora. "If you speak of such things in front of the servants, it will cause more gossip! Lord Thomas could be here to see Cameron, not ask for my hand!"

"Cameron is in town, so I do not think that is the reason," Theodora countered, then added, "I have one caution to make before you speak with him, cousin."

Katherine let out a breath of impatience. "What is that, Dora?"

"If you are thinking of forgetting our plan, I would advise that you don't." Her lips curved in a false smile. "Nothing stays secret forever. One day Thomas could find out the truth of what we were going to do, and the result will be the same. He will be devastated, and the whole Thornton family will be affected by it."

The impact of what Theodora was saying took her breath away. "Are you making a threat, Dora?"

Her cousin's face was blank. "Of course not, Kate. I'm surprised you would have to ask!"

But it was a threat, and Katherine knew it. What she couldn't figure out was why Theodora was so adamant they proceed with the plan. Why was the Thorntons' ruin so important to her?

Shaken and suddenly afraid, she turned and made her way carefully up the steep incline, for the first time in a long while praying as she went. She prayed with all her heart Theodora could not turn against her but feared that, given the right circumstances, she would.

Chapter 8

The moment Katherine walked into the castle, her mother was there, grabbing her by the arm and all but dragging her to her father's study. Though she was talking erratically and too excitedly for Katherine to understand every word, she did hear something about dresses, flowers, and posting banns. That was all she needed to hear.

Apparently Theodora was right.

"Mama, please!" she protested, making her mother come to a stop. "Let me take a moment to catch my breath."

"Now you must listen to me, Katherine." Her mother took both her shoulders in her hands, gripping firmly. "You are to say yes, do you understand me? Do not do anything to make this fine gentleman change his mind."

Katherine once again felt the pressure of what she was about to do. "Perhaps he is not the man for me, Mama. Perhaps he is not what he seems. Should I risk being shamed for a second time?" she asked, her words spoken out of panic.

"He is just a man, Katherine, and, of course, probably has his faults, but that is not the point." She let go of her daughter's shoulders and folded her arms across her chest, giving her a stern look. "If you marry him, then it will dispel the ugly rumors, and we can once again mingle in polite society unencumbered. As is our right, Katherine." She whipped a handkerchief out of her pocket and began dabbing at her face. "As is our right!" she whispered fervently, almost as if she were trying to speak it into existence.

Katherine was even too nervous to be bothered by her mother's dramatics. All she could think about was how angry her parents would be if she followed through with the plan. She knew it might even backfire on them and further lower them in society's eyes.

"Well, don't stand there, Katherine. Go in! Your father and Lord Thomas are waiting for you!" her mother urged in a shrill voice, pushing her toward the door.

Katherine managed to open the door and enter without stumbling, and as expected, there Thomas stood with her father, laughing together as if they were already old friends.

"Ah! Katherine, you are here finally." Her father spoke first. He motioned for her to come closer. "I believe Lord Thornton has something he would like to speak to you about." He shifted his broad grin and shining gaze between them both. "I will leave you two alone."

"Papa!" Katherine called out to him in alarm. "I don't mind if you stay!"

Immediately after the words were out of her mouth, she felt foolish for saying them. Thomas was staring at her with a frown, and her father appeared as though he wanted to strangle her. He didn't say a word to her, either. He merely backed out of the room, closing the door soundly behind him.

"Are you all right, Katherine?" Thomas asked, his voice hesitant.

It hurt to see Thomas standing there dressed so handsomely in his dark brown coat, buckskins, and Hessians—boots that were kept in the finest polish she'd ever beheld.

"Are you going to look at me or just stare at my feet all morning?"

Her head popped up, and she felt her face grow hot. "I'm sorry. I am a bit distracted this morning." She scanned the room, then motioned toward two chairs that stood in front of her father's heavy oak desk. "Did you want to sit down?"

Thomas smiled at her as he took a step closer. "I do believe you are nervous, Katherine." He took her hand and kissed her knuckles. "I do not think it would be hard to guess why I am here."

Katherine took a moment to regain her wits after his gentle kiss. If kissing her hand made her heart beat so fast, what would a true kiss do to her?

"Uh—yes, I think I do know," she answered after a moment. "What are you doing?" she asked when he sank down to one knee, still holding her hand.

He smiled sweetly at her. "I am kneeling before you, my dear Katherine, offering you my heart and my name if you will have them."

Katherine could not help the tears that filled her eyes. She wanted nothing more than to accept his proposal and admit she loved him in return. But with Dora's threat playing in her mind, she was torn about what she should do. "I—I, uh. . ." she stammered.

When an answer was not forthcoming, the smile left his face and was replaced by an air of trepidation. "Katherine?" He stood up slowly. "Have I misread your feelings for me?"

"No!" She found herself crying out. "I mean—"

"I know what you mean," he interrupted with a jubilant grin. "It must be that I have proceeded so suddenly—"

"Yes!" She grabbed on to his excuse. "We have known one another for such a short time! Perhaps we should get to know one another better."

Thomas laughed at that statement and brought her hand to his mouth once again. "You are anxious!" he surmised. "Don't be, my lady. We will have a wonderful life together, and I promise you'll never have to endure being snubbed at a party or have your name bandied about in degrading terms. Not as long as I am there to protect and defend you."

After that touching speech, Katherine knew no woman alive would respond differently than she. "I'll marry you."

He became still, her hand still safely enfolded in his own. "You will?"

She took a breath, tried not to think about what would happen in the future, and nodded. And perhaps she wanted to do a little pretending, too.

"Katherine," he murmured, his eyes full of emotion as he drew her to him. Her eyes grew large as she realized he intended to kiss her.

"Kath—!" Her sister barged through the door and froze when she saw them in a semiembrace. "Aha! I've caught you again, and this time I do not think he was aiming for your hand!" she charged loudly, her eyes full of curiosity.

"Lucinda! What are you doing in there?" Her mother's voice echoed from the hallway; then she, too, was standing there staring at the couple.

Thomas had already stepped away from her but was still holding her hand.

Her father appeared; both parents looked back and forth, trying to gauge the couple's demeanor. "Might we deduce that by your holding hands there is to be a wedding in the near future?" Katherine's mother asked carefully.

"Indeed, there is!" Thomas answered with elation.

"Capital!" her father exclaimed, stepping forward to shake hands with him and give Katherine a kiss on the cheek.

Her mother's reaction was, of course, more dramatic. "Ooh!" she cried. Large tears formed in her eyes. Waving her handkerchief about, Lady Montbatten hurried over to Thomas, put her hands on either side of his face, and whispered emotionally with a properly shaking voice, "Welcome to the family, Thomas. And please call me Mama!"

Thomas had a bemused expression on his face as she kissed each cheek, then clutched her handkerchief to her mouth as if to hold off a sob. She then moved on to Katherine to give her a hug.

Of course, no one but she heard her mother whisper, "Excellent, dear. You have saved us all!"

⌒∽∞

Thomas stayed at Ravenhurst Castle for a little while longer as the family talked excitedly of their engagement. Even Theodora had seemed excited about it and kept giving Katherine a strange smile, almost as if she were communicating her approval of the event.

Something about Katherine's older cousin bothered him greatly, but he could not put a finger on why. He seemed to remember knowing her several years ago, but he could not remember in what circumstance. He thought it might have been in the village of Malbury where he grew up, but he couldn't be certain. Obviously it had not been a memorable meeting, and she *was* several years older than his twenty-seven.

Once he reached his home, Thomas took a few minutes to think about what to say to his brother. He had rushed to the castle in haste and out of anger, but he could not be sorry he had asked Katherine to marry him. His argument with his brother only hastened him to do what he desired to do in the first place.

He was to marry Katherine Montbatten, the woman he truly loved with all his heart.

If his brother could not accept it, then that would be something left for Nicholas to deal with. His brother had found true love and happiness; now Thomas had, also.

But surely his brother would come to accept his choice. They were both Christian men, and they knew God put people in their lives according to His will and not the dictates of men.

"Are you going to stand out here all day, or have you gathered enough courage yet to face me?" Nicholas spoke from behind Thomas, startling him.

"It's not courage I am gathering, brother," he countered. "I'm trying to remember my defensive training from the war in case you decide to try a hit at me."

Nicholas chuckled while shaking his head. "I suppose you've gone and done the deed, haven't you?" he said, getting to the point of the matter.

Thomas lifted his chin. "I have." The two men stared at one another. "Will this drive a wedge between us, Nick?"

Nicholas glanced away for a moment, and when he looked back, Thomas saw the emotion he was fighting hard to hide. "I suffered for a year thinking my only brother had been taken from me. Do you honestly believe I would allow anyone—even an ex-fiancée—to drive a wedge between us?"

Thomas was blinking back tears of his own as he and Nicholas embraced. Then with a hearty slap on the back, Nicholas declared, "Come! We must go and tell Tyler he will soon gain not only a new mother but a new cousin, as well!"

Thomas's eyes widened. "Then it is true? I am to be an uncle?"

Nicholas nodded proudly. "Yes, and this time I will not hire a nanny who repeats the same word with every sentence! I was almost driven mad when Mrs. Sanborne was living at Kenswick!"

Thomas laughed and led his brother into the manor. "I think she is quite endearing."

Nicholas snorted. "Why does that not surprise me?"

⥱⥊

"What are you doing back down in the moat?" Theodora called from above. Katherine squinted up from her seat on the ground where she had been trying to sort out her feelings—in peace.

"I am trying to think, if you do not mind," Katherine returned waspishly, not caring whether or not it angered Theodora.

"But I do mind!" Katherine turned in time to observe Theodora stumbling down the incline again—invading her sanctuary. "We must discuss where to go next with our plan."

Katherine drew her knees up and buried her head in her folded arms. "I do not want to discuss it. Not now!"

"Yes, now!" her cousin's shrill voice demanded. "Cameron has returned from town, and it is the perfect opportunity!"

Katherine's head snapped up. "What does Cameron have to do with this?"

Theodora smiled as she peered down at her. "He is the second part of our plan, dear cousin. Cameron will not be happy about your engagement since he truly hates all the Thorntons for what they did to you."

"What *he* did, Dora. Nicholas. He's the only one who hurt me," she corrected.

"That is neither here nor there, Kate. What matters is that Cameron is bound to stir up trouble. He's already issued two challenges to the earl. He was humiliated by his not accepting, so I would wager he will turn his anger toward Lord Thomas."

Katherine stared at her cousin with horror. "Are you hoping Cameron will shoot Thomas in a duel?"

Theodora laughed. "Of course I am not saying that." She shrugged. "But if one does occur. . ." She let her sentence drift off to be left to Katherine's imagination.

Katherine jumped up with her hands on her hips. "And what if it is Cameron who is shot or even killed?"

"Perhaps they'll choose swords! You know how good Cameron is with those!"

Katherine began to walk away from Theodora, back up the steep hill. "Your words are evil ones, cousin, and I will listen no longer."

Theodora was clambering to keep up, but she'd gone only a few steps before she tripped and rolled a short way back down the incline. "Aren't you going to help me?" she screeched when Katherine glanced back but kept on walking.

Katherine did not answer her, so upset was she over Theodora's callous attitude. In fact, she didn't even see Cameron until she collided with him.

"Oh! I did not know you were there!" Katherine gasped as she grabbed onto his strong arms.

Cameron smiled fondly at his sister as he helped her gain her balance. "I am afraid I was preoccupied myself, wondering what all the screaming coming from the moat was about."

Katherine sighed, feeling a little guilty. "Theodora fell partway down the ditch, and I was so angry at her that I did not stop to help her."

"I do not know why you put up with her at all, Kate. I've never met anyone quite so unpleasant as she!"

Katherine stared up at her brother, who was two years older than she and whom she had always admired. He was a big man, muscular from working with his horses and fencing, and so very handsome with his curly golden hair and light green eyes. From her earliest memories, she saw Cameron as her protector, someone who was kind and gentle with her but would fight to the death if anyone or anything tried to harm her.

That was why she was so terrified to tell him about the engagement. She had no idea of what his reaction would be.

"Theodora has no one else, Cameron—you know that. I fail to notice her undesirable qualities, I suppose," she said in response to his comment.

"You are a far better person than I, Kate," he said with a grin, as he tucked her hand into his arm and began escorting her to the castle. "Now tell me—what is all the excitement about around here? The servants are running about like mad and whispering, and neither Papa nor Mama has time to answer when I ask. They all refer me to you. So what is going on?"

"I have become engaged, Cameron," she said quickly.

"That is wonder—"

"Stop!" she interrupted with a cry, halting their walk. "First let me tell you who the man is."

"Kate, do not be so anxious. I know I am protective of you, but I promise I will accept anyone who has broken with the attitudes of the ton and has chosen to pursue you," he tried to assure her.

"Remember you promised, Cameron, for the man is Lord Thomas Thornton."

It was as if a thundercloud came and sat upon her brother's head. "Surely you cannot be that stupid!" he roared, shaking her hand from his arm and glaring at her as if she were poison. "The Thorntons are our enemies! What can you be thinking?"

Kate tried to reach out to her brother, but he backed away from her. "Please, Cameron, Thomas is not like his brother. He—"

"Kate, has it become this desperate?" he asked in a calmer voice, as he appeared to be trying to fight his anger. "Do you believe Thornton is the only man who will ask for your hand?"

Kate's eyes filled with tears at seeing her brother's disappointment. "It is not like that, Cameron."

"Then how is it?" Cameron charged but turned away, as if trying to collect his thoughts. "If I had known this earlier, then I would deal with it, but now I cannot. I have to finish out the semester." He pointed his finger at her sternly. "But I will see to this matter, Kate. Do not get married before I return!"

If her brother only knew about the plan. Katherine contemplated telling him, but because she was beginning to like Thomas, she did not. Perhaps she was holding out for a miracle.

"And how long will you be gone?" she asked faintly.

"Four weeks."

Katherine and Cameron separated when they entered the castle, for he had to instruct the servants on his luggage.

What she didn't expect, after he had gone from her sight, was her mother rushing toward her. "Is Cameron in his room?"

Katherine blinked with puzzlement. "Yes, but—"

"Lucy has told me about your conversation!" her mother said in a loud stage whisper.

Katherine gaped in amazement. "That little scamp! Was she eavesdropping on me?"

Her mother waved her handkerchief back and forth, giving Katherine a dismissive glance. "That is inconsequential at the moment, dear! What's important is that we must set the date of the wedding posthaste!"

"What do you mean?" Katherine asked, fearful of the determined gleam in her mother's eyes.

"I mean that we must set the wedding date for the thirteenth of June. It will give us four weeks to plan it!"

Katherine shook her head, feeling herself being sucked deeper and deeper into trouble. "It is too soon, Mama. You must let us have time to know one another!"

"Get to know him after you're married. It is what I did and what my mother before me did. It is simply the way of things, dear," her mother instructed her with a shrug. "And besides, we have to do this before Cameron arrives and tries to challenge him to a duel."

Chapter 9

Where did North pop off to?" Christina asked the next morning when they were all sitting down for breakfast. She was quite stunning in her light green morning dress that complemented her red hair and bright eyes. Though Thomas could tell she had polished up a bit from when he first met her again at the wedding, after knowing her in his younger days, she still had the ability to say and do the oddest, most unladylike things.

Just the day before, he'd found her in his stables inside Sultan's stall, examining his front leg. She had gotten completely dirty from head to foot and was busy smearing a smelly mixture on his leg. She'd explained later it was a medicine to help heal strained muscles—that his horse had been "standing oddly" were her words.

Despite her unladylike behavior, she was still one of the most unusual and charming women Thomas had ever known. He was glad his brother had pushed aside society's expectations and married the vicar's daughter. She obviously adored him, and Thomas wondered if Katherine would be the same type of loving wife that his sister-in-law was to his brother.

"North is always traveling here and about, visiting his friends before he embarks on his trip to America," Thomas explained. "He tells me he will be stopping by Kenswick Hall in a fortnight or so."

"Excellent," Nicholas stated in approval. "He was a good friend to me during my dark time when Father died and I thought I'd lost you, too. I'm glad he's been here for you, also."

"Indeed," Thomas agreed. "And though I know he was disappointed he could not go to America months ago because of the war still raging, I am glad for myself he's been able to visit us here at Rosehaven and in London."

"I wish he wouldn't go over there!" Christina interjected, surprising both brothers at the irritation that was behind her words. "He needs to stay here in England and find a nice girl to marry!"

Thomas was vexed by her outcry, but when he looked toward Nicholas, he saw his brother was not. "Ah." He nodded sagely. "Still holding out hope for your friend Helen, are you?"

"Who is Helen?" Thomas asked.

Christina bristled and shot her husband a piqued glare. "Helen is my very best friend, and she happens to be in love with North."

"Helen is the daughter of Mr. Rupert Nichols, a very nice gentleman farmer but poor. North knows his obligations. His family has a tradition of marrying either royalty or the highest of noble families; it is what's expected of him," Nicholas gently reminded his wife.

"You did not do what was expected of you! Did he not, Thomas?" She suddenly turned to Thomas, peering at him with expectant eyes.

Thomas looked from Christina to his brother. "I don't think I want to answer that. Nicholas may try to challenge me to a duel or something."

Christina gasped, and Nicholas seemed irritated. "Thomas, you know that was a long time ago! He is a Christian man now," she explained in her husband's defense.

"I was only teasing, Christina," Thomas said, knowing his brother had changed from the angry, bitter man he had been after the war when those duels had taken place. He then said, with a twinkle in his eye, "Besides, while he is good with pistols, I am better with the sword. So you see—it would not be a fair fight either way."

Christina started to say something, but she closed her mouth as suddenly as she had opened it. "You are trying to get me off the subject, are you not?"

Thomas grinned, not feeling the least bit guilty for it. "Yes, did it work?"

"No, and I still—" she started to say, when Nicholas broke in.

"Getting back to the subject of marriage, are you still in agreement your engagement should be a long one?" Nicholas gave Thomas a look that only older brothers could get away with. A look that told him since their father was gone, he was the one dispensing guidance, so Thomas should adhere to it.

Thomas didn't require his brother's interference, however. Because of Katherine's inconsistent behavior, he, too, saw the need of waiting a bit to know her better and she, him. "I think I shall suggest we wait for at least four months. Perhaps in that time I can get to know Cameron, too, and bring some sort of mending to my relationship with him."

"I think that is wise," Nicholas told him, and Thomas could tell he was still not pleased with the whole situation.

"I hope you will be happy, Thomas, as Nicholas has made me happy. I believe God leads the right person into our lives, and when He does, we know it." She reached across the table and put her hand over his. "Do you know, Thomas? Do you have the feeling God has sent her to you?"

Thomas smiled. "Indeed, I do. Even when she was engaged to Nicholas, I thought she was a special person. And when I met her again, it was as if the whole room darkened and one lone light shone directly from Katherine to me." He squeezed her hand gently. "I know God has sent her to me."

Christina's eyes filled with tears. "Oh, my. That was quite a romantic thing to say, Thomas. You should be a poet." She pulled her hand back and started dabbing at her eyes with her napkin.

Nicholas frowned. "You've said the same thing to me, Christina! It doesn't seem quite as special if you are going to be spreading the sentiment to every poor sap who pours out his heart to you!"

Thomas threw his head back and laughed. "You have never been accused of being romantic! Love must be blind after all," he roared, laughing harder when Nicholas jumped up from his chair and leaned menacingly over the table.

Expecting such a reaction, Thomas was quick to push his chair back and stand away from Nicholas.

"I am a changed man, little brother. Tell him I'm a changed man, Christina," Nicholas ordered in a loud, commanding voice.

"He's a changed man, Thomas," Christina parroted dutifully, but the sincerity of the statement was lost when she, too, started to snicker. "Now sit down, dear, before you do something to make us both liars."

Nicholas dragged his glare away from Thomas to his wife. Suddenly he grinned, letting them know he'd been teasing them both. "I'll sit, but you must promise not to pay him any more compliments," he groused but with a playful gleam in his eyes.

"I promise." She turned and gave Thomas a stern frown. "You sit down, too, Thomas, and behave yourself. I fear I must take back the compliments, but I'm sure you will understand."

"I think I do—" he began to tease as his butler, McInnes, came into the room with a slight cough.

"I beg yer pardon, my laird, but dinna ye sae ye'd be wantin' ta see the *Times* this morn?"

Thomas nodded. "Of course, McInnes. Bring it to me."

The wily Scot who'd been butler at Rosehaven for four years walked with his usual swagger and dropped the paper beside his employer's toast. "Ye might be wantin' ta look o' page four, my laird," McInnes whispered in his ear, and before Thomas could question him on it, he was out of the room.

"I still don't understand why you have a Scot for a butler. I don't believe they have the proper disposition for such an important duty. Did you know he scolded me yesterday for getting dirt on the rug after my morning ride?" Nicholas told him, clearly irritated by the incident.

"Hmm." Thomas barely heard what his brother was saying since he was so intent on turning to page four. "McInnes seemed quite insistent I read something. . . ." His voice drifted off as he read the small item in the center of the paper. "What are you both doing on the thirteenth of June?" he murmured, a little perplexed and just a little pleased by the turn of events.

Nicholas appeared curious. "Why do you ask? What is on page four that has your butler so interested?"

"The engagement has already been published in the *Times*, and it seems the date is only four weeks away on June thirteenth."

"Who is responsible for this?" Nicholas asked.

Thomas stared at the paper without seeing it as his mind pondered the news. He rubbed his chin thoughtfully, then brought his gaze over to his brother. "I believe I shall pay a visit to Ravenhurst Castle to find out."

❧

"I'm sorry, my lord, but Lady Katherine is unavailable," the Montbattens' butler told Thomas, the same thing he'd been telling him for three days. "Perhaps if you'd like to leave your card or a note?"

Thomas stared at the tall, solemn man and contemplated that the man might possess no personality whatsoever. If Ambrose, as he was called, had one, he'd surely never shown it to him. He'd been to the castle a few times and had surely known of the engagement, and still he treated Thomas as if he were an ordinary caller.

"What of her parents? Are they at home?" he persisted, tired of whatever game was being played at his expense.

"They are in London, my lord. I believe they left two days ago."

Thomas thought something was significant in that piece of news. "And Miss Vine? Is she available?"

"Yes, she is."

Thomas stood staring at Ambrose, who merely stared back at him, expressionless as usual. "Ambrose," he finally said, his voice strained with ire. "Can you please let me come in to speak with Miss Vine?"

The butler nodded regally. "Of course, my lord." Ambrose backed up from the threshold and motioned Thomas inside.

He had to wait only a few minutes in a small sitting room before Theodora came unhurriedly into the room. It was odd watching the woman, because her eyes and her expression and tone did not match. It was as if she were a walking contradiction from what she was saying and what she felt. Thomas had the uncanny feeling that Theodora despised him; yet she always seemed to smile at him, and he knew she urged Katherine his way by her insistent whispers and unsubtle hints.

Why? Why was she anxious for Katherine and him to make a match? What would she gain from it?

Something had to be motivating her, he realized. Perhaps God was leading him to find out or maybe even help the woman. He did not want to judge her, so perhaps if he tried to befriend her, he could understand her more.

The thin woman curtsied, and Thomas nodded his head respectfully her way. "My lord," she began. "I was surprised you wanted to see me. Is something amiss?"

Thomas watched as she walked to a chair and sat down on it. It was the largest chair in the room, and when she looked up at him, it appeared as though she were sitting on a throne holding court. Shaking the absurd thought from his mind, he smiled at her, then took the chair next to her. "I came to inquire after Katherine. I've tried to see her but have only been told she is not available. Frankly, Miss Vine, I was wondering if she might be ill or something similar to that."

The woman's lips pursed, and Thomas thought if it were possible, steam would be coming from her ears for how upset she seemed. "I'm afraid I do not understand, my lord. I was under the impression Katherine was riding with you every day since your engagement."

Thomas sat back on his seat, dumbfounded by this information. "I have not seen her since the day I asked her to marry me."

Theodora startled him by quickly standing and walking to the window. He turned in his chair to see what she was doing. "I hope I didn't upset you, Miss Vine. It's just that I'd like to know why Katherine is lying to you about seeing me, then ignoring me when I call."

Thomas saw her bony shoulders lift and go back down in an apparent sigh. Slowly she turned and faced him, all traces of anger gone from her face. "I believe Katherine must be experiencing prewedding jitters, my lord."

That did make sense, but Thomas could not get rid of the feeling there was more to it. "I suppose so, but that would explain only why she has been hiding from me. Why would she lie to you?"

She shrugged as she came and sat back down in the chair. "I must confess, I have encouraged a relationship between you both all along."

"Did you?" he murmured.

"Yes, because I had heard you were a good man and someone who would disregard the gossip that has been spoken of her."

Thomas nodded. "I appreciate your confidence in me."

For a moment, he thought the woman grimaced, but when he blinked, a pleasant expression was clearly shown on her face. Perhaps he had only. . .imagined it.

"I am on your side, Lord Thornton, and will do everything I can to calm her fears so she will speak to you." She stood, and Thomas deduced their little tête-à-tête was over.

He stood. "I thank you, Miss Vine. I shall call again tomorrow." He started to go, but she stopped him.

"Wait!" He turned, and she motioned toward the window. "The moat—or the ditch, rather. I saw her in there by the rear bridge when I glanced out of the window a few moments ago."

Thomas blinked with bemusement. "I'm sorry—did you say 'moat'?"

Theodora sighed with an expression of long-suffering. "Unfortunately, yes. She likes to go and sit at the bottom, and—well—I don't know what she does. Thinks or something."

Thomas smiled at the odd woman. "Excellent. Again you have my thanks."

He didn't wait for a response as he hurried from the castle and walked around until he came to the rear bridge. As Theodora had told him, Katherine was there, lying with her back propped against the incline, staring off in front of her.

He was halfway down when she saw him. "What are you doing here?" she asked in a panicked voice, scrambling to her feet.

"I'm here to find out why you have been avoiding me." Thomas came to stand in front of her. "Are you having regrets?" he added quietly.

Katherine began studying the ground as she folded her arms at her waist in a defensive move. "I don't know what you—"

"Look at me, Katherine!" he demanded softly, as he took her arms and brought himself closer to her. "First I find that you—or someone—has published our wedding date without consulting me, and now you are ignoring me. If you did not want to marry me, why did you set the date for the thirteenth of June?"

"I didn't!" she cried, her expression surprisingly defiant. "My mother did that."

Thomas stared at her for a moment, trying to understand the emotions whirling about in her eyes. "Are you doing this for your mother? Because that is no reason to go into marriage. I—"

"No. I'm not doing this for my mother." She closed her eyes, and when she opened them, she gazed directly into his. "I'm just scared, Thomas. I'm scared of—" She stopped, as if she were unable to find the right words.

Thomas thought he knew the answer. "You're scared I'm going to leave you as Nicholas did."

She frowned and started to say something, then stopped. She chewed at her bottom lip as he waited for her to respond. "I—yes—yes, you are right. I'm scared of being hurt."

Thomas smiled, relieved. "My darling, don't be scared. You must realize I love—"

"No! Do not say it! Please!" she cried, breaking his hold on her and putting her hands over her mouth in an appearance of fear.

"Katherine, why should I not say it? If it is because you are not sure of your own feelings, then I am content to wait until you can say the words. But there is no reason not to express my own."

She was the picture of misery, staring back at him with a stark expression that tore at his heart. "I do have feelings for you, Thomas. I am just afraid, as you said."

"My sweet Katherine," he called out softly, closing the space between them again. "I would not have asked you to marry me if I believed otherwise."

They stood so close, not touching, but he could feel her breath and smell the sweet fragrance of the roses she had pinned in her golden hair; and he imagined he could hear the rapid beating of her heart—or was it his own?

"Thomas," she whispered, her voice sounding as if she were perplexed, unsure of how she was feeling with him so near.

"Katherine," he answered her, and he finally did what he had most wanted to do since he gazed at her across that crowded ballroom. He took her face into his large palms and lowered his lips to hers. He could hear her quick intake of breath, then the soft sigh as she pressed in to kiss him back.

Tenderly he kissed her mouth, delighting in the poignant connection so evident between them. It was a sense of belonging, a sense of knowing they were meant to be. Thomas felt her tremble, and sensing she must be frightened by the emotions of such an ardent and loving connection, he left her mouth to plant a kiss on her cheek, then her ear before folding her into his arms.

His heart ached that so many problems seemed to plague their relationship, and as they embraced, he sent a silent petition up to God to give Katherine peace and assurance.

After a moment, she stepped away from him, but he moved to take her hand, unwilling to sever their poignant encounter.

"We should not have—" she began in a shaky voice.

"Do not say it, Katherine. You are going to be my wife! It's perfectly acceptable for us to have moments alone together and even share a simple kiss." He gave her hand a gentle squeeze. "I pray you will have no more doubts or fears about us, Katherine. I love you," he stated emphatically, and this time she did not stop him, only stared at him with an indecipherable expression. "Let that be your comfort. Let that be your assurance."

She didn't say anything for a few moments as her gaze lowered to their clasped hands. "I don't think I've ever met a man like you, Thomas. You seem too good to be true—everything that is good and kind." She shook her head as if confused.

"Katherine, do not put me on a pedestal. I have faults like any other man. If Anne were here, I'm sure she'd give you a long list of complaints against me as a husband." He reached out and lifted her chin so she was looking at him. "Will you come to Rosehaven tomorrow? I have decided the manor needs a little sprucing up and want your input since you shall be mistress there," he told her, changing the subject.

She paused as if grappling with her answer. "I will come, though I am not very talented in the art of decoration," she answered finally.

He brought her hand up and caressed her bare knuckles with a soft kiss.

"It does not matter. It will be your home, and you should have a say on how it should be styled."

He had a moment of foreboding as one of those fearful expressions crossed her pretty features. But when she nodded, he put it out of his head, intent on enjoying every second with his soon-to-be wife.

Chapter 10

"What game are you playing, Katherine?" Theodora snapped as soon as she entered the bedroom.

"What are you doing in my room, Theodora?" Katherine countered, not in the mood to deal with her overbearing cousin.

"Don't be coy with me, Kate! Why have you been lying to me, and why did you give instructions to Ambrose to say you were unavailable?"

Katherine walked to her dressing table and began taking down her hair since it had become loose from the wind. "I don't want to go through with this anymore, Dora. I wonder why I agreed in the first place!" She all but threw the hairpins on her oak dressing table as she spoke.

She heard Theodora sigh and come walking up behind her where her cousin could see her in the large round mirror. "Because you wanted to right a wrong, Kate. A wrong that Lord Nicholas Thornton wants to forget," Theodora added quietly.

Katherine's head snapped up, and she stared searchingly at her cousin through the mirror. "What have you heard?"

Theodora turned away with a shrug and with a show of nonchalance picked up a comb from the dressing table, pretending to study it. "It's only servants' talk, you understand. But it's been told to me the earl was heard trying to talk Thomas out of marrying you, that he didn't trust you or something like that." Her eyes slowly rose to Kate's. "He even threatened Thomas. That is why Thomas ran over here in such a hurry to ask you to marry him, dear. He was merely defying his older brother." She put the comb down, bending closer to Katherine's ear. "It makes you wonder if he wanted to propose or was doing it to spite Nicholas Thornton."

Katherine frowned as she looked down at her dressing table, breaking the intense stare. She tried to remember the kiss and the lovely words Thomas poured out to her just moments before, but her bitterness toward Nicholas rose up, making it hard to remember anything but the hurt he'd caused her.

She had been so sure of Thomas's feelings. But now, in light of this news, she had to wonder if he had other motives.

And Nicholas. How dare he try to dissuade his brother against seeing her! He was the one who ruined her good name and made her the subject of ridicule. Why would he not want her to have some sort of happiness in life even if it was with his brother?

The moment she thought that, she felt hypocritical. She wasn't being sincere with Thomas. Did Nicholas suspect she might be using his brother for revenge?

"Oh, what a horrible quandary we find ourselves in, Theodora. God will surely punish us for our deceit!" she cried, throwing her hands over her face.

"Stop the dramatics, Kate. You are beginning to sound like your mother," Theodora said in her practical way. "We must continue to advance our plan." She pulled Kate's hands away from her face. "You must not ignore Thomas any longer. In fact, you must do all you can to reassure him of your feelings—or rather your supposed feelings," she amended.

Katherine thought about that. Not about deceiving Thomas but about how lovely it would be to allow herself to act like his true fiancée—to pretend they would truly be getting married and setting up a household. She could help him with the decorations to his house and get to spend time with him—even if it was only for four weeks.

Katherine felt like a different woman the next day when she met Thomas at his manor. Though Rosehaven was a smaller estate than his brother's Kenswick Hall or any of her family's many properties, the three-hundred-year-old manor had seven bedrooms, a large foyer with an appealing double curved stairway, and a lovely sitting room with a full wall of windows that looked out over the garden. Thomas mentioned this room could be exclusively her own since it adjoined his study and small library.

And for a moment, Katherine let herself dream of painting the room a muted shade of blue so it would appear to be an extension of the sky outside the windows. She could imagine herself sitting on a plush sofa with needlepoint or perhaps reading a book. Thomas would come in often, because he did not want to be without her too long, and when they would have children, there would be blocks and dolls strewn about and perhaps a rocking horse in the corner. . . .

"So what do you think?"

Katherine started as she realized he must have been talking to her and she'd not heard a thing he had said as she studied the room. "I beg your pardon?"

Thomas smiled as he walked over behind her, putting his hands on her shoulders, and began to speak softly into her ear. "I know that look. It is the look all women get when they see a room they'd like to change."

Katherine boldly reached up and put one of her hands over his. "You are right. It is such a lovely room, but—"

"But you can improve it," he finished for her.

She laughed softly. "Perhaps."

He turned her around so she was facing him, and his striking blue eyes studied her. "There is something different about you today. You seem more at ease, happier."

It was so bittersweet to see the relief in his eyes, knowing that in four weeks he would despise her very existence. "I've just decided to enjoy our time together," she told him evasively, not wanting to lie anymore. "And I am quite anxious to help you decorate your lovely manor."

He chuckled as he took her hand and walked her out of the room. "Good, because I have arranged a meeting with merchants for fabrics and furniture and also a seamstress with different patterns for draperies you can choose from!"

All morning long, they talked with the merchants and seamstress, choosing various styles of goods for the manor. Katherine began to realize she actually enjoyed envisioning and suggesting how each room should appear and the major changes that should be made.

Because she'd not been in town, only taking the road between their two estates, she had not heard the reaction of their peers or neighbors. She had not even thought about them since the engagement was announced.

That was why when Sunday came around and Thomas escorted Katherine as well as her sister and cousin to church, she was so surprised by the response they received immediately after stepping out of his carriage.

Not only were the villagers there, wishing them congratulations, but members of the ton who were not even part of the church's parish were there, also. The most surprising thing was that the gentlemen who had snubbed her just weeks before at the ball were treating her as if nothing had happened.

"What hypocrites," Thomas muttered for her ears only when they had finally broken away and taken a seat in the abbey. "I know I will have to repent for contemplating this, but I would like to take my fist to each one of the rakes who treated you so shamefully before and are now bowing to you like simpering idiots!"

Katherine had to cover her mouth with her gloved hand to keep from laughing aloud. "Please, don't do that. Then we'd have to deal with another scandal!" she whispered back.

"Who is an idiot?" Lucy asked her in a too-loud whisper that caused the people in the two rows in front of them to turn and look at them. She was sitting on the other side of Thomas and apparently straining to hear what was being said.

"Shh!" Katherine scolded.

And before she could say anything else, Thomas put his arm around Lucy and whispered something in her ear. After that, she sat up in her seat, staring straight ahead.

Katherine shook her head in wonderment. "What did you say?"

"I bribed her," he admitted. "I told her if she was quiet the rest of the service, I'd let her pick a name for my other Arabian."

Knowing her sister's love of horses, she understood how she could be bribed, but what amazed her was that Thomas, who hardly knew her, had been sensitive enough to notice. He had shown the same awareness of her, too. When they were working on his home, he would make sure his cook always made her favorite scones or brewed her coffee instead of tea.

After the service, the ladies were invited back to dine at Rosehaven for a luncheon. Theodora, much to Katherine's surprise, stayed very much subdued, not giving her the usual meaningful glances or hurried whispers. But then she knew her cousin had no reason to say anything because Katherine was playing the part of Thomas's loving fiancée to the hilt.

That was because she so much wanted to be his fiancée in truth. She could admit that. She just didn't know how she could make it happen without Theodora causing trouble.

And Katherine knew her cousin would if she even mentioned she was thinking of changing her mind. How could she not have seen how obsessed Dora was to have revenge on the Thorntons? Her cousin's desire for revenge was not merely to avenge Katherine—she knew that now. But why was this important to Theodora? What would she gain?

She was thankful that, as soon as they arrived at Rosehaven, Mrs. Sanborne was there with Tyler to take her mind off her troubles. Eagerly she reached for him, but the woman held her off.

"Wait, my lady! You must see his stupendous surprise!" Mrs. Sanborne placed the toddler on the floor, and she watched with pride as he wobbled over to Katherine, then grabbed her skirts before he fell.

"He's walking!" she exclaimed as she bent to pick him up. She turned to Thomas, who did not look surprised at all. "When did he start walking?"

"He has been trying to walk all week, but last night he finally was able to walk from Mrs. Sanborne over to me without falling. We wanted to surprise you," he informed her, his eyes glowing with pride. "I was beginning to worry since he is over a year and still only crawling, but I guess he wanted to take his time."

"Of course he did!" she exclaimed, kissing him on the cheek. "You just wanted to do things your way!"

He jabbered some unintelligible syllables in response, making them all laugh.

After lunch, she, Theodora, and Lucy walked down to the stables. Her sister had informed her she had to "talk" to the horse to be able to name her.

Katherine decided to take Ty with them in his pram. When they arrived, she was about to enter the stables with Lucy, but Theodora stopped her. "Lucy, why don't you go on in, and we'll follow in a moment?" The younger girl merely shrugged her shoulders and skipped away from them.

Katherine had hoped to avoid any conversation since she'd succeeded in doing so for the last couple of days. Being with Thomas all day certainly gave her an excuse to do that.

"What is it, Dora?" she asked, trying not to seem put out.

"I just wanted to say you are proceeding excellently!" Her eyes glowed. "He doesn't suspect a thing!"

"If you say so, Dora. I really don't think we should be discussing this here, however." She glanced about them to emphasize her point. "Servants do talk, you know."

"I know, I know," she muttered irritably. "I wanted to tell you I have—well—you might say I've added another ingredient to the pot."

Katherine's heart started beating rapidly. "What have you done?" she asked faintly, almost afraid to hear the answer.

"I've written Cameron," she informed her with an evil grin. "And when he gets the letter, I suspect we shall see him before his semester is finished."

Katherine shook her head in horror. "Do you have no thought for what might happen to either of them, especially Cameron? If he challenges Thomas to a duel, he might be killed!"

Theodora dismissed her words with a defiant lift of her pointed chin. "You worry about things that might never happen, Kate. Stop being so dramatic!"

Kate knew her mother would be furious when she found out, and the sad thing was that it would probably be blamed on her, not Theodora. There was only one thing to do. She was going to have to find a way to tell Thomas and convince him to try any nonviolent things he could to dissuade Cameron from challenging him.

Time is on my side, she thought with some relief. He would not be able to leave school unless he arranged to take his exams early, and that would only cut one week from his four. She'd need that time to think of what to do.

"Theodora, I beg you—do not take it upon yourself to do anything else!" she implored. "Do not forget we are in this together."

"You don't forget this is all a charade, Kate," she spat back. "Those adoring eyes you keep sending him better be make-believe!"

At that point, Ty began to fuss and started trying to climb out of the pram. She grabbed hold of his restlessness as an excuse to get away from her cousin. "Are you wanting to see the horse, little Ty? Let's go see the horsey!" she told him in a singsong voice, as she pushed the carriage into the stables and away from Theodora.

She was relieved to find her cousin had gone when they finally came back out. After they rounded the corner to the front of the manor, however, she saw one of the groomsmen leading a carriage and four horses toward her.

She started to ask the servant whose carriage it was, but once she saw the crest on the side of the black, shiny vehicle, she knew.

It was the Earl of Kenswick's crest.

Nicholas Thornton must be inside with Thomas!

Panic seized her, but peering down at Ty, she knew she must go back in, that she couldn't stay out in the sun much longer.

"Hey, whose black, shiny coach is that, do you think?" Lucy asked, always the curious one.

"It is Lord Nicholas Thornton's coach."

She looked down at her sister and watched her eyes register with recognition. "Wasn't he the first man you were supposed to marry?" she asked bluntly.

Katherine bit her bottom lip as she unconsciously gripped the pram's handle tightly. "We really must work on your tact, sister dear," she murmured, her eyes trained on the front door she had to enter.

Lucy made an unladylike snorting noise. "I think you have larger problems than my manners, *sister dear*," she retorted.

"Please, Lucy. I'm scared to go in. I don't want to face him," she admitted, her voice growing hoarse with tears.

Then her sister, who was usually a thorn in her flesh, surprised her by reaching over and putting her hand over Katherine's clenched one. "You have Thomas now. Think of how lovely it is you have such a wonderful man you'll marry soon; then perhaps Lord Nicholas will not matter anymore," she said matter-of-factly in a voice beyond her twelve years.

Katherine smiled down at her sister with amazement. "You really are quite smart, you know that?"

She took the compliment as if it were her due. "I know." She then pointed to the pram. "Do you want me to take the pram, or do you want something to hide behind?"

"Maybe *too* smart," she muttered, throwing her sister a frown. "I'll take the pram, thank you." She proceeded determinedly to the door.

McInnes showed her to the parlor, where they were gathered, and once they noticed her standing in the doorway, all talking came to a stop. Uneasiness filled the room as Nicholas and his wife stood. Thomas stood, too, and came immediately to her side.

"I didn't know they were coming," he whispered in apology as he put a hand at her back and ushered her farther into the room.

Katherine forced herself to look at Nicholas, then his wife. She was surprised to find the bitterness she thought would arise did not consume her as she'd expected. Perhaps it had been her little sister's words that had done the trick; she did not know. But, as she turned from Nicholas's strained expression to his wife, who was smiling uncertainly at her, she felt strangely calm and—

Free.

"You know Nicholas, of course, but I don't believe you have met his wife,

Christina," Thomas said quickly, as if he were in a hurry to break the awkward silence.

Katherine curtsied, and Christina did the same. "It is nice to meet you, Lady Thornton. Thomas speaks very highly of you," Katherine said first.

The uncertainty left Christina's pretty features as she smiled at her. "Please call me Christina, and I am very honored to make your acquaintance, also!"

Christina, Katherine could tell immediately, was so different from any of the women she knew from the ton with her open smile and readable face, but she also finally understood why Nicholas had chosen her. Her uniqueness had apparently been what he had needed to shake him from self-destruction. Something Katherine had been unable to accomplish once he returned from the war.

Nicholas, however, did not share his friendly wife's openness of expression or eager acceptance. He even put a hand on Christina's arm when she stepped closer to Katherine to speak to her as if to protect his wife from her!

Offended by his action, Katherine stayed only a short time more before making her excuses to leave. Thomas stood ready to escort her out when Nicholas stepped forward.

"I would like to walk Katherine out, if you have no objections," he said to Thomas, but his eyes remained watchful and, to Katherine's dread, mistrustful as he trained them solidly on her.

Chapter 11

The moment Nicholas had passed through the door with Katherine and her sister, he asked Lucy if she would give them a moment so he might talk to Katherine alone.

Lucy grudgingly agreed, and suddenly they were alone for the first time since the night he'd broken their engagement. "I won't mince words, Katherine. I need to ask you why out of all the men in England have you chosen my brother to become engaged to?"

She stared at him, aghast at his nerve. "You of all people should know I did not have 'all the men in England' to choose from, thanks to you!" she snapped back.

"So you are using him because you have no other recourse?" he persisted.

Katherine had to take a few breaths to calm the anger that was boiling inside her at his nerve. "How dare you?" she said slowly and distinctly so he could understand every word. "You have no right to question anything I do. I have been through untold anguish, not because of a broken heart"—she wanted to make that clear—"but because the backlash of your actions has ruined my good name. You should be apologizing to me as you told my father you wanted to do, instead of accusing me of using your brother."

They stared at one another for what seemed like centuries before she finally saw a shift in his expression. "I apologize, Katherine," he offered, astonishing her. "I did not mean to come down on you so hard. I—" He stopped and seemed to be thinking of the right words to say. Something that was uncharacteristic of the old Nicholas. "I just don't want to see my brother hurt. He's been through so much, and I suppose I simply want to protect him."

"I'm not going to hurt Thomas, Nicholas. I love him." As soon as she spoke the words, she realized they were true. She did love Thomas Thornton, and she wanted to marry him.

Nicholas, never one to miss much, narrowed his eyes at her. "You seemed surprised by that admission."

She blinked in wonder and looked up at her former fiancé. "I suppose I am," she admitted. "I mean, I knew I was fond of him, but—I truly do love him."

"You haven't told him?" Nicholas was back to sounding protective again. "Whatever were you marrying him for if you did not love him?" he demanded.

Katherine was not intimidated. She folded her arms about her waist and stared him squarely in his blue eyes. "We didn't love each other when you proposed to me," she reminded him.

Nicholas had the good grace to look away in discomfiture, but then he brought his eagle gaze back to her. "I still do not have a good feeling about this match—I won't deny it." He sighed. "But I will say no more about it."

She let out a breath. "Thank you."

"Unless you give me cause, of course," he added, making her want to slap him.

"Kate!" Lucy called to her, as she came running to where they were standing on the steps. "Theodora wanted me to let you know the carriage is ready."

"Nicholas, I must bid you good day, but before I go, you need to know, although I hated you for what you did at the time, I can now say thank you. If you had not stopped our getting married, then I would not have met the right man for me."

"Nor I the right woman," he said in agreement. He surprised her by taking her hand and bowing over it. "I wish you happiness, Katherine. And if it is found with my brother, then I cannot begrudge it."

She gave him a tired smile. "Be well, Nicholas," she said quickly as she bobbed a curtsy, then turned to leave.

Excitement churned in her chest as she walked briskly to the carriage. She was in love! For the first time in her life, she loved a man who truly loved her back.

She had so much to think about—so much to contemplate and plan for. But one thing was certain. Under no circumstances could she tell Theodora about her change of heart. On her wedding day, she'd just have to be surprised when she walked down the aisle and took her place by Thomas.

Where she belonged.

⌘

"Ye look tae be a bit out o' sorts, my laird," McInnes observed from his post by the doorway, watching Thomas pace back and forth in the foyer.

"He's more than out of sorts, Mr. McInnes," Christina spoke up as she came down the stairs. "He's in love."

"Ah!" The big, middle-aged man nodded sagely as if that answered all his questions. "And tae a verra fine lassie, if ye don' mind me saying so."

Thomas heard both of their comments, but his mind was on what was going on outside the manor. "What do you think they are talking about?" He stopped to run a hand through his thick, brown hair, causing it to stand on end.

"Thomas, would you please relax? He is only trying to bring some sort of conclusion to what transpired between them a few years ago," Christina explained reasonably. "Nicholas has felt great guilt over what he did, and I know he only wants to apologize."

Thomas shook his head. "I don't know, Christina. He does not want this engagement between Katherine and me. I do not want him to say anything that will cause her to have second thoughts."

Christina walked up to him and laid her hand on his arm. "Thomas, surely her feelings are not so fragile. She has chosen to marry you, so she must love you. Nothing Nicholas could say will change that."

Thomas's worry only increased as he listened to her. Katherine had not told him she loved him. He did not have that particular reassurance.

All three of them heard the handle of the door being pushed, and McInnes was quick to grab hold of his end and open the door, causing Nicholas nearly to stumble. After he'd regained his balance, he shot a sharp glare at the Scot. "Does he always hide by the door to scare any who might want to open the door themselves?" he growled, directing his question to Thomas.

" 'Tis my job, my laird, tae to be ready and waetin'." McInnes stared back, not cowed by the earl in the least.

"You obviously do not understand the proper conduct of one in your position! If you were in my employ—"

"You would fire him, then rehire him in the next breath as you've done your butler and valet a thousand times," Christina interrupted her husband's tirade in a matter-of-fact tone.

Thomas wasn't sure, but he thought he heard McInnes make a comment about "the overbearing English" before he excused himself from their company.

"Nick," Thomas called out loudly to interrupt the whispered argument his brother and sister-in-law seemed to be having. "I would like to know what was said between you and my fiancée."

Nicholas gave his wife a warning look that seemed to promise they would resume the argument later, but Christina only smiled at him in her charming way. "Before I answer that, I would like to know why you would marry a woman who has not even declared her love for you. Did you not tell me your second marriage would be for love?" Nicholas charged, his frown deepening with every word.

Thomas froze, astounded he even knew. "Katherine told you she didn't love me?" he asked, horrified at the possibility.

Nicholas shook his head in disgust. "No, little brother, she told me she did love you but that she hadn't told you." He snorted. "I told her it was not very—"

"Stop!" Thomas shouted, pushing out his hand toward his brother. "*Katherine*—told *you*—that she loved *me*?"

"Yes, and I told her—"

"She told you—but she didn't tell me," he stated slowly as he tried to understand the reasoning behind his fiancée's withholding this from him.

"Yes, yes, and I—"

"Nicholas, will you stop for a moment?" Christina scolded her husband, grabbing him by the arm and giving it a small shake to get his attention. "Can't you see he is in shock at what you've told him?"

Thomas rubbed his forehead. "What does it mean, Christina, when a woman loves you but does not share it with you?" He pointed to his brother. "Instead she tells her former beau about it!"

Christina left Nicholas's side and came to take her brother-in-law's hand. "Dear Thomas, it simply means she is afraid to expose her feelings to you. As you grow closer and come to trust one another, she will tell you."

"I have to wonder if she is playing at some sort of game," Nicholas stated baldly.

"Nicholas!" Christina gasped. "Consider your words!"

"What are you implying?" Thomas responded at the same time.

Nicholas held out his hands in supplication, his expression apologetic. "I did not mean to sound so accusing, but I cannot keep my concerns silent. Not when your happiness is at stake, Thom."

Thomas's anger dissipated at seeing the concern in his brother's eyes. "Nicholas, you act as if I am some schoolboy who cannot think for himself." He kept his voice gentle. "I love Katherine Montbatten, and now that I know she loves me, there is no reason to worry."

A self-deprecating smile curved Nicholas's lips. "Then forgive me for prying," he said, but he snapped his fingers as though he'd suddenly thought of something. "Just one thing. I heard Katherine's sister say Theodora was waiting for her. Who is Theodora?"

"She is Katherine's spinster cousin. Vine, I believe her family name is." Thomas became curious. "Why? Do you know her?"

Nicholas shook his head. "I don't think so. I do remember, though, that Father was seeing a local woman years ago after Mother died. I believe her name was Theodora."

"Well, I daresay, there must be quite a few ladies with that name. And, besides, this one doesn't seem the type who would have attracted someone like our father. Keeps to herself, this one does," Thomas commented.

"Mmm." Nicholas looked thoughtful, and Thomas wondered if there were more.

❧

"My dear, you must see the wedding clothes I had made for you!" Her mother held up one garment after another in Katherine's room. Her parents had arrived from London while they had all been at Thomas's manor. "And this"—she paused and held up a beautiful satin gown with pearl accents on the collar, the high waist, and the sleeves—"is your wedding gown. Isn't it stunning?"

Katherine took the gown from her mother's arm with wonder and admiration. "It is a gown made for a princess," she commented in an awed whisper, her fingers reverently brushing over the lovely pearls.

"It is a gown made for a duke's daughter," her mother haughtily corrected. Her attention was caught by Theodora sitting quietly by the bed. "And don't sulk, dear. I did get one for you, too." She pointed to a deep golden gown with ecru-colored lace over the bodice.

Theodora stood up and walked over to the gown. "Thank you, Your Grace. It's quite stunning," she said, a rare smile on her face.

"Well, of course it is, dear. You are Raven's first cousin and have been an excellent companion to Katherine. It is the least I can do."

As her mother chatted on, Katherine watched Theodora take the gown, then hold it up and glimpse herself in Katherine's oval mirror. Theodora, with her plain gray gowns and her unflattering hair pulled back so severely, had never struck her as someone who would get misty-eyed at a pretty frock.

But then she hadn't truly known her cousin very long. Theodora had come to live with them right after the broken engagement because Katherine's mother thought she needed someone to be with her. Before that, she'd seen her cousin at family gatherings and never paid much attention to her. She did know there was a time when Theodora did not seem so plain—even when she remembered her mother mentioning that Dora was close to becoming engaged, but apparently it hadn't happened.

Had she been jilted as I have? Katherine wondered suddenly. Perhaps that was why she was so determined for her to go through with the plan.

But later, all sympathetic thoughts she may have had for Theodora left Katherine when her cousin began mapping out their plan for the wedding day.

"Now I believe the best thing for you to do is get dressed and pretend you're running late." She glanced down at her notepad and made some sort of mark upon it. "I will tell your family to go on to the abbey, that I'll make sure you get there on time. That is when you will leave and—"

Katherine held up her hand, confused. "Leave? And go where?"

Theodora smiled. "This is where Cameron comes in. When he arrives in a few days, we will tell him of our plan and have him acquire the necessary transportation to get you to the estate in Wales."

Katherine sighed, trying to be patient. "Dora, why do I need to leave?"

Theodora smiled at her as if she were a tolerant schoolmistress trying to teach a slow pupil. "If you stay here, your parents might come back to the castle and make you go through with the marriage. This way you will be gone, leaving a note saying you realized you did not love Thomas and you couldn't go through with the ceremony."

Suddenly Katherine could not take discussing the plan of revenge anymore. "Dora, I just remembered I need to do something at the abbey," she said hurriedly as she walked to the door.

"What? Should I go with you?" Theodora called after her.

"No!" Katherine cried as she whirled around and held out her hand. "It is something I must do alone." She continued in a slightly calmer voice as she kept backing up.

Theodora tried to argue the point, but Katherine's hands found the handle of the door. She pulled it open and ran quickly out the door, then out of the house.

She didn't understand what or who was compelling her to go to the abbey, but Katherine knew with all her being she had to go there. She had to make things right with God and beg His forgiveness for what she'd planned to do.

It took her only fifteen minutes to walk to the quaint stone abbey and into the cool interior of the empty sanctuary. Tears were already pouring down her face as she ran to the altar and fell down on her knees.

And she prayed. She prayed God would forgive her for the angry thoughts and words she had said about Nicholas and his family. She asked God to bless the love she had for Thomas and make their marriage a strong one, despite the falseness that had been a part of it in the beginning.

Most of all, she thanked God for sending her Thomas and making what she meant for bad turn out so wonderful.

"Lady Katherine, is there anything I can do for you?" She heard the vicar's voice through her sobs and felt his comforting hand upon her shoulder as he knelt beside her.

She lifted up her head, wiping her eyes in the process. "I've been a wicked person, Reverend," she told him, her voice thick and shaky with tears.

The vicar, an elderly man with a shock of curly white hair, nodded sagely. "We all can be a bit wicked now and then. The important thing is you've acknowledged your sin and you've come to the best place to make things right." He patted her on the back. "Did you ask God for forgiveness?"

She nodded with a hiccup. "I want Him to, more than anything."

"That's good, child," he assured her, his eyes crinkling at the corners as he smiled. "Now the only thing you can do is accept His forgiveness and be careful in the future to be a better Christian person."

Katherine felt as though a weight had lifted off her shoulders. "Oh, I will, Reverend. I shall endeavor to be the very best Christian woman I can be." Then she added, "And the best wife and mother, too."

"Ah! That is correct! I have a wedding to perform in a few weeks. Very fine man you're marrying. Very fine."

Katherine impulsively hugged the vicar, then jumped up from where she'd knelt. She offered a hand to the slim, short preacher and helped him stand, also. "Thank you so much for your comforting words, Reverend. They have helped me tremendously."

When she left the old building, Katherine, for the first time in two years, felt so splendid inside, so full of hope.

The only wrinkle in her happiness was Theodora and her brother, Cameron. But she would not worry about them today. Today she was going to bask in the wonderful feeling that she was finally free from her bitterness and need for revenge.

Chapter 12

Thomas was astounded at the change that had come over Katherine in the last three weeks. She was no longer uncertain in her manner or constantly changing in moods as she had been when they'd first become reacquainted; now she was the loving, caring person he'd always dreamed she'd be.

Katherine, too, had been a tremendous help in the redecoration of his manor, putting her style and special touches in each room of the house. Thomas could not walk into a room without seeing something his lovely fiancée had added or rearranged, and it thrilled him to his very soul to know she was making Rosehaven her home, too.

And then there was Tyler. His son could not have been more attached to Katherine, even if she'd been his real mother. And she treated him like a son, instructing him, dressing him, and even discussing with Thomas about his future education.

Their lives could not be more perfect, except for one little detail.

She had not told him she loved him yet.

He realized they'd not had much time to spend alone, so perhaps the opportunity had not arisen for her to pour out her feelings to him. He knew also that she had shown her love for him in her smiles and the way she freely touched his arm or hand.

Perhaps he wanted too much. After they were married, they'd have plenty of time for talks of love and romance.

Another problem he had encountered the day before was a visit from Katherine's father. The duke had asked him all sorts of questions about whether or not he and Katherine were getting along and if he had anything he needed to tell him before the wedding took place.

Thomas tried to get to the bottom of such an odd interrogation by his future father-in-law, but the duke would not tell him if anyone had talked to him. In fact, Thomas was going to discuss this with Katherine, but all thoughts of the concern left his mind when he saw her.

"We have finally hung the drapes in the library!" Katherine declared, bursting into the room with her sister behind her. "It took us over three hours, and though half your staff threatened to quit, we finally got them up there!"

Thomas chuckled. Both Katherine and her sister were covered with dust. "How did you get so dusty?" He stood up from his desk and walked toward them.

"It is the dust from the old curtains!" Lucy said. "Katherine was trying to direct one of the servants on how to bring the curtain off the rod, when the whole thing fell right on top of my sister." She sneezed then and wearily rubbed her nose. "Unfortunately, I happened to be standing right by her."

"Well, for all your hard undertaking, let me ring for some hot tea and coffee to help calm your—er—dusty nerves." He laughed and pulled a cord beside the grand fireplace in the room.

"Not funny, Thomas. We are truly quite worn out from the ordeal." Katherine started to lower herself onto the red velvet sofa but stopped. "I forgot I cannot sit—your furniture—"

"Is cleanable," he finished for her, placing his hands on her shoulders and gently pushing her down. "You, too," he said to Lucy. He held out his hand to her, but the young girl shook her head.

"If you don't mind, I want to walk down to the barn and see about Rosie," she told them.

Thomas looked at Katherine with puzzlement. "Who is Rosie, Lucy?" He turned back to her when Katherine only shrugged.

Lucy smiled with pride. "Rosie is the name of your other Arabian! Remember that you told me I could name her? I named her after your home, Rosehaven Manor." And before Thomas could say anything else, she skipped out the door that led to a side entrance and was also a shortcut to the stables.

"I am so sorry, Thomas. Of course you should name her something else."

But Thomas shook his head. "No, I promised. But perhaps I can add another name later to make it more fitting, like Desert Rose or something similar."

A knock sounded at the door before Katherine could comment. "A compliment to your staff, Thomas," Katherine told him admiringly. "I've never seen tea delivered so quickly!"

Thomas shrugged, though puzzled. "Perhaps they were anticipating my wanting it. . . ." He walked over and opened the door to the study. It was not the maid, however, who stood there.

McInnes wore the strangest expression Thomas had ever beheld on his butler's face before. It was a warrior's expression, one hard and ready for battle.

"McInnes? Is something wrong?"

" 'Tis an enemy a' yer gate, laird," he whispered menacingly, his jaw muscle flinching with emotion. "If you'd like, I'll taek care o' him fer ye!"

Thomas shook his head in confusion. "What enemy, McInnes? Who are you talking about?" He looked down and realized his butler was wearing a kilt. "McInnes? Why aren't you wearing your uniform?"

" 'Tis the colors o' the clan McInnes, laird. We always wear 'em when trooble is cooming." He leaned forward, and for a second Thomas thought he heard the music of ancient bagpipes off in the distance. " 'Tis her broother, laird.

'E's coom begging fer a fight."

Then he suddenly understood why McInnes seemed worried.

Apparently Katherine's brother, Cameron, the Marquis of Sherbrooke, was standing at his door and probably none too pleased to hear of the engagement.

"Thomas, what is the matter?" Katherine asked, coming to stand beside him. She, too, gaped at his butler with astonishment.

"Your brother is here."

Katherine's face turned pale, almost white. "Oh no, Thomas. Please let McInnes send him away. I'm afraid of what he might do," she begged him, clutching his arm.

Thomas patted her hand with reassurance. "Katherine, I cannot hide in fear of him. The sooner I deal with him, the sooner you and I can move on with our lives."

"Show him in, McInnes," he ordered. "Try not to manhandle him too much."

"Aye," the Scot answered with his thick brogue. "I'll get 'im fer ye."

Thomas was a little uneasy at the smile of anticipation on McInnes's face but dismissed it when he looked down at Katherine's troubled features.

"Katherine, please don't worry," he said, trying to soothe her, and led her to a settee. "I'm sure we can discuss our differences like reasonable—"

"Take your hands off my sister, Thornton!" a booming voice commanded from the doorway. Thomas turned in surprise and saw a giant, blond young man bearing down on him with fist closed and ready.

"Cameron, no!" Katherine jumped up and put herself between them.

Cameron paused and took a moment to glare at his sister in disgust. "Get out of the way, Katie, and let me deal with this vermin face-to-face."

Thomas agreed. "Yes, do sit down, darling." He gently moved her aside, ignoring her protest. "I don't believe I've had the pleasure of meeting you," he told the angry man drolly, determined he was not going to reciprocate his fury.

"Save your niceties," Cameron growled, taking a menacing step closer. "Let's settle this like gentlemen, shall we? Pistols. At dawn."

Thomas almost laughed at the absurdity of the challenge. Cameron Montbatten was a young man, probably a couple of years older than Katherine's twenty, and still had much to learn about how a true gentleman conducted himself. But he held on to his bemused mirth and was careful not even to smile, lest he humiliate the brother of his future wife. As it was, he wished he could give the young whelp a good lashing for his impudence.

"Sherbrooke, may I ask just what offense I have committed against you or any member of your family?"

Cameron's clenched jaw jerked with annoyance. "I offered you a challenge, my lord. Will you or will you not accept it?" he demanded, ignoring Thomas's question.

Thomas folded his arms and gave the young man a narrow-eyed stare. "Not until you tell me what I need to know."

"Because your family has caused great harm to my sister's reputation!" he roared, his face a picture of incredulity that he'd have to explain such an obvious reason.

Thomas shook his head and turned from Cameron, walking across the room to motion for the maid, who was standing with uncertainty at the door, to bring in the tray bearing the pots of tea and coffee.

Once she'd set it down and exited the room, Thomas picked up a cup and saucer. "Would you like tea, Sherbrooke? Or do you prefer coffee as Katherine does?"

Cameron appeared as though he would explode any minute. "Tea? Have you not heard a word I've been saying, or"—he stopped, and a sneer spread across his face—"or are you too much of a coward to face me on the field?"

This time Thomas did laugh; he couldn't help it. "Sherbrooke, let me make a few things straight with you," he said, pouring Katherine a cup of coffee. "First of all, I am not the one who hurt or brought shame upon your sister. And, second of all, I am not about to maim or kill my future wife's only brother." He winked at a worried Katherine. "Bad way to begin a marriage, don't you think?"

"How dare you laugh at me!" Cameron charged, shaking a finger at Thomas. "I am sincere in my challenge, and though you did nothing directly, I declare you are just as responsible since you did nothing to stop your brother from doing the deed!"

This time it was Katherine who spoke up. "Cameron, Thomas had just enlisted in the Royal Navy at the time and was preparing for sea." She walked over to him. "Please say no more, brother. This is none of your concern."

Cameron suddenly turned his rage on Katherine. "What is wrong with you, Kate? Have you no standards at all? Did you not learn your lesson the first time?"

Thomas lost his humor when Cameron grabbed Katherine's arm. He put down the cup and went to take Katherine's other arm. "I've had enough, Sherbrooke. We'd like your blessing, but we don't need it. Your father has given his consent, and that is all we need to get married. Now let go of her arm," he ordered the man, his voice quiet but deadly.

Cameron was young but apparently not stupid. Resentfully he took his hand away and stepped back. "So you will not meet me at dawn?" he persisted.

Thomas sighed, trying to maintain his patience. "Of course not."

"Then let it be publicly known to you I protest this union and will never accept it!" he stated emphatically.

"Cameron!" Katherine cried. "Please, do not say such things!"

But her brother's expression did not soften as he looked from one to the other, then turned and stalked out of the room.

"I'm so sorry, Thomas," Katherine told him. "He's usually a mild-mannered gentleman. I can't understand why he won't see reason."

Thomas put his arms around her shoulders and kissed the side of her head affectionately. "I am not worried, Katherine. I just do not want you upset about it."

She looked up at him with such feeling that it caused Thomas's chest to constrict with emotion. "I am not going to let anything ruin our wedding day, Thomas. Not even my hotheaded brother."

Thomas smiled, and though he truly wanted to kiss her, he restrained himself, knowing that in three days she'd be his to kiss and hold whenever they desired. He took her hand instead and led her back to the settee. He handed her the coffee he'd poured earlier, then made himself a cup.

They chatted about the changes they'd made to the house; then he remembered the visit her father had paid him.

"Katherine, I had the strangest visit from your father yesterday. Did you know he was here?"

He saw the surprised expression on his fiancée's face. "No, I did not. What was it about?"

Thomas took a sip of his steaming coffee and leaned forward. "He kept asking me if everything was right between you and me and if I had anything to confess to him before we married. Do you know if anyone has said anything to him—anything at all to make him doubt my sincerity to marry you?"

～❧～

Katherine willed herself not to panic upon hearing of the reason behind her father's visit. *Theodora*. It had to be Theodora's doing.

She forced a smile, trying to make him think nothing was wrong. "He is just protective of me, Thomas. You know how fathers are," she equivocated.

Thomas nodded, and a sad smile curved his lips. "Yes, I do know. I'm just sad to think my father couldn't be here for the wedding. He always liked you, you know."

Katherine smiled, thankful the subject had been changed. "Why don't you tell me about your father?" she urged him, honestly wanting to know more about the man who sired such a wonderful son.

After that, she didn't stay at Rosehaven much longer.

A half hour later, she and Lucy were in their carriage going home. Her main mission was to find Theodora and confront her with her suspicions. Had Theodora spoken to her father? There could be no other explanation.

Chapter 13

O f course I'm the one who has been talking with your father," Theodora admitted without the least compunction when Katherine questioned her. "I tried to talk to your mother also, but we both know she hears only what she wants to and blocks out all the rest."

"Dora, making Papa worried is not going to help—" she tried to reason, but Theodora cut her short.

"I am doing what we had decided *you* would do, cousin dear!" she charged with a sharpness to her tone Katherine did not like. "Putting doubts in your parents' heads about him will help your explanation when you run away from the wedding! You know this, yet you are doing nothing about it!"

Katherine wearily put her hand to her head, trying to decide what to say and what to do. "Dora, I know we agreed to this, but you must know how busy I've been at Rosehaven."

Theodora made a disbelieving sniffing noise. "That is another one of my concerns, Kate. Either you seem to be playing your part as the loving fiancée so well as to rival any of the actresses on the London stage, or you are beginning to believe the lie. Please, tell me you haven't forgotten our objective!"

Katherine turned from her cousin so she could not see the truth written on her face and walked over to peer out the window. Pushing the lace sheers aside, she muttered, "I don't know what you mean."

She waited for a few long, unbearable moments for her cousin to respond and at the same time dreaded her speaking.

"You have changed your mind, haven't you?" Theodora said softly, her voice filled with disbelief. "Answer me, Kate! Have you changed your mind?"

Katherine could keep up the charade no longer. Since she'd come to the conclusion she loved Thomas and had made her peace with God, she had gone to great lengths to avoid Theodora; the few times they'd talked, she would say very little. It was time for this whole despicable plan of revenge to come to an end.

She turned slowly and looked the older woman directly in her eyes. "Yes, Dora. I have changed my mind. I'm in love with Thomas and want to marry him."

Theodora began to laugh but not with happiness. It was a crazed sort of laugh that sent chills down Katherine's spine. "You have changed your mind, just like that, eh?" she said in a shrill voice and snapped her fingers for emphasis. "And you thought I would sit back and let you?"

THE ENGAGEMENT

Katherine froze. Was her cousin a little mad? She'd known Theodora had been emphatic and oddly possessed as they planned the revenge upon the Thornton family, but she had not considered her obsession was unnatural.

She wondered again why this mattered so much to Theodora.

Katherine took a breath, then licked her lips nervously. "What do you mean by that, Dora? Are you planning to tell Thomas about our plan? I plan to tell him anyway, so your threats won't work!"

Theodora smirked, her plain face becoming ugly. "I'll do whatever I have to do, Kate. Remember that." She walked closer, and Katherine tried to back up but realized with the window behind her that she had no way to escape her cousin. "I will not let you marry him," she growled no more than an inch from Katherine's face.

"You are scaring me, Dora." She tried to keep her voice steady and not show the fear churning inside her.

Theodora surprised her by backing up a little and smiling pleasantly. "Don't be a ninny, Kate. I was just teasing you," she explained as if nothing out of the ordinary had just occurred.

But Katherine wasn't fooled by her words or seeming innocence. Theodora Vine was not the teasing sort. All Katherine wanted to do was get away from her, so she pretended to accept her explanation. "Of course you were." She carefully walked around her cousin and opened the door. "I've had a tiring day, Dora—if you don't mind leaving so I can wash up and possibly nap before dinner."

Her cousin smiled at her, but her eyes were hard and cold like ice as she nodded and walked to the door. "Don't worry, Kate. All will be as it should," she said cryptically as she left the room.

Katherine closed the door and leaned against it, her mind racing as to what to do. Part of her wanted to go to Thomas right away and tell him the truth—the plan of revenge, her change of heart—everything.

But another part of her was afraid that if she did tell him, he'd call off the wedding and walk out of her life forever.

Closing her eyes, she prayed, "Please, Lord, guide me in the way I should proceed. I do not want to lose Thomas, not after You have helped me overcome my bitterness and unforgivingness. Help me know what to do—"

A knock sounded at her door, startling her, for she thought it might be Theodora again. "Yes?" she called.

"It's me," Lucy answered from the other side.

Katherine sighed, not wanting to deal with her sister at that moment. "Lucy, I was about to take a nap. Can you come back later?"

"Not unless you want me to tell Mama about the plan," she said in a loud whisper.

Her eyes wide with shock, Katherine threw open the door and dragged her sister inside. "What do you know about that?" she charged.

Lucy shrugged off Katherine's hold on her arm and walked to the bed, plopping down on it. "I was listening at the door," she explained, as if it were the most obvious answer in the world.

"You little scamp!" Katherine roared. "Can I not have any privacy?"

"Not until you move out," Lucy answered. "*If* you move out, that is," she added, her voice mysteriously low.

Katherine shook her head, wondering what her sister would do with the information she had. "Lucy, if you overheard, then you must have heard me tell Dora I will not go through with our plan of revenge. I truly want to marry Thomas."

"It was a stupid plan to begin with," she said critically. "I can't believe you conspired to do anything with Theodora anyway. Can't you tell she doesn't like you?"

Katherine had begun to realize this but was surprised to hear Lucy state it with such conviction. "How do you know this?"

"She resents coming to live here with our family and being the equivalent of a servant." Lucy paused. Katherine waited for her to explain how she would know this. "I heard her tell that to Aunt Constance when she visited last Christmas. Of course our aunt chastised her for speaking so forthrightly, but I heard it all the same."

Katherine sat on the bed next to her sister, her mind trying to think back on all the times she and Theodora had spent together. In hindsight, she could recall times when Theodora's behavior could be interpreted as resentful. "I guess I never realized—"

"You were too busy feeling sorry for yourself," Lucy supplied.

"Are you here to make me feel guilty?" Katherine frowned at Lucy.

The younger girl shook her head. "I'm here to make sure you marry Thomas and not jilt him at the altar."

"Of course I am marrying Thomas. I love him."

Lucy smiled brightly and jumped off the bed. "That is all I wanted to know, because I thought it would be quite fun to come and stay with you at Rosehaven in the summer and on holidays!"

Katherine stared at her sister in bemusement. "Behave yourself and keep your mouth shut, or you will never get to come!" she threatened with a reprimanding expression.

Her sister, apparently not bothered by the stern warning in the least, merely grinned at Katherine and skipped out of the room.

"Brat," Katherine muttered, thinking her sister was out of earshot.

"I heard that!" came her sister's reply as she poked her head back inside the room with a pouty pucker on her lips.

"Good!" Katherine said before closing the door firmly in Lucy's face.

～

After the meeting with Katherine's father and the confrontation with her brother, Thomas knew he needed to get away from Rosehaven and go to Malbury, where the Kenswick estate was located, to talk with his brother. It wasn't that he doubted Katherine's feelings for him again. On the contrary, when she'd left his home earlier, he felt the affection she had for him, although she did seem concerned about her father's visit.

No, it was that the whole engagement—and even before—had been riddled with misgivings and reservations—things that shouldn't normally be part of a relationship.

Every day he prayed he could be the father Tyler needed, the husband Katherine desired, and most of all that the little worries and uncertainties would not plague their union as they did now. He knew God had put Katherine in his life. Only God could know what kind of woman both he and Ty needed.

It was just that. . . Thomas dropped his head into his hands and groaned, so very weary of trying to reason it all out.

Finally he could feel the carriage slowing, so he peered out of the small window to determine where they were. It was now dark, but because of the full moon, he could see the majestic site of Kenswick Hall, high upon the hill. He'd spent the majority of his childhood in the old hall, and it never ceased to bring him comfort whenever he would visit.

Because of the late hour, Pierce, the family butler who had been there since Thomas was in his teens, seemed quite put out at having to get out of bed to answer the door. Thomas could tell his clothes had been hastily thrown on, for his shirt was buttoned all wrong and half his thinning hair was standing on end.

"Pierce!" he greeted him. "Sorry to wake you, old man; but I had this need to come to Kenswick, and it just happened to be at a late hour."

Pierce was in no mood, obviously, to act as though he were thrilled. "Could the 'need' not have waited until morning, my lord?" he asked grimly.

Thomas laughed, feeling better already. "Is my brother in bed yet?"

Pierce shook his head. "No, my lord. I noticed they were still in the library on my way to answer the door."

Thomas shook his head with mock disapproval. "It wouldn't hurt him to answer his own door once in a while."

"Beg your pardon, my lord," he returned stiffly. "He is the Earl of Kenswick! He will not open his own doors—not on my watch."

Thomas laughed. "Go back to bed, Pierce. I'll see myself in." He stepped over the threshold onto the marble floor of the foyer.

He glanced back and noticed Pierce still held the door open and was looking out into the night.

"What are you waiting for, Pierce?"

Pierce turned his way. "I was thinking perhaps you brought Master Tyler with you, my lord."

Thomas shook his head with regret. "I'm sorry, Pierce, but I left him at home with Mrs. Sanborne. It was to be such a quick trip that I didn't want to unsettle him by the hour-long carriage ride."

Pierce had such a disappointed look on his long, thin face that Thomas wished he'd brought his son. Nicholas had told him stories about how the butler, as well as many of the staff, had all pitched in to care for the infant when he had first been brought to Kenswick Hall.

"Cheer up, Pierce. In two days' time, Nicholas and Christina will bring Ty back with them from my wedding, since they'll be watching him while I'm on my wedding trip."

This cheered the older man up immensely. Thomas was still smiling about it when he walked into the library and found his brother at his desk reading something. Christina was in the room also, holding some sort of bird.

"Thomas! What a surprise!" Christina greeted him, though she remained seated. "What brings you to Kenswick?"

Thomas's eyes remained on the object squirming around in her arms. "Is that a chicken?" he asked, unbelieving.

"Don't look so shocked, Thom," his brother commented drolly before Christina could answer. "Last week it was a rabbit, and the week before, a goat ate half the drapes in the dining room."

"Oh, it did not!" Christina cried defensively. "It only nibbled on the fringe."

"I stand corrected!" Nicholas said with a grin, as he stood up and walked to his brother. "Welcome to the Kenswick Animal Menagerie!" He threw his hands wide. "You never said why you are here. Don't you have a wedding to get ready for?"

Thomas hugged his brother and tried to kiss Christina on the cheek, but when the chicken tried to peck him, he blew her a kiss instead.

"To tell you the truth, I came because I am a little weary, I suppose." He and Nicholas sat down in chairs across from one another, and he went on to explain the confrontations with Katherine's father and brother.

Nicholas seemed thoughtful for a moment, as if he were weighing his words. "Please don't take this the wrong way, Thom, but I have felt unsettled by this whole engagement, as you well know. It just seems odd Katherine would show interest in you when I'd heard she hated me and the entire Thornton family for what she'd suffered."

"Nicholas," Christina said, throwing him a warning look.

Thomas, however, held up his hand to her. "It is all right, Christina. I understand what he is trying to say." He turned back to his brother. "When I first encountered her again at the Beckinghams' ball, I, too, thought it odd she seemed so drawn to me. But you have to realize, Nicholas, there was such a strong connection between us. Perhaps she felt it as intensely as I."

Nicholas nodded. "Perhaps you are right. I pray you are right, for I truly want your life to be a happy one."

Thomas smiled at his brother warmly. "I know you do." He slapped his hands down on his legs. "I've been meaning to ask you, since we are speaking of my life, have you removed the monument yet in the family cemetery bearing my name and announcement of death?"

Nicholas shifted in his chair and looked away. "Uh, not yet, I—"

"He hates to think of destroying it, Thomas, because he worked hours on designing the monument and the statue that bears your likeness upon it," Christina supplied helpfully.

Thomas was astounded by that news. "I did not know you were the one who sculpted it! I had assumed you commissioned it."

"Well, I—"

Christina sighed, interrupting her husband once again as she got up and walked over to the mantel above the fireplace. "He usually carves figurines. He created all of these."

Thomas joined her in admiring the stunningly accurate statuettes of various animals. Each was made with careful detail.

"Is there anything else I should know about you?" he asked teasingly as he studied one particular figurine of a tiger.

"I am sure if you remain at Kenswick long enough, Christina will divulge about everything you ever wanted to know," Nicholas said with mock annoyance.

Christina made a huffing sound of protest. "You make it sound as if I talk too much!"

When Thomas exchanged a knowing look with Nicholas, the brothers suddenly found themselves pummeled with throw pillows.

⬚

The next morning, after a restful sleep, Thomas decided to walk through the small, quaint village of Malbury before he rode back to Rosehaven. He thought he would speak with the vicar, who also happened to be Christina's father, and walked the short distance to the cottage that sat adjacent to the church.

Reverend Wakelin seemed to be the same as when Thomas was only a boy. He was now gray and his face lined with wrinkles, but he still exuded energy and a charisma that made him seem younger than his years.

"Lord Thomas!" he greeted before the vicar's housekeeper could even announce he was there. He was coming from his study and rubbing his eyes, making Thomas think he'd been studying. Christina had told him her father would sometimes forget even to eat when he began digging for information for one of his sermons.

"Reverend Wakelin, sir, it is good to see you," Thomas returned his greeting while shaking his hand. "Did I come at a bad time?"

The vicar waved off his concern. "Of course not. In fact, I needed to take a break, so your visit is more than welcome." He motioned toward a side door. "Come! Let's go into the parlor."

Thomas smiled as he followed. "Is it the one with the lovely paintings your wife painted?"

"The very same," he answered, swinging the door open. There on all four walls hung some of the loveliest paintings Thomas had ever beheld. He'd remembered seeing them as a child but could appreciate the talent behind them more now that he was older.

"They are quite amazing, sir," Thomas commented reverently as he studied one in particular. It was a self-portrait of Mrs. Wakelin holding the baby Christina.

"Please sit and tell me of your upcoming wedding!"

Thomas sat on the sofa and leaned toward the vicar with arms propped on his knees. He told him of the frustrations he'd experienced during his engagement, not mentioning the confrontation he'd had with Cameron. He thought that was better left silent.

"Let me ask you what I asked your brother when he came to me for Christina's hand in marriage." He adjusted his wire-framed spectacles and leaned back in his chair. "Do you love her?"

A smile lit Thomas's face as he thought of his beautiful Katherine. "With all my heart," he answered.

The vicar shook his finger at him. "Then that is all that matters. There is something that happens when two people vow before God to love and cherish one another, especially if they have a relationship with God and mean it with all their hearts. It bonds them together, and when there is trouble, whether it be family or outsiders, those vows will ring out in your heart, reminding you that with God you can make it."

Thomas could not wait until those vows were indeed spoken and Katherine was truly his. "I understand what you are saying, Reverend. I do trust in God—I suppose I learned to when I was hanging on to a piece of wood, praying I wouldn't drown in the ocean!" They shared a chuckle, and Thomas stood. "I just need to pray Katherine does not want to bring her companion and cousin, Theodora, to live with us!"

A strange expression passed over the vicar's face as he stood with him. "Theodora, did you say?" When Thomas nodded curiously, he continued. "What is her surname—do you know?"

"It is Vine."

"Vine. . .Vine. . . ," the vicar muttered, scratching his head as if to jog his memory. Then his eyes widened. "Theodora Vine! You have a connection with her, I believe."

Thomas did not think he heard the vicar right. "I beg your pardon, sir? I?"

The vicar nodded. "Well, actually, it was with your father. I believe your father had called on the woman, a spinster, I believe, for a few weeks. It was two or three years after your mother passed away."

Thomas searched his memory. "You know—I believe Nicholas had told me something similar, but we did not think it could be the same woman! What happened to the relationship?"

"Hmm." The vicar hesitated. "I know she was younger than he, but that is not uncommon. I believe he told me she seemed a bit unstable." He nodded vigorously. "Yes, that was it. She was the type of woman who constantly demanded his attention, and when he stopped seeing her, she tried to sneak into his London town home with a knife. Your father, of course, did not press charges, but she was strongly urged by the local authorities to keep away from the earl or else they would go public with the incident."

Thomas frowned. "I wonder why he never told us about the knife episode."

"You were away at school and involved in your own lives. He didn't want you to worry about him, I suppose."

Leaning forward, Thomas told him, "Reverend, this woman has been Katherine's companion, and I've had the feeling she was pushing Katherine to do something. I don't know what it is, but it can't have been good," he added slowly, as he hastened to figure out what to do.

The vicar looked at him, his gray eyes deeply serious. "If I were in your shoes, I would urge Lady Katherine to be careful. Miss Vine is the type of woman who could make life unpleasant for anyone who crosses her."

Thomas thought of the way Theodora seemed to try to control Katherine, and his heart pounded a bit faster. If Katherine decided to go against her cousin, whatever that might be, it could be dangerous for her.

Thomas thanked the vicar and left. All the way back to Rosehaven, he tried to convince himself Katherine would be all right since their wedding was only two days away. After that, Thomas would make sure Theodora never bothered either of them again.

Chapter 14

For a day and a half, Thomas had tried to see Katherine, but it was to no avail. She was either being fitted into her gown or involved in settling in the many relatives who had arrived at Ravenhurst Castle to attend the wedding. He, too, had guests at Rosehaven, which included North, his brother and sister-in-law, and his aunt Wilhelmina.

It bothered him, however, that he did not get a chance to speak with Katherine about her cousin, and when he shared his concern with North, his friend assured him he was no doubt worrying over nothing. But he wasn't reassured, especially when his brother voiced his own worry about Theodora. And when he awoke the morning of his wedding, it was not with the anticipation he should have had, but instead he felt a deep foreboding.

His feelings were evidently transparent, for when he joined his family for breakfast, his aunt Wilhelmina picked up on his strange mood. "You are marrying into one of the most prominent families in England, and yet you seem forlorn this morning," she observed in her usual straightforward manner. "If you are concerned at her present social standing, Thomas, I should not worry. Your marrying her has elevated her reputation considerably."

It was Nicholas who responded to that comment. "Aunt Willie," he emphasized, knowing she hated being called that nickname. "None of us is concerned about social standings where marriage is concerned," he stated firmly.

His aunt sniffed. "I daresay you aren't, as you readily proved from your match!"

A stunned silence fell around the table, most everyone aghast that she would be so bold in her criticism. But it was not surprising she felt that way. Thomas knew when his brother had announced he would marry Christina, a common vicar's daughter, Aunt Wilhelmina had tried to tear them apart.

"You go too far, madam!" Nicholas glared at her across the table. He started to leave when his wife grabbed his arm.

"Oh, do sit down, Nicholas. Her words do not bother me in the least," she told him, looking from her husband to his aunt. "Lady Wilhelmina, if you cannot curb your comments and speak of more pleasant things when you are in our presence"—Wilhelmina gasped, but Christina kept talking—"then we shall not let you visit us when our son or daughter is born."

"That is marvelous!" North spoke up. "Congratulations to you both!"

"You're having a baby?" the older woman asked faintly, clutching her hand at her chest. "This means he will be heir to your title."

Thomas shook his head, as he surmised what this meant to his society-driven aunt.

"Yes, if it is a boy," Nicholas answered, his voice and demeanor now calmed, thanks to his wife.

"Then we have so much to plan for!" She clapped her bejeweled hands together. "We must have the right nanny and then governess—and, Nicholas, you know you must send him to Eton because—"

"We will deal with that as it comes, Aunt," Nicholas interrupted, then looked at Thomas. "What I am concerned about right now is Thomas. You never did tell us why you seem so upset this morning."

Thomas sighed, pushing his food about on his plate with his fork. "It's just a feeling I have—I don't know. I suppose I'm a little out of sorts since I have not been able to talk to Katherine in two days. I really would like to warn her about her cousin."

"Thomas, you shall have all the rest of your life to talk to her," Christina reminded him gently. "In a few hours you shall be her husband, and it will be within your power to make sure Theodora stays well away from her."

"You are right, Christina," Thomas said, feeling a little better. "I guess I do not want anything to happen to stop us from getting married."

Nicholas stood and put his hand on his brother's shoulder. "Thom, trust in the love you have for one another. I may not have been completely behind this relationship in the beginning, but I do know she spoke the truth when she told me she loved you. Believe in that, little brother."

Thomas held those words close to him as he, with the help of his valet, dressed in his new black suit, with its gray vest and snow white cravat tied expertly at his neck. Christina pinned a pink rose on his lapel; then they, along with Mrs. Sanborne and his son, left in his brother's grand carriage and traveled to the abbey where the service was to be held.

⁓

Katherine stood in front of her mother as they stared at their images inside the oval mirror in Katherine's bedroom. She was in awe at how the stunning satin gown with its empire waist and wide, pleated skirt transformed her into the bride she'd always dreamed she'd be. The circlet of pink roses around her head, with the lace veil that streamed behind her, completed the look.

"You are so beautiful, dear." Her mother sniffed and put her arm around her shoulders and gave her a loving squeeze. The other hand was dabbing madly at her moist eyes. "I shan't get through the ceremony without staining my own gown with tears—I just know it!" she declared with typical dramatic flair.

It took great concentration for Katherine not to roll her eyes in exasperation.

"Mama, I am sure your dress will hold up fine," she assured her dryly. "And, besides, the pink color complements your features quite a lot. I daresay there will be many comments made about how young it makes you appear."

Her mother immediately stopped crying and nudged Katherine aside a bit so she could see her own image fully. "Do you think so, dear?" she asked breathlessly, tugging at the neckline, then smoothing the skirt. "Yes, I do believe you are correct, Katherine! It is a very good color for me."

Katherine hid her smile behind the bouquet of flowers she'd taken from her nightstand. "You must remember to tell your dressmaker of this so she might search for more fabric of the same hue," Katherine added, feeling a bit guilty she was teasing her mother, though the woman was oblivious.

Lady Montbatten breathed in quickly in a small gasp, and her eyes grew wide. "I shall do that first thing Monday morning!"

"Here you are!" Lucy cried as she came bounding into the room with her usual burst of energy. She, too, was dressed in pink with her thick, blond curls tied back with a large, matching ribbon. When she saw Katherine, her eyes stared at the veil and ran down the length of the gown to her sister's satin slippers. "You look so beautiful!" she whispered in admiration.

"Oh! Why, thank you, dear!" her mother answered, making the sisters glance at each other with surprised humor. "I was just going down to write a note to my dressmaker about it." She started out of the room but paused to look at Lucy with a critical eye. "Do something with her hair ribbon, Katherine. It appears a bit disheveled!"

"Do you think she is really that capricious, Kate?" Lucy asked with a grin when their mother was out of earshot.

Katherine shook her head with a chuckle. "I don't know. I once thought she may only act that way because it allows her to get away with things a lady normally wouldn't, but now I'm not so certain. She would have to be the world's greatest actress to carry off such a charade over our whole lifetime."

Lucy walked over to her, and Katherine began straightening her ribbon. "Have you seen Theodora this morning?" she asked her little sister. If anyone knew, it would be Lucy.

But the younger girl shook her head. "I haven't seen her since last night, but I did notice Cameron is here."

Katherine was astonished at that news. "I thought he said he wouldn't come."

"You know Cameron," Lucy said with a grown-up tone to her voice. "He pouts, but he loves you too much to snub you on your own wedding day."

Katherine smiled. "I'd hoped he couldn't stay away." She bent and gave her sister a kiss on the cheek. "There you are. Now go down and make sure Theodora is not about causing trouble, will you? I'll be down in a moment."

"I hope she'll be so upset because you are not going along with her plan that she has decided to go away somewhere and not attend the wedding!" Lucy stated fervently.

"Now, Lucy, behave yourself!" she called after her sister, but because she ran out of the room so fast, Katherine was doubtful she even heard.

Katherine's maid came in and applied the last touches to her blond curls. Ten minutes later she was fully dressed, so she made her way downstairs to let her family know she was ready to leave for the church.

But when she stepped into the library where her parents were supposed to be waiting, she suddenly froze.

No one was there but—Theodora.

An uneasy feeling settled over Katherine as she stepped farther into the library, nervously searching about the room. "Where is everyone?" she asked, keeping her voice as steady as possible.

Theodora's lips curved into the most frightening smile Katherine had ever seen. A chill ran down her spine as she tried to assure herself it was only her imagination that made Theodora seem so daunting.

"They have gone to the abbey," she answered coolly. "I told them I would ensure you arrived safely and on time." She let out a small laugh. "But, of course, you won't."

Katherine felt panic building in her chest, and she took a deep breath to try to calm down. She thought about the servants and decided, if she had to, she would scream for their help. "Dora, I told you I had changed my mind, and I meant it," she said firmly, her eyes trying to gauge the distance between herself and the door.

As if reading her thoughts, Theodora began to circle her, putting herself between the door and Katherine. "Ah, but that is not what we planned, Kate. You know that." Theodora stepped closer to the door. "The Thorntons must pay, and this is the only way to do it," she stated as if it were the most rational explanation in the world. "You see, I was once involved with Nicholas's father."

Katherine stood staring at her cousin with unbelief. "What? I never heard about—"

"Of course you never heard about it!" she snapped. "I was staying in Malbury when we met, so very few people knew. He led me to believe I was special to him, then he threw me over for no reason!"

Katherine raced to try to reason with her. "I understand how he must have hurt you, Dora, but this is not going to change your circumstance. This will not make either one of us happy!"

Theodora sneered at her as she clutched the handle of the door. "It will make me happy to see those high and mighty Thornton men suffer as I have suffered! It will make me happy!" she repeated, almost as if she were trying to convince herself of that fact.

Her cousin appeared to be quite mad, completely beyond reasoning. But Katherine was desperate to try. "Please, Dora. When Thomas and I are married, I will help you make another match! We'll arrange parties, get you a new wardrobe—"

"Stop it! Just stop it!" Theodora cried, jerkily shaking her finger at Katherine. "It is too late for that! This is the only way!"

Katherine stood there for a second, stunned when Theodora slipped out of the room, slamming the door behind her. When she heard the key jiggling in the lock, Katherine snapped out of her stupor and ran to the door. She pounded on it with all her might. "Theodora! Let me out! Ambrose! Let me out of here!" she yelled, hoping the butler could hear her, knowing Theodora would not listen.

"There is no one to hear you, Kate!" Her muffled voice came through the thick wood of the door. "So scream your little heart out. It will do no good!"

Katherine continued to scream and bang on the door until she had no strength left. With tears streaming down her face, she finally shuffled over to a chair and fell into it, covering her face with her hands. Heavy sobs shook her thin frame as she contemplated what Thomas would think once she did not show up for their wedding.

⁓

Thomas scanned the congregation for the twentieth time in ten minutes, then checked his watch again. Where was she? Nervous sweat beaded on his forehead.

He wasn't the only one who was wondering about his absent bride. He heard scattered whispers throughout the building and saw heads turning to check the entrance to the abbey.

Where was Katherine?

Finally he walked over to Lord and Lady Montbatten. "Your Grace," he addressed Katherine's mother. "Are you sure Katherine had a way to the abbey?"

Lady Montbatten seemed a little nervous herself. "Yes, Thomas. Theodora assured me she would see Katherine arrived safely and on time."

Thomas directed his gaze to the back of the abbey to the person he'd noticed the last time he'd looked for Katherine. "Your Grace, Theodora is"—he paused, overwhelmed by the same foreboding he'd felt that morning—"Theodora is here."

"What?" Lady Montbatten cried, as she turned in her pew and looked toward the back of the church. "Something is not right here!" She jumped from her seat and hastened to where Theodora was.

Thomas followed her, praying his instincts were wrong but knowing they were right.

Katherine had apparently jilted him.

"Theodora!" Lady Montbatten whispered in a hiss. "Where is Katherine?"

THE ENGAGEMENT

Theodora shifted her eyes from Lady Montbatten to Thomas, her face full of innocence. "She sent me on to the church. She told me she would soon follow."

Thomas didn't understand what was going on, but he knew Katherine would not be coming to the abbey, and he knew in his very soul Theodora Vine was part of the cause.

Katherine's mother sighed. "Well, she must have gotten held up for some reason! I'll send Raven to get her and bring her back here," she insisted. "Wait a few more minutes, Thomas. I'm sure we'll have her here as soon as possible."

Thomas didn't say a word. He merely walked back up to the altar, told the crowd the wedding would be delayed a few moments until the bride arrived, then stood beside the vicar—

And prayed he was wrong and she'd come.

Chapter 15

Katherine cried so much she finally fell into a restless sleep. She'd done all she could think of: yell, bang on the windows and door—

Pray—

Nothing seemed to work. She had felt so helpless, so despairing. How would Thomas ever understand any of this? How could he forgive her part in it from the beginning?

"Katherine!" a loud voice bellowed over her, causing her nearly to fall out of the chair. "What are you doing here?" her father demanded, once she had looked up at him with bleary eyes.

She pushed her tangled veil out of her face and tried to get her bearings. "How did you get in?"

Her father blew out a breath of frustration. "How do you suppose I got in, young lady? I opened the door!"

Katherine shook her head, knowing she must not have heard him right. "But it was locked!"

For the first time in her life, her father directed a frown of pure disappointment upon her. "It was not locked."

"But—"

"Do not insult me by lying, Katherine. I've been looking for you for over forty minutes around the property, thinking you might have been kidnapped or crashed in your carriage. But when I realized the carriage had never left the stables, I came inside to search for you." He shook his head. "I never thought you'd do something like this, Katherine. I am ashamed of you."

Tears were once again spilling from her eyes. "Papa, you don't understand. Theodora—"

"Yes, she informed me you sent her ahead to the abbey. She's also been looking about the house for you!" He stared at her as if he didn't know her at all. "Did you do it for revenge? Did you plan this whole thing to bring shame upon the Thornton family?"

Katherine grabbed her father's arm, her eyes pleading with him to listen to her. "No! Papa, you must hear me—"

"Instead," he continued as if he didn't hear her, "you have brought more shame upon this family."

With that, he shook off her hand and walked to the door.

"Papa! I didn't do this deliberately! Papa!" she yelled, but he never turned back as he left the room.

Katherine rubbed her eyes, trying to clear them. Walking out into the hallway, she turned in the direction her father had taken. Abruptly she stopped, realizing that speaking to her father was not her top priority. Instead, she ran in the opposite direction to the front door.

Perhaps if she spoke to Thomas, she could explain. Make him understand what had happened.

She did not know what compelled her to stop by the abbey first, but she asked her coachman to do that very thing.

As she let herself into the church, she was assaulted by the sweet smell of the roses her mother had decorated with. On each pew end was a small bouquet, and in the very center of the altar was a huge arrangement with both pink and white roses intertwined with the same colored ribbons.

Her attention, however, was not on the beautiful décor, but on the right front pew. Thomas was there, bent over slightly; his eyes seemed to be focused straight ahead, staring at—nothing.

Her heart felt as though it were breaking as she slowly walked up to where he sat. The floor creaked beneath her slippers, but he did not turn or make any movement of acknowledgment at her presence.

A few feet from him, she stopped. Taking a deep breath, she called softly, "Thomas."

He stood then and slowly turned toward her, his face swathed with hurt and betrayal. Those blue eyes that had gazed lovingly into hers only a few days before now stared with stark coldness.

"Thomas, listen," she began, her voice shaking. "This was Theodora's doing. I tried to—"

"I can't believe I've been so gullible," he ground out bitterly, making a slashing movement with his hand. "I had a feeling all along you and your evil cousin were up to something. I never dreamed you would go to such elaborate lengths." He ran his hand through his already mussed hair. "Or perhaps I did but did not want to believe it," he added with a self-deprecating murmur.

"It's not like that, Thomas." She realized it was time to tell him the truth. "You see, I did set out to hurt you, but I changed my mind after I met you. It's just that Theodora would not accept it. She locked me in the castle. I couldn't get out!"

"You mean you set out to convince me to marry you, all along knowing you would never go through with it?" he asked, focusing on her first sentence. He appeared confused. Katherine hurried to explain.

"Yes, Thomas, but I changed my mind! Don't you understand? I was hurt and bitter over what happened with your brother and how the ton turned against me. Theodora convinced me this was the only way to avenge myself. But I couldn't do it."

An appearance akin to revulsion spread across his face as he stared at her. "That you could even think of hurting an innocent man, a man who was falling in love with you, horrifies me, Katherine. You are not the person I thought I knew."

With one last look, he brushed past her. Katherine turned and ran after him. "Thomas, I've changed! I fell in love with you, too. I even asked God for forgiveness for the sin I had planned to commit! Please, believe me."

He kept walking, and she followed him outside, into the shaded courtyard of the abbey. She expected to see his coach waiting for him, but when she saw only a horse, she thought his family must have taken it back to Rosehaven. He stopped and turned toward her when he reached the animal. "You know, Katherine, I have waited weeks for you to tell me you love me, but you didn't. You can perhaps understand why I'm having trouble believing you now."

"Thomas!" she cried, tears pouring from her eyes as she watched him mount his horse and snap the reins to urge him forward. "But I do love you, Thomas. Believe me. Please, believe me."

Katherine realized her words were falling on deaf ears. As he galloped away, she fell to her knees, her wrinkled wedding gown spread about her as great sobs shook her body.

"My lady!" her coachman called, running to her.

"I've lost him," she muttered incoherently. "I can't believe I've lost him—"

"I'm sure 'tis not as bad as all that, my lady." He managed to lift her to her feet.

Katherine allowed him to lead her to the carriage and tuck her in safely. She lowered her gaze to her gown and saw the dirt stains that now marred the once lovely satin material.

She wished with all her heart God could remove the stain in her heart as easily as her maid could remove the stains from her wedding dress.

❧

"Are you all right, Thom?" Nicholas entered the sitting room where his brother was staring out the window.

"Have you come to say 'I told you so'?" he asked bitterly, wishing everyone would go home.

Thomas heard Nicholas sigh and his footsteps come nearer to him. "I think you know better than that," he answered quietly, making Thomas feel shameful at his malevolent attitude. "The vicar came by a minute ago, but I told him you weren't receiving anyone."

Thomas nodded, his eyes still fixed ahead, staring at nothing. "I appreciate that."

The brothers lapsed into silence, then Thomas saw Nicholas move beside him on the other side of the wide picture window. "He did say, however, that he saw you talking to Katherine outside the church." Nicholas cleared his throat as he cut his gaze over to his brother. "Well, no—that is not exactly what he said. I believe he told me you were yelling, and she was crying, running after you." Nicholas turned to stare fully at his brother. "What happened? Why didn't she come?"

Thomas made himself face his brother. "You were, indeed, right when you said it seemed an odd coincidence she happened to turn her attentions to me. She was conspiring with her cousin, Theodora Vine, to get me to the altar so she could call it all off, thus vindicating the hurt you caused her. In other words, she was using me to hurt you."

Nicholas shook his head, dumbfounded. "You can't be serious! I thought she'd turned to you because you were the only man available to her, not because she had a malicious agenda!"

Thomas closed his eyes briefly and tried to block the sharp pangs of hurt and disappointment that pierced his heart and soul. Instead, he tried to focus on the emotion that was easier to express—his anger. "I cannot believe I have been so foolishly misled," he spat out, talking more to himself than to Nicholas. "I knew something was amiss; yet I kept pursuing her and trying to make it work."

Nicholas gripped his arm. "Thomas, you are not a fool! You simply loved her, and you cannot be faulted for that!"

"I even prayed I could be the right man for her, Nick. In my stupidity, I assumed God had put us together and she would be the perfect mother for Tyler and all our children to come." He swallowed hard, trying to chase away the bitterness that seemed to clog his chest and throat. "She seemed to love Tyler, Nick. How could I have misunderstood?"

"God can work this out, Thomas. What did she say to you? Why, if her plan was to abandon you at the altar, did she show up later? Surely by staying around she would have to bear the chastisement of her father and mother."

Thomas had a picture of Katherine's tear-stained face as she pleaded with him to forgive her. "She said she had tried to make it to the wedding because she had fallen in love with me and had changed her mind about her plan." He let out a snort of disbelief. "She had the audacity to blame her absence on Theodora locking her in a room. Why wouldn't the servants let her out then?" he asked, throwing his hands up in the air.

Nicholas frowned thoughtfully. "But, Thomas, what if it's the truth? Katherine is not an evil person by nature. I could quite believe bitterness made her concoct the plan, but guilt and love for you would not let her go through with it."

Thomas was not ready to hear reason. He turned his heated gaze to his brother. "She purposely tried to get me to fall in love with her, and I"—his voice cracked, and he paused a second before continuing, his voice more solemn—"and I did, Nick. I love her still, and one day soon I will forgive her misdeeds against this family and me. But I will never allow her back into my life again."

Nicholas slammed his hand down on the white, wooden window seat, startling his brother. "Don't do this, Thom," he growled at him. "Remember what bitterness did to me? Dwelling on bitterness and anger separates you from everyone you love, and most important, it will separate you from God." He took Thomas's shoulders in his hands and shook him gently. "And living a life without God's love is the coldest, most miserable world you could possibly live in."

Thomas shook off Nicholas's grasp. "First you warn me against her, and now that she's shown herself to be conniving and untrustworthy, you want me to give her another chance. What do you want me to do, Nicholas?" he asked, feeling the desperation of his situation closing in on him.

"You must do whatever you feel God needs you to do," Nicholas answered, his eyes and voice intense. "Push away the hurt and emotions, then do what your heart is urging you to do."

Thomas did not have to look deep within himself to know what he should do. He loved Katherine with all his heart and soul. Nicholas did not realize how tremendously he wanted to believe her, wanted to be assured she truly loved him.

But he could not go to her. Perhaps it was pride or some other strong force that kept hardening his heart from believing her, but it was there.

"I can't do anything right now, Nick." He finally spoke the only truth he knew at that moment.

Nicholas sighed and put his arm around his brother for a brief hug. "I will pray you do it soon, then."

"Please, give my apologies to your wife and North that I cannot entertain them tonight. I fear I need to be alone," Thomas said once they stepped apart.

Nicholas nodded. "We had all planned to leave in the morning." He walked to the door but turned to give his brother a look of concern. "I will come if you need me. North wanted me to convey the same message to you."

Thomas nodded and watched him leave. After that, he did not know how long he stood and stared out the window, replaying the day over and over in his mind, reliving each and every horrible minute of it.

His thoughts were interrupted when Mrs. Sanborne hesitantly entered the room, asking if he'd like to tuck his son into bed as he did every night.

He almost declined, but suddenly he had an urge to hug his son, to tell him he loved him no matter who did or did not come into their lives.

Chapter 16

The scene that followed the next day was not a pleasant one. Katherine had finally admitted to her father her and Theodora's plan. She also told him she could not go through with it. She explained that her cousin had locked her in the room, but because the room had been unlocked, he had not believed the last part.

That did not mean he would allow Theodora to get away with what she'd done.

He summoned Theodora into his meeting with Katherine, and she knew the older woman had some idea of what it was about by the speculative gleam in her eyes as she entered the study.

Katherine prayed that whatever excuse her cousin gave, it would not be more convincing than the truth she'd already told her father.

"Theodora," Lord Montbatten began, his tone hard and serious as he looked up at her from his desk chair. "Sit down, please. I have something I need to discuss with you."

The usually collected woman appeared very nervous as her gaze darted from Katherine back to Lord Montbatten. "Your Grace, if it is about the wedding, I tried to bring Katherine with me, but she—"

"Theodora!" he thundered, causing her to cease her prattle. "Do as I have asked and sit down!"

With pinched lips, the older woman did as he ordered and sat on the edge of the leather chair across from him.

The Duke of Ravenhurst minced no words. "Because of your dire situation two years ago, I allowed you to come live with us and be my daughter's companion. And though I knew about all the trouble you had caused the late Earl of Kenswick, I had your promise you would behave in a ladylike manner, helping my daughter through her difficult time."

"Yes, Your Grace. I fully appreciated your generosity—"

"You do not 'appreciate' anything, Theodora Vine. I believe you actually resent the post you have been given here," he inserted forcibly.

Theodora's face held an innocent expression Katherine knew all too well was faked. "But, Your Grace, I—"

"Because of this latest scheme you and my daughter have conspired, I can no longer allow you to stay and influence any more members of this family."

All manner of pretense left Theodora's face, and a look of pure hatred masked her features. "How easy it is for you to throw away an unwanted, poor relative. You sit in your many homes and castles and presume to cast judgment on all you deem undesirable." She stood, her fists balled tightly at her sides. "What about your own daughter? She has obviously planted all sorts of lies in your mind against me. Did she also tell you of her own deceit?"

"Theodora, I told him everything," Katherine answered. "I am taking no fault away from myself in the plan. I only wanted him to know I had decided not to go along with it. I told him the truth."

Theodora threw back her head and let out a crazed laugh. "*Your* truth, Katherine. That does not mean it is the real truth!"

"Enough!" Lord Montbatten roared. "I do not know what is going on here, but I only know I will not tolerate this any longer!"

"I will not allow you to throw me out, sir. I will leave on my own accord. You do not have all power over me, you know!" Theodora declared in a triumphant sneer as she spun around and started out of the room.

"I am afraid I cannot allow you simply to walk out of here when you can easily come back to harm either Katherine or anyone else in the family."

Katherine turned to her father in surprise and saw Theodora also looked very confused. "What do you mean by that?"

"I have arranged for you to leave here with my sister and travel with her to France. She is a widow, as you know, and needs help with her eight children. I told her you would be available."

Theodora was not cowed by his arrangement. "You cannot make me go with her! I will simply refuse! Do not think I am completely without friends or resources. I will go elsewhere."

Lord Montbatten leaned forward as he narrowed his sharp gaze on his cousin. "You either go with her, or I shall tell the authorities to renew the charges against you because you have conspired to bring ruin to a member of the ton."

Katherine suspected Theodora knew she had no recourse. The older woman marched out of the room but not before she stopped where Katherine was sitting and smiled at her coldly. "Welcome to the world of spinsterhood, where you are at the mercy of self-serving relatives who care nothing for you except what you can do for—"

"That is quite enough, Theodora!" Lord Montbatten roared.

"Good-bye, Dora. I hope you'll be happy," Katherine told her quietly. For the first time, she truly felt sorry for the woman and prayed she'd allow God to come into her life and help her.

But for now, Theodora only sent her a heated look before sweeping through the door.

THE ENGAGEMENT

When Katherine awoke the next morning, her aunt had left with Theodora.

After that, the matter was dropped, but it was clear she would bear the result of her actions for a long time.

And she did. For in the two weeks that followed, Katherine was sure she had never felt so alone in her entire life. Though she'd once again tried to explain what had happened, neither her father nor her mother spent any time with her. At dinner she was largely ignored, except for Lucy's attempt at bringing her into the conversations. But even then, all would fall silent; then they'd begin a new subject—one she could not be part of.

Katherine knew what their silence was about—though they believed Theodora had kept her from attending the wedding, the whole event would not have happened if the two cousins had not contrived the scheme in the first place.

Lucy was most surprising at her acceptance that Katherine was truly sorry for her deeds. Even Cameron, before he'd left a week earlier, had told her that while he still despised Nicholas Thornton, he was sorry she had been hurt over the ordeal.

He was not, she noted, sorry the Thorntons were embarrassed over the situation.

As she paced back and forth in the foyer of the castle, waiting for a reply to the letter she had sent Thomas, she wondered if this letter, too, would be rejected as all the others had.

Day after day she'd written him, and every time her letter came back with the seal still intact and unread.

Christina, Thomas's sister-in-law, had even written her a letter, urging her to try to see Thomas and mend the relationship. *He's not doing well,* she wrote in her scrawling handwriting. *He won't even allow Nicholas to come out to Rosehaven to see him.*

She went on to tell her own story of how she had to badger Nicholas into opening himself to other people again when he'd returned from the war. Even when he rejected her, she had gone to his house, finding excuses to run into him until he finally gave in to her.

So, just two days ago, Katherine had tried to do as Christina suggested. She went to his house and told McInnes she would sit on the front step until he came out and talked to her.

Apparently the picture of her sitting alone deep into the afternoon and the beginning of night could not induce him to care enough to speak with her. She finally left, her faithful coachman having waited for her all day to take her home.

The large brass ring on the outside of the main door to the castle sounded loudly inside the marbled foyer. Katherine ran to the door as Ambrose opened it and took the letter from the boy who had delivered it.

She held her breath as Ambrose closed the door and turned to her, handing her own letter back to her. There was pity in the older man's eyes as she slowly took the folded papers bearing her intact seal.

Though tears stung her eyes, she avowed she would not cry in front of her father's servants anymore. She'd done it so much that he'd sent the doctor over to check her "mental health."

She wasn't crazy; she was just so desperate to get in contact with Thomas. Somehow, some way, she had to let him know she would not give up on her love for him.

Deciding she had to get out of the castle for a bit, she ran to get her light shawl from her room and headed out toward town.

She was surprised to see Lucy by the gate that surrounded their property. She was without her governess or a maid, which meant she had sneaked out without her parents' permission.

"Where are you going alone?" Katherine asked in her typical big-sister voice she knew irritated her little sister.

She saw a bit of guilt on Lucy's face as she answered evasively, "I just wanted to be by myself for a while. Perhaps pick flowers near the forest."

Katherine, in a hurry to get away, was in no mood to argue with her sister, so she gave in to her. "Well, do not stay out too long. Mama will worry if she chances to look for you."

A satisfied smile curved Lucy's lips as she skipped off without so much as a thank-you.

Katherine let go a deep sigh as she began the short walk to the village. She noticed the summer flowers blooming in full color around her, and that went to great lengths to restore her spirit.

At moments, during the two weeks, she had felt so alone and wondered if even God had abandoned her. But surrounded by His beautiful plants and trees and the warm sun shining on her face, she knew He had never left her. He was in everything around her, reminding her that when she was down, He'd be there to lift her up.

At last she entered the village, and her reception by the people of the village would probably have been laced with more frostiness had she not been above most of them in station. As it was, they were polite but not talkative, and Katherine could not blame them for their judgment. She had done a very bad thing; even if the end result had not been her fault, she had brought it on herself.

She had gone into the bookstore, which usually never failed to take her mind off her problems, but today it did not. She wandered around for about ten minutes, then decided to stop by the village inn to get a cup of coffee before she started back on her journey.

Katherine had walked only a few feet when unexpectedly a man stepped directly in front of her from out of a shop. She stumbled to gain her balance, and when she looked up to mumble an apology for not seeing him, she froze.

There Thomas stood, staring at her with as much surprise as she was at him.

"Thomas! I can't believe it is you—"

Before she could finish her sentence, he turned away from her, giving her the rudest direct cut she'd ever received from anyone.

Ignoring the pang of hurt that pierced her heart as he walked away, she tossed all protocol to the wind and ran after him, not caring that she was making a spectacle of herself.

"Thomas! Please talk to me!" she called as softly as she could when she finally reached him and grabbed hold of his arm. He stopped when he felt her and after a tense moment turned and stared coldly into her tear-filled eyes. "Why won't you let me explain? Why won't you at least give me a chance to—?"

"I know all I need to, Katherine. Frankly, anything you could tell me right now I would be disinclined to believe." She gasped, and he became grimmer— seemingly more determined. "I'm sorry, but that is how I feel."

"But I told you I had changed my mind!" she cried fiercely, hoping he'd see the love pouring from her gaze—from her expression. "I love—"

"Do not speak of it, Katherine!" he insisted in a stern whisper. "It is over and done with. Now please, cease in your attempts to contact me."

"I won't!" she declared. "I will not give up on us, Thomas. Not until you listen!" Her voice had risen to the point that anyone coming onto the street could hear every word.

He merely shook his head at her, disappointment etched on his handsome face. "Katherine, you need to stop. You are embarrassing yourself and me. Good-bye."

She watched with disbelief and a wounded heart as he turned from her. It was pride that held her back this time. She'd pleaded with everything in her, and he'd rejected it.

She had nothing else to give. No more words to say.

He'd given up.

Perhaps she should, too.

Suddenly she became aware that everyone who had been in the village shops was now lined on the dirt street, staring at her as if she were mad.

Everything, even her dignity, had now been stripped from her. Gathering as much fortitude as she could, Katherine held her head straightforward as she walked down the street, ignoring the glaring eyes and curious faces.

Once she was out of their sight, she allowed her tears to fall, but she vowed it would be the last time she'd allow herself to cry over Thomas Thornton.

She had only God now. He loved her. He had forgiven her.

It was a good start.

∽∾

Thomas felt as though his heart were breaking into pieces as he turned from Katherine and walked away.

He'd been so close to forgetting his pain, forgetting his feelings of betrayal, and simply pulling her into his arms. He loved her so much it had been agony turning her letters away each and every day.

But his pride had stood in the way. His manly pride that stopped him from forgiving her as he knew he should.

Deep inside, he knew she wasn't lying to him when she declared her love. But he could not believe no one could have heard her cry out, if Theodora had indeed locked her in the room.

It had been the one sticking point as he'd deliberated over the circumstances of that day. The Montbattens had more servants than anyone he knew. He could understand Theodora's fooling one of them into going along with her plan, but the entire staff?

Not likely.

If only he knew for sure. Could he know?

He entered his manor and stopped when he saw the uncomfortable expression on McInnes's face.

"What is it, McInnes?"

" 'Tis tha' young lass, my laird. I couldna turn tha' puir thing aweey," his butler said hesitantly, motioning toward the sitting room Katherine had liked so much.

Thomas looked at the open doorway but could not see inside the room. Was he talking about Katherine? Surely not, he tried to assure himself. There was no way she could have beaten him to the manor.

"What poor thing—I mean, who are you talking about?" he amended, shaking his head, confused.

"He's talking about me," a familiar voice spoke, and Thomas glanced back over and found not Katherine but her sister, Lucy, standing in the doorway. She was not wearing her normal carefree, happy expression; instead she looked upset, with her arms folded and her toe tapping the floor in annoyance.

"Lucy? What are you doing here?" he asked, walking with her back into the sitting room.

He showed her to one of the plush seats her sister had picked out for the room and sat across from her. Lucy seemed to take an enormously long time in smoothing her skirts and getting settled in the chair. "I have come on a matter of great importance," she announced formally, her expression more adult than child.

Thomas didn't want to upset the girl, but he was in no mood to discuss her sister. "If this is about Katherine, Lucy, it is none of your business—"

"Oh yes, it is my business!" she declared, interrupting him. "You don't have to listen to her crying all day long and holding those sad little letters you return to her unopened." She took a breath and scowled at him. "Hasn't she suffered sufficiently? Or are you going to let her go on like this indefinitely?"

Thomas tried not to be stirred by Lucy's words, but the vision of Katherine holding those letters and tears streaming down her face made him feel ill.

"It is my intention to go on with my life, Lucy," he told her gently, not believing his own words. "Your sister will, too."

Lucy shook her head sadly at him. "It wasn't her fault Theodora locked her in the room. My cousin had even made sure every servant was out in the garden, setting up for the party." She sniffed. "I can tell you Ambrose was none too happy about that. Said it was quite beneath his dignity."

Every muscle in Thomas's body froze at her words. He didn't take a breath as he contemplated what that meant. "I beg your pardon, but did you say there were no servants in the house? None at all?"

"None!" Lucy assured him. "I know because Theodora bragged about it to Cameron—because, of course, he was glad the wedding didn't take place," she said matter-of-factly. "And when I asked Katherine about it, she said Theodora told her the same thing. My sister yelled and pounded on the door until she grew tired and cried herself to sleep. Theodora came back home with my father, and while he was out looking around the estate, she came in the house and secretly unlocked the door so it would look as if Katherine had deliberately stayed home from the wedding."

Thomas closed his eyes as he thought of what Katherine had gone through, especially when he did not believe her. "Lucy, do your parents know any of this?"

The young girl nodded her head, her bright golden curls springing about with the movement. "Yes, but I am not sure they believed her about the house being empty. I've tried to talk to them, but they won't listen," she said as if she were terribly put out about it. "Father keeps telling me he is too busy to talk, and Mother keeps crying and lamenting how they will never be able to face the ton again." She leaned forward and with a serious face confided, "It's quite daunting to live in a household where everyone is so caught up in their own feelings they won't let anyone help them feel better."

Thomas stood up and put out his hand to her, pulling her up with him. "I have to go to Katherine," he said quickly, knowing he could wait not a minute longer.

Lucy's eyes lit up with hope. "You are going to forgive her?"

Thomas put his hand on her smooth jaw with affection. "I will do better than that. I am going to ask *her* to forgive *me*."

Lucy nodded sagely. "Excellent plan. I think that will do quite nicely."

Thomas smiled at her and gave her a big hug. "Would you like to ride with me back to your home?"

Lucy surprised him by declining. "Oh, no. I sneaked out to come and plead Katherine's cause to you. So I will have to sneak back in!"

Thomas laughed and walked hurriedly with her out of the room.

Chapter 17

Thomas decided to take Sultan since the horse could get him there faster than a carriage or walking. As the wind whipped through his hair and clothes, Thomas prayed it wasn't too late. He knew he'd hurt Katherine today by his coldness and by allowing her to make a fool of herself in front of the entire village.

He was so caught up in his thoughts that he didn't see a low branch hanging over the path. Leaves and dense branches hit him squarely in the face, almost knocking him off his horse.

He slowed Sultan down a bit and gingerly touched his stinging cheek. He checked his hand and saw a smear of blood on his fingertips. Thomas grew aggravated at himself for letting the mishap occur. He needed to present a good picture of himself when he arrived at the castle, and here he was, his hair askew, his clothes riddled with leaves and bark, and his face bloody.

Not exactly respectable standards.

But it really didn't matter, he tried to assure himself as he took out a linen handkerchief from inside his coat pocket and held it against the scrape on his face. Urging Sultan on at a slower speed, he knew the only thing that mattered was making Katherine believe how sorry he was for doubting her.

In hindsight, Thomas wished he'd heeded his brother's advice and tried to remember the time he'd spent with her in the weeks leading up to the wedding. Now he could remember how loving she was with him, how caring she was toward Tyler, and how beautifully her eyes lit up when they had shared that kiss.

He'd taken great measures not to be so forthright again, but he had wanted to kiss her. He had wanted to take her in his arms, and now he had no doubts she wanted to be near him as much.

Once he arrived, he handed over Sultan to a stable boy with instructions to wait a moment before taking him to the stables, in case Katherine would not see him.

A less than friendly Ambrose opened the door and reluctantly showed him in, making him stand in the grand foyer to wait for the duke.

He was taken aback when the duke rushed into the room, spouting apologies even as he came through a doorway. "I am so glad you've come, my lord. I must apologize again for my daughter's behavior. She used to be such a good girl and—"

Thomas held up a silencing hand. "Your Grace, please," he interrupted before he became irritated that the man would say anything else about his daughter. "I did not come here for apologies. I came because I must see Katherine!"

The duke frowned and gaped at him in a moment of stunned silence. "What happened to you, son? Were you set upon by highwaymen?" he asked as he took in Thomas's rumpled clothes and scraped face.

"It was a branch," he muttered, agitated at having to answer when he needed to speak to Katherine. "Now about your daughter, Your Grace, I—"

"Why do you need to see her? Hasn't she tried to apologize to you in letters?"

"Yes, and I thoughtlessly sent them back unanswered," he admitted. "But you have it all wrong, Your Grace. It is I who need to apologize to her. I had thought she was lying when she said Theodora had locked her in her room."

The duke shook his head. "Yes, yes, but I still am not sure I believe that. Surely she couldn't have routed all the servants out of the castle! It's been my belief Katherine stayed home, and by the time she realized she wanted to marry you, it was too late. So she lied," he theorized.

"But she didn't," Thomas insisted, hoping he could set the matter straight. "Theodora admitted to Cameron she had done the deed and devised a scheme to get all the servants out of the castle so she could accomplish it. Katherine apparently cried until she finally fell asleep in exhaustion."

"Oh, dear. I feel quite guilty for not believing her. I have been quite severe upon her for the last two weeks," the duke told him, his gray eyes troubled.

"Ambrose told me Katherine had not returned home from her trip to the village. Do you know where she might have gone?" Thomas asked, his voice growing more urgent as the need to see Katherine increased.

He was devastated when the duke shook his head sadly. "I am afraid I don't know. You can wait for her here if you'd like."

"No," Thomas answered emphatically. "I have to find her. I have to let her know I believe her."

"You might find her either in the moat or by the bridge that spans the narrow part of the lake, my lord," Ambrose answered, stepping into the room.

"The moat? Do you mean my daughter spends time in that great ditch around the castle?" the duke asked, clearly distressed by this. "She would almost have to use her hands to get in or out of there. Quite unladylike! Quite!" he stressed, apparently already forgetting he owed his daughter an apology.

Lucy was right about her parents. They were not the most attentive in the world. "Regardless, Your Grace, I will go and look for her."

He turned and walked toward the door Ambrose already held open for him. "I pray good news about renewed wedding plans will follow upon your return, my lord," the old butler whispered.

Thomas paused a moment to pat him on the arm with an assured smile. "I'll do my best, Ambrose!"

"Excellent, my lord."

The moat, unfortunately, was empty, so Thomas ran down to the lake, stepping over bushes and foliage, praying he wouldn't trip and further injure himself.

He came upon the clearing and beheld the shimmering waters of Ravenhurst Lake. The sun's reflection cut a bright path across the ripples made by the wind, and Thomas felt compelled to follow that path with his eyes.

There in the distance, through the trees, he could make out the curved bridge and someone sitting on its railing.

Horror struck his heart as he saw it was Katherine and she was leaning forward as if to jump in.

"Katherine!" he yelled as he ran along the lake's bank, waving his hands, trying to get her attention.

Her head popped up, then she glanced around as if trying to find the source of the noise. Her gaze landed on Thomas as he came barreling out of the trees.

Her surprise over seeing him startled her so much she began to tip forward. A yelp escaped her throat as she grabbed onto the railing, steadying herself.

Thomas's mind was not thinking rationally, and his first thought was that she was about to throw herself off the bridge. He sped to the bridge, and before she could say anything, he grabbed her waist and pulled her from the bridge. "Don't do it, Katherine," he whispered with great anguish in her ear, holding on to her with her back to his chest. "I could not bear it if you were gone from me."

"Thomas?" He heard her call out softly, and with a smile, he hugged her closer.

"Yes, darling?"

"Let—me—go!" she demanded, putting more emphasis on the last word as she broke his hold on her and whirled around to face him. Thomas was shocked by the anger blazing in her golden eyes.

"Katherine, I've come to tell you—"

"I don't care what you've come to tell me, Thomas. You nearly scared me to death." She pointed jerkily to the railing. "I could have fallen off this bridge!"

"But I—" He stopped when he realized what she'd said. With a questioning frown, he shook his head in confusion. "I thought you were about to throw yourself from it. I came to rescue you!"

Katherine stared at him as if he'd completely lost his mind. "Why would I throw myself off the bridge?"

"Because of how I treated you in town."

She gaped at him. "You think I would kill myself over you?"

Thomas had the grace to blush at such a bold assumption. "Well, I—"

"Thomas, you truly must think I am stupid." She shook her head in disgust. "First of all, I would never think of killing myself over anyone, least of all you. And second, if I did, it wouldn't be jumping off a bridge into two feet of water," she said, her eyebrows raised and her hands folded over her chest.

Thomas glanced over the railing and, upon seeing the muddy bottom, looked back to Katherine. "Then forgive me, Katherine. I did not stop and think about anything when I saw you leaning over. Especially when I have something of great importance I must speak to you about."

Katherine eyed him with a wary expression. "What could you have to say that you haven't already said?"

Thomas prayed God would help her understand and forgive. "Lucy told me Theodora admitted to your brother she locked you in the room, then sent the servants from the house so they would not hear you call out," he explained, his voice rushed.

He expected her to be happy he finally believed her. In that moment, he realized his understanding of the female mind was limited.

"I had already told you it was Theodora's fault!" she snapped back.

"But you didn't tell me about the servants," he tried to reason. It seemed perfectly logical to him.

"You should have believed me in the first place, Thomas Thornton. Instead, you stood there and peered down your nose at me and passed judgment. I told you I loved you, and you threw it back in my face. *Then* you humiliated me in front of the whole village."

But he stood there and allowed her to voice her anger, knowing he deserved every accusation.

"You are right. I—"

"Do you know how much I have cried?" She continued, ignoring his attempt to talk. She was pacing back and forth on the small bridge. "And now you think I should fall at your feet in gratitude because you have decided to believe me. And not," she added, "because of anything I have said. Oh, no. But you *do* believe my little sister."

"Katherine, please. Everything you are saying is the truth. But I think I knew all along, in my heart, that you loved me. It was just my pride that held me back."

She whirled around and narrowed her eyes at him. "And where is that famous Thornton pride now? Hmm?"

He held her gaze for a moment, and despite the anger on her face, he could see the hurt and love in her eyes. "My pride is lying at your feet, my beautiful Katherine," he answered her softly. "I know I should have listened and trusted you." He walked closer to her slowly, as one might approach a scared animal.

"But if you'll forgive me, I will vow to you, in the presence of God, that I shall trust you with my whole heart from now until I die. I will protect you and never doubt your love for me, my son, or any of the children we will have."

She still was not giving in, but Thomas could see her indecision. "*If* we have children."

"*When* we have children, Katherine." It was a promise. "I want us to marry and start creating our life together as quickly as possible. We have already missed two weeks, you know."

Tears filled her eyes, and he could tell she was fighting her emotions. "I do not know how I should bear it if you did not truly believe I love you. I had set about to do a horrendous deed to you and your family. How can you forgive me?"

Thomas smiled, taking her hands into his own and pulling her closer to him. "As I have studied the scriptures and realized how Jesus forgives our sins, He expects us to do no less. For me to hang on to my hurt and anger over what you and Theodora had planned would be to rob me of a life of joy with a woman God has put into my life. I believe you when you say you realized you loved me and could not go through with it. But more than that, Katherine," he whispered before he kissed her bare fingers, "I believe that even if you had not loved me, you would not have gone through with it."

Through her tears, Katherine smiled up at him with an expression of relief. "You're right. I felt so convicted from the very beginning. God was trying to talk to me, and finally I broke down and asked for His forgiveness. He truly changed my heart, Thomas. He took away the bitterness I held toward your brother so I could truly love you without any hindrances."

Thomas could hold back no longer. He felt as if a great load had been taken from his shoulders as he leaned down and pressed a jubilant kiss to her waiting lips. "Will you marry me, Katherine?" he asked.

She nodded as new tears streamed down her rosy cheeks. Only this time they were happy ones. "Yes! Oh yes, I will marry you!" She threw her arms around him, and he held her tight for a long moment.

Finally he leaned back and said, "Let's do it right now."

She searched his eyes as if trying to gauge his meaning. "Do what right now?"

"Get married!" he exclaimed and laughed when her eyes widened. "The vicar still has the license, and the banns have already been posted. We can marry right now, just the two of us."

She smiled, then seemed to think of something. "We can't marry without Ty! He must be here with us!"

Thomas's grin could not be any larger. "You are right! Let's go to the vicarage and let the vicar send one of his servants for Mrs. Sanborne and Ty."

Katherine tucked herself back into his embrace, laying her head upon his chest. "I cannot wait to be your wife, Lord Thornton."

He kissed the top of her head. "And I cannot wait to call you Lady Thornton!"

She looked up to smile at him but just as abruptly frowned. "Thomas? What happened to your face? Were you in a fight?"

Thomas shook his head. "I was in such a hurry to find you that I'm afraid I met head-on with a tree limb." His smile was self-deprecating as he explained.

Katherine grinned and gently touched his scratched cheek, which had finally stopped bleeding. "You show no scars or signs of wounds from your time spent in the war or during your shipwreck, but now you'll have a tiny scar on your handsome face, all because you were in a hurry to see me." She smiled brilliantly at him. "I believe I like the sound of that. When I tell Lucy, she will declare it your most romantic gesture to date!"

"I am wounded, and you are pleased about it," he observed, slightly bemused. "Will I never understand the workings of the amazing female mind?"

She smiled smugly at him, hugging him once more. "Of course not, silly. Can any man?"

⤳

Katherine had never felt so loved as she stood beside Thomas, holding the dark pink roses he'd picked for her in the vicar's garden. Beside them stood Mrs. Sanborne, who, at first, had tried to hold Ty but finally allowed him to toddle over to his father, where he clung to his leg, swinging back and forth.

It was a little chaotic, but when Katherine gazed up at Thomas as he slid the diamond-encrusted family ring on her finger, she knew she was destined for a wonderful life.

At last the moment came when the vicar announced they were man and wife. Thomas held her face in his hands and whispered, "Lady Thornton." He kissed her then, and the thrill of it made Katherine a little dizzy with excitement. That quickly turned into embarrassment when the vicar had to clear his throat in a subtle hint they should bring the kiss to a close.

Katherine was the one who stepped away, but her embarrassment changed to humor when she realized Tyler had been standing, watching them quietly the whole time. When Thomas finally looked down at him, he held up his hands as if to say "I'm next!" Thomas obliged by lifting his son into his arms and kissing him soundly on the cheek.

Mrs. Sanborne was the first to speak. "Oh, I don't think I have ever seen such a stupendous ceremony." She dabbed at her eyes. "It was stupendously moving."

Katherine and Thomas shared a grin. "You are right on that score, Mrs. Sanborne. It was stupendous."

"Now, to deal with my parents. You do know they will be, and I will use my mother's words, 'extremely vexed'!" Katherine told him as they walked out of the abbey.

"No more so than Nicholas and Christina. I fear we might have to throw a ball or something as a peace offering."

Katherine gazed up into those Thornton blue eyes that were so filled with love and happiness and thought she couldn't possibly be happier. All the hurt and loneliness she'd been through seemed to melt away, and she was left with a hope for the future that seemed so bright and overflowing with promise. A future that included God and a life built on a solid foundation. She would never forget or cease to be thankful God had not only forgiven her misdeeds but had restored to her the only man she had ever loved and allowed her to be a mother to his sweet son.

Smiles radiated on their faces as they entered the carriage. Soon they were on their way to Ravenhurst Castle to announce their marriage to her parents.

She hoped her mother had her handkerchief ready.

Remember Me

To Josie Delonie Kennedy, my grandmother.
And special thanks to Julie Rice and Melissa Alphonso for coming to my rescue
and helping me with this project.

Chapter 1

1815

Trevor "North" Kent, the Duke of Northingshire, breathed in the fresh sea air as he relaxed against the smooth railing of the ship that was carrying him to America. His blond, wavy hair, which he'd allowed to grow longer during the voyage, was blowing about his face, tickling his nose as he focused on enjoying his last day aboard ship. They would be pulling into port in the morning; and although the voyage had been a long one, it had been one of much-needed peace and relaxation, something North hadn't even realized he required until he was away from England.

For four years, he'd been planning to make the trip, where he was to join his cousins on the sugar plantation that he'd invested in with them. But because of the war with England, travel had been made impossible. Then there had been a personal matter that had caused him to want to reschedule his trip, also, but it had since been settled to his satisfaction.

The delay had also let him go to the aid of his two best friends: Nicholas, the Earl of Kenswick, and his brother, Lord Thomas Thornton.

The two brothers had been through war, the death of their father, Thomas's shipwreck, and, through all that, raising Thomas's motherless son. North had been there for both of them, giving them advice or just being a friend when they needed it. But now both of them were happily married to two wonderful women, and North was glad to leave the men in their capable hands.

All North wanted was to spend time on the plantation and be free from anyone's problems, except maybe his own. His two cousins were married and hopefully didn't need his advice or support with anything dealing with the state of one's mind or happiness.

Now his own happiness was another kettle of fish altogether, and North had high hopes that he, too, would be able to find love and happiness in his future.

But at the moment, his only concern was how he was to travel and find the plantation, which was located some forty-five miles southwest of New Orleans. He'd sent a message to his cousins telling them of his impending arrival, but the captain had told him that because of the war, mail was slow. It had to be routed through ships going to other countries since there was no travel directly from England. His own journey had been made longer when he'd had to travel to France to board one of their ships.

"The captain has just informed me a storm is headed our way." A Scottish-accented voice spoke beside him, stirring North from his thoughts.

North turned to Hamish Campbell, the minister who was traveling to Louisiana to be the new pastor of a church there. They'd become friends during the long voyage, and North wondered at the troubled look in the older man's eyes. "Well, it is too early in the season to be a hurricane, so I would imagine that it'll pass over us quickly. We are very close to the port, so I don't think there is cause for too much worry," North tried to assure him.

Hamish gripped the railing in front of him as though it were a lifeline. "I know you might think me daft for saying this, but I'm not sure I'll make it to Louisiana."

North stifled a sigh as he felt the need to comfort yet another friend. He knew God was the compelling force in his life who urged him to reach out to people, but he sent up a quick prayer that the Almighty would see fit to give him a little break during his stay in Louisiana.

"Hamish, my dear fellow, these ships are built to withstand storms. Are you sure you are not just experiencing a case of nerves about your new post?"

"Not at all," Hamish insisted, as he reached into his plain, brown coat and pulled out a small, worn Bible. He held it against the rail in both hands, his thumbs stroking the leather cover reverently. "It's. . .it's more of a feeling, I suppose. I've been sensing for some time that my time on earth is almost at an end."

Hamish's words put a chill in North's heart as he struggled to understand. "You are not so old that you will soon die," North reasoned. "And, too, why would God send you all the way over here if He did not mean for you to become the pastor of the church at Golden Bay?"

Hamish didn't answer for a moment. The slightly balding man, who was near North's size and height, just stared off into the now choppy sea as if contemplating his next words. Finally he muttered something that North couldn't decipher and turned to him, his eyes serious. "I think it has something to do with you."

North raised a dark blond brow. "I beg your pardon?"

Hamish nodded his head. "Yes, that must be it! I have felt compelled to befriend you ever since I boarded the ship." He held up his Bible in a strange moment of contemplation and then thrust it toward North, hitting him in the chest. "Take it, please!"

North's hand automatically caught the Bible, but he immediately tried to give it back to Hamish. "What do you mean, 'Take it'? Will you not need this to construct your sermons and what have you?"

Hamish ignored North's attempt to return the small book and turned back toward the railing. "I will not be needing it, I fear. I beg you to take it and—"

Hamish's plea was interrupted when one of the ship's crew ran over to them and gave a brief nod to North. "Your Grace! The captain's askin' all to clear the deck." He pointed out to the increasingly rough waters. "We're lookin' at some bad weather ahead. You could be washed overboard."

North agreed with the young sailor, but when he motioned for Hamish to begin walking toward their cabins, his friend shook his head and pointed to one of the chairs a few feet away from them. "I must retrieve my spectacles. I left them lying on the chair," he insisted as he began to head toward the chair and away from shelter.

The wind was picking up, and North could hear large waves hitting against the ship's hull. It seemed as though the noonday sky had gone from sunny to almost dark in just a matter of minutes. North knew he could not leave Hamish alone, so he tucked the Bible inside his coat and began to walk quickly to him, although the swaying of the ship was making the task very difficult. The ship jolted sharply, and Hamish stumbled and then fell. North was able to grab hold of a deck chair and steady himself before moving to where his friend had fallen.

"Are you all right?" he called loudly over the wind.

Hamish nodded as North helped him stand back up. "I didn't realize the weather could change so fast," he commented as they again steadied themselves against the swaying deck.

North focused on getting them to the chair to retrieve the small, wire-framed spectacles. Once they were finally in Hamish's possession, North led him to the railing. "Use the railing to steady yourself and follow me," he yelled as he looked back to make sure the older man was holding on. Together they began the trek back to their cabin.

A large wave slapped hard against the ship, spraying them both with water. North found it hard to hold on with the chilling wetness making both the railing and the deck slippery. Finally they were mere steps away from the door that led to their cabins. North glanced back to see how Hamish was faring, but his attention was caught by the vast wave that was several feet above the ship and heading straight toward them.

He tried to yell for Hamish to hold on, but there was no time. The water hit both men with more force than either could withstand. As the water swept over the ship, North could feel his body being picked up. Panicked, he tried to keep his head above the water while at the same time looking for his friend. But then pain exploded in the back of North's head. Though he tried to fight unconsciousness, the pain was too great.

His last thought was a prayer that Hamish had somehow managed to keep from being washed overboard.

⊗

Two Weeks Later in Golden Bay, Louisiana

The large and rather bored-looking alligator barely glanced in Helen's direction, despite her yelling and waving a broom about like a madwoman to shoo him away from the house. After about five minutes of this, Helen finally gave up. She plopped herself down on the grass, not even giving a care to her dress as she would have months ago, and glared at the huge reptilian beast.

Before coming to America three months earlier, Helen Nichols had not even heard of an alligator, much less thought that she might stand so close to one.

No, Helen, a gentleman farmer's daughter, had been brought up in her native England with no more cares than what pretty ribbon she'd wear for the day. It had sounded like such a grand adventure when Claudia Baumgartner, granddaughter and heir to the Marquis of Moreland, approached her with the offer of paid companion to her little sister, Josie, in America. Claudia had explained her parents wanted an English girl to provide not only companionship to the lonely girl who lived on her parents' plantation, but also to instruct her in the proper ways of a lady.

But adventure was not the only thing that compelled Helen to leave her family and friends behind. It was the same reason she ventured often to her best friend Christina's home when she heard a certain person had arrived. It was the reason she allowed Christina, who was also the Countess of Kenswick, to provide her a whole new wardrobe for the London season, even though she was mostly snubbed by those who were of much higher class. It was the first thing she thought of in the morning and what she dreamed of at night.

Helen Nichols was in love with North, the Duke of Northingshire.

And the duke was traveling to America, just twenty or so miles from where she was living in Golden Bay.

Helen knew it was foolish to believe that she would even see North while he was staying at his plantation. Yet she knew the Baumgartners, her employers, were acquainted with North's relatives and held out a small hope they would at some point socialize with one another.

She didn't even know if North had arrived in Louisiana. So day after day, she'd keep a keen ear out to hear any news about the Kent plantation. So far, though, she'd heard nothing.

"What are you doing?" A young voice sounded behind her. Josie Baumgartner, Helen's precocious thirteen-year-old charge, skipped around and plopped down in front of her. With wildly curly brown hair, freckles, and a mischievous gleam constantly glowing in her hazel eyes, Josie looked just like the wild child that she was. In fact, Helen despaired of ever turning the young girl into anything remotely resembling a proper lady. She liked to ride astride horses, fish while wading in the swamp, and climb trees. Those were the seminormal things she did. The other activities consisted of playing practical jokes, collecting every creepy-crawly thing she could find, and voicing her opinion about every subject her father and mother would bring up at the dinner table, usually expressing an opposing view.

But despite her incorrigible behavior that would likely leave most of English society agog, she was an extremely likable girl with a personality that made it hard to reprimand her or be angry with her for long.

Helen sighed as she answered Josie's question. "I am trying to get this big lizard to move away from the front door so I can go into the house." She pointed at the ugly beast. "But it seems he is determined to ignore my commands."

Josie giggled. "We have five other doors, you know. Why don't you just go through one of those?" she reasoned in her drawn-out American accent.

Helen sniffed. "It's the principle of the thing, my dear. I will not be ruled by a slimy green creature!"

Josie jumped up and crept closer to the alligator, though still at a safe distance. "Did you know they eat small animals? Dorie LeBeau said one ate her cat once."

Helen shivered with disgust. "Well, that's just uncivilized, isn't it?"

Josie turned back to Helen with a look of long-suffering. "You think *everything* is uncivilized if it's not from England."

Helen stood and brushed off the skirt of her gown. "Well, of course I do," she stated matter-of-factly. "We're the most civilized people in the world!" She had a brief recollection of Christina and herself running about the countryside with dirty dresses and faces. They were forever rolling about with puppies and kittens and trespassing on others' property to climb their trees. Not a very civilized way to behave for a couple of young ladies.

Helen wisely kept the memory to herself.

"Well, we can go get Sam to come over here and kill it. They make for pretty good eating, you know," Josie said, interrupting Helen's thoughts. Sam Youngblood was a Choctaw Indian who lived on property adjoining the plantation. He also fancied himself in love with Helen and was forever trying to barter horses or cows with Mr. Baumgartner for her. He said it was the Choctaw way.

Helen told him the practice of bartering for a woman was just plain barbaric!

Helen shivered again as she got back to Josie's comment. "*Ladies* do not eat—"

"I know, I know," Josie interjected. "Ladies do not eat *anything* that *crawls* around on its belly. It's *quite* uncivilized!" she mocked, using Helen's higher-pitched English accent.

"Scoff if you must, but you will do well to—"

"Miss Helen! Miss Josie!" a male voice called out from behind them. They turned to see George, the Baumgartners' house servant who usually ran their errands in town, running up the dusty drive.

Though the Baumgartners owned many slaves to run the vast plantation that consisted of thousands of acres, a sugar mill, the slave and servant quarters, not to mention the huge three-story white mansion, they had freed many of those who worked in the house and the higher-ranking field hands. The Baumgartners were good people who treated every worker and slave fairly, but Helen secretly felt the whole slave system was unjust and inhumane.

"What is it, George?" Josie asked as he stopped before them and tried to catch his breath.

"The preacher. . ." His voice cracked as he took another deep breath. "They found him. He ain't dead like they thought."

Helen and Josie exchanged a disbelieving look. "You mean he did not drown as we were all told?" Helen attempted to comprehend. Just over a week ago, the people of Golden Bay had been informed that the preacher for whom they'd been waiting had fallen overboard with another man and had drowned. The Baumgartners, LeBeau, and Whitakers were all distressed and saddened, since it was these neighboring families who had gotten together to build a church and then pay for his voyage from Scotland.

If this news was true, they wouldn't have to go to the trouble of searching for another minister!

"A couple of fishermen pulled 'im out of the gulf and took 'im back to they cabins 'bout thirty or so miles from here," George explained. "They sez that he didn't wake up fer about fo' days, but they found a Bible on him that had his name on it. They sez he didn't know who he was when he finally woke up, but after they told 'im his name and that he was a preacher headed for our town, he seemed to remember."

Josie clasped her hands together. "Why, that sounds like a bona fide miracle!" she exclaimed. "Is he in town? Can we go see him?"

"Yes'm, Miss Josie, you sho' can. That's why I ran back lickety-split." He ran the back of his sleeve across his beaded brow. "They's wantin' the mastah to come out and give 'im a proper welcome with any food or house gifts to help 'im get settled."

"Oh, this is exciting, isn't it?" Helen whispered eagerly as she looked from George to Josie. "It will be so refreshing going to a proper service again instead of waiting for the circuit preacher to pass by. It will be just like it was in—"

"England! We know; we know," Josie finished for her with exasperation. "Let's just hurry up and tell my parents so we can meet him!"

It didn't take long for the family to assemble the goods they had set aside for the new preacher and to load their wagon and carriage. Ten or so minutes later, they pulled into the small town that consisted of the blacksmith, a general store, and the newly built church. The town was actually owned by three plantations, unlike many others along the river that were self-contained. The three families signed an agreement that they would share the profits from the businesses, as well as the labor to keep them running.

There was already a small crowd in the tiny yard of the church, with its small parsonage on the side. Mr. and Mrs. Baumgartner stepped out of the carriage first, followed by Josie and Helen.

As they drew nearer, Josie walked on her tiptoes, trying to see over everyone's heads. Helen, herself, tried to see around them but could only see the top of a man's head. In fact, the hair was such a pretty golden blond, a person couldn't help but notice through all the dark heads gathered around him.

Helen was finally close enough to see better, and as the crowd parted, she was disappointed to see the man's back was turned as he spoke with Mr. Baumgartner. She studied his longish, wavy hair, then the width of his broad shoulders for a moment. He seemed almost familiar to Helen, as if she had met the gentleman before, yet she was sure she had never heard of a Hamish Campbell until she had arrived in Louisiana.

"Oh, I wish Papa would turn him around so we could see him! I had imagined he would be an older man, but he appears to be younger than I thought," Josie whispered as their neighbors chatted excitedly around them.

"Indeed," Helen murmured, as she tried to inch her way closer to him. She noticed he was quite tall. Though they seemed to be a little ragged and faded, his clothes were very well made, cut like those worn by the nobility.

When she finally was able to hear him speak, Helen suddenly realized who the preacher reminded her of.

He was the same height and build and sounded just like. . .North, the Duke of Northingshire.

Helen briefly rubbed her brow, thinking that of course she must be mistaken and perhaps had been in the sun too long. The preacher was supposed to be a Scotsman, and the accent she thought she heard was clearly a cultured English one.

"Ah! Here are my wife and daughter," Mr. Baumgartner said, motioning toward Helen's direction. "Let me introduce you."

As she began to turn, Josie bumped her as she scrambled to go to her father, and then Mrs. Baumgartner stepped in front of her, again blocking her view. She heard the man speak to her employer and his daughter and again was struck by his rich voice.

I just miss North. I am clearly hallucina—

"And this is Josie's companion, Miss Helen Nichols, who has come from England and been with us for three months now," she heard Mrs. Baumgartner say, as she stepped back. For the first time, Helen got a view of the tall man's face.

For a moment Helen said nothing, frozen by the sheer shock of seeing the man before her.

It *was* North!

And he was smiling pleasantly at her without so much as a gleam of recognition shining in his light blue gaze.

"Pleased to make your acquaintance, Miss Nichols," he responded smoothly with a nod.

Helen was horrified that he did not recognize her. She had spent many hours in his presence in the past and thought it humiliating that she didn't seem familiar to him at all. But then she had a second thought: *Why is he pretending to be a preacher?*

Confused, she found herself blurting, "North? Do you not remember me?"

Chapter 2

An immediate hush fell over the group as every eye turned to stare at Helen, including North. Helen focused only on him as she watched the strange expressions move across his handsome, strong face.

At first it appeared to be fear, then it went to what looked like confusion, and then it was as though a mask fell across his face, shielding her from his thoughts entirely. He seemed to compose himself as he nervously glanced around the group and then turned his gaze back to Helen.

His eyes were unreadable as he smiled at her and finally responded. "Of course I do. It's just. . .I suppose it has been quite awhile, hasn't it?" Helen wasn't sure if he was telling or asking. Neither would make a bit of sense to Helen since she'd only seen him four months ago. "It is good to have a friend nearby," he finished cryptically, perplexing her even more.

She was about to ask him what he was doing here, but he turned from her suddenly, stopping any further communication between them.

Doubts assailed her as she thought maybe the man wasn't North after all. Perhaps he had a cousin who looked like him.

But then, she amended her thoughts, why did he pretend to know her?

Oh, it was very vexing on her nerves to reason his behavior all out in her mind.

"You know him?" Josie exclaimed, startling Helen back to the present. "Why didn't you tell us you knew the preacher?"

Helen shook her head absently as her eyes stayed on who she was sure was the Duke of Northingshire. "I didn't know his Christian name. I've always called him North," she lied, since she knew very well that his name was Trevor Kent and certainly *not* Hamish Campbell!

Josie frowned. "You addressed a preacher by calling him North? That's strange and not at all the civilized thing for a lady to do." She paused for effect. "According to you."

Helen licked her lips nervously as she tried to answer without too much lying involved. "I knew him when he wasn't a minister." She finally dragged her eyes away from the confusing man and tried to appear nonchalant. "I don't suppose I knew him as well as I thought." That was an understatement!

"Well, you shall have plenty of time to get to know him in the future," Josie reasoned, as she took Helen's hand and pulled her toward the nice lawn beside the church. "Let's sit over there and wait for my parents."

Helen agreed and allowed Josie to pull her to the white wooden benches, which were placed under a great oak shade tree.

As soon as they sat down, Josie immediately brought their conversation back to the preacher. "Don't you think he is the most handsome man you've ever seen? And to think you know him!" she expressed in a lovelorn tone. She sat up and looked at Helen as if she were suddenly hit with an idea. "He is unmarried, and you are unmarried! You would make a great match!"

If only it could be so, Helen thought longingly. But until she figured out why North was pretending to be someone else, she could not even wish for it. "Josie, he did not even recognize me. How could you think he would want to marry a lady who has made no lasting impression in his mind?" She sighed. "Besides, I am here to work and teach you to be a lady. Wishing that I would fall in love with North just so you will not have to learn your lessons on etiquette will only bring you a headache."

Josie sat back on the bench and groaned. "Why does being a lady seem so *boring?*"

Helen hid a grin. "One day when you become interested in a young man, he'll expect you to act like a lady, and then you will thank God I bored you so!"

"I will never be interested in boys!" she declared.

"That is too bad, for I have a feeling you will grow up to be quite a lovely woman one day." A man's voice spoke beside them.

Startled, Helen turned and looked up to find North standing over her. "North!" she exclaimed automatically but then quickly amended, "I'm sorry. I mean *Reverend.*"

He seemed preoccupied as he presented her a small smile. North quickly stepped closer, whispering in an urgent voice, "I must speak to you alone, Miss Nichols." He nervously glanced around as if to see if anyone was watching him and then looked briefly at Josie. "There is some very important information I need, and I'm positive that only you can help me."

Helen felt butterflies of excitement fluttering about in her chest, just as she always did when North spoke to her. It didn't matter if he was acting like the craziest man alive or that he was pretending to be a minister, which Helen imagined was a big faux pas in God's book! All that mattered was North, the love of her life, had asked to talk to her. Alone!

She jumped up with more enthusiasm than was warranted, for she startled both Josie and North. "Of course, you can speak with me!" she said brightly as she reached down to pull Josie up from the bench. "Please be a dear and excuse us, will you, Josie?" She threw the request to her charge without so much as a glance and then latched her arm around North's elbow. "Let's walk, shall we?"

North looked a little dazed but gave her a tentative smile. "Not too far.

I would not want to bring suspicion on your character or mine. I may not remember much, but I do know that talking alone with a young woman out in the open public is considered a social blunder if she is not accompanied by a chaperone."

Helen stopped suddenly upon hearing his words, let go of his arm, and turned to stand in front of him. "Did you just say that you might not remember much?" She shook her head. "What does that mean?"

North stood there, staring down at her, looking more handsome than ever before. His countenance, however, was not the easygoing and self-assured gentleman she'd known in England. Instead he looked tired, confused, and not at all the confident man he should be.

He took a deep breath as he stared off to his left for a moment, then slowly brought his gaze back to her. "I do not remember who I am." Helen gasped, but North held out his hand so that he might continue. "I apparently fell off the ship that I had been on during a storm. Two fishermen dragged me out of the water and brought me to shore, where I finally came to my senses. But that is where every one of my memories begins. I wouldn't even know my name except I had a Bible inside my coat that had the name Hamish Campbell etched into the leather."

Helen could not even speak for being so dumbfounded by his story. She had never heard of a person forgetting his own name and past. "So you don't remember anything? Not your family, friends, or any sort of past memory?"

He shook his head as he walked past her to lean against the oak.

"And no one knows you've lost your memory?" she asked as she walked over to him.

"No, I didn't want to make everyone think I'd lost my mind or had become crazed." He took a minute to rub the back of his head, then continued. "To tell you the truth, when the fisherman who I was staying with finally told me he'd found out where I was heading and that I was to be the vicar of a church in Louisiana, I felt even more confused. I pretended, however, that I suddenly remembered." He looked back to Helen. "That is why I am so anxious to talk to you. You know who I am. You and you alone can tell me about myself, what kind of family background I have or anything that might possibly help me to remember. . . *something*!" His eyes bore into hers as if he were trying to read her thoughts. "You can also confirm I am indeed who they say I am or if it is some sort of mistake." He paused and seemed to try calming himself with a deep breath. "Helen, am I the Reverend Hamish Campbell?"

Helen opened her mouth to inform him that he definitely was *not* the good reverend but stopped before any words could escape. A thought suddenly seized her—a truly wicked thought.

If North knew he was a duke—a nobleman—sixth in line to the throne of

England, then Helen could never hope to win his affections, for he would be socially far above her station.

But as a reverend. . .

Oh, surely she could not consider it, much less go through with such a deed! But she could not help it. If North believed he was a reverend, then he would be in the same class as she. The barrier of position and means would no longer be an obstacle, and the brotherly affection North always showed toward her could change into something more if he believed he was Hamish Campbell.

"Miss Nichols? Were you indeed telling the truth when you said you knew me? You suddenly seem confused about. . ."

"You are!" she blurted out before she could think twice about it. "I. . .I mean. . .you are. . .the reverend. . .Hamish Campbell," she stammered, as she began to already feel the weight of the lie she had just told.

He let out a breath as he ran a hand through his shimmering blond curls. "I was hoping. . ." He paused and began again. "I don't know what I was hoping. It's just that I do not feel like a Hamish Campbell. I cannot imagine choosing to be a vicar, either. I do have a sense I am a follower of God and have attended church in my past, but. . .being a vicar does not seem to. . .*fit*!" He threw his hand in the air with frustration.

If he only knew! Helen thought guiltily. "What sort of man did you imagine yourself to be?"

North seemed to think a minute before he answered. "I really don't know, except I look at my clothes and, though they are faded and worn from being wet and then dried in the sun, I somehow know they are very finely made and that the fabrics are not something a poor man would wear." He held up his long, lean hands. "I look at my palms and see no evidence of calluses from hard work."

"Perhaps you spent your time in studying and contemplation," Helen inserted.

"I suppose you could be right, but it doesn't explain the clothes."

All the lies were making Helen very nervous, and she wasn't finished telling them yet. "Perhaps your family is somewhat wealthy, but as you were the youngest son, you chose the church as your occupation," she improvised.

He raised a dark blond brow. "Perhaps? You mean you don't know?"

"Uh. . ." Helen scrambled to answer him without telling another lie. "We were introduced through a mutual acquaintance and saw each other only a few times after that," she answered truthfully.

His expression fell to a frown. "Then you don't know me well enough to tell me anything significant?"

Helen breathed a sigh of relief, hoping that this revelation would stop his questions. "I am sorry, but no." She looked toward the crowd and noticed the Baumgartners were looking her way. "I'd better go. My employers are about to leave."

She started to walk off, but he stopped her by touching her arm. "Wait! May I ask you one more question?"

Seeing the confusion in his beautiful blue eyes, Helen could not turn down his request. "Of course you may."

"Everyone keeps telling me I have journeyed here from Scotland, yet I clearly do not have a Scottish accent. Do you know anything about this?"

This question she could answer truthfully. "Actually, I do. You were raised in England, but later when your family bought an estate in Scotland, you would spend summers there. I suppose you've moved back there recently." She felt compelled to put her hand over his. "Good-bye, Nor. . .er. . .I mean, Reverend. I'm sorry I was not more helpful."

He gave her a small, preoccupied smile, nodded, then stepped away from her.

Helen took one last look back before she ran to where her employers were waiting for her. As she suspected, they were full of questions.

"You must tell us how you know our new preacher, Helen!" Mrs. Baumgartner ordered immediately as they settled in the carriage. Imogene Baumgartner looked much younger than her forty years. Though she didn't have the style the ladies in England had in the way of clothes or hairstyles, she was always very prettily dressed in her flowered cotton and linen gowns that she so preferred, her dark brown hair knotted low on her neck.

Robert Baumgartner, on the other hand, sat quietly, as he usually did whenever his wife was going on about something, preferring the solitude of his thoughts as he looked out of the carriage window. Helen often wondered if he regretted his choice of marrying the daughter of his father's butler. After all, it caused him to be disinherited by his father and, in turn, to renounce his claim to the title of Marquis of Moreland. Josie had told Helen they'd taken his small inheritance from his mother and moved to America soon after.

It seemed like such a grand love story, and since Helen was also in love with a man above her station, it gave her a small hope her own life could have a happy ending with North by her side.

"Helen, dear?" Mrs. Baumgartner prompted, shaking Helen from her thoughts.

After remembering her employer had asked how she knew North, Helen answered, "I knew him briefly through a friend." She wished Mrs. Baumgartner would take the hint that she did not want to talk about it, but the woman was very persistent when she wanted to know something.

Imogene stared at her as if waiting for more, but when Helen remained silent, she tried again. "He certainly was wearing a very fine suit of clothes to be a poor vicar. I almost had the feeling when studying his bearing and regal pose that he might be a nobleman!" She leaned closer to Helen from across the carriage. "Do you know if he is indeed from a noble family?"

Helen could feel sweat beading on her forehead, and it wasn't just because of the humidity. "I know he is from a wealthy family."

That answer seemed to be enough for Imogene. She leaned back and folded her arms as if pleased with herself. "Of course he is. I am quite good at spotting a gentleman of means." She paused and frowned. "Although he must be quite a younger son and not entitled to the wealth if he has chosen to be a clergyman."

"Must he?" Helen answered, trying desperately not to lie.

"Well, of course he must!" Imogene declared. "But his misfortune is our good luck. I had not looked forward to trying to find another vicar to take his place."

The questions seemed to be at an end as they rode the rest of the way in silence. But Helen's reprieve was only a brief one.

"Helen, it just occurred to me he might be a good match for you!" Imogene exclaimed as they exited the carriage.

Josie piped up. "I had told her the same thing!"

Imogene clasped her hands together as if thrilled with her idea. "You are a gentleman's daughter, Helen, and he is a gentleman! If you married him, you could stay right here in Golden Bay with us. Wouldn't that be just the thing?"

Just thinking about living in the rugged, swampy lands of Louisiana forever made Helen shiver with horror. But on the other hand, if she could spend her life with North by her side. . .perhaps it might not be so bad.

"I barely know him. . . ," she prevaricated, but Imogene was not one to let anything distract her.

"We have all the time in the world for that!" she declared as the carriage slowed to a stop in front of the home. "Leave it to me, dear, and you shall see yourself wed by fall!"

As Helen climbed out of the carriage behind Imogene and Josie, she wished her employer's words could be true, but if North remembered who he was before he could fall in love with her, her hopes of even being his friend would be permanently dashed.

Chapter 3

The more North learned of his life, the more confused he became. Many days and long hours since he was rescued, he tried to find just the tiniest of memories, just the smallest tidbit to help him feel less lost, less bewildered.

The only information he'd heard that felt as though it belonged to him was when Helen Nichols had called him North. The more he said it to himself, the more the name seemed to fit him, as though he'd finally had one little piece of his missing life back.

But saying it did not bring back any more memories or any other sense of familiarity like he hoped and prayed it would. There was nothing in his mind other than a few memories since he'd awakened. The rest was this large, gaping black hole that refused to give up any answers.

Now as he sat in the tiny house the church leaders had shown him to, with its two rooms divided only by a large piece of cloth, he felt more out of his element than ever.

Since he had nothing but his deep-down gut feeling to rely on, North assumed he had never lived in such a small, barren house, nor had he ever known anyone who had. Before they had left him, he'd been shown the barn behind the house, where a cow and a few chickens were kept. He trusted the feeling of dismay that washed over him when they told him the animals would give him all the milk, eggs, and poultry he could eat.

They actually expected him to *milk* the cow and somehow get eggs out from *under* the chickens. Then, if he actually wanted to *eat* chicken, he would have to *kill* one to have it?

Appalling!

He almost told them so, but when they said that North should be familiar with the animals since he had been raised on a farm, North bit back any retort he had been about to make.

Helen Nichols had left out that little piece of news. If his family had been wealthy, why would he be milking his own cows?

Confusion crowded his mind as he thought about it. Perhaps they'd lost their money, he tried to reason, which is why he never tried to pursue a deeper acquaintance with Helen Nichols.

Oh, yes, those thoughts had run through his mind when she'd informed him they barely knew one another. The very first thing that popped into his head was he must have been a blind fool to let such a beautiful, delightful woman slip in and out of his life so easily.

And she *was* beautiful, with her inky black curls that fell about her rosy cheeks and those dark blue eyes that seemed to look right though him, straight to his heart.

When he realized he was contemplating pursuing a woman instead of focusing on his immediate problem, he jumped up from his hard, wooden seat and stomped out of the cottage.

As he breathed in the cooling air that the darkening sky had blown in from the gulf, North strove to find some sort of peace, anything to take away the uncertainty plaguing his heart and mind. Spying the church that was in front of his cottage, he began to walk toward it. The church leaders had told him the building had been used seldom, only when a traveling preacher was in the area.

North thought it looked as lonely as he was, standing there empty with its freshly painted walls and its dark, gleaming windowpanes. Again North tried to look inside himself, to find some sort of connection with the church, to feel the calling he must have had—but he came up empty.

God must surely have some reason for taking away his memory, North tried to rationalize. Perhaps in his forgotten past he needed to learn a valuable lesson, or perhaps someone's life would benefit from his dilemma. Of course, he couldn't think of one thing that would benefit anyone, but he was only a man; God was all-knowing, so there must be a reason.

Briefly North reached out and braced both hands on the smoothed planks of the church. "Help me, dear Lord, to remember. If I have been called by You to serve as Your minister, then I want to know that certainty once again. I am frightened by what lies ahead of me, Lord, and I have an idea that I don't feel this way normally. But most of all, dear God, please do not let me fail these people." He stopped as he once again felt the enormity of his situation bearing down on him. "In Jesus' name. Amen." He finished quickly and backed away from the church.

He was about to walk back to his cottage when the sound of horse hooves broke the calm silence of the night.

North immediately recognized the two-wheeled, small curricle as being one of excellent quality, though he wished he understood *how* he knew this! Instead of focusing on the frustration that was boiling up within him, he watched as a tall, slim, brown man climbed down from the conveyance and walked toward him. The man was dressed in a black suit with a fluffy white cravat tied at his neck. North noticed there was an air of self-confidence about him in his walk and posture, and he wondered, not for the first time, about the class system within the slave and nonslave community.

"Reverend Campbell," the man's deep voice sounded as he gave him a brief bow. North returned the gesture, and the man continued. "I've been sent by Mr. and Mrs. Baumgartner, sir, of the Golden Bay plantation. They would like to extend to you an invitation to dine with them this evening."

Food! It was the only thing that stood out in North's nutrition-starved mind. He was invited to eat food he wouldn't have to cook, milk, or kill.

⨋

"Oh, this dress is wrong!" Helen wailed as she stood in front of her mirror, critically surveying the light blue taffeta. "The ribbon is wrinkled, and the material just droops in this heat!" She dramatically grabbed two handfuls of hair on either side of her head. "And just look at my hair! It will do nothing but curl! I look like a ragamuffin."

Millie, the young slave woman who served both Helen and Josie, propped her hands on her slim hips and made a *tsk*-ing noise as she shook her head. "Miss Helen, I don't know what's wrong with yo' eyes, honey chil', but there ain't nothin' wrong with that dress or yo' hair." Millie took Helen's arm, pulled her away from the mirror, and directed her to sit at her dressing table. "Now yo' jus' got yo'self all in a lather 'cause o' that young man who's comin' to dinnah, tha's all! Now sit still and let me fix yo' hair up real pretty."

Josie took that particular moment to let herself in the room without so much as a knock. "I knew it! I knew she was sweet on the preacher!" she crowed with delight.

Millie stopped brushing Helen's hair to shake the brush in Josie's direction. "Miss Josie, I done tol' ya and tol' ya. You gonna listen at the wrong do' one day, and it's gonna get yo' in a mess o' trouble!" She pointed the brush to the chair next to Helen. "Now sit yo'self down, and I'll get to yo' hair next."

Josie did as she was told because Millie, slave or no, just had the kind of voice you obeyed. It was then Helen noticed the dress the younger girl was wearing.

"Josie, you can't wear that old dress to dinner!" she blurted with horror.

Josie frowned as she looked down at the plain beige dress made of slightly wrinkled cotton. "What's wrong with it? I've worn this to dinner lots of times, and you've never said anything about it."

Helen took a deep breath to calm her nerves, and then in her best teacher's voice, she instructed, "When guests are dining with your family, you must dress in a more formal manner." She noticed Millie looking for a hairpin and opened her drawer to find one for her. She then continued. "Especially when you have a guest like the d—" She stumbled over the word *duke* and quickly corrected herself. "Er, North."

Josie let out a breath to show her frustration with the whole conversation. "He's just the preacher. It's not like he's the president of the United States."

No. More like the Duke of Northingshire. If Helen's nerves were this frazzled with trying to keep her story straight and not saying the wrong thing, how was it going to be in front of North?

What a mess she'd gotten herself into!

In the end, Josie kept her plain dress on, and with her hair done up "pretty" by Millie, Helen decided, droopy or not, her dress would have to do, also. She noticed as she approached the three adults that the Baumgartners wore their usual casual attire; and when she saw North, she was glad they did.

Of course he would have no other clothes! How silly of her not to remember that all his belongings had not been brought from the ship. And even when they were, would he realize the garments belonged to someone else? Would she remember that his own trunks contained the finest clothes England had to offer and not those of a poor vicar?

She had to remind herself not to get into a mental tizzy as she walked up and greeted him.

"Hello, Reverend," she greeted, as she tried to ignore the guilt she felt over calling him that false title. "Are you getting settled in?"

The smile he gave her was lacking in confidence, and his words were those of someone putting on a brave front. . .and failing at it. "Uh, yes, I think so. I'll just need time to adjust to the. . .uh. . .culture change."

The Baumgartners all laughed at that, and though Helen joined them, it was only out of politeness. Since she, too, was still experiencing quite a culture shock, it was difficult to joke about it just yet.

They were all seated in the dining room, which boasted a long table that could easily seat sixteen people. Helen was not accustomed to such extravagance, since her own family manor was of modest means. Neither was she accustomed to all the house servants who worked around the clock to make sure the family had all they needed.

No, she wasn't accustomed to such a lifestyle, but she knew North was. This was apparent only to her as she watched him walk into the room without so much as blinking at the expensively carved furnishings or the heavy blue brocade-and-satin drapes framing the ten large windows in the room. The only thing that caused him to pause was when he noticed the large cloth-covered fan above the table that was framed in the same carvings as the table and chairs. Attached to the fan was a blue satin cord that ran along the high ceiling all the way to the corner, where a small child was pulling it, causing the fan to swoosh back and forth, creating a breeze.

"Remarkable" was the only comment North made as he seated himself by Mrs. Baumgartner and across from Helen. There was a smattering of small talk as they were served their first course, and Helen noticed North was clever enough to keep the conversation off himself by inquiring about the plantation and Mr. Baumgartner's plans for it. Under normal circumstances, it might have been enough; however, North had never dealt with Imogene Baumgartner.

"Oh, enough about business! You must tell us about yourself, Reverend. I quite expected you to have a Scottish dialect and am curious as to why you do not," she voiced, interrupting the gentlemen's conversation.

Helen could actually see the nervous sweat start to bead on North's brow as he paused before answering. "I was raised in England but spent summers with my family in Scotland. I later moved there, but my accent was already established," he answered, parroting the explanation she'd given him earlier.

"And what town were you from in England?" she persisted.

North glanced briefly her way, and Helen could see the rising panic in his eyes. He had no idea where he was from, and Helen scrambled for a way to answer for him. Her only problem was that by saying the name of Northingshire, it might make him remember suddenly who he was. So she thought of the town next to it.

"Lanchester, isn't it? In County Durham? I believe you mentioned that town when we last saw one another," she blurted out, and from the odd looks by the Baumgartners, she knew her answering for him in such a forceful manner seemed quite odd.

But North adeptly smoothed the awkward moment, as would anyone used to handling all manner of social affairs. "Yes, I used to call Lanchester home. Excellent memory, Miss Nichols," he answered easily. Helen was amazed that, though he couldn't remember his own name, he still acted like the nobleman he actually was.

Helen prayed his answers would satisfy Mrs. Baumgartner, but to no avail. "And your parents, are they still living?" Imogene asked.

Once again, his panicked gaze flew to Helen, and once again, she intervened. "Oh, I meant to tell you how sorry I am that I was not able to attend your father's funeral." Helen looked at Mrs. Baumgartner, who she noticed was looking a little put out by her interruptions, and added, "It was influenza. His mother, however, still lives in Scotland."

North seemed to be digesting what she'd just said, and Helen had to add one more lie she would have to beg forgiveness for later. In truth, she didn't know how his father had died. She only knew he'd become duke at the age of ten.

North's panic was now curiosity as he looked in her direction, and she could tell he was trying to remember what she'd told him.

"Really, Helen!" Mrs. Baumgartner scolded, causing both of them to look to her. "I really think that the Reverend Campbell can answer my questions himself."

"I'm sorry, ma'am," Helen apologized as she forced herself to look contrite. In truth, she was just plain stressed by the position she'd put both North and herself in. But it was too late to fix it now! What was she to do? Quickly she scrambled to find a reasonable, believable explanation for her behavior. "I suppose I am just excited about seeing a familiar face from England."

Helen couldn't have come up with a more perfect excuse. Immediately Imogene's expression changed; she thought she knew a secret as she slid her gaze from North to Helen and back again. "Of course you are, dear!" she crooned as she put a hand to her chest and sighed. "I forgot you haven't had a chance to reacquaint yourselves."

"So do you holler when you preach?" Josie piped up in her usual straightforward fashion.

"Well, my word, Josie! What a thing to ask!" her mother reprimanded her.

The thirteen-year-old shrugged. "Well, the preacher at Joseph's church down the bayou hollers. Joseph says it is because the preacher wants to make sure the devil knows they won't fall for his tricks."

Helen quickly covered her mouth with her napkin to conceal her laughter, and when she looked across the table, she noticed North was having a hard time containing his own.

"Maybe it is because sometimes the preacher believes his *congregation* is hard of hearing when he sees them doing something that isn't right," North suggested when he had his laughter under control.

Josie nodded sagely, unaware she was entertaining them all. "You could be right, Reverend. So *do* you holler, too?"

North appeared to think about it and then answered, "I don't believe I have ever hollered in church."

Helen had to cover her mouth again when she pictured North "hollering" at all. He was much too dignified. Again, North slid his gaze Helen's way and shared a smile with her.

Their look apparently did not go unnoticed, although it may have been misread. Surprising them all, the usually silent Mr. Baumgartner spoke up. "Why don't you walk him out to the bayou, Helen, and show him our newly built pier? It is a full moon tonight, so there should be plenty of light. It will give you two a chance to get reacquainted." He took a drink of water and then continued. "I'll have Joseph follow you at a distance to act as a chaperone."

Helen stared at her usually quiet employer, and she was further surprised when he gave her a brief wink that only she could see. "All right," she murmured, looking back at North. "Would you like to see the bayou?"

A look of pure relief relaxed North's strong, manly face, and a smile curved his lips. "Only if you tell me what a bayou is."

They all laughed at his comment, and Helen stood up from her chair. "It will be better if I show you."

❧

In a matter of moments, Helen and North were walking the path that led out to the pier.

"I want to apologize for putting you in the position of having to answer for me," North told her as he looked over at her, admiring how the moon illuminated her soft features. "But I thought you said you didn't know much about me." He hoped she knew more than she let on, not only for the sake of getting his memory back, but because it might mean that she'd been interested enough in him to find out.

She didn't answer right away, and when she did, there was regret on her face as she gave him a quick glance. "I'm afraid I told a small lie in there just now." She blew out a breath and stepped in front of him to stop him from walking. "I lied about your father."

He had trouble focusing on what she was saying, so drawn was he by her beauty and the soft tones of her voice. But when he did realize what she'd said, he frowned in confusion. "What are you saying? That he is alive?"

She seemed horrified by his question as she put her hands on either side of her face. "Oh no! I didn't mean that. . . . I mean. . .he is deceased." She shook her head. "Oh, dear! I meant he didn't die of the flu like I said. I hope I did not give you false hope."

North reached out and took her hands from her face, squeezed them, and let them go. "You didn't injure me, Miss Nichols. When you said my father had died, I instinctively knew you were right. I can't explain how I know this, but it was the same when you called me 'North.' " He thought for a moment. "Do you know my mother?"

Helen looked regretful when she shook her head. "I'm sorry, but no. I never met her, nor do I know anything about her."

He sighed. "It seems a shame not to remember one's own mother." He smiled at her wistfully. "It seems a shame not to remember you, either."

Helen looked up at him for a moment, making North wish even more for his memories back, if only the ones he had of this lovely, enchanting woman who was gazing into his eyes. Then she seemed to grow uncomfortable with the intimacy of their situation. The moment was over when she turned to resume their walk to the pier.

When they arrived at the pier, she announced to him that the stream of water that looked like a small river was the bayou they had spoken of. From there, she explained, smaller ships and barges could move their sugarcane out to the gulf.

They discussed the merits of such a waterway awhile longer but soon fell silent. Helen and North stood there a moment, letting cool air off the bayou's water flow over them as they breathed in the sweet smell of the magnolia blossoms on the nearby trees.

"Did you know my house has only two rooms?" he commented, finally breaking the silence with an odd subject.

She looked up at him and laughed. "I beg your pardon?"

He held up two fingers to her but kept his gaze looking over the water. "Only two. A bedroom and a living room that has a large fireplace from which I am supposed to cook my meals."

From the corner of his eye, he saw her cover her mouth to hide her smile. "Oh, dear. I didn't realize it was so small," she said in a muffled voice from behind her fingers.

"Can you tell me, Miss Nichols: Have I ever lived in such a small house before?"

"Uh. . .no," she answered with certainty. This time a giggle escaped.

"No, no. Go ahead and laugh. I expect I shall get used to it. At least that is my goal."

She laughed, and he joined in with her. It went a long way in releasing the stress he'd felt ever since arriving at Golden Bay.

"I must have been prepared for such a life of imposed poverty. Why else would I have journeyed to such a primitive part of the United States to be their pastor?" he said after their laughter had subsided.

He watched as apprehension seemed to cloud her eyes for a moment. She looked away quickly but then looked back up at him. "North. . .I mean. . . Reverend. . ."

"Please call me North," he insisted, since it was the only thing that made his life seem real.

"North," she said his name softly. "There is something I need to tell you—"

"Can you tell me something?" he interrupted, barely hearing her words. He knew he had to ask his next question, because it had burned constantly in his heart since the moment he laid eyes on her. "Did I ever call on you or ever do anything to make you think I wanted to see you more?"

"No, but you really must hear what I—"

"You see, that is what I cannot figure out." He continued, as if she hadn't spoken. "Why didn't I call on you? Did you have a beau, or for that matter, *do* you have one?"

She stood there frozen, as if shocked by what he was asking. "I've never had a beau."

Elation swept over North as she spoke those precious words. It suddenly didn't matter why he had not pursued her in the past. There was nothing stopping him now.

"Excellent!" he exclaimed with a wide grin. He held out his arm to her. "Shall we go back to the house?"

She did as he asked, but he could tell she didn't understand his response or his delight. That didn't matter.

It wouldn't be long until she realized he was determined to be her first and *only* beau.

Chapter 4

When North awoke the next morning, he was disappointed to find his memory had not improved. He didn't even feel as though he was close to remembering anything. He tried to recall if he'd dreamed of anything, and yet he knew his dreams had only consisted of one thing. . . Helen.

In his dreams, she was smiling and gazing into his eyes; North was fairly sure it wasn't a dream of his past with her, but a dream of what he wished would happen.

Slowly North pulled himself from his bed and once again found himself shocked by the bareness of his surroundings. *Would Helen want to live in such conditions?* He obviously was not a man of great means, nor would ever be if he continued on his current course as a minister, so would such a life be acceptable to her?

He had not even thought about that, possibly because this life seemed so unreal to him, as if he were walking in someone else's shoes. It would seem more reasonable for him to believe he was a wealthy man instead of someone who was used to doing without.

He realized he never fully discussed his background with Helen. Perhaps she could fill in the missing information and provide insight on his exact status in life. If he had money, where was it and how was he to get it? He thought about writing his mother about it, but then he would have to explain about his lapse in memory.

There seemed to be no solutions in sight.

The strange, foreign feelings he'd been experiencing all morning only increased when he pulled on the plain cotton shirt and britches he'd been given by one of the church members. They were slightly tight around his broad shoulders and a tad long in the leg, but it was the quality that made it seem so odd. If he lived and helped out on a farm, wouldn't he be used to dressing like this?

How he wished he could find just one answer.

He walked around the cloth that divided his room from the living area. There was a basket of food items set on the table, and the only thing he could manage to eat, since it required no cooking skills, was the plums. The rest of the bag contained rice, potatoes, dried beans, and a few jars of figs, which North instinctively knew he did not like.

253

Since his stomach was growling, he knew that he was left with only one choice: He would have to go out and gather some eggs and get milk from the cow. Then, of course, he'd have to figure out how to actually cook the eggs.

Taking a deep breath for fortitude, North stepped out of the house, walked across his front porch, down the steps, then behind the house to the small barn.

The first thing that greeted him was the cow. She had such a baleful look on her face, as though she were afraid he was about to have her butchered. North decided right then and there the cow would be called Queen Mary, after Mary, Queen of Scots, because he had an idea that is what the martyred queen's face must have looked like when she was being led to her execution!

"Look here," he spoke to the wary cow. "I don't have the slightest idea what I'm about, so if you'll be patient with me and let me take some of your milk, I'll let you have all the grass you can eat. Do we have a deal?"

Queen Mary continued to stare at him without so much as a blink. "Come on, give over, old girl," he urged as he patted the coarse hair on her back. This time the cow just turned her massive head away from him and let out a long breath. "Hmm, not very trusting, I see."

"Are you expecting her to just hand over her milk in a bucket?" a young voice asked from the doorway. Embarrassed, North jerked around to find Josie and Helen standing there smiling at him.

"How long have you two been standing there?" he asked carefully.

"Long enough to see you know nothing about farm animals," Josie answered, only to receive a nudge from Helen.

"Josie, don't be indelicate," Helen scolded.

North held out his hand. "No, don't correct her, for she is right. I fear that I will starve for my lack of animal husbandry knowledge."

Helen and Josie giggled at his pitiful expression. "You won't this morning!" Helen told him, holding up a cloth-covered basket that smelled delightful. "We have brought fresh muffins and milk, so your. . .uh. . .Queen Mary, is it? Your Queen Mary will not have to be bothered this morning."

Hunger overcame any embarrassment North might have been feeling. He quickly led them to the benches under his oak tree. It wasn't until he had finished off two of the muffins that he was able to talk.

"These are quite delicious!" he complimented with a satisfied sigh as he reached over to take another.

"I knew you would like them. Christina told me you once ate a whole plate of them," Helen told him, as she brushed the crumbs from her light pink skirt. Today she was clad in a short-sleeved cotton day dress, and her hair was tied back with a matching pink ribbon. It was a simple gown suited for the hot, humid weather that also suited Helen's beautiful, creamy skin, black lash-framed eyes, and pink lips.

His ears perked up at hearing a name she had not mentioned before. "Christina? Who is she?"

There was a stillness that came over Helen that North did not understand. It was as though she had said something she shouldn't, yet it didn't make sense. How did Christina fit into both their lives?

"She is a girl I grew up with," she answered vaguely and quickly. She then jumped up from her seat and said in an edgy tone, "I have an idea! Since I grew up on a farm, I could show you how to milk the cow." She started walking toward the barn. "There is no time like the present," she yelled over her shoulder.

North didn't know what to think of her behavior. Confused, he looked at Josie, and the young girl just shrugged. "She only becomes nervous and does crazy things when you're around, you know," she explained in a conspiratorial whisper. "The rest of the time she is extremely proper and concerned at all times about being a lady."

Hmm. Interesting. Perhaps Helen liked him as much as he liked her.

That didn't explain the evasiveness about her friend Christina, though.

"Let's go learn to milk a cow, shall we?" he asked Josie as he extended his hand to her.

Josie, clearly not thrilled by that prospect, rolled her eyes and sighed. "Oh, all right. But I'm almost sure this is not on the list of ladylike duties I have to learn."

North laughed as he led her to the barn. "No, probably not."

How could I be so careless? Helen lamented, as she paced back and forth in the barn. The more information she offered, the more he was going to want to know, and the more lies she would have to tell.

Oh, this was truly the most awful idea she had ever schemed! Once North found out how much she deceived him and concealed from him, he would never want to see her again! Last night she had tried to tell him the truth, but he wouldn't listen. And she couldn't tell him now because Josie was with her.

Helen was caught in a web of her own making, one that was created for the cause of love but was truly selfish at its very core. All because she wanted something she couldn't have.

"We're here for our lesson!" North announced cheerfully as he and Josie dashed through the barn door, startling the cow and upsetting the three chickens sitting over in the corner.

Helen looked at the cow and wished she hadn't been so hasty in her suggestion. Though she'd seen cows being milked a dozen or so times by her father's servants, she'd never actually milked one herself. "Well. . . ," she sounded, stretching the word out as she thought of what to do. "We need a bucket, but I don't see one."

Josie snatched a bucket that was hanging from a nail on the wall beside her. "I found one!"

"Wonderful," she replied, trying to sound confident as she took the bucket from her charge. "Well, now we need a stool."

"Like the one there beside the cow?" North asked. Helen looked keenly at him to see if he was on to her, but she couldn't tell whether he was teasing her or not.

"Uh, yes. There it is." She slowly edged her way to the side of the cow, praying the animal would not be difficult. She carefully sat down and stared with much apprehension at the cow's underparts in front of her.

She was going to have to touch the animal for this to work, and she didn't want to touch it at all. She remembered petting a cow once, but that was the extent of it. She had never touched the underbelly of one.

She glanced back at North, who had come to stand behind her, and once again, he seemed truly interested in what she was doing. "Are you all right?" he asked when she looked back at the cow and then to him once more.

"Oh, yes. . .yes. . .I am fine. I just wanted to make sure you were paying attention," she answered.

"You have my full concentration," North assured.

"Capital, just capital!" she murmured between gritted teeth. Taking a deep breath, she slowly reached out and took hold of the cow. The cow stirred a little, but that was all.

She tried to pull like she had seen the servant do, but no milk came out.

"Trouble?" North asked.

Helen ignored him as she pulled again, and still nothing. Three, four, then five times she tried but only succeeded in making the cow become irritable.

Finally she couldn't take it anymore. Helen jumped up from her seat, causing the stool to fall back, the cow to move around, and the chickens to be once again upset.

"I don't think she's in the mood to be milked," Helen said quickly, as she brushed at her skirt, then tried to push a few stray hairs away from her face.

North folded his arms and appeared to study the cow. "I wasn't aware that cows needed to be in the mood."

"Yeah, I've never heard that, either," Josie added. "Are you sure you've milked a cow before?"

Putting her hands on her hips, Helen held her chin up with as much bravado as she could muster. "Actually, no. But I've seen it done plenty of times." She tapped her fingertip on her hips. "Enough to know when a cow is in the mood to be milked or not!"

North narrowed his gaze at her, but she could see the humorous gleam shining in his eyes. "So how do I know when she's in the mood?"

Helen suddenly realized he'd known all along she was faking it. She pointed her finger at him and charged, "Why didn't you tell me you were on to me? You actually let me touch that...that...thing!"

Both Josie and North were doubled over laughing by this point. "I can't wait...to see how...you do...with the chickens!" he said between laughs.

Helen smiled confidently as she marched over to one of the hens and deftly slipped her hand under the chicken and quickly withdrew it, holding an egg triumphantly in the air. "Now let's see you try," she challenged, knowing what the outcome would be to a novice.

Just as she thought would happen, North walked over to the hen, poked and prodded through its feathers and, instead of an egg, got a painful peck on the wrist for his efforts.

"Oh, dear," she said with mock innocence. "I fear you did not do that correctly."

North frowned as he rubbed his hand. "I take it you've done this before?"

"Many times."

North grinned at her, and her heart did a flip-flop. To finally have all his attention directed at her, after many months of having him be merely polite to her while she pined away for him every time she saw him, was a heady experience indeed. The sight of him being so natural and at ease, standing in a barn surrounded by chicken feathers and a smelly cow, made her wish he were truly who he thought he was—a simple preacher.

While it was true that North was always a very nice man despite his exalted position in society, he always seemed to be aware of and took care with everything he did—every move he made. He seemed bound by the dictates of his society and the boundaries of the English society, or the ton, as they were called.

Now he didn't have those restrictions on him. There was no one watching how he dressed or with whom he kept company. There were no responsibilities on him since he didn't realize that he had the burden of taking care of four estates and watching after his many investments, not to mention the people who depended on him for their livelihood. He thought he was simply a country preacher whose only worry at the moment was probably the sermon he would have to preach on Sunday and how to get his cow to give milk.

Despite his confusion, he seemed relaxed and content.

Because of his confusion, there was nothing keeping him from hiding his interest in her. There was nothing keeping him from smiling at her and looking at her as though she was the most important person to him.

But that doesn't make it right, said a tiny voice, which she knew was the conviction of God nudging at her heart. He deserved to know who he was. His cousins deserved to know that their family member was still alive and well.

"Shall we begin again?" he asked, breaking her from her musings. "Perhaps if we three put our heads together, we can figure out how to milk this cow."

Laughing, Helen agreed, and so did Josie. Of course, the younger girl was up for anything that kept her from her lessons.

For about an hour, they worked on the poor cow. They finally got some milk out of her, but Helen had a strong suspicion that it was because the animal got tired of their pulling and prodding!

The difficult part, however, was dodging North's probing questions and her trying to answer without actually lying. "So Christina is married to a man named Nicholas who is a former soldier?" He repeated what she'd just told him, and Helen could tell that he was trying to see if the names were familiar to him.

"Nicholas and Christina are the Earl and Countess of Kenswick, you know," Josie informed him, much to Helen's dismay. She'd forgotten all about telling her of them. She quickly looked at North to see if he recognized any of these names.

North's brow furrowed as he stood up from his seat by the cow. "They're nobility?" he asked curiously, and Helen couldn't help but breathe a sigh of relief that his thoughts had taken a different direction from what she imagined he was thinking.

"Yes," Helen affirmed as she walked over to the chickens and finished gathering their eggs. "Christina is only a vicar's daughter, but Nicholas fell in love with her despite the ton's objections."

"Ah, you tell the story with a wistful sound in your voice," he said with a grin. "I gather you thought the whole affair was sentimental and romantic."

She handed the eggs over to Josie, who ran out of the barn to take them to the house. "As a matter of fact, I did," she answered with a raised brow, challenging him to say something against her romanticism.

"I'll bet when the censure came from England's society and his family, it did not feel quite as romantic as they dreamed it would be. Marrying against one's own class can cause a great deal of heartache for all involved." He stopped and blinked. "Well, I say! I don't know where that little insight came from!" he retorted with a chuckle.

Helen laughed in return, but it was a hollow gesture. If he felt that way now, he'd still hold to those convictions once he got his memory back, she realized. Perhaps North, as a duke, didn't want to shake up his life unnecessarily whether it was for love or not.

"I don't think that particular thing is something we have to worry about, do you?" he teased, but she could see the interest for her burning in his gaze as he looked at her. How she wished things could always be as they were now.

"We'd better get this milk stored to keep it cold," she said instead of answering his question.

If she thought North would not notice her evasiveness, she was wrong. As he picked up the bucket of milk, he gave her a long look that let her know she would not be able to avoid his questions forever.

Chapter 5

A loud knock awoke North the next morning, and with a jolt, he was sitting up in his bed, scrambling to get his bearings. His bleary eyes scanned the room, and he noticed that it wasn't even light outside yet.

Who in the world would be out at this early hour? Where were his servants, and why weren't they doing something about the loud noise?

Bit by bit, the fog of sleepiness lifted, and he remembered where he was. He remembered *who* he was. . .at least he remembered who everyone *told* him he was.

"Hamish Campbell. I am Hamish Campbell, the vicar of this hot, muggy spot of America." He recited this to himself to try to lift the odd confusion that had come over him since he'd awakened. For a moment. . .he felt different somehow. Not at all like Hamish Campbell, the humble, poor preacher of Golden Bay.

He remembered thinking that his servants would answer the door. He wondered why he would automatically think he had servants to see after him. Did he once have them in England and Scotland?

Once again, several loud raps sounded on his door. North grudgingly pulled himself out of bed and quickly donned his plain, wrinkled clothes.

When he finally opened the door, he was surprised to find a tall, slim, black man dressed in a fine brown suit with a darker brown-and-black-striped vest over a snow-white shirt and expertly tied cravat.

"*Bonjour*, Monsieur Campbell," the man greeted in a crisp, confident tone as he bent in a short bow. "I am Pierre LeMonde, a freedman from New Orleans and currently in the employ of Mr. Robert Baumgartner. I am versed in all manner of household chores and have been at Golden Bay to teach their household staff the correct methods in which to carry out their duties. I not only speak excellent English but also French, which is my first language."

Slightly bemused by the lengthy, confusing speech, North automatically responded to his last statement without any thought. "Bonjour, monsieur. *Heureaux pour vous rencontrer,*" he replied in French, telling him he was pleased to make his acquaintance.

"*Et vous aussi,*" Pierre answered, and North understood him to say that he was pleased to meet him, too.

But he didn't know *how* he knew this.

Would a simple preacher know this? Was this something one learned at seminary or university?

"I'm sorry, monsieur, but are you all right?" Pierre asked, bringing North's attention back to the present.

"I think I am a little unclear as to why you are here," he told him bluntly, still shaken from discovering yet another odd piece of the puzzle that didn't seem to fit in with what he knew of his life.

"Miss Helen Nichols informed her employers you were in need of. . .how shall I say. . .domestic help."

North grinned at the man's effort at being tactful. "She told you about the fiasco with the cow and chickens, did she not?"

Pierre put his hand against his mouth and let out a little cough. "Uh-hum. Well yes, monsieur, she did."

North laughed as he stepped back and motioned for the man to come into his small house. "I will take help any way I can get it, even if I have to promote my embarrassing moments to get it."

Pierre smiled broadly as he entered the house. He inspected the room and then quickly turned to look at North with the same critical eye. "You are not what I imagined you'd be," he said finally, his deep tone thoughtful.

Intrigued, North cocked his head to one side as he asked, "Why do you say that?"

Pierre shook his head as he shrugged his slim shoulders. "I have been in the employ of some of the richest families of south Louisiana. English, Spanish, and French—it does not matter. They all had the same quality about them, the same air. They spoke differently—they walked differently than the average man or woman." He motioned his hand in a sweeping gesture toward North. "You possess these same qualities."

North scampered to remember what Helen had told him. Did she say his family was or had been wealthy? Oh, yes. She had been very vague as to the exactness of his financial status. So instead he went with his intuition—what he felt deep in his heart. "I am from a wealthy family," he answered, praying it was not a lie.

Pierre lifted an eyebrow as he nodded his head slowly. "Then that explains it. And you gave up your comfortable life for God's calling," he reflected aloud. "Very noble."

If only he could feel the calling, North thought sadly. He must have felt the zeal that had caused missionaries and preachers through the centuries to leave their friends and family to do the work of God. All he felt was scared and uncertain about his ability to minister effectively to these American people.

"I'm just doing the will of God," he said to Pierre, and as he said it, he knew that statement to be true. Somehow, some way, God had a plan, and North was a big part of it.

"Then you are fortunate," Pierre told him, his face solemn. "There are many of my people here in this country who cannot be free to do work such as yours but are bound by the dictates of their masters."

North nodded. "It is indeed a travesty. I would think, however, you are not sitting idly by," he guessed, sensing Pierre would be one who worked behind the scenes, trying to help those slaves whom he could.

Pierre pretended to straighten the cuffs of his sleeves and nonchalantly answered, "I have no idea what you mean, monsieur."

At that moment, North heard his stomach growl, reminding him of his hunger. He started to ask Pierre if his talents extended to knowing how to cook when another knock sounded at the door. Shaking his head, North lamented, "Americans are certainly early risers!"

Pierre smiled as he breezed past North, heading for the door. "Allow me, monsieur."

This time there were two men at the door, and both were holding either end of a large trunk. Pierre spoke to them briefly, then turned back to North to inform him that these were men from the New Orleans port.

"Excellent!" North exclaimed. "Just put it on the table there." The men did as asked, and Pierre gave them water for the journey home.

After the men had gone, Pierre helped North bring the trunk into his small room and then, much to North's eternal thankfulness, left him to make breakfast.

North didn't open the trunk right away. For a moment, he stood there contemplating what the old, beat-up trunk might hold. Would there be mementos inside to help him remember? Would the smell of the clothes or the sound of the trunk's creaking hinges unlock the closed doors of his mind?

He put his hands on the scuffed metal that framed the lid and slid them over until they reached the latch. Carefully he lifted the lid and waited for something familiar to wash over him.

It never came.

It was a trunk filled with clothes that seemed as though they belonged to a stranger. There was nothing vaguely familiar about them. Not even the smell of them gave him the tiniest twinge of remembrance.

Disappointment struck North to his very soul as he slumped down on the bed, his shoulders bent in defeat. He wiped his hands down his face, then through his hair as he tried to assure himself it did not mean anything, that his mind just hadn't healed sufficiently to get his memory back.

Curiosity, however, soon overpowered his disappointment. North stood again and started sifting through the contents of the chest. Perhaps if he could not remember, he could at least try to piece together certain aspects of his life.

Underneath a small stack of neatly pressed white shirts, North found four very worn books. But when he saw the titles and the authors, he was more confused than ever. The first three were religion-based writings by Jonathan Edwards, an evangelist from the Great Awakening period in America, and John Wesley, the man responsible for starting the Methodist movement in England. Curious, North just stared at the books as he tried to comprehend the greater meaning behind his apparent choices in literature.

Was he a Methodist or part of the Church of England? North could not remember how he obtained the information, but he knew the Methodists in England were a religious people only just tolerated by society. The Church of England would not accept their teaching in their chapels and abbeys, so they would meet elsewhere, constructing their own buildings and oftentimes moving to America, where they could worship without censure.

North understood their ministers spoke passionately when they preached, which caused many to call them radical, or religious zealots. North was aware, however, he didn't feel this way about them but only felt a curiosity when he thought about it.

He truly wished he could remember what denomination he was! What if he taught something that this particular congregation did not agree with?

It was just one more thing he'd have to ask Helen about and pray that she knew something about it.

Setting those books aside, he then noticed the title of the fourth book, and he immediately smiled. Daniel Defoe's *Robinson Crusoe*, he intuitively knew, was one of his favorite stories. Perhaps it may have been the catalyst to bringing him to America.

A shimmer of shining metal caught the corner of his eye, and he looked down to notice a gold frame peeking out from under a folded pair of britches. North set the Defoe book aside and reached for the frame.

As he got a better look at it, he saw it was a double-oval frame that contained two miniatures of a man and a woman. North concentrated all his energies into the study of the small portraits as he moved his gaze from the brown-haired man's eyes and smile to the pretty woman's red curls and delicate features.

It struck North right away that neither of them had blond hair. As a matter of fact, neither even looked like him.

North didn't know why this upset him, but it did. In fact, he was more affected by the miniatures than by any of the other disappointments he'd yet encountered.

Agitated, he gripped the frame and began to pace the room. Closing his eyes and gritting his teeth, he focused hard, trying to make his mind remember something. . .anything!

Absolutely nothing was achieved except perhaps a headache from the pressure of trying.

Walking to his window, he pushed the light blue cotton curtain aside. His eyes focused on the church, which was situated in his direct line of view, and then he did the only thing he knew to do.

Pray.

"God, I cannot understand why I can't remember. I cannot understand why I become more confused looking at my own belongings. Most of all, I cannot understand why I don't feel like Hamish Campbell." He took a breath and lifted the miniature up to the sunlight. Thoughtfully he rubbed his thumb along the edges of the frame. "I can only conclude that You have a purpose, Lord, and need me to fulfill it. I will endeavor to feel honored You have chosen me for Your task, and please forgive me when I have felt otherwise since I arrived in Golden Bay. I will strive to do my best for You, dear God. Please help my faith to stay strong." He ended the prayer and stayed a minute more, gazing out the window, letting the heat of the sunlight bathe his face and rejuvenate his spirits.

In fact, he felt so much contentment in his heart that he wasn't even fazed when he tried on his clothes from the trunk and found the shoulders were just a little tight and the arms just slightly too long.

Apparently I had an atrocious tailor in Scotland was his only thought as he made his way to the kitchen and to the delicious food Pierre already had spread on the table.

❧

"Josie, a lady never grabs the body of her teacup with both hands!" Helen stressed as she was unsuccessfully trying to tutor the young girl on the correct way to take tea.

Josie looked at Helen with a typically bored expression on her features. "Which would you prefer: my picking the cup up by the handle and dropping it, getting tea everywhere, or would you rather see me using both hands to make sure that doesn't happen?"

Considering the cost of the teacups they were using, the young lady had a point. But Helen couldn't tell her that.

"Josie, if you practice, you will be able to hold on to your cup without dropping it and look elegant at the same time," she instructed patiently, knowing Josie was barely paying attention. The younger girl kept looking out the window with a longing expression. She cleared her throat to get Josie's attention. "Shall we begin again?"

Josie sighed with vexation. "Why don't we go visit the reverend and see how he's getting along? It's been over a week since we've seen him," she said, suddenly perking up.

Helen wanted more than anything to go but knew it was wiser to stay away. It was getting more and more difficult to live with the lie she had told him. Seeing him only compounded her guilt. "Josie, please. . . ," she began only to be cut short.

"Can't we go fishing instead? Sam is going to be there, and he was going to show me how to use crickets for bait."

Helen shuddered at her words. "Your fascination with that Indian is beyond the pale! Young ladies do not go traipsing around alone with young men who are not in one's family!"

Josie's chin rose, and Helen knew she wasn't going to back down. "You just don't like Sam because he keeps wanting to trade horses for you."

"Exactly! He is a barbarian!" In truth, Helen was a little fascinated with Sam, the tall, red-skinned man who dressed in his leather-fringed britches and only covered his upper torso with a closed vest, leaving his arms bare. It was even a little flattering he seemed so taken with her.

Josie slumped in her chair and folded her arms defiantly. "I should have been born an Indian; then I wouldn't have to learn all these dumb rules."

Helen smiled. "I'm sure there are a whole different set of rules you would have to learn as an Indian girl."

Josie's rebuttal was stopped short when her mother breezed into the room at that moment. "I just received a note from Pierre that all is going well at the Reverend Campbell's house," she informed them as she waved a small piece of paper in her hand.

Helen stood and looked at her employer gratefully. "Thank you so much for sending help," she told her earnestly. "I saw he was unfamiliar with animals and even how to prepare his own meals, so I feared he would starve without immediate assistance."

Imogene raised an eyebrow as she studied Helen with a critical eye. She made Helen feel like the woman could see straight inside her mind. "I see I was right in my assumptions."

Helen could feel her heart beating with nervousness. "I beg your pardon?" she said, hoping she was misreading the direction of Mrs. Baumgartner's thoughts.

"You have feelings for Hamish Campbell!" she declared with certainty. "Your eyes light up when you speak of him, and an inner joy exudes from your heart and into your words. I would even be so bold as to say that you were in love with the reverend even before you came to Louisiana. Am I right?"

Helen tried to swallow the lump in her throat, but she was so frozen by what she should say next, she was unable to accomplish the task. She said the first thing she thought of, hoping her words would defuse Imogene's assumptions. "I can honestly say that I am not in love with Hamish Campbell." She was only in love with Trevor "North" Kent.

She must have sounded convincing, because Imogene frowned with confusion. "Are you absolutely sure?" she asked but then continued without an answer. "Perhaps you have not realized your feelings for him yet! Of course!" She clapped her hands together. "You need time to sort them out!"

Did a girl really need time to realize that she had found her true love? The moment Helen had laid eyes on North, she knew he was the only man she wanted to be her husband, the only man she could love.

"You can only be sure of your feelings if you spend time with him!" She patted Helen on the cheek and spun around to walk toward the door. "Don't worry, dear! Leave it to me. You'll realize he is your one true love in no time!" she exclaimed over her shoulder as she left the room.

Bemused by Mrs. Baumgartner's words, Helen could only liken the feeling to being run over by a buggy.

"You may be good with manners and such, but you are wretched at handling my mother," Josie spoke from behind her as Helen still stood staring at the door.

Blinking, Helen finally turned and looked at the younger girl. "I don't suppose you can give me any pointers on how I should do that, can you?"

Josie's smile was one of pure cunning. "Only if I can go fishing with Sam today."

Plopping back down in her chair, Helen waved her hand toward the door. "Just go," she told her in a tired voice, and in just a matter of seconds, the girl had flown out of the room and down the stairs.

Helen thought about all that had transpired since she had arrived in Louisiana and wondered if things could become any stranger. Here she was in love with a man who had no memory and whom everyone believed was someone else. She was trying to hide the fact that she was in love with him, but now Imogene Baumgartner was determined to see them together.

Why am I fighting this? Helen thought, but deep down she knew the answer. Guilt was holding her back. Guilt over lying to poor North about who he really was.

The whole purpose of making him think he was Hamish Campbell was to have a chance at winning his heart. But even if he never got his memory back, could she live with such a lie hanging over her head? Could she even keep up the charade without anyone finding out?

She imagined telling the vicar from her village, the Reverend Wakelin, about her deceptive deeds and wondered what he would say. Helen knew he would be very disappointed in her, because she was growing more and more ashamed of herself.

Chapter 6

Pierre!" North called out as he entered his house, holding a basket of eggs. He'd been in Golden Bay nearly two weeks now, and dealing with the animals was still a daily challenge. "I got out every single egg without damaging myself in the process!" he announced proudly as he put the basket on the table.

Pierre peered over his shoulder as he knelt in front of the fireplace, where he was adjusting the metal rack mounted inside. "Very good, monsieur. Perhaps tomorrow you will be able to get a little more than half a cup of milk from the cow."

North laughed at Pierre's droll tone. "Could you let me savor my small victory before criticizing my failures?"

"I am just helping you to strive for more, monsieur," Pierre countered with laughter in his deep voice.

"Well, I am about to strive to write my first sermon, so if you'll excuse me, I'll go and get my Bible."

"It is Saturday!" Pierre exclaimed with disbelief. "You are only now preparing your sermon?"

North stopped in his tracks and looked to Pierre with concern. "That's not the way it's done?" he asked cautiously, not thinking about his words.

Pierre blinked at him and paused a minute before asking, "You don't know?"

North felt like a fraud. Here he was pretending to be the person he really was. . .except he couldn't remember being that person. And if everyone knew he couldn't remember, then they would either think he was crazy or doubt his ability to lead them.

Which would be a proper assumption in his case because he had no idea how to be a vicar and no inkling as to whether he was even good at public speaking. Maybe the reason he came all the way to America was because everyone back in Scotland thought he was a terrible preacher.

"Uh. . .my experience has been somewhat. . .limited," he finally answered with the biggest understatement of the decade.

Pierre's right eyebrow rose in query. "How limited?"

"Practically nonexistent."

Pierre just stared at him for a moment, making North wonder what he was thinking. Would he go tell the Baumgartners that he was a fraud? A novice who had no business pretending he knew *anything*?

Then Pierre suddenly turned from him, and his shoulders began to shake. North peered closely at him, and when he'd walked to face Pierre once again, he realized the man was laughing!

"I'm sorry, monsieur, but you English are very funny," he said, as tears started to run down his dark cheeks. "I wish I could be in that church tomorrow. It would be more—" He interrupted his own sentence as he tried desperately to hold on to his usual dignified disposition. "More entertaining than watching you milk that poor. . .cow!"

North sighed as he watched Pierre sit down at the table and completely cover his face as his whole body shook.

North wished he could see the humor of the whole situation. He could use a good laugh.

Leaving the still-laughing servant in the kitchen, North dragged his feet into his bedroom and took the Bible from his night table. He opened the book at random, praying for divine intervention, and landed in the book of Exodus. He read the story about how Moses led the children of Israel out of Egypt and how their disobedience kept them in the desert, which should have taken them a short time to go through, for forty years.

He sat there for a moment and thought about how that story could be used in a sermon, but then he had a horrible thought. What if he had done some incredibly bad thing or had been disobedient to God before he came to America? Perhaps God was punishing him for this.

Perhaps he would be stuck in a wilderness of forgetfulness for forty years like the children of Israel!

Looking back down at the faded pages of the Bible, North quickly flipped the pages away from that particular book. He decided it would be best to look for something else.

He looked through several passages, and none seemed to be right for his first sermon until he found the book of Job. Here was a man who had lost everything but still would not blame God for any of his misfortunes. And in time, God restored him above and beyond his former glory because Job stayed faithful to God.

North rubbed his chin as he thought about how Job's life was similar to his own. Everything had been stripped from him, so if he continued to keep his faith in God, perhaps He would restore to North what he had lost.

He determined he would build his sermon around the story of Job. North felt that since he was so affected by the story he would have the passion to convey the lesson to others.

Encouraged that he had a theme for his message, he took several sheets of paper from his trunk and went to the kitchen with pen and ink in hand.

"You look pleased with yourself," Pierre observed. "I will assume it is because you have found a theme for your sermon?"

"Yes, you may assume," North said with a relieved smile. "I am speaking about the life of Job and how we should keep our faith in God when things go wrong in our lives."

Pierre looked impressed. "An excellent topic. How will you begin?"

North thought a moment. "I will open by reading the scriptures." He opened his bottle of ink, situated his papers just so, and dipped the tip of the pen into the bottle.

"And then?"

North looked up as Pierre sat across from him. He had on the same suit as yesterday, and North couldn't help but notice his own servant dressed better than he did.

"Then. . .I will put the story into my own words—explain it, if you will."

He began to write down the scripture reference in his bold, yet expertly done, script.

"Ah. . ." Pierre sounded thoughtful. "And where shall you go from there?"

North smudged his paper when his hand jerked at Pierre's words. "I should have more?" Suddenly the process seemed complicated again.

"*Oui*, monsieur. What you've described will take less than seven to ten minutes. It will need to be a great deal longer than that."

North looked from the near-empty paper to Pierre with dismay radiating from every pore of his being. "I don't suppose you could. . . "

Pierre made a *tsk*-ing sound. "I write very poorly, monsieur. And besides, if I do it for you, it would not be from your heart but mine."

North sighed and ran a hand through his wavy blond hair. "Yes, I suppose you're right," he conceded, although he wished he knew what to do.

Helen suddenly came to mind, and he wondered if she could help him. Of course she had been to church before, so perhaps she could give him an idea of what to do. And besides, she was the only person who would understand *why* he didn't know what to do.

He quickly gathered his papers and put the top back on his ink. "May I borrow your barouche, Pierre?"

Pierre seemed taken aback by his sudden change. "Of course, but why?"

"Because I'm going to see Helen. She'll be able to help me."

Pierre helped him don his coat and put his things in a leather satchel, which North had found near the bottom of the trunk. "Perhaps there are other reasons you want to see the pretty lady?"

"Mind your own affairs, Pierre," he ordered as he walked briskly to the door.

He heard Pierre shout as he closed the door. "But yours are so much more interesting than my own!"

North's heart was beating excitedly as he knocked on the Baumgartners' door. Just the prospect of seeing Helen once again seemed to reduce him to a nervous schoolboy with his first crush.

Of course, since he couldn't remember even going to school, she would actually be the first.

A tall black man dressed in fine black attire greeted North with a solemn nod and asked him the reason for his visit.

Before he could answer, Imogene Baumgartner came hurriedly down the staircase to greet him. "Reverend Campbell! How wonderful you have come to visit us."

They both nodded to each other in lieu of a curtsy or bow. "Good morning, Mrs. Baumgartner. I came by to see if I might have a word with Helen."

North was surprised to see the older woman's eyes light up. "Of course you did!" she exclaimed as she put a hand against her throat and looked at him as if she knew a secret. "Our Helen is a very special lady, if I might be so bold as to say." She leaned forward and whispered, "But I think you are already aware of that."

North was well aware Imogene Baumgartner was not a lady of high society. Pierre had told him about her being the daughter of a servant in England and that Robert Baumgartner had given up everything to marry her. But despite her obvious lack of ladylike behavior, she was a very engaging woman who quickly endeared herself to all those she met.

Again, North had no idea how he understood the differences of society and their behaviors. He couldn't even remember if he'd been considered a gentleman or simply a rich commoner. And there was a difference. Whereas a gentleman was born to his distinction whether he was wealthy or poor, a commoner, no matter how rich, could never hope to be recognized on the gentleman's level.

In America, however, it seemed that whoever had the most money or the drive to better themselves could achieve anything they wanted.

So North supposed it didn't really matter what he was, as long as he worked hard to establish himself and proved himself worthy to be called a minister to the Golden Bay people.

North smiled at Imogene, leaned forward, and whispered back to her, answering her assumption. "You are correct. I think Helen Nichols is a very lovely girl."

Imogene giggled with girlish delight, and North smiled with her, enjoying the merriment dancing in her light hazel eyes. "Why don't you wait right here in the library while I go and tell her you are here." She directed him to a small room off their grand foyer, just beyond the staircase.

North remained standing after she had left and looked with startled interest about the room. It was indeed a library with shelves made of what looked like heavy oak, but there were no more than twenty books spread about them as they circled the room. The rest of the space was taken up by potted plants, figurines, and a few miniatures.

"It seems sort of an atrocity to call this room the library, doesn't it?"

North turned toward the female voice that he was coming to recognize so well. He took a moment to admire how Helen had left her dark curls to flow around her shoulders, complementing the light violet of her morning dress. "Indeed, it is," he agreed. "It seems to be nothing but old books of poetry, scientific works, and. . ." His voice drifted to a pause when he noticed a stack of books in one far corner that seemed to be newer than the rest. "What are those over there?"

Helen smiled. "Those are mine. I'm afraid I wasted a lot of time in England reading and not applying myself to other studies as I should have."

Suddenly a thought popped into his head, and North spoke it without realizing what he was saying. "Of course! I remember you like to read gothic romance novels; am I correct?"

The moment those words were out, they both froze—staring at one another in unbelief.

"How do you know that?" she finally asked, her voice sounding almost fearful.

North shook his head in wonderment. "I don't know. The information just appeared in my mind like a memory normally does."

"Well, do you remember anything else?"

North closed his eyes and tried to concentrate on the memory he just had but could remember nothing else. He opened his eyes and sighed. "Absolutely nothing."

Helen looked at him with sympathy. "I'm sorry, North. I'm sure more memories will come to you. Perhaps if you try not to think about it so much, you will one day remember everything."

"I suppose you're right," he readily agreed. It just felt so good for that tiny moment to have a true memory of something. It was like God giving him a small gift to get him through the day.

"What's that in your hand?" Helen prompted as she spied the satchel he had taken from his shoulder.

"Ah yes." He'd almost forgotten his reason for being here. "I've come to ask for your help with my sermon." He dipped his hand into the satchel and brought out his papers. "Since I can't remember preaching or even hearing a sermon, I don't have the first idea how to go about constructing one."

He watched as Helen smiled prettily and crossed her arms in front of her in a motion of confidence. "Well, Reverend, you've come to the right person!"

Helen was still a little jittery after North told her about his memory. Sure, it was a tiny memory, but who knew what he would remember next?

This was bad—very, very bad. *She* was bad for even creating this situation. But what could she do? If she told him now, it would not only confuse him but also upset the whole town!

She was trying to calm her nerves when he asked her the one thing that would help take her mind off her problem.

He needed help with his sermon. She could do that!

Helen motioned for North to sit at the desk by the far wall, and she pulled a chair beside him. "Can I assume you have a little knowledge in the area of sermon writing?" North asked as he reached over to take a Bible down from the shelf behind him.

"My best friend's father is a vicar. Every Saturday Christina and I would take his notes in his very sloppy script and rewrite them so that he could see them better from the pulpit," she explained. "I know exactly the structure in which he wrote all his sermons. They would have one major scripture reference and at least three points. At the end, he would bring it all together and bring out one last nugget of truth, maybe other scriptures in the Bible that might tie in with his first one. He was a very respected and widely known vicar in our parish."

North seemed surprised by her information. "You don't know how relieved I am that you seem confident in how to do this." He paused for a moment. "Uh. . .Helen, this congregation here in Golden Bay. . . Are they a Methodist congregation? That is to say. . .am I a Methodist?"

Helen shrugged her shoulders. "Actually, it is a sort of blended church. There are a few Methodists, Baptists, and members of the Church of England, as the Baumgartners and I are. I'm almost certain you are, as well." Actually she was *very* certain he was, but she'd already told him that she knew little about his personal life.

For over an hour, they labored side by side, working with his passage from Job and choosing points that best brought out the lesson he wanted to be most understood.

When they had finished, he leaned back in his chair and stretched his arms forward. "I think I could use some fresh air," he said with a yawn.

Helen thought about how humid it had been outdoors earlier when she'd stepped out for a moment, and she smiled. "I don't know if *fresh* is the appropriate description of the Louisiana air, but I do concede that it would be nice to walk around a bit."

Together they stepped out onto the porch, which wrapped around the house, and made their way down the ten or so steps, following the path to the pier.

"So what caused you to leave England and journey to this place?" North asked as he picked up a long, thick stick from the path and then used it as a walking cane.

There was no way Helen could tell him the truth—that she'd come to America because she had hoped to see him. "Well, I suppose it sounded adventurous," she answered, giving him only half the truth. "My best friend had gotten married, and I suppose I just wanted a change of setting. My parents were hinting around for me to marry a young farmer in my village, and I just didn't want to settle for someone I didn't love." She shrugged her shoulders. "When Lady Claudia told me about the position of being a companion for her little sister, I felt God was opening a door for me. So here I am."

"Well, might I be so bold as to say I am eternally grateful that you did not settle for the farmer, or else I might have never seen you again," he said in a teasing tone as he looked down at her with appreciation.

Helen could feel her cheeks reddening, and she quickly looked away before he could read her true feelings. She knew he liked her, but it would be hard to explain the feelings of love she carried for him so soon.

North, however, was adept at stemming the awkwardness as he changed the subject to her earlier comment about Lady Claudia. She was trying to explain that Claudia, Robert Baumgartner's elder child, had been accepted by her grandfather to inherit the title of marchioness after his death, when something large moved in their path, blocking the sun.

Helen knew, before she lifted her gaze, who it was.

Standing before them with all the confidence a chief of his tribe would possess—wearing his usual buckskins and vest—was the Choctaw Indian Sam Youngblood. In his hand were three ropes that led to the horses situated behind him.

Helen could sense the moment North noticed him, and after a period of stunned silence, he barked out, "*What* is *that*?"

Chapter 7

Helen glanced back and forth between the two men nervously; and if she were pressed to describe their first reaction to one another, it would most definitely be *hostile*.

Even *that* would be an understatement.

As soon as the words had left North's mouth, Helen feared Sam would surely take offense. And if his flaring nostrils and narrowed, angry eyes were any indication, Helen knew she was right in her assumption.

Realizing she would have to try and unruffle the Indian's feathers, so to speak, she began to walk toward him. Helen had only taken two steps when she was suddenly jerked back by North and pulled to his side.

"What are you doing? That is a savage!" North barked, sounding as though he were horrified at even being in Sam's presence.

Knowing how Sam usually liked to play up to people's stereotypical thinking that all Indians were uneducated, barbaric, and dangerous, Helen knew he was probably already thinking of what to do to shock North even more.

"But, North, he's. . ."

"They've been known to scalp a fellow before he could even let out a scream," he stressed in a low voice, all the while keeping his eye on Sam. "They also like to take white women back to their camps and use them as their slaves."

Helen stopped short of rolling her eyes. "You know this, but you can't remember your own name," she whispered back with exasperation. Then in a louder voice, "North, if you'll just let me intro—"

"Why don't we start walking toward the house very slowly? Perhaps he'll leave us alone." He started to pull her to walk around Sam, when the Indian suddenly pulled out the long knife that had been strapped to his hip.

As Sam made a show of examining his blade, flashing the metal against the sunlight, Helen noticed North appeared to be growing more apprehensive by the minute.

"All right, you've had your fun, Sam. Now put the knife away," she called out.

Sam scowled at her. "But I haven't even shown him my frightening war cry," he complained.

North looked at her with disbelief. "You *know* him?"

Helen's arm was starting to hurt as North unconsciously kept tightening his grip. "If I vow with all sincerity that he will not scalp us, will you let go of my arm?"

North immediately let go, his face matching the apology he offered her. "Please accept my forgiveness; I did not realize. . ."

"Are you hurting my woman?" Sam roared angrily, as he stomped over to where they were standing.

Helen groaned, holding out a hand to stop the tall man. "Will you cease calling me your woman?" she lamented. "I've told you time and time again that—"

"I demand to know what he means by the words 'my woman'," North interjected, his question directed to Helen but his eyes steady on Sam.

Helen put her hands on either side of her face and shook her head. "Oh, dear! This is getting dreadfully out of hand. If you both would stop and listen—"

"I have tried three times to barter a trade between myself and Baumgartner for Helen," Sam started to explain in his blunt way.

"You've done *what*?" North interrupted, but Sam, unfazed, continued.

"He has rejected all my offers, but this time I don't think he will." He waved a hand back toward the black horses. "This time I have brought not two, but three of the finest horses around this area. I do not think he will refuse."

"Trade. . ." North choked as he listened to Sam. "That is the most preposterous thing I have ever heard. You can't be serious," he barked and turned to Helen. "Tell me he isn't serious."

"Sam, I told you our people do not trade women or even men for horses or anything else! It's just simply not civilized."

Sam scoffed at her words, which he'd heard many times before. "I have seen white men barter for the black men and women," he countered. "I see no difference!"

How can I argue with that? Helen stared at Sam, disconcerted. "Sam, I am not for sale, and there is no more I can say about it. Mr. Baumgartner, even if he wanted to, could not trade me to you. He doesn't own me."

"I can't even believe I am hearing this conversation. Why are you trying to reason with him?" North said, exasperation threaded in his tone.

"This is none of your business, white man!" Sam barked, his eyes glaring at North.

Helen quickly jumped in, in an attempt to defuse whatever was happening between the two mistrustful men. "I haven't introduced you two, have I?" she asked brightly as she stepped between them, causing them both to back up. "This is Sam Youngblood, Reverend Campbell. He lives just across the bayou. Sam, this is my friend, North. He is the new preacher in town."

Suddenly the hostility left Sam's face, and he smiled broadly. "You are a preacher?"

North seemed unsure of how to react to the Indian's sudden change of attitude. "Yes," he answered after a brief pause.

Sam nodded as he zeroed in his focus on Helen, his interest in her shining in his dark, mysterious eyes. "That's good. Because if I can't barter for Helen, then I suppose I'll have to get her another way," he stated.

North tried to move around Helen, but she kept sidestepping him. Finally he just pointed to Sam over her shoulder. "And what other way would that be?"

Helen moaned, "Oh, dear!" She looked over her shoulder and saw Sam was actually enjoying the fact he was upsetting North.

Sam shrugged, and with a sigh that sounded as though he was quite put out, he answered, "I'll have to woo her into marrying me, I guess."

"Mar—" North choked on his words again. "Did you hear what he just said?" he practically shouted at her.

Oh yes, she'd heard, and she was just a little perturbed at his seeming reluctance to try to court her. It didn't matter that she didn't want him to!

"You don't have to seem as though it would be a great hardship to woo me!" she scolded Sam. "You were certainly willing to give up your best three horses for me, so what is the difference?"

North, standing behind her now, tapped her on the shoulder and whispered forcibly in her ear, "Helen, do you hear what you are saying?"

"It's a lot less work!" Sam answered over North's whisper.

"Well, I never!" Helen huffed, insulted by his words.

"So can you marry us?" Sam asked over her shoulder to North, ignoring Helen's outrage.

"Absolutely not!" North stated with a steely resolve.

"I never said I would marry you!"

"Why not?" Sam pressed, his question not directed at her but at North again.

"I am not marrying anyone, so please stop discussing a wedding that will never happen!" she yelled at them both as she backed away and glared with hands on hips.

"Do you always yell like this? I'm not sure I want a wife who is so loud," Sam observed with a sudden frown.

Helen tapped her fingers on her hips. "Then I shall make sure to yell at you every time we meet!"

Sam scowled at that answer. North smiled at her with admiration.

Both men were driving her crazy.

Without so much as another word, she whirled around, tossing her dark curls behind her, and marched to the house.

❧

North watched Helen flounce away, and he couldn't help but admire her spunk and the way she had stood up to Sam. She would indeed make a fine wife, but not to the Indian. No, she would make a very fine wife for a man like himself.

At least the man he imagined he was, he amended, as he thought about how his own past was still a mystery.

"So I have competition for Helen Nichols," Sam commented, as though he already knew the answer.

North answered anyway. "No, because you have no chance in winning her heart." It was an overconfident statement for which he had nothing to back it up except his own hopes for Helen.

Sam stared at him as if he were trying to decipher the truth. "You believe you do?"

North smiled a confident smile filled with determination. "I know I do."

North returned the Indian man's stare measure for measure. Finally Sam answered with equal conviction, "We shall see, preacher man." And with that he nodded his head and turned to gather his horses.

As North began to walk back toward the path that Helen had taken, he realized he actually liked Sam, despite his fondness for the woman of North's choice. He found he looked forward to learning more about Sam's culture and way of life.

Did Indians of his tribe actually scalp people?

It wasn't hard to locate Helen after he'd reached the plantation house, because she was sitting on the front porch with Josie sipping tea. The first thing he noticed was that she'd tied back her beautiful black hair with a ribbon.

Pity.

"I was wondering if you two brutes had killed one another," she told him, as he walked up the many steps to where they were seated.

"Let's just say we had a few things to talk over," he prevaricated.

"Did he show you his big knife? I once saw him cut a snake clean in two with one swipe!" Josie threw in, apparently not wanting to be left out of the conversation.

"Never mind about that!" Helen waved toward the younger girl as if dismissing her words. "What possible things would you have to discuss with Sam?" she demanded to know.

North had to try hard not to smile at her curiosity. "I believe the subject revolved around"—he paused for effect—"your marriage."

"My *marriage*!" she gasped, coming out of her chair and nearly spilling the tea on the wooden floor.

"You're getting married?" Josie queried in an excited voice. "Who are you getting married to?"

"Nobody!"

"Wait and see."

They spoke at the same time, and Josie clapped her hands with delight. "I'll bet it's Sam! He's been in love with Helen since she got here!"

"But she's not in love with *him*," North answered without thinking, only realizing until after he spoke how self-assured he sounded.

One should never, ever presume to tell a woman what her feelings are, he remembered too late.

She gasped with incredulity at his words. North couldn't help but admire how beautiful she looked even when she was angry. "Perhaps I want to marry Sam!" she stated, emphasizing each word.

North knew good and well she didn't, but it didn't stop him from feeling irritated that she'd said it. "You've turned him down three times!" he countered with a snap of his fingers, remembering his earlier conversation with Sam.

Helen looked less angry, as if she thought she had the upper hand in the conversation. Almost deliberately she began to study her nails. "Maybe I was holding out for four horses."

The whole conversation seemed so silly that North began to laugh. A quick glance at Helen told him that she, too, found the whole exchange ridiculous. Soon they were both laughing.

"I don't know what is so funny," Josie huffed as she stood up from her chair. "If you don't want the horses, I'll take them!"

That just made them laugh harder.

Chapter 8

It was with great excitement that Helen and the Baumgartner family dressed for church the next morning. In fact, the whole area was abuzz with anticipation of finally having church services and their very own pastor. Weddings would not have to be delayed, and funerals could finally be done properly, with a minister presiding over them instead of someone just reading scriptures. There had been no one for spiritual guidance and no one qualified to go to for clarification on certain scriptures.

Among the females in the area, however, their excitement was not focused so much on the spiritual benefits but rather on the fact that he was young, single, and extremely handsome. Helen didn't really want to listen to that particular rumor from Imogene as they walked into the church, but there was plenty of evidence to support it when they entered and saw every female in the church dressed fancier than Helen had ever seen them.

Helen was amazed at the elaborately decorated bonnets that all seemed to match their frocks perfectly. It was almost like being transported back to London, so stylish they all looked. She glanced down at her own gown, which was nice with its pink flowers at the bodice and flowing cream taffeta below the high waist, yet it wasn't as stylish and well made as most of the dresses in the room. Even her bonnet, though one of her finest, seemed dowdy in comparison.

These were like all the society ladies whom North was used to being around in England. Would the sight of them jog his memory?

As she thought of North, she looked around but was unable to see him among the twenty or so people there in attendance. Helen took her seat beside the Baumgartners in one of the middle rows. It was then that she saw North enter the church from the side door by the pulpit.

She was only able to partially see his face as he took a seat in the front pew, and she wondered why he didn't look about the room at all. In fact, he seemed a little tense as he faced forward, not speaking to anyone.

Helen glanced to her side, and Josie, too, seemed to be studying North's strange behavior. But before Helen could whisper anything to her young friend, Ollie Rhymes, the self-appointed hymn leader from the Hill plantation called for everyone to stand and turn to hymn number 23. It was then that Helen noticed the handmade booklet with words to songs written out in plain script and tied together with a heavy string. Since she was sitting on the end and there was only one booklet per pew, she was unable to sing the words to the unfamiliar song. It really didn't matter because poor Miss Ollie sang like an injured housecat, and since she was hard of hearing, her volume was one of gargantuan proportions.

Though Josie was all but holding her ears as she grimaced with mock pain, Helen barely gave Miss Ollie a glance, her gaze still fixed on North. *What is wrong with him?*

"What's wrong with him?" Josie echoed her thoughts, talking louder than a whisper as she tried to make herself heard over the caterwauling.

Helen noticed the disapproving frown from Imogene directed at her daughter, so she just shook her head in lieu of an answer.

Finally Miss Ollie ended the song, and Helen could almost hear the audible prayer of thanks from everyone in the small church as the petite, elderly woman stepped down from the pulpit.

Miss Ollie smiled and nodded toward North, giving him his cue that it was his turn.

Apparently he didn't know the cue.

North just sat there, and after a few seconds, the congregation started whispering and moving around.

What *was* wrong with North?

Finally Miss Ollie apparently got tired of standing there and smiling at him. She went over to him, slapped him on top of his shoulder, and said, "It's your turn, sonny."

This time North responded with a jerk as if he had awakened from a dream. He quickly stood and looked around nervously. Stiffly, he walked to the pulpit and put down his Bible and notes.

It seemed like an eternity passed as he slowly flipped through his Bible, adjusted his papers, then cleared his throat at least four times.

"Has he ever done this before?" Josie whispered, still too loud. A smattering of laugher trickled from the people sitting around them as they heard her comment.

"Shh!" Helen sounded sharply as she prayed North would be able to calm down and begin his message.

Finally he read the scripture passage they'd chosen together. His voice sounded steady and strong as he read expertly from his Bible, and Helen started to relax.

He was doing fine. Of course, he could do this! He was, after all, a duke!

Unfortunately, poor North didn't have any idea who he was or what he was capable of. For after he read the scripture, he looked up at the crowd, looked back down at his Bible, and. . .

Nothing! He seemed unable to speak another word.

North was so seized with self-doubt that he couldn't seem to get another word out! He just couldn't seem to fathom why he had chosen the occupation of clergyman when he was so obviously afraid of speaking in public.

Wouldn't it be something that comes naturally? he wondered hurriedly as he struggled to get hold of his panic. But then nothing else had come naturally. Not taking care of animals, providing for himself without the help of a servant, and certainly not writing sermons. Why should he believe this would be any different?

Nothing felt right. His collar was too tight, his shoes were actually a little too big, and he thought he might have gotten a splinter in his hand when he stepped up to the pulpit and ran his palm on the top of the wooden surface.

Read! Just read your message. It is all written out for you, he told himself so sternly that he feared he'd spoken it aloud. But when he looked at the congregation, they merely seemed curious and puzzled as to why he was just standing there, not saying anything.

He didn't want to tell them of his memory loss, because they would believe him to be crazy. If he didn't control his fear, they were going to come to that conclusion anyway!

Taking a deep breath, he prayed he would find a peace and be able to proceed. And miraculously God must have heard, because he was able to take a deep breath, his heartbeat slowing down so he could focus.

He lifted his gaze and saw Helen's concerned eyes fastened on him. A feeling like North knew he'd never felt before seemed to hit him square in the chest and straight to his heart. But it didn't make him more nervous; instead, it gave him a greater peace, knowing she was there to support him.

He smiled at her but quickly moved his gaze about the room so as not to let anyone think he was flirting with a woman in church and in sight of everyone. When he briefly looked back at her, she was returning his smile, looking quite relieved that he seemed to be all right.

He looked back down at his notes and began to read. He kept trying to stop and make comments on what he was reading without having to look directly from his notes, but he couldn't seem to think of anything. So he read. And read.

And read.

He didn't *once* look up.

He finished the sermon in what he was sure was record time for a clergyman. In fact, the whole thing including the scripture reading could not have lasted more than ten minutes.

When he finally spoke the last words on his page, he looked up to find everyone staring at him with sort of a dazed expression on their faces. Not knowing what else to do, he quickly bowed his head and said a closing prayer, which sounded amateurish at best.

The members of his congregation were as polite as they could be as they filed out of the building, shaking his hand as they passed him. Every once in a while someone would actually tell him that his sermon was good, and North had to wonder if God wouldn't mind the lie so much since they were only trying to be nice.

Finally Helen was standing before him, giving him a smile that could only be described as one borne out of pity. *Splendid,* he thought grimly. The woman for whom he carried great affection felt sorry for him.

"You did it!" she whispered with encouragement. "It can only get easier from here."

North didn't feel quite so optimistic, but he did manage to murmur, "Thank you."

"You read really fast," Josie offered. She was wearing the same expression as Helen.

Helen nudged the younger girl and scolded, "Don't say that, Josie. He read quite nicely."

"I was trying to compliment him!"

North stemmed whatever Helen was about to say by stepping up and putting his hand on Josie's shoulder. "Thank you, Josie. You are very sweet," he told her, touched that she, too, was trying to help him feel better.

The sermon *really* must have been appalling.

"Reverend Campbell! Will you join us for our noonday meal?" Imogene asked, coming up behind Helen and Josie. "We have invited the whole church to come and picnic with us on our plantation."

There was nothing North wanted to do less than be around the congregation, but he saw no way to bow out graciously. "Of course I'll join you."

"Excellent!" Imogene exclaimed with a smile. "Then would you mind taking the barouche with Josie and Helen? I'll ride with my husband in our carriage."

He told her he would, and when everyone had exited the church, he closed it up and headed for the barouche, where Helen and Josie sat waiting for him.

Helen's face blossomed into a breathtaking smile when she saw him. North suddenly didn't care that he had embarrassed himself or that he would still have to face his congregation once again.

He was about to spend another day with Helen.

Nothing else mattered.

⤚∕⤙

All through North's sermon, Helen couldn't help feeling responsible for putting him through the whole tedious ordeal. She felt such admiration for him because, even though he didn't know what he was doing, he was willing to give it his best efforts.

In fact, Helen realized now that she hadn't really known North at all back in England. She had only been taken with his good looks and charming ways. She had never seen the giving, caring person who was nervous about public speaking and so determined to do what he thought was right—to be the man everybody thought he was even though he didn't feel like Hamish Campbell.

He was truly a good, decent man. A wonderful Christian man.

She didn't deserve him, but she couldn't tell him that. She couldn't tell him any of the truths she, and only she, knew to be true, because it would not only hurt him but everyone she respected in Golden Bay.

Helen felt terrible she had let things go this far. When she first thought of lying to him, she never stopped to consider the consequences. All of her reasoning was based on herself.

Now all she thought of was North. Every night she prayed not that God would forgive her but that He'd help her find a way of helping North get his memory back without hurting him too much in the process.

Unfortunately it sounded like an insurmountable task.

"All right, ladies. You are being too quiet, and Josie keeps smiling politely at me as if she's been instructed to do so," North said suddenly, breaking the long silence as they rode toward Golden Bay plantation. "Why don't you just give me your honest opinions? Trust me, it could be no worse than what I have already thought of myself."

"Well. . ." She hesitated, desperately trying to think of something positive to say. "You have a very nice voice for speaking. It's deep and very pleasant to listen to."

North threw her a look that told her he knew she was evading the question. "Wonderful! I read swiftly, and I have a pleasant voice. Anything else?"

"You could use some practice," Josie told him bluntly, making Helen groan with embarrassment. "Well, it is the truth, and that is what he asked for, isn't it?" she tried to reason after Helen glared at her.

"Josie, don't you remember our lesson on tact?" Helen stressed, then threw North an apologetic smile. "A lady does not voice every thought that pops into her mind!"

"Please don't scold, Helen," North interjected. "She is quite right. I do need practice."

Helen thought a minute about how the Reverend Wakelin prepared for his sermons. "If you start writing it tomorrow, perhaps by the time the week rolls by, it will become familiar to you. Perhaps it will help take away your nervousness and give you more confidence."

"Yes! And then you can practice your sermon on us!" Josie added excitedly. "We shall be your congregation, preparing you for the real one on Sunday."

North looked over at Helen, and she found herself moved by the appreciation that was radiating from his beautiful blue eyes. Her heart ached with all the love and affection that seemed to grow each time she was in his presence. There was a hope inside her that still refused to die.

A hope he really could love her and desire to marry her.

"Would you mind doing as Josie has suggested?" he asked, still holding her gaze as if he, too, could not look away. "I wouldn't want to bring a conflict between you and your employers."

"Oh, don't worry about that," Josie answered before Helen could speak. "Mama has been hinting around to Helen that you would make her a good husband." Josie ignored Helen's horrified gasp. "I know she will agree to let us visit you."

With a face she knew was flaming red, Helen watched North's expression to gauge his reaction. She was relieved when he appeared to be happy with that news.

Helen's gaze slowly lowered to Josie, and she saw the young girl looking at her with a sheepish expression. "I'm in quite a lot of trouble, aren't I?" she whispered in an apologetic voice.

"You can be assured of it," Helen whispered back as they entered the main yard of the plantation.

Helen scanned the lawn and noticed for the second time just how many young women were in attendance. Most of them she'd never seen before this day.

And when the sound of the carriage drew everyone's attention, every single female smiled and began to walk straight for the barouche.

There was only one word running through Helen's mind, and it wasn't a nice one.

Competition!

Chapter 9

H ello, Reverend Campbell!" said the one with the huge blue bonnet decorated with lighter blue flowers.

"Yoo-hoo! Over here, Reverend," said the brunette in the bright yellow dress.

"I truly enjoyed your sermon this morning," said the one with the light blond hair as she fluttered her eyelids.

What a liar! Helen thought mean-spiritedly, her mood darkening with each little shrill giggle. He had barely handed Josie and Helen down from the barouche before the ladies surrounded him, all giving North one simpering compliment after the other.

North looked a little dazed, as he appeared to be trying to make sense of their words, since they were talking all at once.

Helen and Josie were both wearing frowns as they watched him being led from them over to where the table of food was set.

"It's like watching a bunch of crabs all trying to grab hold of a baited string at one time," Josie commented. Since Helen had no idea what she was talking about, she would have to take the younger girl's word for it.

"He's certainly not fighting off their attentions," she observed but then felt petty for voicing it aloud.

"I think he's just overwhelmed!"

"Hmm." Helen sounded skeptical as she continued to watch North. They were actually preparing him a plate of food, each one adding to it. They were creating a small mountain not even three men could possibly eat.

"Girls! You've lost him!" Imogene cried for their ears only as she came running hurriedly up to them. "Helen, you must do something!"

She had to be joking! "Mrs. Baumgartner, what can I possibly do? He doesn't seem to mind the attention," Helen told her, and again she heard the jealousy in her tone.

Imogene waved her hand as if to refute her words. "Of course he does." She sucked in a loud breath. "Did you see that?" she asked excitedly as she pointed in North's direction. "He's looking around. . . . See! He looks like he needs rescuing! So *go!*"

All Helen saw was North looking at the pile of food on his plate with something akin to horror and then peering around for a place to sit. That was quickly resolved for him when the blue-bonnet girl led him to an empty table.

"I'm going to get something to eat," Helen said instead of responding to Imogene's urgings. Determinedly she began to walk toward the table of food.

"But, Helen!" Imogene pleaded after her. Still, Helen doggedly kept walking. It took a lot of willpower not to look at North when she passed his table, which was now occupied by all the ladies.

"Helen!" She thought she heard him call, but it could have only been her wishful thinking.

These women were ridiculous in their behavior, Helen observed as she heard them giggle and chatter. In England, never would a girl go up to a man she hadn't been introduced to and speak to him.

It was too bad North couldn't remember that!

Or maybe he did, she amended her thoughts, as she plopped the food on her plate without really paying attention to what she was getting.

She found a table on the other side of the lawn from where North sat with his admirers.

When she realized she had scooped a large amount of collard greens onto her plate, a vegetable that was her least favorite food, she sighed and pushed her plate away. She really wasn't hungry anyway.

She was jealous, and it was silly to feel that way, really. Everyone believed North to be their clergyman and wanted to know him better. And since there was quite a shortage of young, marriageable men in the area, they probably all had higher hopes they could know him *much* better.

" 'It isn't ladylike to pout,' " Josie quoted, as she sat beside her while placing her plate of food on the table. Helen could tell Josie had managed to fill her plate without her mother looking on, for it was filled with slices of cake and pie. " 'It puts one's face in an unattractive position and causes tiny lines to form between one's eyes. . . .' " She paused from her speech, in which she used an exaggerated English accent, and thought a moment. "Or was the 'lines between the eyes' thing for when one is jealous *and* angry?"

Helen sighed. "I suppose I have become a bit fond of North." She nibbled on a piece of bread and then noticed the boiled crawfish on her plate. *How did that nasty little creature get there?* She could never understand how civilized people could get so much enjoyment out of cracking open the outer shells and biting the meat out of the tail with their teeth.

She knew ladies of London's society who would faint dead away at the sight of such a spectacle.

"I may be only thirteen, but I am not blind, Helen. I could tell you were in love with him the moment you realized who he was on that first day. Even Mother agrees."

She spoke like a woman of twenty! "You are too young to know what love is," Helen countered as she carefully picked up the crawfish by one of its pinchers and tossed it onto Josie's plate.

"Oh, thank you!" Josie automatically responded. And just as Helen knew she would, she cracked and peeled the shellfish in no time at all.

Helen shuddered.

"I do know about love." Josie picked up the conversation after she had wiped her hands on her cloth napkin. "My father left behind a title and his father's riches because he loved my mother. One day I'll find love like that." She sighed dreamily as she said this, and Helen didn't remind her of her earlier statement about not even liking boys.

Helen also didn't mention the fact that Josie's father wasn't exactly poor after he was disinherited, either. She wondered if he'd have married Imogene if there had been no inheritance from his mother and if they'd had to start from nothing. She looked across the lawn and saw Robert walk by his wife at that moment. Before continuing to where his friends were standing, he put a hand on her shoulder and squeezed it. A sweet gesture. Perhaps he would have married her no matter what.

"I hope you will find true love, Josie," Helen said instead as she finally allowed her gaze to settle on North. She was startled to see him staring straight at her. She glanced around him and noticed there were other people besides the young women around him now.

North smiled at her, then looked back to the man on his right, who appeared to be speaking to him.

Helen sighed dreamily, already forgetting her earlier jealousy. That smile from North had undone all the hurt she'd felt over being pushed out of the way by the other girls.

It was then she became aware that the blond girl with the fluttery eyes was still sitting next to him. North was looking at her, and she seemed to be telling him something.

Suddenly Helen was struck by a horrible thought. What if North fell in love with someone else? Not only would it make Helen terribly sad, but it could also spell disaster if North got his memory back!

If he fell in love with any of these young ladies and even married one of them, he could wake up one day and realize his whole life was a lie. He and his future wife would be devastated. It would be more disastrous than if he married Helen.

Steps had to be taken to ensure this did not happen!

She was going to have to embarrass herself. There was just no other way about it!

"I'll be right back!" she told Josie as she jumped up from her chair, then all but ran over to where North was sitting. . .still talking to *Blondie*!

What do I say? What do I do? she asked herself over and over as she drew nearer to him. It had to be some reasonable excuse to pull him away from his table and from *her*!

"Uh. . .Reverend. . .uh. . .Campbell!" she stuttered as she tried to catch her breath and remember what to call him. "I. . .uh. . ."

She drew a complete blank. She glanced about the table and noticed every eye was on her, curious as to what she was about to say.

"Uh. . ." Nothing. She wondered if this was how North felt this morning when he was trying to deliver his sermon. Her eyes strayed to the blond, and there was a certain smirk about her rosy lips that suggested she knew what Helen was up to.

"What's wrong, Miss Nichols?" North asked, his tone more questioning than concerned.

"Uh. . ." She stalled again. She glanced at the blond again and noticed she was back fluttering her eyes at North, trying to get his attention.

It was the eye-fluttering thing that inspired her.

She began to bat only one of her eyes. "My eye!" Batting one eye was not an easy thing to do. "I believe there is something in it."

North looked at her with a somewhat bemused expression. "It looked fine just a moment ago."

"It comes and goes," she answered quickly, realizing how ridiculous she sounded. But since she had begun the ruse, she might as well finish it. "Would you mind stepping over there in the sunlight and looking at it for me?" She pointed to a spot far from the shaded area they were seated in.

"Pardon me, but might I be of some help?" the man beside North questioned, finally bringing all the attention off Helen and onto him. "I am Dr. Giles. I have a practice in New Orleans, but I come through Golden Bay every month to check on everyone here. Why don't I take a look at it?"

"Oh. . ." Helen sounded like a deflating balloon. Just like her bright ideas! "I suppose that would be all right," she relented after coming up with no reasonable excuse to turn down his offer of help.

"I'll walk with you," North chimed in, and Helen could have kissed him. Did he know what she'd been up to? "I will hold your hand while the doctor performs the surgery," he added teasingly. One quick glance at his eyes told her she hadn't fooled him one bit.

"Never take the eyes lightly, Reverend," the doctor cautioned, unaware of Helen's subterfuge. "One tiny shard of wood or glass can cause a world of damage."

"Of course, Doctor," North answered contritely as they followed the older man, who was dressed rather more like the dandies of the English ton than the usual American mode of dress she'd seen thus far. His coat was a rich gold color with red trim at the sleeves and lapel. The vest underneath matched the ruby color of the trim and was made of shiny brocade. Considering every other man at the picnic wore more somber colors in shades of black, gray, and brown, he quite stood out.

Helen felt ridiculous as Dr. Giles examined her eye. He kept making the sound *mm-hmm*, and she wondered if he actually saw anything.

He didn't. "I'm afraid I cannot tell you the source of your irritation," he finally told her, looking perplexed.

Helen could have told him her source of irritation had blond hair and was flirting with the man she loved. Instead she thanked him for at least going to the trouble of examining her. "Perhaps the wind blew it out," she offered.

He accepted that it could have happened, and both she and North walked him back to the table.

Blondie was still there. Waiting. She was already smiling at him, and the fluttering eyelids would certainly be next! "Nor. . .uh. . .Reverend! Would you walk me back to my table? I just wanted to have a word with you for a minute."

North didn't even look surprised by her request. "Of course. Will you excuse me?" he asked to the table at large, and Helen was glad to notice he didn't so much as glance at the blond.

"If you wanted to talk to me, Helen, there was no need to go to such theatrics. Next time, just ask," he told her in a low voice as he smiled at her, flashing his even, white teeth.

Helen's face felt heated with embarrassment. "I noticed the blond girl was so ill-manneredly monopolizing all your time, and so I thought that since you might not know how to extricate yourself without hurting her feelings, I tried to do it for you," she offered, the lengthy explanation hardly making sense even to her.

But North agreed. "Aye, I was feeling quite uncomfortable. I might not remember much, but I do know the young ladies here are not skilled in the art of ladylike manner or etiquette. These are some of the finest families in the area, and yet I do not understand why this facet of their children's upbringing is overlooked."

"Many of the English families are not former nobility such as Robert Baumgartner is but have come from little or nothing and become wealthy with hard work. I've heard the Creole plantations are a little different because more of them are from aristocratic families hailing from mostly France and Spain." Helen shrugged. "That is why I am here. The Baumgartners wanted to make sure their younger daughter was taught those things."

They both looked to see Josie still sitting at the table, stuffing cake into her mouth. Helen noticed there was white frosting smudged on both cheeks, and she, along with North, began to laugh. "Whether she will follow your teachings is quite another thing altogether."

Helen laughed more. "I'm afraid you are right. Even her sister was having a tough time adjusting to all the rules of society when last I saw her." Helen thought about the beautiful and friendly Claudia Baumgartner whom she'd met while visiting London with Christina. "Claudia is determined to be the lady that her grandfather, the Marquis of Moreland, wants her to be, yet I can't help feeling she's very unhappy. It's like seeing a caged tiger at a circus that you know just longs to be free."

"Did I ever meet her?" North asked, and Helen remembered that indeed she had seen him talking to her once.

"I believe you had been introduced," she answered truthfully, for she had no idea if he was better acquainted with her or not.

North and Helen sat down at the table, and Josie chose that moment to get up, announcing she was going for another round.

North laughed. "She is going to be sick."

"Not if Mrs. Baumgartner sees her!" Helen peered over her shoulder to where Josie had just reached the dessert table. Just as she knew she would, her mother was there to intercept and lead her over to the regular food.

They chatted for a moment, topics ranging all the way from the weather to the people they'd met in Golden Bay. Finally their words drifted away, and for a sweet moment, they sat looking into one another's eyes, neither looking away. Helen was surprised to have no feeling of awkwardness, and she got the impression he felt the same.

"Helen, if I may be so bold as to ask this, what is there between you and me?" he suddenly came out with, surprising them both. He sat back, rubbing a hand over his face. "I am sorry to have spoken so forcibly out of turn," he began to apologize.

"No, it is all right," Helen expressed, her heart pounding with fear and expectation all at one time. "You cannot remember anything, so—"

"But you see, it is not that reason for which I am speaking." He looked around as if to see if anyone had heard his impassioned statement, and then let out a breath. "I am experiencing feelings for you I feel did not just begin when I first saw you two weeks ago. It's as though my heart remembers even though my mind cannot. I know we did not act upon them, but was there a mutual attraction between us?"

Helen could only be confused by his words. North had never given her any indication he felt anything but friendship for her when they were in England. He thought her pretty—this much she knew from Christina—but wouldn't she have sensed anything deeper from him? When he looked at her with his dazzling, friendly smile, wouldn't she have read something more in the depths of his blue gaze?

She had certainly looked hard enough for any sign, any shred of love or deep affection.

She had lied to this man and misled him on so many things. And even though she had the golden opportunity to make him believe there was more between them so that he would feel more confident to pursue her, she just couldn't tell another lie.

"I will tell you honestly, North, that I never knew you thought of me as anything but a friend. If you felt more, then I was not aware of it," she told him, careful not to mention her own feelings.

North shook his head. "I know I must have, Helen. The question is, why did I not act upon it? Why did I not call upon you and pursue what I know I must have been feeling in my heart?"

Helen tried to comprehend what he was telling her, but she couldn't believe it. Surely he had to be wrong! North had feelings for her when he knew he was a duke?

Helen thought back on the times she last saw him and realized that he started to avoid her at the balls she would attend. He would say no more than a few words before he'd excuse himself to go talk to a friend and such. Could it have been because he liked her more than he should yet saw no hope in it?

Helen looked at North, with his lock of golden hair falling in a wave over his brow and the stylish yet simply made suit, which was tight about his shoulders. His handsome looks and elegance did not fit the image everyone had put him in. They thought he was a clergyman, so they did not look past that title to grasp that this was no ordinary, common man.

"Perhaps your family would not have approved of me. I am, after all, just a gentleman farmer's daughter. They could have been pressuring you to settle on a woman of means," she offered truthfully.

"Hmm," North sounded, rubbing his chin thoughtfully. "I had not thought of that. It would seem like, judging from my attire, my family may have been in a financial quandary. Perhaps they were pressuring me to find an heiress," he murmured more to himself than to her, as if he were trying to reason it all out.

Abruptly he raised his head and smiled like a man who knew all the answers. "I have it all figured out!" he declared.

Helen felt as though her heart had fallen to the pit of her belly. "You remember everything?" she asked, trying not to sound dismayed by that prospect.

North, however, shook his head. "Unfortunately no, but I have been struck with insight! I know the reason I came to America!"

Helen blinked, trying to adjust to the path their conversation had taken. With North, she felt like she was often riding on a wild carriage ride, not knowing where they were heading or what sudden turns they might take. "It wasn't to be their preacher?" she offered, interested to know what scenario his mind had conjured up.

"Helen, I chose Louisiana because I knew you were going to be here!"

Chapter 10

One week then two passed, yet Helen could not stop thinking about North's words at the picnic. Though she tried to dissuade him from his reasoning, he would not be influenced. To him, everything made perfect sense, and he treated his "epiphany," as he called it, almost like it was a true memory.

Helen frankly did not know what to do or say when North wanted to talk about it. Which he did—quite a lot. He wanted to know about each meeting they had, what they said, and how they treated one another.

It was so taxing on her poor nerves that Helen began to make excuses to stay away from his house. But that didn't work because he would just come down to the plantation to see her. It was an easy thing to do since he had an ally in the house, namely Imogene Baumgartner.

One good thing that happened was that North's preaching, thanks to Josie and Helen's helping him prepare, was greatly improved on the next Sunday, and one might say even inspiring on the third one. He seemed to be acclimating himself within the community as he visited families and prayed for their sick. As odd as it was, he seemed to be thriving in the occupation he was never meant to perform.

Helen would give herself headaches at night just thinking about the what-ifs. What if he never got his memory back? Would he be happy and content as Hamish Campbell? What if he didn't remember until he was fifty? Would he want to rush back to England and try to acclimate himself to his old life, or would he decide to continue as a preacher?

Helen was certainly no philosopher about life's mysteries, but it sure opened her mind to possibilities outside what she'd always known. She even raised the question to herself as to whether God had, indeed, meant for North to take poor Hamish Campbell's place.

But He didn't mean for you to lie and break one of His commandments, a voice would always remind her whenever she began to justify herself and her actions.

A knock sounded at her door, pulling Helen from her pondering. It was Monday morning, and she was supposed to have been brushing her hair but had, as usual, gotten lost in her thoughts.

After Helen called out for her visitor to come in, Imogene Baumgartner walked into the room, her face clearly upset. "Helen, I have just heard the most devastating news," she stated right away, her voice full of sorrow as she pulled a chair up so she could sit beside Helen.

Helen immediately thought of North. "Has something happened to Reverend Campbell?" she cried, not even realizing how easily his false name just rolled off her tongue.

Imogene quickly assured her that wasn't it. She placed her hand over Helen's and told her, "It concerns Lord Trevor Kent, the Duke of Northingshire, who is related to our friends at the Kent plantation."

Uh-oh, Helen thought with mounting dread. In the few weeks North had been in Golden Bay, not once had she considered that if North were here, everyone else in the world would presume he was dead. How incredibly selfish and single-minded she had been!

"I'm afraid he has been declared missing and assumed to be dead," Imogene said gently, speaking the words Helen had already assumed would be the news. "I believe Josie said you knew him?"

Helen glanced at her and then quickly lowered her eyes, hoping to give her employer the notion that she was shocked by the news. "Yes, but I knew him only as an acquaintance while I was in England," she said softly and carefully, trying not to lie yet not wanting Imogene to know of her feelings for the duke.

"Oh, then I am truly sorry," she offered in condolence as she patted Helen's hand again. "I have often heard from the Kents of what a fine man he'd been and how generous he was to his friends and loved ones. I had been hoping to meet him."

Helen listened to Imogene and heard her sigh sadly. "He was very nice to me when I first met him," Helen said, feeling like she needed to say something. In truth, she felt sick inside as she thought of his poor relatives and what they must be going through. Then she asked, trying to keep the worry from her voice, "Have they notified his family in England?"

She was relieved when Imogene shook her head. "No, they said they would search a little longer before they sent word. They are hoping against all odds that he still lives."

Helen wanted to cry. What was she to do now? Again the situation had grown more complicated.

"Well, I'll leave you to your grooming," the older lady said, as she got up from her seat and straightened the bow on the high waist of her fawn-colored morning dress. She was almost at the door when she seemed to suddenly remember something. "Oh! I also wanted to ask a favor of you."

Helen, still overwhelmed by this latest obstacle, nodded absently.

"Pierre, poor dear, is sick this morning with what appears to be some sort of stomach ailment. Is there any way you and Josie could take the barouche and make sure Reverend Campbell has all he needs today? Pierre tells me he still burns everything he tries to cook, and I know you have some knowledge in this area. . . ?" She let her voice drift off in a question.

Helen managed to curve her lips into a smile that she truly did not feel. "Of course I'll go."

"Excellent! I normally would have one of the house servants go, but since I know you like to spend time with him, I didn't think you would mind," she told her in a gentle, teasing tone and then left the room.

Yes, Helen loved spending time with North; but the more she was in his presence, despite their growing feelings for one another, the more she got the feeling that a future between them could never be.

⤞⤝

There was a great deal of self-pity in North's thoughts and even in his walk as he practically dragged himself from his little house out to the barn. He'd sat in his house an hour after he'd received word that Pierre wouldn't arrive, hoping someone would be sent as a replacement.

No one came.

So he came to terms with the fact that if he didn't go out and retrieve the milk and eggs himself, plus get a slab of bacon from the underground ceramic urns that served as a way to keep his food cool, he was going to starve.

Well, he amended to himself, he would certainly be very hungry. That would lead to his being cranky, and he would be unable to begin to study his new sermon for the upcoming Sunday.

Since he was actually beginning to enjoy his studies of the Bible and finding just the right message to share with his congregation, he decided to search for nourishment.

So here he was, about to enter his least favorite place in this world. . .his barn.

He had to admit he was getting better at milking the cow, although he managed to connive Pierre into doing it most days.

Thankfully, this morning Queen Mary must have "been in the mood" because she gave over her milk without a lot of fuss. The chickens were another matter altogether, however. They seemed not at all like themselves; instead, they were restless, jittery, and unwilling to part with their eggs as usual.

He finally managed to grab a few but not without war wounds to show for his struggle.

He'd no sooner swung open his heavy barn door when he spotted the source of his chickens' anxieties. There, stretched out straight with his mouth wide open toward North, was the most ferocious, ugly beast he'd ever encountered.

Alligator!

What had he heard about them? His mind raced. Did they attack? Did they eat humans? The creature chose that moment to snap his jaws shut and crawl forward a couple of inches as if showing North what he was capable of.

North didn't doubt him one little bit!

The wise course of action at this moment, he knew, would be to get away from the alligator as quickly as possible. The problem was that when the reptile moved forward, he blocked the door from being shut, and there was no other door in the barn.

Except. . .

North glanced around to gauge the distance between himself and the ladder to the loft. From there he could try to jump out of the hayloft door.

Hopefully he would not break a leg and arm in the process!

As he turned and sprinted toward the ladder, he held tight to his bucket of milk and basket of eggs. Climbing was a lot more difficult with them, but there was no way he was letting that beast take what he'd worked so hard to get!

Once he was out of harm's way, North watched the alligator to see if it would go away.

It didn't.

For what seemed like hours but actually was only minutes, the creature just lay there, not moving one muscle, despite the fact that his animals were all restless and moving about noisily.

Even *they* recognized danger.

After a few more minutes, North concluded he was going to have to try to jump from the loft. For all he knew, it might be days before the creature would decide to leave.

It took him a moment to locate a rope to lower his items. He was in the process of tying them together when he heard a movement from below. Quickly North scrambled to the loft door leading to the outside and peered down.

He nearly toppled out of the small door when he spotted Sam cradling the now-dead alligator in his arms as he walked out of his barn.

"What are you doing here?" he barked brusquely. He suddenly felt ridiculous, hiding up in his hayloft while the Indian had taken no more than a few seconds to take care of the problem.

Sam didn't so much as glance up as he tied the reptile to the back of his horse. The black gelding stirred in protest because of the weight of his new passenger. "Rescuing you from an alligator, preacher man," he answered sardonically, as he checked then double-checked his knots.

North, feeling less than a man, backed away from the small door and, with his milk and eggs, made his way back down the ladder. He placed his goods down on a table and then walked out to meet Sam. North noticed him examining his small garden.

"I have something to put on the soil of these carrots that will help them grow," Sam offered. Again he hadn't even looked up to see North walking toward him, and North was sure he hadn't made a sound while walking on the soft grass.

"Thank you, but I have my own way of gardening," he answered, knowing it was childish but finding it hard not to show his irritation where the swaggering Indian was concerned.

North heard Sam make a snorting sound, which just made him more irate.

"How many gardens have you planted?" Sam asked, this time standing up and looking straight at North. The Indian had an unnerving stare.

North couldn't know for sure, but he was almost certain he'd never even *walked* around a vegetable garden in his entire life. "Is there a reason for this visit?"

Sam smirked at him, still giving him that odd stare. It made North, for the first time, wonder if he'd been a violent man in his past, because he truly wanted to hit him.

The truth was, however, that North felt strangely inferior to the Choctaw. He seemed to be a man of the earth, capable of defending, feeding, and protecting himself and anyone he cared about. He appeared comfortable with this wild, untamed land, whereas North constantly felt like an outsider.

North was smart enough to know he shouldn't compare himself to the Indian, because they were raised in two different worlds and taught very different things, but he found he did anyway.

He hated not being able to do simple things for himself. He even had trouble dressing himself and was almost certain he'd had a servant to do it for him in Scotland.

He didn't want to be pampered and waited on. He didn't want the kind of life he saw the plantation owners leading, where servants or slaves did everything for them and they did nothing for themselves.

"In your country, what do you do when another man wants the lady who you want?" Sam asked, bringing North's attention back to the smirk he was still sporting.

North had a feeling this was the reason why Sam had come. "The lady chooses the one she loves," he stated with confidence, knowing with all his heart that Helen was falling in love with him. It was in every glance, every smile she gave him. As far as he was concerned, Sam wasn't a rival for her affections.

Sam surprised him by bursting out with a loud, mocking sort of laugh—the kind that really set North's teeth on edge. "You let your women decide? Your people do things peculiarly!"

"And just how do *your people* do things?" North countered. "Throw the women over your horses and whisk them off to your caves until they relent?"

"Since we don't have caves in Louisiana," Sam began, his voice slow and deliberate as though he were talking to a child, "we issue a challenge to our opponent."

North didn't like the sound of that. With a disapproving frown, he told him, "Are we talking about a duel? Because I am most certain they are illegal."

Sam sighed and looked skyward as if trying to hold on to his patience. "This is another thing that irritates me with *your* people. You jump right away to the worst conclusion." He turned and walked back to his horse and withdrew a bow. "This is what I am talking about. A challenge. A contest to see who the better man is."

North eyed the bow and made every effort to pretend to be unfamiliar with one. He knew instinctively that he was familiar with how to handle the weapon. "You want to challenge me to an archery contest?" North asked, to make sure he understood that they weren't going to be shooting arrows at each other. "And if I don't know how to handle a bow. . . ?"

Sam shrugged, his overconfident smirk back on his face. "There are always guns or knives."

North wanted so badly to accept the Indian's offer and show him that he was just as much of a man as Sam was. But he had the distinct feeling Helen would not be pleased, and neither would his congregation, once they found out their preacher was in a contest to win a girl's affections!

"Well, Sam, as interesting as that sounds, I will have to turn your offer of challenge down," he told him and watched the Indian's face turn to disappointment.

North couldn't help but wonder if the Indian was trying to befriend him in his own odd little way. "But I would love to join you for target practice sometime. Maybe even try my hand at hunting," North impulsively offered, just to see if he would accept.

Sam appeared interested but only after he studied North a moment, unsure of the preacher's motives. "I will come by in two days," he told him and then pointed toward the alligator. "I'll bring you half of the meat I get from the alligator tail, too."

Alligator tail? North didn't say a word. He didn't want Sam thinking he was less of a man because he'd never eaten any. He'd eat every bite if it killed him!

Sam gathered the horse's reins and began to walk off when he unexpectedly stopped and turned for one last comment. "I am still determined to marry Helen Nichols, preacher man," he stated, wanting that particular point understood.

"So am I," North countered, knowing he truly did want nothing more than to marry Helen.

They exchanged a measuring look, and then without another word, Sam grinned and turned to walk away.

Both were surprised to see Helen come from around the house with Josie.

"Sam!" she exclaimed, clearly shocked to see him. "What are you doing here?"

"Alligator hunting" was all Sam said as he walked past her, tugging his horse behind him.

Helen opened her mouth as if to say something as she turned to watch him walk away, but no words seemed to come out.

"Did you really go alligator hunting, Reverend North?" Josie asked, using her own version of his name, as she ran up to him, her long, bound hair bouncing as she went.

North reached out and gave her hair a playful yank that made her giggle. There was absolutely no way he was going to tell them what really happened. A man had to maintain some sort of dignity. "Something like that."

"You weren't fighting with him, were you?" Helen asked as she, too, walked up to meet him. "Sam can be a little overbearing, but I wouldn't let him aggravate you. He lives by a whole different set of rules than any other man I know."

North reached out and pulled a ladybug off Helen's shoulder. It was interesting to note that she didn't flinch or jerk away from his touch. Instead she looked at his hand and smiled as the red bug flew away. "Sam *is* very different from most white men," he noted, watching to see what her reaction would be to his next words. "Some women like the outdoorsy, rough-and-tough type that he is."

He almost laughed when Helen actually shuddered. "I don't know of any woman who enjoys polite society and gently bred manners who would want Sam as a husband!" she stated emphatically.

"I would!" Josie piped up, causing both of the adults to gape at her with astonishment. "He wouldn't care if I had any manners at all!"

Helen shook her head disapprovingly. "You will not get out of learning your lessons on the art of curtsying today, so stop trying."

Josie made a *humph* sound and folded her arms defiantly at her chest. "Why do I need to learn that? I'm an American! We don't bow down to anyone!"

North exchanged a long-suffering glance with Helen; then she looked back down and answered, "Your sister will one day be the Marchioness of Moreland. She will have to bow before the king, and you and your parents will have to do the same thing."

Josie rolled her eyes and made a growling noise. "I'm going to talk to the chickens. At least there I don't have to be polite or remember my manners."

Helen and North laughed softly as the young girl stomped into the barn.

"You know, if Sam can wait a bit, Josie just might be the perfect match for him," North observed. "But you can't always choose the person you fall in love with. And if he is truly in love with you, he might not want anyone else."

North saw a sadness fall over Helen's face as she murmured wistfully, "That's true."

He bent his head toward her and brought her chin up so she was looking directly into his eyes. "Helen," he began, almost afraid to ask the question. "Were you once in love with someone?"

She just stared at him for a moment, and North wasn't altogether sure she was going to answer him. But finally she did, and the answer hit him squarely in the heart. "Yes, once. A few years ago."

His hand was still on her chin, and she didn't seem to mind when his thumb began to softly caress the skin along her jawline. "What happened?"

"Nothing. He was not a man of my station. In fact, he was way above it." She paused as if she were gauging his reaction. "He was a nobleman, and though we were friends, he chose not to pursue a relationship outside of that friendship."

A fire lit within North's heart, and indignation for her hurt flowed from his lips. "That is preposterous!" he articulated passionately. "To throw away a chance at love that may only come once in one's lifetime, just because of one's birth, is an injustice to God and all He created us to be."

He spoke it with such fervor and with such vehemence that North had the feeling he'd grappled with this very situation before; only it had been he who'd faced such a decision.

He realized then that Helen was looking at him as if she didn't believe a word he said.

Chapter 11

Helen could only stare at North with marked disbelief as he moved his hand from her chin to run it through his hair in a gesture of perplexity. It wasn't so much what he said but *how* he said it. It was like someone trying to make a case for himself.

What *did* that mean? Did he once grapple with the same feelings—go through the same situation?

Helen could barely think it, although she couldn't help but hope for it.

Had he been in love with her after all?

But another thought followed directly after that one—if he *had* been in love, he hadn't acted on his feelings. In fact, he'd even started seeking her out less and less at gatherings.

What did *that* mean?

Finally she voiced part of her musings. "You speak as though you have struggled with this dilemma yourself. Did you remember something?"

She held her breath until she saw him shake his head no. "It's odd, really. I feel as though I've made the same argument before, but where? Had you once told me this? Is that what I'm remembering?"

Helen shook her head. "No, I've never told anyone except my best friend, Christina." And she had always tried to discourage Helen from letting her attraction to North grow, for she feared Helen would be hurt.

North looked so confused and seemed to be trying hard to remember something that would make sense to him. It compelled Helen to reach out spontaneously to hold his hand. The gesture seemed to freeze North for a moment, as his eyes focused on their hands.

Uh-oh. She was being too familiar. Too forward. "I'm sorry, I didn't mean. . . ," she began to ramble as she tried to pull her hand away, but he held fast and interrupted her.

"No! Please. . . ," he cried softly as he looked directly into her eyes, his own searching as if trying to decipher her thoughts. "I like it that you feel so comfortable with me."

She smiled shyly, aware of the change of mood between them—of how important this particular moment seemed to be. Her feelings were so overwhelming to her that she had to remind herself even to breathe.

"I just need to ask you one thing," he said softly, pulling her closer to him.

"Are you still in love with the nobleman?"

Now that is a tricky question, Helen thought, panicking for a brief instant. But as she thought of the man she knew in England versus the man she knew him to be here in America, she knew she could answer truthfully. "No, my feelings are not what they were."

North emitted a breath of relief as he looked down for a moment and took her other hand, bringing both of them to his lips. "Helen, you must know of the growing feelings I have for you." She nodded jerkily, still having a hard time comprehending she was standing so close to North. "I would like to openly begin calling on you," he explained. "That would mean everyone would know you and I have an affection for one another, and that includes the congregation. You might come under some scrutiny, so I wanted to warn you beforeha—"

Helen stopped him by putting her fingers over his lips. "Yes," she gushed excitedly, unable to contain her joy.

He took hold of her hand again. "Are you sure?"

She nodded, and they stared into one another's eyes again. Helen forgot that almost everything about their relationship was built on a lie. She forgot the guilt she'd been under and the fear of what might happen in the future. For this one moment, she was going to revel in the love she had carried for so long for this man and remember it when she was old and alone with nothing but memories to get her through.

North leaned forward to brush a stray hair that had blown across her cheek, and when Helen turned to see what he was doing, they found themselves nose to nose.

North paused and looked at her searchingly. And whatever he'd been looking for, he must have found, for he gently pressed a kiss to her lips.

Helen held tight to his hand as his mouth gently caressed hers. Her heart was beating madly, and her mind was swirling, trying to reconcile her old emotions with the brand-new feelings she was experiencing. All the romance and gothic books she had ever read had not even been close to describing the feeling of being in his arms and being kissed by him.

Perhaps God felt sorry for her a little bit, and since He knew she would probably never live down the scandal of what she'd done to North and therefore never find a man who would want to marry her, He was giving her this little bit of bliss to live the rest of her life on.

Helen almost protested when he finally drew his head back and smiled at her. But the wonder in his eyes filled her heart with gladness as he gazed at her one last time before stepping away.

Helen suspected that North must have kissed a half-dozen or more women in his lifetime. But he didn't remember any of them, and kissing her was like his first time.

"I can't wait to tell Mama you kissed him!" Josie exclaimed, causing them to jump farther apart and guiltily look at the young girl.

Helen swallowed and threw North a nervous glance. "Uh, Josie, it might not be a good idea to tell your mother about this."

Josie frowned. "Oh, why not? I have to tell somebody!" She smiled, apparently coming up with a better idea. "I know! I'll tell Sam!"

"No!" Both Helen and North yelled out to her at the same time.

"You don't want to hurt his feelings, do you?" Helen tried to reason in a softer tone.

"Well, what good is it for me to know if I can't brag about knowing something that no one else knows?"

Helen sighed, rubbing her temples, wondering if the child could ever be tamed. "Josie, later we shall discuss the merits of guarding our tongues."

"Why don't the two of you get the milk and eggs from the barn, and I'll get the bacon from the urns," North suggested, as he must have known Helen was growing weary of dealing with the young girl.

He knew her so well. "Yes, let's do that!" she agreed, eager to take everyone's mind off the kiss they had just shared.

Well, maybe not everyone should forget. Helen certainly could never forget it, and she had a feeling North wouldn't, either. Now if only Josie *would*!

The two of them took North's food into the kitchen, and she began to prepare the skillet over the fire. A knock sounded at the door.

Josie ran to open it. "Hi, Mrs. Chauvin!" she greeted, and Helen could hear a female voice telling her something from outside.

Helen got up and walked to the door to find Marie Chauvin standing there, holding what looked to be a letter.

"Oh! Hello, Helen," Marie greeted, surprised at finding Helen in the preacher's house. "Is the reverend here?"

Helen wondered what Marie was thinking. The middle-aged French woman, who was petite in stature and a little plump, was the wife of the area blacksmith and one of the nicest ladies Helen had met in the area. She was the perfect person to handle everyone's mail because she was not a gossip or nosey by any means. She knew the woman would not draw false conclusions and think the worst. However, Helen wanted to make it clear why she was here at North's house.

"He is around back, I believe. Josie and I were sent by Mrs. Baumgartner to make sure Reverend Campbell had breakfast. Pierre is sick and unable to help him today."

Marie smiled at the explanation, seeming to accept it at face value. "Ah yes. I know my husband would not be able to do one thing for himself if I were not there to do it for him. He'd probably starve."

Helen chuckled. "It was the same with my father," she told her. She looked down at the paper Marie was holding. "Did you need to tell him something? I know that he should be back any minute."

Marie smiled and waved the note in front of her face. "No, no. I'll just leave this with you, and you can pass it on to the reverend. I believe it's a letter from his sister, judging by the name and the postmark from Scotland. I remember my husband telling me he'd mentioned living with his sister in some of the correspondence we had with him."

It took everything in Helen to hide the dismay she was feeling as she reached out and took the letter.

She and Marie exchanged a little more small talk, which she could barely remember later; then Marie left.

For a moment she found herself just staring down at the letter with the scratchy penmanship addressed to Hamish Campbell. She couldn't help but feel sorrow for his sister and the fact that somehow she had to be told her brother was missing or most probably dead.

But how could Helen do that without North trying to write her back?

The web of deceit and the problems it was causing were growing thicker and more intricate every single day. When she got one thing under control, something else would pop up that made the situation worse.

"How come he never mentions his sister?" Josie asked. Helen could tell she was dying to read it.

So was Helen.

"Perhaps it makes him sad to talk about her since she is so far away," Helen prevaricated. She noticed how easily false excuses just rolled off her tongue.

That definitely wasn't a talent to be proud of.

She then realized she had to give the letter to North when they were alone so he didn't make a slip and say he didn't know he had a sister or something equally as telling. Helen truly wished she could just hide the letter from him and write one back to the woman, giving her the bad news.

But Marie might ask him about receiving it. Then Helen would be in even more trouble.

What a calamity!

"Josie, would you see to the fire while I go and show this to North?"

In typical fashion, Josie made a face of protest but did as she was asked. The younger girl was obedient for the most part, even though she was extremely vocal about her opinions.

North was just coming up the side steps of the porch when Helen met him. He smiled at her in a way that let Helen know he was still thinking about their kiss and the new commitment they'd made to one another.

It was such a thrilling feeling to know he liked her so much.

It was just too bad their relationship was built on nothing but deceit.

"North, Marie Chauvin came by to give you this. I wanted to make sure Josie wasn't around so you wouldn't be surprised to know that it is probably from your sister."

North looked at the letter she was holding out without even trying to take it from her. In fact, he looked at it as if he didn't want to open it at all.

His eyes flew back to hers, questioning. "I have a sister?"

Helen scrambled to find the right thing to say. "I didn't know," she explained, going with the truth. "I've never heard you mention a sister."

North looked back down at the letter, a frown of concentration on his face as he was trying to remember something. . .anything!

Slowly he reached out and took it from her. He read the name *Fiona Campbell* written above the seal. For a moment he seemed as though he wasn't going to open it.

Finally he lifted the seal and quickly read through the brief letter. "It is from my sister," he told her, his eyes still focused on the paper. "She writes that all is well in Melrose and for me not to worry about her. She says she has recently been called upon by a local sheep farmer whom she knows I would approve of." North looked up at Helen with troubled eyes. "She urges me to write back as soon as possible, Helen, but how can I when I can't even remember her?"

Helen's heart broke at the misery pouring from his voice and the despair in his eyes. Reaching out, she put her hand on his arm in a comforting gesture. "I will help you write it. There is no reason to tell her you've lost your memory. Just tell her about your church and the people living here."

He smiled at her and placed his hand atop hers. "I will tell her about you, too," he said low and tender.

Helen thought that was the sweetest thing she'd ever been told. Unfortunately she would have to find a way to make sure any letter that was written would never make it to Fiona Campbell's door.

She smiled at him, trying not to show how unsettled she was by this latest problem in her life. "Why don't I come by tomorrow and help you write it?"

He grinned broadly at her. "Why not today? Or are you just trying to come up with an excuse to see me tomorrow, also?" He tucked her hand in his arm and began to lead her to the door.

Actually she needed time to come up with a plan. She did, however, like being with him any time she could. "I don't think I'll answer that, for I fear you are becoming too sure of yourself!"

North laughed as he opened the door and allowed her to enter first. "Ah! So that is the reason for the delay!"

She pretended to sniff at his comment as she stuck her chin up and looked down her nose at him. "Nonsense! Josie and I have lessons to finish, that is all."

"Ugh!" Josie sounded with more than a little disgust. "She never forgets!" she exclaimed with marked disbelief as she set the skillet down noisily on the metal rack of the fireplace.

Helen exchanged a look with North, and her heart skipped a beat when he teasingly winked at her. "Perhaps tomorrow I can talk her into a picnic that would take up most of the afternoon and therefore most of your lesson time," North suggested to Josie but kept his gaze on Helen.

Helen pretended not to like that idea. "I don't know. . . ."

"Oh, please say yes, Helen. A picnic sounds like such fun!" Josie pleaded, practically jumping up and down with excitement.

Helen thought a moment and then smiled at Josie. "I know! I can teach you how a lady makes polite conversation during a picnic or some other sort of gathering. I have so many—"

"Do you see what I mean, Reverend? She never lets me take a day off from my studies!"

North bent down to Josie and whispered in her ear, though it was plenty loud enough for Helen to hear. "Perhaps I can distract her tomorrow so you can play or go fishing."

He straightened and looked back at Helen. She hadn't even realized how much time passed as they stared into one another's eyes until Josie pulled on North's coat and motioned with her finger for him to bend down to her.

With an equally loud whisper, she told him, "If you could just keep staring at her like that for a few more hours, I might be able to miss today's lessons, too!"

North laughed, and Helen felt her face heat up with embarrassment. With determination, she grabbed the basket of eggs and made her way to the skillet, ignoring North when he asked her if she knew what she was doing.

Chapter 12

The next morning, North woke to the wonderful smell of bacon frying and the sound of a French song being badly sung, bringing him to the conclusion that Pierre was in his house.

"Good morning, monsieur!" The smiling black man greeted North as he walked into the room. Pierre had just placed the freshly fried eggs on the table.

"Good morning, Pierre," he greeted as he looked at his friend carefully. "Are you quite sure you are well enough to be here?"

"Of course," he assured him. He set a glass of milk beside North's plate. "It was only one of those maladies that lasts about three-fourths of the day. By the time the sun had started setting, I was feeling better."

"Well, I said many prayers for you, and I'm ashamed to say some of them were very selfish ones on my part," he admitted honestly with a sheepish grin. "I hate to admit it, but I am not a man who is used to taking care of himself."

Pierre sat across from him and sipped on a cup of coffee, a beverage he was often fond of drinking. "You are not telling me anything I do not know, monsieur."

North frowned. "Am I so obviously inept?"

Pierre held up his hand and shook his head. "No, no, monsieur!" he assured. "But I see what no one else sees since I am here all day." He seemed to study him through the coffee's steam. "You seek to change, monsieur?"

North leaned forward, eager to talk to someone about what he'd been thinking over. "I do, Pierre. I suppose I've had things done for me all my life, and now that I'm here"—he threw his arms wide—"I see men who are well respected who do things for themselves. They are not waited on hand and foot!" he finished in an impassioned voice. He was discomfited to realize his voice had risen, and he was practically shouting.

But it didn't seem to faze Pierre. "If you are determined to change, then you can change, but it will take dedication," he stated firmly. "The important matter here is that you show a desire. Most men are satisfied to stay where they are and settle for what life has brought them."

Pierre was truly an amazing person. If all men were as passionate about what they believed and what they wanted out of life as he was, the world would be a greater place to live. Every day he and North talked about everything from the war to slavery and politics and even debated the merits of Cajun French cuisine versus true French. Pierre had an opinion for everything and profound insights about things North was sure he'd never even thought about.

They even discussed God and the Bible, and even then, he loved to hear Pierre's convictions about certain matters and how he was so careful to live his life the way he felt God was leading him, taking advantage of every open door.

That was the way North so wanted to be. He wanted to be a man God could look down upon and say, "He is a man after My own heart!"

The two of them chatted a bit more, and then Pierre remembered something. "Oh yes! I forgot to tell you I received good news yesterday. My sister, who lives in New Orleans, had a fine baby boy. It is her first boy after giving birth to four girls, so everyone is happy about the *le petit garçon*," he told North proudly and went on to tell what else his sister had written in a letter. North barely heard him.

A baby. North suddenly had a flash of a genuine memory of holding a baby. Afraid to even move lest he do something to make the memory disappear, North slowly closed his eyes and concentrated on what he was seeing in his mind.

He was in a garden filled with brightly colored flowers, and he was dressed in a very fine navy suit. A baby in a linen dressing gown was in his hands, and he was holding the infant up, talking nonsense to him, causing the dark-headed child to laugh.

He wasn't alone in the garden! With him were a man and two ladies. The man with dark brown curly hair was chatting with a lovely redhead. He knew instinctively they were in love with one another.

Suddenly the other woman, a beauty with wisps of black curls falling about her rosy cheeks, sat beside him. He looked over to her and felt a tugging at his heart like it always did whenever she was around. She reached for the baby, and he gave him to her. He watched her lovingly kiss the infant on the head.

"North?" She looked up at him, and he noticed it was his Helen.

"Monsieur Campbell?" Pierre called out again, causing the memory to suddenly come to an abrupt halt. "Sir, are you all—"

"Wait a moment, Pierre," he said urgently as he put his fingers at his temples and tried desperately to bring the memory back.

"If you are ill with a headache, I. . . ," the servant tried again, but North interrupted with a shake of his head.

"No, no, it's not that," he said, sounding defeated. He knew the memory was lost for the time being. "I was remembering. . . ." He stopped when he realized what he was about to confess, then quickly thought of something else to say. "I was remembering something I told Helen," he said instead. He got up quickly from the table, not even noticing he'd barely touched his breakfast.

"Where are you going?" Pierre asked, also getting to his feet.

"Pierre, I'm sorry, but I need to ride over to the Golden Bay plantation. There is something I need to ask Helen about," he called out as he ran to his room to find his coat. He knew he wasn't making any sense, but he couldn't explain, either.

He dashed back out and found Pierre just leaning against the table, watching him—and looking at North as if he'd lost all his senses. "You have to go. . . right *now*?"

North smiled apologetically as he glanced at the table and saw his uneaten meal. "I'm sorry, but it's important."

"You're not asking her to marry you, are you?" he asked suddenly, his voice wary.

North opened the door and turned to grin at his friend. "Not today," he answered mischievously. "Oh! Is there any way you can prepare a food basket for three? I've invited Helen and Josie for a picnic today."

Pierre barely got a nod in before North was out the door and running to the buggy in which Pierre drove over every day. He'd been told he could use it anytime he needed.

He was so eager to see Helen and ask her about his memory that the usually short trip seemed to take longer. It did, however, give him time to dwell on the images for a bit longer, to study them and try to figure out what he saw and how he felt. The main question that burned in his mind was the obvious one. It was the one thing he wanted to know before he asked anything else about Helen being in his memory.

Whose baby was he holding?

Finally when he had arrived, North jumped from the buggy and threw the reins to the stable boy who had come running up to meet him.

Luckily Mr. and Mrs. Baumgartner were either out of the house or busy with other things, so he was able to instruct the servant to fetch Helen right away for him without having to make small talk with her employers.

He was pacing back and forth in the library when she breezed into the room, her expression indicating her surprise. "North! What are you doing here so early?" He swung around to see her and noticed her hair was totally unbound and flowing around her face and shoulders. She had always had at least the sides of it pulled back before, so it fairly took his breath away to see it in its natural state.

"Your hair. . . ," he murmured, feeling a little dazed and momentarily forgetting what he'd come for.

Immediately her hands flew up to her head, and she began pulling it back. "Oh no! I ran out of the room so fast I forgot about my hair!"

"No!" he cried, putting out his hand to stop her. "It's. . .it's fine, I assure you."

She gave him a look that said she didn't really believe him, but she decided to let it drop. "Well," she said, as if not really knowing what else to say. "Would you like to sit down?" She motioned toward cushioned chairs that faced one another.

North spied a sofa on the other side of the room that was more to his liking.

"How about there? We have a view of the window."

They both walked over to it and sat close together. North turned slightly askew so he could better see her, then took one of her hands. "Helen, I remembered something this morning, and I need to ask you about it."

North felt Helen stiffen at his words, and he assumed it was due to the excitement that he could actually be getting his memory back.

"Oh?" she said, and North got the feeling she was a little nervous about what he was going to say.

❧

Helen had never been more nervous in her entire life. What had he remembered? How *much* had he remembered?

"Did you remember. . .everything?" she asked carefully

She was a little relieved when he shook his head. "No, actually it was only a small segment, but it really brought a lot of questions to my mind."

Helen swallowed, knowing this was not going to be easy. "All right. Suppose you tell me about it."

North explained what he'd seen of the three people being there and the baby. Helen knew exactly what he was talking about.

"First, I guess my biggest question is, whose baby was I holding? I think I was calling him Ty?" He shook his head as if the details were a little sketchy.

Helen nodded, feeling safe to answer that one. "Yes, that was Tyler Douglas Thornton, Nicholas and Christina's nephew. They were raising him for a while when everyone had thought Nicholas's brother had been lost at sea," she explained, hoping she wasn't giving him too much information.

But North only nodded thoughtfully and looked a little relieved. "I'll admit the baby had me worried. I'd wondered if you'd been married before and had a child or if I had. But then, of course, that is silly. You would have told me anything important such as that," he stated assuredly.

If he only knew what I've been keeping from him, she thought shamefully.

"I was friends with Nicholas, wasn't I?" he asked, as he seemed to be figuring things out.

"You were best friends," she affirmed. "Are you remembering anything else about him?"

He shook his head. "No, but when I think about him, I feel a strong bond between us." He smiled. "And I think you can guess who else I saw in that memory."

Helen could still remember the day like it was yesterday. It was probably the second time she'd ever talked to North, and she'd been so excited. "You saw me," she said with a wistful smile.

North rested his arm along the top of the sofa and touched the back of his hand to her smooth cheek. "I saw you," he confirmed, his voice husky with emotion. "I remember what I felt, too, when I looked at you. You had taken the baby from me and were holding him in your arms, and it made something in my heart yearn for things I'd never really thought of before."

Helen could hardly believe what she was hearing. This was a memory from North the nobleman, not North the commoner. "What was that?" she asked breathlessly, so anxious for his answer.

His hand reached back to cup behind her ear, sending goose bumps down her spine. "I wanted a family. A wife, a child." He frowned, as he appeared to be analyzing his memory again. "You know, it's so strange. There are so many pieces missing, but I'll just tell you what I remember feeling." He took a breath. "I remember looking at you and feeling such a strong attraction, but coupled with that was a sort of regret or. . .or maybe it was indecision. I just don't know. But it was like I had feelings that I believed could not be realized or shared."

"You've spoken of this before," Helen broke in, unable to stop herself as she remembered an earlier conversation.

"I know! But this time I felt it even stronger than before," he stressed, seeming so desperate for answers. "Why did I feel this way? I know we've been over this, but what was keeping me from pursuing a relationship with you?"

Tears began to sting the backs of Helen's eyes, and she quickly looked down so that he wouldn't see them. This was the frustration she had always felt when she was in his presence, and, too, here was the answer she'd always looked for.

And maybe she knew it deep inside all along.

He had wanted her but was not willing to defy society to have her.

"I can't tell you that," she answered finally as she looked up at him. The sudden anger she felt over his inability to take a chance had dried up all her tears. "I had no idea you felt that way, North. You never, ever let me believe you wanted anything more than friendship."

He turned more so he was almost fully facing her. Cupping both hands on either side of her face, he asked urgently, "What was the obstacle? Was it my family? Was it because I knew you loved someone else?"

Tears came to the surface again, and this time she could do nothing but let them fall. "I can't tell you that. Only you can know the answer," she said softly, her voice small and broken.

He stared deeply and intensely into her eyes, and she noticed his own seemed a little misty. "I don't know what it was," he said, his voice husky with emotion that she'd never heard before. "However, I will promise you this. When my memory returns and I find out what the barrier was that kept me away from you, I vow to you now that I will never let it come between us again."

Guilt and shame ate at her soul as she tried to shake her head, yet he held fast to her. "You can't make that promise," she cried, trying to speak sense to him. "Perhaps it was insurmountable."

She nearly started crying again when he smiled at her with wonder and love shining so brightly in his eyes. "Helen, I promise," he stated emphatically. Then as if to seal his word, he pressed his lips to hers in a solid, strong kiss that lasted only a few seconds but spoke more than words could ever say.

North reached into his coat pocket and produced a white handkerchief, and he proceeded to gently wipe the remaining wetness from her cheeks. "You're even beautiful when you cry," he teased.

"No, I'm not," she said, then sniffed and tried to look down.

North took her chin and brought her face back up. He appeared to study her skin carefully. "Well, there is the matter of the red nose." He nodded in mock seriousness. "Yes, the red nose definitely brings the compliment from beautiful down to merely lovely."

She laughed and slapped his hand away. "You're horrid," she laughingly charged.

He laughed and tucked his handkerchief back into his pocket. "Why don't we get a little fresh air while the temperature is still cool outside?"

Helen nodded, eager to take her mind off North's troubling vow. "I'll dart upstairs and get my shawl."

❧

North followed Helen out of the room and watched her as she disappeared up the staircase.

He leaned on the railing, daydreaming about the poignant moment they'd just shared when a stern voice spoke behind him.

"That was quite a display back there," Imogene Baumgartner said crisply. North turned to see her looking every bit an irate guardian, with her lips stretched in a thin line and her blazing eyes narrowed on him with more than a little distrust.

"I beg your pardon?" he asked, although he knew she had seen the kiss. But had she heard what they'd said?

"Let's not play games, Hamish." He noticed she'd dropped the "Reverend." Not a good indication. "I saw you kissing her, and as I am Helen's guardian, I have a right to demand what your intentions are toward her."

Well, that was an easy question. "I love Helen and intend to marry her."

That took the wind right out of Imogene's sails. "Oh," she said, sounding quite deflated.

North stepped closer to her, his face set in a sincere, heartfelt expression. "Mrs. Baumgartner, what you saw in there was me reassuring Helen that my feelings for her are real and my intentions are true. I do intend to court her in a proper fashion before I ask for her hand, but there is no doubt in my mind Helen Nichols will become my wife."

Imogene just stared at him unblinkingly for a moment with her hand at her throat. Suddenly tears were pouring from her eyes. "I haven't heard such a romantic speech since Robert proposed to me even though he knew his father would disown him!" she blubbered. "I knew. . .I just knew you were the right man for our Helen!" She was crying so much that North felt compelled to reach back into his pocket and bring out his slightly soiled handkerchief again.

He gave it a wary examination, shrugged his shoulders, and handed it over to her.

Imogene never noticed.

Chapter 13

Helen, North, and Josie spent most of the morning down by the pier. After a spirited lesson in archery, which Josie was already pretty adept at, thanks to Sam, North sent for the basket of food from his house so they could have their picnic by the water.

"This chicken is delicious!" Josie said enthusiastically as she bit into a chicken leg, not caring that the juice was running down her chin.

Helen had a brief, uneasy moment while she wondered which one of North's chickens they were actually eating, but it truly was so delicious that she soon forgot to worry about it.

She did chide Josie for her unseemly manners. "Josie, please use your napkin. You are about to stain that dress, and you know how Millie fusses," Helen warned.

Hearing Millie's name mentioned did what Helen hoped it would do. Josie immediately wiped her mouth and started being more careful with her food.

North exchanged a smile with her, and though they'd exchanged pleasantries and small talk, she could tell he very much wanted to ask her more questions about his memory. It was difficult to do so with Josie around, however.

Finally he seemed to think of something he could ask in Josie's presence. "Oh yes! I meant to tell you I started the letter to my sister last night."

Helen took a sip of water and hoped she didn't look as though she were dreading the topic at hand. "You did? What did you say?"

North leaned down on the blanket, propping himself up with his elbow. "I confess I didn't get very far into it. I still need your help with it."

"Please tell me about your sister!" Josie insisted with interest. Helen knew that the girl missed her own sister dreadfully. "What is she like? Is she younger or older?"

Helen didn't have a clue, so she was powerless to help him. She watched as a glimpse of panic flashed on his face but was quickly masked. "Uh, let's see. . . ." He stalled as he threw a pleading look to Helen. "She is younger. Yes, I have a younger sister," he stated as if he were trying to convince himself. "And. . .she's nice! Really and truly nice."

Josie looked at him with a scowl, clearly not pleased with the lack of details. "Well, what else? What does she like to do for hobbies or entertainment?"

North thought again and suddenly smiled. "She likes to knit! She is knitting me a sweater and plans to send it to me as soon as she finishes it."

"Oh," Josie responded with lackluster. Abruptly she brightened and asked another question. "Does she like puppies?" Helen knew exactly where this line of questioning was heading. Josie's friend Sarah had received a puppy for her birthday, and now Josie wanted one, too.

Imogene was scared to death of anything with four legs, except maybe a horse.

"Uh. . ." North hedged. "I suppose so." When Josie turned her head to grab another plum from the basket, North mouthed *"Help me"* to Helen.

What was she supposed to do? She didn't know the woman, either!

"Josie!" Helen exclaimed quickly, as she saw the younger girl's mouth open, ready to ask another question. "Didn't you want to go fishing today? I believe Joseph said he would take you out in the pirogue."

Those were the magic words. Josie loved nothing better than to paddle down the bayou in the small boat where she might get to see an alligator or snake. "He did?" she gushed as she jumped up, throwing crumbs all over them. "I'm going to go pull on some britches!"

Helen knew she should say something about dressing like a boy, but she decided to let it be. Being able to talk to North alone was more important than what the little girl wore. "Just don't let your mother see you dressed that way."

"I'll sneak out the back way," she yelled over her shoulder as she raced to the house.

"I hate to disillusion you, but it's not going to be easy to turn her into a lady. I wouldn't be surprised if she deliberately sought to marry an Indian or even a more common man to avoid any sort of etiquette altogether," North commented as they watched Josie disappear from sight. He sat up and began to put the uneaten food back into the large wicker basket.

Helen sighed and reluctantly agreed. "She's already threatened it, but I just keep hoping something will change her mind."

North chuckled. "Like what? Holding out for a miracle, are we?"

Helen shook her head and with a secret smile answered, "No, just a man." North raised his brows in question, and she explained, "All it will take, once she's a little older, is for a young man to totally captivate her. She'll strive to do everything she can, including remembering all the proper behaviors that I have taught her, just to show him she's worthy of his attentions."

North just stared at her as if he'd never heard of such a thing. "Is that what you did? When you wanted to attract the nobleman you've spoken of?"

Oh, dear! She hadn't meant for the conversation to take this turn. "I've always wanted to better myself," she replied truthfully. Christina was forever teasing about how Helen loved to know about the aristocracy—how they dressed and the way they conducted themselves and spoke.

It was ironic that for all those years she'd wished to marry a nobleman so she could live in the society she so admired, and she now wished North would remain a simple country preacher so they could continue to live their lives uncomplicated by titles and riches.

A disturbed look fell across North's face as he looked back down at the basket and started moving things around. "You will not be 'bettering yourself' if we marry," he said gruffly. "I do not want to be the person you settle for because you have no one else."

Helen couldn't help but notice how ironic his words were, considering who he really was. "Oh, North." She whispered his name softly as she stalled him by putting her hand atop his. "Every day that I am in your presence, I feel like a better person. You are the kindest, most thoughtful, gentlest man I have ever known. You make me laugh, you listen to me, and I can feel you truly care for me, as much as I do you. That is more important than riches or what place you hold in society."

A wide smile stretched across North's handsome face as he peered at her with teasing, narrowed eyes. "You've never told me you care for me. I could see it sometimes when you would look at me, but I like hearing you speak it."

She knew she was blushing, but inside she also felt another pang of shame. The more serious their relationship became, the worse it would hurt when he got his memory back. "Why don't we finish your letter?" she quickly asked, trying to change the subject.

North shook his head at her as if letting her know he knew what she was about. "All right, we'll leave that discussion for another day," he conceded, but she knew he would not be put off for long.

They worked on the letter and finally were able to construct one to North's liking. Thankfully, he didn't seemed to mind, either, when Helen offered to mail the letter herself. She'd hold on to it for a while before writing another one telling Miss Campbell that her brother was missing at sea.

They were just gathering their picnic supplies when a pebble suddenly dropped in Helen's lap, startling them both. "Where did that come from?" Helen exclaimed as she began to look about.

Sam Youngblood stepped out from behind a tree, and he didn't seem happy as he took in the scene before him.

Helen quickly sat back, snatching her hand away from North and receiving a frown from him by doing so.

Excellent. Now both men were unhappy with her.

She was about to ask Sam what he was doing skulking about when he tossed another pebble into her lap.

"Sam, is there a reason for you throwing rocks at Helen? I have to tell you, in our culture, it is not considered polite," North told him, as he stood, then reached down to give Helen a hand up.

Once again Sam eyed their briefly clasped hands with suspicion. "It is my observation that your people consider many things impolite," he countered.

North murmured, "So we're back to the 'your people' issue, are we?"

Helen wondered what that meant as she looked back and forth at the two men. At first she thought North was a little angry at Sam's presence, but now both men seemed to be just bantering with one another as if they enjoyed it.

How much time did these two spend together? Helen wondered, perplexed.

"In our Choctaw culture, throwing pebbles at a woman's feet means you are declaring your intention to marry her," Sam explained as he looked over to Helen and smiled.

Helen had to acknowledge that Sam was actually quite a handsome man, with his dark, golden skin and his straight, black hair that fell to his shoulders. He was quite muscular, too, she easily observed since his attire was minimal, at best. All her life she'd been around men who wore several layers including a shirt vest and sometimes two coats. The American Indians certainly liked to keep things simpler. . .and cooler, it would seem.

"And just what is the woman supposed to do? Throw them back if she doesn't want you?" North asked. He seemed more curious than offended by the fact that Sam was still pursuing her. Didn't he care?

Sam shrugged his shoulders to North's question. "If she agrees to engage herself to the man, she looks at him and acknowledges his presence. If not, she simply ignores him and walks away." He pointed at Helen and smiled. "Since she is looking at me, I'll assume we will soon be wed."

Helen gasped, just a little embarrassed at being caught staring. "I didn't know the rules!" she cried defensively as she threw up her arms. "It doesn't count if I'm not aware of such a custom!"

"Why not?" Sam asked.

Helen gasped and for a moment was unable to speak from being so flabbergasted by the whole thing.

It got worse when North started laughing.

"What is so funny?" she demanded, exasperated.

"You have to admit that throwing rocks at a woman as a way to propose marriage is exceedingly amusing."

"No more than some of the silly customs of your people. I've heard you organize a whole party of people and dogs just to hunt down one little fox. And then you don't eat it!" Sam expressed, clearly disgusted by the waste.

North's laughter turned to interest. "Speaking of hunting animals and such. . . You know, I've thought about the alligator you killed, and I was wondering exactly how you went about doing it."

"Well, I—"

"Pardon me, but could we please get back to the subject at hand?" Helen asked loudly, feeling a little left out. Wasn't she usually the center of both their attentions? What was happening here?

Both men looked at her blankly. It was North who replied, "I'm sorry, Helen. What were we talking about?"

She glared at both men. "It doesn't matter. Please continue with your manly talk of hunting and killing. I'll just gather the picnic supplies and be out of your way!" She let out a dramatic sigh as she whirled around and began to stack the soiled plates, not caring that she was close to cracking them from the force she was using.

As she moved on to the silverware, she realized she no longer heard them talking. Helen wanted so desperately to turn and find out what they were doing, but she was determined to ignore them.

She couldn't believe it when she felt another pebble hitting her back. She whirled around to fuss at Sam and demand he stop doing that, when she saw it wasn't the Indian at all but North who was standing there, tossing a pebble back and forth in his hands and smiling at her. Astonished, she couldn't hold back the giggle that bubbled from her throat.

North grinned as he slowly tossed his last pebble at her feet. Helen looked to see if Sam was still around but noticed he had already disappeared, leaving them alone.

Her eyes returned to North's, and she sauntered over to him. "Are you acknowledging my presence?" North asked teasingly, repeating Sam's words.

"Yes, but throw any more rocks at me, and I just may throw some back."

North laughed again as he helped her gather the remaining picnic supplies and then headed back to the plantation.

⚬⚬⚬

A few days later, North was told to go to the bedside of John Paul Hughes, a young man who was a member of his church and the son-in-law of Silas Hill of the Hill plantation. He'd been accidentally shot while hunting, and the doctor was unsure whether he would live or die.

For two days, North did nothing but stay by that young man's bedside, read his Bible, and pray. It was a true test of his faith, as the time seemed to stretch endlessly for himself as well as for the young man's family. He prayed he was saying the right things to them and doing all he needed to do in comforting them.

Finally John Paul's fever broke, and he awoke at the end of the second day. Once the doctor told everyone that his wound had no infection and it seemed he would live, North made his way home with Dr. Giles.

On the way there, North broached the subject of memory loss and asked if the doctor knew anything about it, mostly how long it usually lasted. The doctor, however, told him he knew very little but had known one man who never regained his memory after falling off his roof.

It was not the encouraging news North wanted. He chose to believe instead that God would bring his memory back in His time.

Once he arrived home, as he was turning the corner at the church, the first thing he noticed was Helen sitting on his front porch with Josie and Pierre. It was the most welcoming sight in North's recent memory, and probably in his life, that he'd ever witnessed.

Helen waiting for him to come home.

He didn't even think as he began to jog toward his house. He leaped up the steps, taking them two and three at a time, and walked right up to Helen. North pulled her up from the chair and enveloped her in an embrace.

He felt her hesitate, but only for a second. Her arms were quick to circle his waist and begin patting his back in a comforting gesture.

They stood there for a moment as he slowly let all his tension and anxiety drain away and allowed himself to be rejuvenated by her embrace.

It overwhelmed North sometimes to realize how much he actually loved Helen and how he needed her in his life. He wanted to spend the rest of his days making her happy and showing her how much he loved and adored her.

Josie's giggle, then Pierre's discreet cough, brought him back to the reality that there were other people around them. He, too, began to become conscious of just how inappropriate his actions were.

He backed away from Helen, giving her and the others a sheepish half grin. "Uh, I'm sorry, but I feel I'm not myself this afternoon. I've not had any sleep since Wednesday."

They may not have totally believed his excuse, but they were willing to give him the benefit of the doubt. Helen quickly took his arm and directed him into the house. "You poor dear! Come and sit down, and Pierre will get you a bowl of soup."

"Yes, of course!" Pierre responded quickly, going to the fireplace, where a huge black pot filled with soup was slowly boiling over a low fire. "You will eat and go right to bed," he instructed North sternly.

North grinned tiredly as he sat down. "You'll get no arguments from me."

Josie slid into the chair beside him and put a comforting hand on his arm. "Shall I go and fluff your pillows and turn back your bed?" she offered, concern clearly written on her small features.

"That would be nice, Josie," he answered, leaning forward to give her a kiss on the forehead.

The younger girl giggled and jumped up to go do the task.

He couldn't help but reach for Helen's hand as she sat by him, looking at him with concern brimming in her eyes. "Have you been here all day?"

She squeezed his hand gently. She began searching his face as if making sure he was all right. "Yes," she answered. "Josie and I wanted to help Pierre clean your house and do some of your chores before you got home. How is John Paul faring?"

"The doctor said he should be fine. But a few times they weren't sure he'd pull through." He stared at her a moment, hoping to convey the feelings he'd felt the last few days. "For the first time, Helen, I finally experienced being comfortable with my occupation. The family needed my strength to lean on and my prayers. I wish I could tell you what peace I felt, as if I were doing something I'd done many times before, performing the deed that God had made me for—ministering to the hurting."

He was about to say more, but Pierre chose that moment to set the bowl of soup in front of him. "We'll talk more about this tomorrow," he whispered before he exchanged a smile with her. He squeezed her hand once more, then let it go to take hold of his spoon.

"Oh, let me get you a slice of bread to eat with that," Helen told him as she got up from her seat to walk over to the counter.

"Just cut a small slice. I'm too tired to eat a lot tonight," he mentioned, then took a bit of the soup, closing his eyes from the warmth and the tantalizing taste of it.

"Yes, Your Grace."

North's eyes widened at Helen's words, and he noticed she, too, seemed frozen, no longer cutting at the bread.

"Your Grace". . . What did that mean? Why was it familiar, and why in the world did Helen say it?

Perhaps he hadn't heard just right. "I'm sorry, did you say—?"

Helen whirled around from the counter, and North was perplexed to see panic flashing in her wide eyes. "Yes! Yes, I was about to quote my favorite verse in the Bible!" she said just a little too brightly.

She is quoting a verse? Now?

" 'Your grace is sufficient for me.' " She misquoted, which North noted.

"Uh, I believe it is a part of a scripture that actually reads, 'My grace is sufficient for thee,' " he corrected, still unable to get rid of the feeling there was something important connected with the words and Helen knew it.

"You know, I believe you're right!" she said, her smile just a little off kilter and forced. She placed the bread in front of him on a small dish.

"You know, I just realized how late the hour has grown!" Helen exclaimed unnaturally loudly. "We'd better get Pierre to drive us home and let you get some rest."

"Helen, are you all right?" North asked, but his question was ignored as she flew to his bedroom to get Josie.

North rubbed his eyes wearily as the words *Your Grace* kept ringing in his head, only it was different voices than Helen's saying them.

"Perhaps you should get into bed, monsieur. I'll be back in a moment to finish cleaning the kitchen," Pierre told him, and North wearily agreed as he watched Helen fly out of his bedroom, towing a reluctant and confused Josie behind her.

"Maybe I do need some sleep," he murmured, thinking that possibly everything would make sense in the morning.

Chapter 14

Indeed, everything did make sense the next morning when North opened his eyes from a restful sleep. The sun appeared to be shining brightly as beams of light pushed through the openings of his curtains. He listened and thought to himself that even the birds seemed a little more cheerful as they whistled and chirped like never before.

In fact, the whole world seemed to be a much brighter and certainly a much clearer place to live on that particular morning.

And it was all due to the fact that North woke up knowing *exactly* who he was.

And it wasn't Hamish Campbell.

Every last memory North had ever collected and remembered was there for him to pull up at will. Suddenly everything made sense, from his ill-fitting clothes and his being unfamiliar with simple chores, to his feeling at odds with his profession and not being comfortable with public speaking.

The only thing that made no sense at all was why Helen played along with everyone's wrong assumption that he was their long-lost preacher.

Propping his hands behind his head, North thought back to their first encounter in Golden Bay and how shocked she'd been when he hadn't remembered her. Suddenly all the guilty expressions that had flashed on her pretty face and the reluctance she exhibited for telling him any information about his life made complete sense.

The little minx! She actually allowed and even encouraged him to believe he was someone else!

Suddenly he laughed as he realized the length at which she'd gone to keep the truth from him.

Was it done so that she might have a chance with him?

It made him smile even more. Of course she would have thought that way. Helen had no idea he'd spent night after night thinking of some way to convince his family to allow him to marry someone several classes beneath him. He'd never been the sort of person to rebel against his position or want to cause dissension in any way; so when he realized he had feelings for Helen Nichols, a poor farmer's daughter, he didn't know how to tell his mother, friends, or peers.

He'd even tried to tell Nicholas, who had himself married a woman who was a vicar's daughter, but Nicholas had laughed off his feelings, telling him he'd get over his infatuation.

But he hadn't. In fact, North had grown more in love with Helen each time he was with her, and he was sure she felt the same way.

He'd made excuses to postpone his voyage to America and had been glad when the war helped to delay the trip. He just hadn't wanted to be away from Helen that long.

Finally he had found a way to go to America *and* make a way to ask Helen to marry him while being away from his peers and immediate family. After speaking with Claudia Baumgartner, Josie's older sister, about her search for a companion for Josie, he persuaded her to seek out Helen for the position.

He reasoned that once he arrived at the Kent plantation, he would make contact with her and convince her to marry him.

He had a feeling that Helen took the position because she knew *he* was coming to Louisiana.

How sad it was they'd both gone to such great lengths to be together. Especially Helen, since she had had no idea how he felt about her.

North sat up in his bed as he thought a moment about all Helen had told him. She'd said she had always wanted to better herself. Even Christina, her best friend, had told him that Helen knew everything about the aristocracy and longed to be a part of that world.

He still loved Helen, no matter how much she had tried to deceive him into thinking he was someone else. She had done it because she loved him. That he had no doubts about.

But he wondered if she would love him without all the riches and the titles in front of his name. What if he truly were Hamish Campbell? Could she live the life of a poor minister's wife?

As North slowly got out of bed, he found it hard to concentrate on anything, much less reason out Helen's feelings for him. He found it a bit difficult to merge his old memories with the new ones because he felt like such a different person than he used to be.

In all honesty, he could remain Hamish Campbell for the rest of his life and be completely happy with that choice.

But he had other people to consider besides himself. He had four large estates that depended on him. If his cousin Wilfred, his next of kin, got hold of them, they would be run to ruins because of his excessive gambling habits.

Then there was his mother, who was the epitome of the proper noblewoman and embraced all of what the ton stood for in style and behavior. But although she could be an extreme snob and terribly bossy, he loved her—even if she did urge him constantly to marry and to marry well.

She would not be happy once he brought Helen home as his wife. But hopefully, after they gave her a grandchild or two, she would forgive him.

As he thought of his family, he tried to imagine what his cousins at the

Kent plantation must have been going through. They had probably gotten word he was missing or even dead.

He wondered again if the real Hamish had somehow made it ashore. The man had seemed so calmly resolute in his belief that he would soon die. Perhaps God had prepared him and given him peace. North truly hoped so.

But somebody had to tell his sister! He realized that since Helen had taken the letter they had written to her, it probably would never be mailed. She must have taken it because she had planned to write a new one, telling Hamish's sister that her brother had been lost at sea.

Poor Helen. The more North thought of the situation that Helen had created and how she must have felt when it grew to be more and more complicated, he really felt sorry for her. But it also made him feel humbled she'd done it all for him. If she'd only known he had planned to court her anyway and to declare his love to her, she wouldn't have had to go to so much trouble.

He began to dress himself, pulling on his simply made clothes, and he realized he would actually miss dressing in the simple garments. His usual suit consisted of so many layers and had to be buttoned, tied, and ironed just so, or a person might find his name gossiped about all over London for not knowing how to properly dress. He did hope his own trunks, bearing his fine garments, had been taken to the Kent plantation. Once he told everyone who he really was, he'd be expected to dress appropriately.

Pulling on Hamish's brown coat, he walked to the window and pulled back the curtain. As he looked out to the little white church in his view, he had a moment of regret that he would not get to enjoy being the town's pastor for very long. He knew it wasn't his calling, but he felt the work so much more worthwhile than anything he'd done before.

He stayed at the window a little longer as he tried to decide his next course of action. The one thing that kept ringing in his head was that he didn't want everything to come to an end just yet. Once Helen knew his memory had returned, she might start treating him differently, and so would everyone else. They would have to become adjusted to his being a duke again, and that would take all the fun and excitement out of their fresh, new relationship.

One more week or two as Hamish Campbell surely wouldn't hurt anyone, would it? he wondered, already liking the idea. He could find a way to sneak off to the Kent plantation to assure his relatives that he was all right, but other than that, he could enjoy being at Golden Bay awhile longer.

⤝⤞

When Helen woke up that same morning, she was a bundle of nerves over what happened with North the night before. He seemed to react to her slip of the tongue so oddly that she feared she had shaken loose some of his memories.

Did he remember he was a duke?

In fact, she had worried so much about it that her head ached. Imogene suggested she sit out under the cypress trees in the swing and let the cool morning air soothe her head.

So far, it hadn't helped. Sitting so close to the bayou, all she could hear were the crickets and frogs making such a loud noise together in a sort of a fast rhythm that it seemed to go along with the pounding of her head. When a woodpecker joined in the chorus, she finally decided a cold cloth in a nice, dark room might be a better choice.

Helen walked back to the house, and when she was almost to the yard, she heard the distinct sound of a carriage coming up the drive. Squinting through the haze of pain, she finally focused on the driver of the barouche.

It was North, she realized in a panic, making the pain in her head worsen.

But as he jumped from the vehicle and ran to where she was, she noticed he was smiling at her and. . .he was holding a bouquet of flowers!

"Helen!" he called as he waved to her. The closer he got, the less her head hurt. It was amazing, really.

Slightly winded but still smiling, North trotted to a stop before her as he held out the bouquet of wildflowers. "I'm so glad I caught you outside. I didn't really want to disturb anyone else," he explained as he looked at her with love shining in his gaze.

Helen was relieved he seemed not to remember her odd behavior from the night before. Perhaps he was too tired to remember anything! "You're here early," she commented, hoping he'd reveal the reason for his visit.

"Yes," he answered cryptically, without explanation. "Is there somewhere we can go to be alone? I know it is an improper thing to ask, but I just had to see you and talk to you this morning."

Hmm. What does this mean? "We can go out on the bayou in Joseph's pirogue," she suggested. In the last few days, Sam seemed to be watching for her at the pier as he kept trying to "woo" her, as he called it, by serenading her with his flute.

"Is that anything like a rowboat?" North asked warily.

Helen laughed and tucked her arm into his. "If you're asking if you have to use a little bit of muscle to make it go, then the answer is yes!"

Minutes later, they were paddling down the bayou, searching for a nice shaded spot to stop for a while.

"Oh, look! There are several large oaks over there and an old root sticking out of the bank to tie the boat to," Helen told him as she pointed over his shoulder to show him exactly where it was.

North almost upended the boat as he moved about the shaky vessel to grab hold of the root and then wrap the rope around it. He looked at her and joked, "I'd better be careful! Last time I fell out of a boat, I lost my memory. I'd hate to see what would happen if I did it again."

Helen looked over the boat and could only imagine what was beneath the murky water. "You'd probably be eaten," she quipped with a shiver.

North chuckled as he climbed out of the boat and then helped her up the slightly steep embankment.

As they walked to the base of a huge, sprawling oak, Helen knew she couldn't have picked a more perfect place for them to sit and talk. It was peaceful and cool under the shading leaves with only small rays of sunlight able to peek through.

North dragged a log over so they would have an elevated place to sit and lean against the tree.

At first North and Helen didn't speak a word—they only sat there enjoying just being next to each other.

"I did a lot of thinking last night and this morning," North finally said in a low voice, as if he didn't want to spoil the mood of their special place.

Helen didn't know what to make of that statement. Did he remember something, after all? Her stomach began to twist in knots with worry. "What were you thinking upon?" she asked, even though she wished only to change the subject.

North sat up and turned so he could look at her. "I thought about you and the feelings I have for you."

Helen's stomach eased a little as he looked at her with such love and gentleness shining in his eyes. "You did?" she asked, unable to say anything else. She wished she could remember some of the clever things her favorite heroines would say during such intimate situations as this.

North nodded and reached to take her hand. As he caressed her palm with his thumb, he seemed to be weighing what he wanted to say next. "And I thought about what your feelings were for me." He continued, watching her cautiously. "Do you love me, Helen?"

Helen's breath caught at the straightforward question. She wasn't expecting such directness from him on such a delicate topic. She felt so conflicted as she looked up at his handsome face. Like a fly caught in the web of a spider, she felt like any move she made would only make things worse. Either saying nothing or confessing would accomplish the same thing.

The truth of the matter was that she did indeed love him with all her heart. There was no way she was going to make him believe otherwise.

"I do love you, North."

A look of pure joy spread in the form of a smile across his face as he let go of her hand and placed both hands on either side of her cheeks. "And I love you, my sweet Helen. You have wound yourself so deeply into my heart, I can't imagine my life without you," he expressed wholeheartedly, then bent forward and kissed her.

Tears borne more of sorrow than happiness stung her eyes, and she returned his kiss, finally letting free all the pent-up feelings she'd kept locked away since she'd first met him. After a moment he moved his lips from hers to string tiny kisses across her cheeks and up to her brow. Then, leaning his forehead against hers, he appeared to be slightly winded. "Marry me, Helen," he said suddenly, startling her so much that she nearly fell off the log.

"What?" she gasped as she pulled back from his embrace. "But you only just asked to court me and—"

He shook his head and interrupted her words. "I know what I feel, and nothing is going to change that!"

He had no idea what he was saying, she thought, growing panicky. "You don't know that for sure, North. Perhaps if we just wait—"

North put his hand over her mouth, a loving smile curving his lips. "I said nothing," he stated firmly and resolutely. "God brought you into my life, Helen. He took a situation that could have been disastrous with my memory loss and then sent you to help me get through it. We were made to live together, raise children, grow old with one another."

Helen looked away in order to try to stop herself from crying again. Once he found out it was she and not God orchestrating this whole situation, he would change his mind about wanting to marry her.

This is such an impossible dilemma, she cried silently, as her panic only grew. If only she had someone to talk to. If only Christina wasn't an ocean away to help her know what to do.

"Helen, I'm sorry," he said gently as he brought her face around with his hand. "I've gotten carried away, haven't I? I've had all morning to think about this, and you haven't had time to let it all sink in."

She shook her head, and a tear escaped despite her best efforts at keeping them at bay. "I'm sorry, North; I guess I am a little overwhelmed."

"And of course I haven't thought about you needing to inform your parents, also," he thought aloud, his hand still caressing her cheek.

Helen smiled as she placed her hand over North's hand. She couldn't help but be amazed at his impromptu proposal and his childlike excitement at the prospect of them marrying. Whenever she had daydreamed about North proposing to her, it was a very dignified and proper picture of North bending down on one knee and placing the family betrothal ring on her finger.

This was so much better than her dreams.

It was just too bad she couldn't enjoy it.

"North, I would like nothing better than to marry you tonight. I want you to know that. It's just that I do have so many things to consider and plan for before we take that step," she finally said, hoping it would stall him long enough for her to come up with a way to tell him the truth.

North gave her a quick kiss on the cheek and then grinned happily at her. "Just hearing you want to marry me is enough for now. I can be patient until you're ready to set a date." He chuckled. "At least I'll strive to be."

As he stood and gave her a hand up, Helen prayed he'd not only be patient but understanding once all was revealed and the truth finally made known.

Chapter 15

Sunday arrived, and North found himself actually looking forward to delivering his message. He had begun studying when he sat with John Paul and decided then to speak about Paul's conversion and how God had used miraculous means to get his attention. He wanted to make the point that God had a plan for everyone, and when we weren't truly listening to what He wanted to tell us or we were going our own way instead of the way He would have us go, He'd use all sorts of methods to get our attention.

He'd had no idea just how much that applied to his life until the day before. God had wanted North to learn something, and apparently it wasn't going to be discovered living as he had been, surrounded by wealth and having everything done for him at just a snap of his fingers. North was ashamed to admit it, but though he went to church and always strove to live right, he had really never talked to God—never really prayed and studied the Bible.

His life had been too busy with social events, his estates, and friends. He had even been caught up in the dilemma of what to do about his feelings for Helen. Instead, he should have prayed and asked for guidance about it. God would have led him to the same conclusion that he'd come to himself: They were simply meant for each other. It didn't matter if they stripped him of his title and he had to live out his days as a poor man. His love for Helen was so much more important.

But of course they couldn't strip him of his title. He was already the Duke of Northingshire, and the worst that could happen would be they'd spend a few years being cut by the ton and passed over when invitations for the season were written. He just prayed Helen could bear up to the snobbery she would face once they returned to England.

England, he thought with a sigh and was surprised to realize he felt reluctant to return. He truly liked Louisiana, even though he stayed sweaty all the time and was constantly battling mosquitoes. The people were truly nice and were more apt to cross social borders than those in his homeland. The only thing that bothered him was slavery. Pierre had made him aware of so many atrocities that most white people just turned their heads to, pretending it was a normal part of life.

Today North dressed in his usual black suit, the nicest one that had been in Hamish's trunk. After running a comb through his thick locks (and making a mental note that he really needed to get a trim), he made his way to the church.

Because the weather was so pleasant and unusually cool for late May, there were more people gathered outside the building. Several people walked up to greet him when he was noticed, including a couple of young ladies who never failed to make their presence known to him. He could now remember other young ladies flirting with him back in England, but he was never sure if it was he or the title they sought. So it was a little flattering that these ladies hoped to catch his attention, even though they knew him to be practically penniless.

Helen obviously was not flattered or amused by the women's attention. He noticed quite a determined glint in her eye as she marched over to him and placed herself directly in front of his admirers. "Good morning, North," she said informally, knowing it would cause speculation from the onlookers, with such a familiar address.

North managed to stifle his chuckle over her territorial behavior but did smile broadly at her. "Hello, Helen," he returned the greeting, playing along with her plan. "I trust you are doing well this morning?"

He was rewarded with a radiant smile. "Indeed," Helen answered, probably not even aware she was looking at him with all her feelings showing clearly on her face.

Of course the same could probably be said of him, too. Their declaration of love was so new and fresh to North that it was hard not to think about it when he looked at her.

"Shall we go inside?" he said quickly before he might find himself doing something stupid like reaching for her hand or kissing her cheek just to be nearer to her.

"I think we might hear wedding bells soon," someone whispered, and he heard a few others agree. Then he thought he might have heard a cry of protest from some of the young ladies walking behind him but thought again that perhaps it was just a bird.

A few moments later, much to the congregation's obvious relief, Miss Ollie sang the last stanza of her hymn and sat down in her pew in the front row. North walked up to the pulpit after that.

As he scanned the room, looking at the faces of those he considered his friends, he felt a real sadness that he wouldn't be with them much longer. Part of him even wished he could continue the work of a minister. It was true he wasn't the best at delivering a message, but he mostly liked just being a regular person, not revered for a title or riches, but counted and respected as one of a small community.

North began his sermon. Because of his renewed confidence from the return of his memory and the fact that he believed in his message so strongly, he was able to preach like never before. In fact, there was a sort of surprised look on the faces of most of the congregation as they stared and listened intently to what he was saying.

Had I been that bad?

When he had finished with a closing prayer, he glanced over to where Helen sat with Josie and the Baumgartners, and he was pleased to see her face beaming with pride.

"That was wonderful!" she whispered to him afterward, when almost everyone had gone.

"Yes, you're like a real preacher now," Josie commented, having heard what Helen had said. She had her bonnet in her hand, holding it by the ties and twirling it around.

"Josie! I do wish you would learn to hold that tongue of yours!" Imogene scolded with exasperation. "And would you put your bonnet back on?"

Josie scowled, still swinging it. "But it's too hot!"

Imogene gave her a narrowed look of warning, which made the little girl quickly plop it back on her head.

"You will dine with us today, will you not?" Imogene queried North. "I would love to discuss some of the points of your sermon I felt were particularly inspiring."

With her comments, as well as most of the congregation's, North felt a little overwhelmed by all of the sincere praise, whereas before it had been halfhearted, at best. "I was hoping for an invitation. There is also something I would like to discuss with Mr. Baumgartner."

"Excellent!" Imogene crowed, clasping her hands together at her chest. "You can ride in the carriage with Josie, and I will ride in the barouche with Robert."

North was able to steal a few moments alone with Helen before Josie joined them. "Helen." He called her name softly as he reached across and held both her hands. "I am going to speak with Mr. Baumgartner today about my intentions toward you and that I've ask you to marry me. I know you have not given me a definitive answer, but I feel we should make him aware of our feelings for one another."

North watched the warring emotions play across her lovely features, and he felt a little guilty himself for not telling her he knew the truth.

"But shouldn't we wait until your memory returns?" she fretted.

"What if it never returns? Could you be happy living here with me even though I can barely remember ever knowing you before?"

"Oh, North, I could be happy with you in any place or any circumstance," she declared so passionately that he couldn't help but feel she was sincere.

"And I, you," he responded softly, wishing he was able to kiss her once again.

They heard a sound outside the carriage and quickly sprang apart, sitting back in their seats. Josie stuck her head in the doorway, laughing. "You were holding hands!" she charged merrily as she hopped aboard the vehicle, stumbling over their knees to her seat beside Helen.

Helen lowered her head to shield a blush as she busily straightened her blue dress. "Whatever do you mean?" she hedged.

Josie looked back and forth between them. "I mean I was peeking at you through the window and saw you holding hands." She then turned all her attention to North, her head bent in a quizzical stance. "And whatever did you mean about remembering something or other? Did you ever remember that you once knew Helen before, when you were in England?"

North sent an alarmed glance Helen's way as he searched his mind for a feasible answer.

"A lady does not skulk about listening at doors and spying on her elders!" Helen scolded in the meantime, obviously trying to change the subject from what Josie had heard. "And I see you've removed your bonnet once again! Whatever did you do with it?"

Josie blushed this time. "I. . .uh. . .tied it on Boudreau's head," she confessed, speaking of Miss Ollie's mule that pulled her tiny wagon. The old mule was famous for getting loose from his fence and trampling the neighborhood gardens.

Although North was relieved to find the younger girl had completely forgotten their previous conversation, he looked forward to the day when there were no more secrets to conceal.

⊛

"What's he saying now?" Imogene whispered as the three females squeezed together in a small closet that connected the library and dining room. The dividing panels were easily removed so they could move forward to peer through the cracks of the closet door. Helen was bent, trying to peek through the keyhole, Josie managed to kneel down below her, trying to get a better view, and Imogene kept pushing against Helen's back, nearly toppling her over as the older woman tried to peer over her shoulder.

The thing they were all agog to witness was the meeting between Mr. Baumgartner and North.

"I don't know. I can barely hear them," Josie complained, as she wiggled around trying to get comfortable and leaned on her mother's foot in the process.

"Oww!" Imogene hissed. "Do take care, Josie!" They all moved around a bit to try to get more comfortable. "How did you know the boards were removable, anyway?"

"I just discovered it one day," Josie answered easily, and Helen could only guess who she was trying to spy on when she made that discovery.

"He just declared he loves Helen and has asked her to marry him," Josie whispered a little louder than she should.

"Shh!" Helen warned. "They will hear you!" She peered again through the crack. "Uh-oh! Mr. Baumgartner is frowning."

"What?" Imogene questioned as she tried to take a look for herself. "What's wrong with him? Has he forgotten what it's like to be young and in love?"

"Oh, wait!" Josie cried, this time in a softer voice. "He just asked him if he is able to afford a wife. They're quite expensive, Father says."

"How dare he say that!" Imogene gasped, and Helen was thinking it might not have been the best idea to invite her employer along.

"Hmm. . . This is interesting. North just told him he has recently found out that he has an inheritance coming to him," Helen told them as she wondered where this news had come from. She'd only read part of the letter Hamish's sister had written. Perhaps he'd learned of it from there.

But why didn't he tell her about it?

"Oh, look. Papa is smiling!"

Helen squinted to see the men shaking hands. "It appears they've reached some sort of an agreement."

"Oh, I wish I could see!" Imogene complained, pushing even more against Helen. To balance herself, she tried to brace her arms on the frame of the door.

"If you truly love her, then you have my blessing, Reverend. I would imagine that, as you are a man of God, you are being guided by Him, so I can do nothing less than to approve of the match, also," Helen heard Mr. Baumgartner say to North.

"Thank you, sir!" North replied, a wide smile on his face. "God has indeed brought us together. In Helen He has given me more than I could ever have hoped for in a mate."

"Oh, that's so romantic!" Josie expressed with a dreamy sigh.

Helen brushed at the tears on her cheeks. "He is so sweet, isn't he?"

"That is wonderful, and I'm sure Helen appreciates hearing the sentiment, as well."

Helen watched with trepidation as Mr. Baumgartner looked straight at the closet they were hiding in. "Don't you, Helen dear?"

Imogene, still trying to see a little better, chose that moment to lean forward and, in the process, caused Helen to lose her grip on the door frame and fall directly into the door.

All three of them tumbled out of the closet and landed in an embarrassing heap at the men's feet.

Since she was on top of the pile, Imogene was the first to pull herself to her feet. "Well, I must say this is very embarrassing!" she murmured as she smoothed back the curls that had come loose from her hairpins.

Helen and Josie managed to scramble to their feet, both ignoring the men's offer to help them up. "We were just. . .uh. . . ," Josie began, trying to excuse her behavior, as usual.

"Eavesdropping, dear. I believe that's what they call it," her father supplied for her in a droll voice.

"Why don't I call for a pot of tea?" Imogene mentioned brightly, obviously hoping to defuse the awkwardness of the situation. "Better yet—I'll go make some myself!" She began to walk quickly from the room, and Josie hurriedly followed her.

"I'll go, too!"

Helen watched helplessly as they left her to face them all alone.

"You know, I really should take my leave," North said as he looked at Helen. "Would you like to walk me out to the stables?"

Helen looked over at her employer, who smiled at her and nodded. "Have a good night, Reverend," he directed toward North.

"I am so embarrassed," Helen groaned, as soon as they walked outdoors. "It *seemed* like a good idea when Josie mentioned the closet."

North laughed. "Well, at least you know we have Mr. Baumgartner's approval. We only need to try to send a letter to inform your parents now."

"Speaking of letters," Helen began as she was reminded about something he'd told Mr. Baumgartner. "You mentioned an inheritance in the meeting."

"Yes, so you don't have to worry about my being able to support you," he said confidently.

He didn't, however, explain *how* he knew it. "Oh, I know you will, but. . . umm. . .did your. . .uh. . .sister write in her letter about it?" she persisted.

"No, I actually remembered something about it."

Helen's heart started beating faster. "Oh? You've had more memories?"

He looked down at her, the full moon reflecting a soft glow on his face. "A few," he said, as if it were nothing of great concern.

She tried to read his expression to get some idea of what he knew exactly, but it was just too dark to tell. "Well, that's good," she commented lamely, unable to think of anything else to say.

"Oh, I also wanted to tell you that I may be going to the Kent plantation soon."

His words caused Helen to stumble, so horrified was she by what he'd just said. "Why?" she asked, her voice noticeably shaky.

"I heard they are the relatives of the other fellow who was thrown from the ship. I thought I would go there to convey my sympathies and offer them any comfort I can."

This is bad. Terribly, terribly bad.

She turned her head away from him to take a few breaths, trying to calm herself. "When will you go?"

"Tomorrow."

All Helen could think of was running away and finding a good place to cry her eyes out. It wouldn't solve anything, but it might help her feel a little better. Then she thought of another solution that could very well help. She needed to pray! Only God could help her find a solution to the dilemma she'd caused for herself and North—not to mention the entire area of Golden Bay.

Complaining of a sudden headache, Helen left him standing at the stable door. When she reached the porch, she realized that she hadn't even told him good-bye.

Chapter 16

Helen spent a restless night tossing and turning as she grappled with what she should do. She had tried to pray, but the guilt she felt was so great.

How could God forgive her when she would never be able to forgive herself?

The more Helen weighed her options, the more she realized there was only one course of action she could take. It was the cowardly solution, but she just couldn't witness the hurt and betrayal in North's eyes when he realized what she had done.

Darkness still filled the early morning as Helen quietly pulled a small bag from under her bed and stuffed as many of her clothes and belongings as she could manage into it. Then, opening the drawer to her night table, she untied a handkerchief that contained all the money she'd earned since coming to Golden Bay. It wasn't a large sum, by any means, but she prayed it would be enough to purchase a passage back to England.

Helen then tiptoed into Josie's room and gently shook the girl awake.

"What. . . ?" she mumbled sleepily, as she tried to open her eyes and adjust to the lamp that Helen had lit beside her bed.

"Shh!" she sounded as she put her fingers over Josie's mouth. "It's me. I need to talk to you."

Josie sat up, rubbing her eyes. She seemed so young in her ruffled sleeping cap and high-necked cotton gown. "What's wrong?" she asked with a yawn.

Helen patted her on the shoulder and regretted she might not see her little friend again. "I have to leave, and I need you to explain to your parents for me."

Quickly she told her the truth of what she'd done and about North not knowing that he was really Trevor Kent. "Everyone will hate me once they find out, so I have to leave," she explained.

"Please don't leave, Helen. Everyone will understand. I won't even complain about my lessons anymore if you'll please stay!" Josie pleaded, tightly grabbing hold of Helen's hand.

Helen shook her head as tears filled her eyes. "I just can't, Josie. I'm so sorry, but I can't," she sobbed as she got up and pulled her hand away.

Josie began to cry, too. "Will you come back?"

"I hope so," Helen whispered as she quickly bent down and pressed a kiss to the little girl's cheek. "Good-bye."

"But Helen. . . !" Helen heard her call out as she ran out of the room and closed the door behind her.

Helen managed to get out of the house without being noticed, but once she'd run a few steps, she realized she had no idea where to go.

Then she thought of the only person who would help her.

Sam!

Although she'd never been there, Helen knew Sam lived down the bayou, so she quickly began to make the trek down to the pier, hoping that she'd be far enough from the house before it became too light.

It was already getting easier to see, as the dark sky began to show streaks of dark pink and orange on the horizon. Helen scurried as fast as she could along the embankment. As she went deeper into the area where the cyprus trees were thick along the border of the property, she could only pray that she wouldn't meet up with an alligator or even a water moccasin. Frankly there were just too many creepy-crawly things to worry about, so if they were around her, she tried not to notice them.

Her running slowed to a breathless stride as the minutes seem to drag by and her bag grew heavier with each step. She felt as though she was now a ways from the house, but there was no sign of any dwelling or camp where Sam might live.

She honestly didn't know what kind of place the Indian would live in. Would it be like the teepees she'd read about? Sam seemed so primitive at times, yet he spoke very well, and Helen always had the impression he was probably more educated and informed on the customs of the white race than he let on.

As the sky began to brighten her path, Helen grew so weary that she plopped down tiredly on a log to rest a bit. Three times she slapped at the same mosquito as she considered she should have come up with a better plan than just running away. If only North hadn't decided to go to his cousins' plantation, then she might have done better, but as it was, there was simply no time to think much less plan.

"Does this mean you've changed your mind?" a voice spoke behind her, startling Helen so much she screamed.

Whirling around, she saw Sam standing there, laughing at her reaction, and that made her mad. "It's impolite to sneak up on someone like that! You nearly scared me to death!" she charged as she placed a hand on her chest as if to steady her racing heart.

Sam raised a black brow as he pretended to check her over. "You look alive enough to me," he teased. With his calm expression, it was quite hard to tell. "So does this mean you want to marry me?" he tried again, this time his expression changing to a hopeful smile.

Helen sighed. "Sam, you know I can't marry you. I don't love you, and I'll bet you don't love me, either."

Sam looked at her as if she were crazy. "A man doesn't choose a wife because of some silly emotion like love! If she's a good woman, hard worker, and likes children as you do, that's all I need." He shrugged. "It's hard to find a good wife with those qualities, you know."

Helen shook her head, needing to get to the point of why she had come looking for him. "Sam, enough about that. I came because I need your help."

He immediately became concerned. "What has happened? Are the Baumgartners all right? That preacher hasn't done anything to hurt you, has he?"

"No!" she quickly assured him. "It's me, Sam. I've done something very bad, and I need your help to get away from here before everyone finds out."

Sam clearly did not believe her. "Helen Nichols, what could you have possibly done that was so bad? You're a good woman."

She quickly blurted out her story, giving him the basic facts and not painting herself as anything but a deceiver and liar. "So you see, Sam, once North arrives at the Kent plantation, he'll know the truth, and then he'll hate me for what I've done not only to him but also the church! The people will be crushed to find out he's not really their preacher."

Sam threw up his hands. "So marry me, and it won't matter if they are upset with you. In time they will forget, and we can have a happy life together."

Helen covered her ears in frustration. "Sam, will you please stop with the proposals! I cannot marry you, for I love North!"

Sam shook his head as if he didn't understand her words. "But since he won't marry you after this, why not me? I may be your only chance to marry once everyone finds out."

She glowered at him. "You're not making me feel better, Sam. Will you help me get back home or not? I'm not even sure I have enough money to get home."

Sam let out a resigning sigh. "I'll help you, Helen Nichols. My cousin is captain of a merchant ship that makes regular trips to France. He doesn't sail, however, until tomorrow. You might as well come home and stay with us until then."

Helen looked at him, confused. "Us?"

"My elder sister, Leah, has a house next to mine. You can stay with her."

"You have a sister?" she asked, a little too surprised, for Sam scowled at her.

"Yes, and I have a mother, father, and two brothers. Did you think I was raised by wolves?"

Helen thankfully didn't have to answer that question, because Sam bent down and grabbed her bag. "Follow me," he said gruffly.

By the time they reached Sam's and Leah's houses, she'd apologized for everything from turning Sam down to thinking he was so barbaric. He finally accepted her apology, but she could tell he was still miffed that he had been unable to talk her into marrying him.

The cleared area where the two very English-looking cottages were set was surprisingly beautiful and unlike any of the homes she'd seen in the area. They were placed side by side and faced the bayou. There was even a path that led down to a large pier and a swing hanging from a large, shady oak. The houses were painted yellow and blue with white trim and shutters. Rosebushes surrounded both residences, along with various other flowers that Helen knew must be tended to every day, for they were so perfectly groomed.

"What a lovely place you have," Helen complimented as he walked her to the yellow cottage. Before knocking at the door, Sam threw her a glance that said all this could have been hers, too.

A tall, very beautiful woman with golden skin and long, black, shiny hair answered the door. She might have looked like any number of Indians in the area except for her startling blue eyes. "Hello," she said hesitantly as she looked from her brother to Helen with a quizzical expression.

"Leah, this is Helen, the woman I've been telling you about," Sam told her in his straightforward way.

Helen, so fascinated by the woman's eyes and the fact she was wearing a pretty morning dress instead of leather, blurted out, "You are not completely Indian!" As soon as the words left her mouth, she started to apologize, but Sam interrupted her.

"I never told you, but my father is an Englishman. He and my mother live in Brighton, England. So you see, I'm not a complete barbarian," he told her wryly.

Helen was trying to digest that startling piece of news when Leah said with excitement, "You are to marry my brother then?"

"No!" Helen said a little forcibly. When she saw Leah's smile turn to a confused frown, she quickly added, "I mean, I've come to ask Sam to help me get back to England," she told her briefly.

"Why don't you brew us some tea, Leah? We will fill you in on the predicament Helen Nichols has made for herself."

Sam certainly has a way with words, Helen thought morosely, as she stepped into the charming cottage and began to tell her story once again.

❧

When North rode from the reunion with his cousins the next morning, he couldn't help humming a happy tune as his borrowed barouche rolled steadily back toward the Golden Bay plantation and back to Helen. The Kents had been so relieved to see he was alive and had tried hard to get him to stay a few more days with them, but he told them that he must get back to settle his affairs and to make the truth known of who he really was.

He was ready to tell Helen that he knew the truth. They'd played games with one another long enough, and he so wanted everything to finally be in the open with no more secrets between them.

When he finally pulled into the front of the plantation, however, North knew right away that something was wrong. Several neighbors were gathered on horses around Mr. Baumgartner, and he seemed to be instructing them to do something for him.

He looked to the front porch and noticed Mrs. Baumgartner hugging Josie, and both seemed to be very worried about something.

And where was Helen? Why wasn't she outside with them?

As he climbed down from his vehicle, Josie spotted him and ran down from the porch, with Imogene following closely behind her. "Reverend North!" Josie cried as she ran straight into his arms. She mumbled something about Helen into his coat, but she was talking too fast for him to understand.

As his arms came around her to try to comfort the hysterical little girl, he looked worriedly at Imogene. "Where's Helen? Has something happened to her?"

"She's gone, North," Imogene told him, using the nickname she'd probably heard Helen speak so often. "She told Josie about your memory loss, but she also told her something else that might come as a big shock to you." She paused, seemingly having a hard time getting the words out.

"I know, Imogene. I know I'm not Hamish Campbell," he supplied for her, and he watched her let go a breath of relief.

"Then you know that you're. . .uh. . ."

"Trevor Kent, the Duke of Northingshire. Yes, I do know that."

"Helen's really sorry she lied to you, Reverend. . . ." She was cut off when her mother whispered something in her ear. "I mean. . .Your Grace?" she called him, wrinkling up her nose in question as if it didn't sound right. "Anyway, she was crying and saying you would hate her after you found out, so she's decided to go away," Josie explained in one breath.

North's heart felt as though it had dropped to his toes. "Gone? Where could she have gone?"

Imogene shook her head. "She told Josie she was going to sail back to England. I suppose she's found a way to get to the port. We're about to send some men down to look there for her."

"You don't hate her, do you? She didn't mean for all this to happen. She was just trying to get you to like her," Josie pleaded, grabbing hold of his coat.

North took the time to comfort the young girl by putting his hands over hers. "I don't hate her, Josie. I know she loves me, and I still love her. But I need to go look for her." He looked at Imogene. "Tell your husband to keep looking around the area just in case she's lost in the swamps or forest. I'll ride down and see if she was able to get aboard a vessel."

"Take a horse from the stables," Imogene offered, pointing to where one of their stable boys was standing. "Tell him to saddle one for you."

In a matter of minutes, North was on a horse and riding as fast as he could toward the port. He prayed he could remember the directions that had been given to him as the horse darted along the unfamiliar wooded path.

He could hardly believe his eyes when a man suddenly stepped into the path of his horse. He barely had time to recognize the man as being Sam, when his horse reared up in fear and promptly knocked him on his back.

Chapter 17

After he finally got his wits *and* his breath back from the hard fall, North pulled himself from the dirt and glared at the Indian, who just stood there staring at him with narrowed eyes. North had been under the impression they had become friends. They'd gotten along famously during their target practice, which had turned into a competitive yet enjoyable archery match.

"What is wrong with you, man?" North yelled at him as he tried to shake the dirt off his coat and britches. "You could have been trampled!"

"I just wanted to save you the trouble of looking for Helen," Sam answered calmly.

North was surprised when Sam mentioned her. "What do mean? Do you know where she is?"

"She's decided to accept my offer of marriage, and I even get to keep my horses." He spoke again with the same even voice. He could have been talking about the weather; he seemed so nonchalant. Didn't he know North was insane with worry?

"You're lying! What have you done with her?"

Sam's eyes flared at the implied accusation. "If you're asking if I'm holding her against her will, well, think again. She came to me, white man!"

North didn't know what to believe. Surely he wasn't telling the truth, he thought, starting to doubt. Surely she couldn't decide to marry Sam just because she thought North would be upset with her?

"Listen, Sam. I am out of my mind with worry for her. If you can drum up any compassion within your heart at all, you'll take me to her. I have to see her," he told him, trying a different approach with the Indian.

Sam seemed to take an exceptionally long time to study him, as if looking for the truth. "You're not going to hurt her, are you? She seems to think that you hate her now."

North shook his head, growing irritated by the long wait. "I love her! And when I find her, *I'm* going to be the one who marries her," he stressed. "Now, please, take me to where she is!"

Sam had the audacity to laugh. "You were a lot calmer before you remembered you were a duke," he told him, then turned his head toward the woods and whistled. One of his prized black stallions he'd been trying to trade for Helen came trotting out to him. Sam hopped into the saddle, motioned for North to follow, and took off at a run.

North snapped his reins and rode with the Indian until they arrived at two pretty cottages in a clearing. North didn't wait for Sam to show him which one Helen was in. He jumped off the horse and began to call her name.

He stopped short when a beautiful Indian woman walked out of the yellow cottage, her brilliant blue eyes studying him curiously.

North found himself just standing there for a moment looking at her. She had the face and hair of an Indian and the eyes and dress of an English woman. *Very odd and yet very striking, indeed!*

"You are North? The English duke?" she asked in a soft American accent.

He nodded. "Yes. Can you tell me where I may find Helen?" He got to his point right away.

She didn't answer him at first but leaned her head to the side in a thoughtful, contemplative sort of manner. "You won't hurt her, will you? Helen said you would be very upset with her."

North frowned with incredulity. "Why does everyone suppose I am a violent man? I just want to take her back to the plantation."

"I've told him that I'm to marry Helen," Sam said loudly, as he walked to stand by his sister. North saw the twinkle of laughter in his eyes, but he was in no mood to play games with the Indian.

The striking woman merely sighed at Sam's words and told North, "My name is Leah, North. . .or should I call you Lord Kent?" She shook her head. "Anyway, wait right here and I'll call for Helen."

North saw her open her door and stick her head in as if to talk to someone. The door opened wider, and Helen reluctantly walked out. Her face was a mask of guilt, and she only glanced once at him before looking back to the ground.

Was it guilt for what she'd done, or had she truly agreed to marry Sam instead of him? He didn't wait to find out! He stormed right up to Helen and grabbed her by the shoulders. Her eyes flashed at him with surprise.

"Tell me that you are not marrying Sam," he demanded, not caring that he might sound like a lunatic.

Confusion creased Helen's brow as she shook her head. "Is this why you are here? You are upset because you believe that I am marrying someone else? Aren't you even upset that I lied to you and made you think you were Hamish Campbell?"

North moved his hands down her arms to link his fingers with hers. "I already knew that, Helen." He brushed her concerns aside, not noticing Helen's fiery reaction to that statement. "Are you or are you not marrying Sam?" he asked again.

It shocked him when Helen let out a cry of outrage and shook off his hands.

"You knew!" she cried. "How long did you know?"

North realized his mistake right away. "Uh. . .I got my memory back the morning after you called me *Your Grace*," he explained carefully.

Helen just stared at him a moment, hurt and anger swimming in her eyes. "And you knew I would be feeling horrible with guilt over it, and yet you said nothing!" He tried to touch her arm once again, but she promptly slapped it away.

"Wait just a minute," North countered, getting a little irritated himself. "*You* are the one who lied to *me*, remember? I was just trying to figure out your motives for deceiving me. *That's* why I said nothing."

"My motives!" she echoed, pointing at herself. "I've been in love with you for two years! I thought you wouldn't consider me for a wife because I'm not of your class, so I simply just made you think you were of *mine!*"

"Are you understanding any of this?" North heard Sam ask aloud to his sister, but Leah told him to shush and kept her eyes glued to them.

Wonderful. In all his born days, he'd never even come close to making a public spectacle of himself.

Until today.

Then North was suddenly struck by something that Helen had told him before. "I am the nobleman you were in love with, aren't I?"

Helen pursed her lips as if she were loath to admit it. "Yes, but as I said, you did not feel the same for me."

"Helen," North said softly as he tried again to touch her arm. He was encouraged that this time she allowed it. "I have been in love with you from the very moment I saw you at Kenswick Hall."

Her eyes widened with surprise and a little unbelief. "But why—?"

North caressed her shoulders as he shook his head shamefully. "I didn't know what to do about you, Helen. I've always done what my family expected me to do. So when I knew I wanted you for my wife, I tried to find a way to make that happen in a place where our every move wouldn't be scrutinized or judged too harshly."

"I don't understand," she began to say, and then her eyes widened with comprehension. "You knew I was coming to America! But how?"

He quickly explained how he talked to Claudia Baumgartner about offering Helen the job of companion for her sister.

"I planned to court you once I had arrived and marry you here. We would have had time to get to know one another and be stronger as a couple to face the criticism of my family and the ton."

Tears filled Helen's eyes as she looked at him with dismay. "You mean I caused all this for nothing? You were intending to marry me anyway?"

North folded Helen into his arms to comfort her. As he glanced over her shoulder, he saw Leah and Sam still standing there watching and listening to everything. Leah was even crying a little, dabbing her eyes with a lacy white handkerchief.

"I've had the time of my life, Helen," he assured her, pulling his focus back to their conversation. "God used this to get my attention and to make me aware of how much I need Him in my life." He leaned back a little and framed her face with his large hands. "It's made me realize, too, I should have never wavered in acting on my love for you."

"Oh, North!" she sighed.

"Oh, my!" Leah sighed with another sniff.

"Oh, brother!" Sam groaned, putting his hands to either side of his head as if the whole thing were giving him a headache. "This is getting embarrassing."

Leah elbowed him. "You're just jealous that you didn't win her."

"No," Sam insisted. "I'm just irritated that I have to start this whole courting business all over with another woman!" With that, he threw up his arms and stomped off to his cottage.

"I'll go get your bag," Leah told Helen, leaving them alone.

North took advantage of their absence. He pressed a kiss to her lips and felt his heart leap when she threw her arms around his neck and kissed him back.

After a moment, he looked down at her and smiled. "Does this mean you are not marrying Sam?"

Helen shook her head, smiling dreamily. "No, I think I will marry you."

"Wise decision."

"I think so."

❧

Two Weeks Later

"You look like an angel!" Imogene sighed as she peered over Helen's shoulder into the mirror. They were admiring the beautiful ivory lace gown that Millie had made for Helen, with its pearl-lined neck and stylish empire waist. Millie came up behind her and placed a crown of pink roses and baby's breath on her dark curls and adjusted the lace veil sewn onto it.

"She sho' nuf is, missus. Sho' nuf!" Millie said as she joined the ladies at the mirror.

"I don't see why I have to have all these flowers stuck in my hair," Josie complained from behind them, causing them all to turn and look at her. She was dressed in pink satin with a circlet of roses in her hair, just like Helen. "I'm not the one getting married, so what does it matter?"

Helen reached for the younger girl's hands and couldn't help but notice how lovely and grown-up Josie appeared in her pretty dress. "But you're my maid of honor! And for that, you get the privilege of wearing roses like me."

Josie let go of her hands and rolled her eyes, letting Helen know the "privilege" wasn't appreciated.

Imogene stepped up to adjust the string of pearls that she'd lent Helen for her special day. "We are going to miss you once you've gone back to England," she said as her eyes grew misty, just as they always did when the subject of Helen's leaving was broached. "It will be quite dull in this big house without you around to cheer us up."

"Yeah," Josie seconded, as she sat down on the window seat. "I won't miss the lessons, but I truly will miss having you to talk to."

Helen blinked back the tears as she rushed to comfort her young friend. "We are to stay for three more months, Josie. We have lots of time to finish your lessons," she teased to brighten everyone's mood.

Josie pretended to be put out by that news, but Helen could see that she was in better spirits.

"We must hurry if we're to get to the church on time!" Imogene said as she looked at the clock on Helen's mantel. "We can't keep Lord Kent waiting!"

Lord Kent. It seemed so strange to Helen to think of North as a duke anymore. Because he'd offered to stay on for three months as the church council searched for another minister, he still seemed like an ordinary person to her.

But he wasn't. And soon, when Helen became his wife, she wouldn't be, either.

Lady Helen Kent, Duchess of Northingshire. Just thinking of the title made Helen anxious—anxious she would have a hard time adjusting to her new life once they arrived back in England. Could she cope with the censure and the coldness she would receive at marrying so far above her station? She prayed every night that God would help her to do so.

That was one of the reasons she and North decided to marry in Louisiana. Their day would not be ruined by gossip and speculation but could be shared with the people they had grown to love in Golden Bay. Helen did feel a little remorse that her mother and father would not be able to see her marry, but she'd promised them in a letter she'd write down every detail to share with them after it was over.

Of course, there was one other reason they were not waiting to marry in England—North simply told her he would not wait that long to make her his wife.

North had teased he was afraid that Sam would talk her into marrying him instead, but she knew that he was just as eager as Helen to start their lives together.

"Well, I think we are finished here!" Imogene announced as she looked Helen over once more. "Are you ready to go meet your future husband?" she asked with a happy twinkle in her eyes.

"I've been ready for two years!" Helen stressed as she took Imogene and Josie by the hands and laughingly pulled them toward the door.

❧

"Are you sure you want to go through with this, monsieur?" Pierre asked as he helped North don his dark gray overcoat.

North smiled at him, purposely misunderstanding his question. "Of course I want to marry Helen. I'm practically giddy with anticipation!"

Pierre narrowed his eyes and wagged his finger back and forth. "No, no. You know what I'm talking about," he corrected, his face quite serious. "You should reconsider having me stand up with you as your groomsman. It will cause some to walk away and not stay for the ceremony."

North shook his head. "That is why we are holding the wedding outdoors under the oaks. I want everyone who I consider to be my friends to attend, and that includes Sam, the servants and slaves at Golden Bay, and *you*. If someone is offended, then they can leave without causing a commotion," North stated firmly as he checked his hair in the mirror of his dressing table. The fancy piece of furniture as well as the tall four-poster bed looked out of place in the small room, but North had wanted it to be more comfortable for the three months he and Helen were to live there. Once his cousins realized that they could not talk him into living at the Kent plantation, they had generously lent him all the furniture that he needed for his brief stay.

"I don't believe I have ever seen such a crowd of people, monsieur," Pierre observed as he peered out the window. "And I see that Helen has just arrived with the Baumgartners."

North's heart skipped a beat at the mention of her name. He hadn't seen Helen in three days because of all the preparations for the wedding, and he missed her dreadfully.

He vowed to make certain that after today they would never have to be apart.

After one last inspection, North and Pierre walked out of his house and made the short trek to where everyone had gathered. He greeted the minister who had driven from New Orleans and then faced his friends and family, waiting for his bride.

There was a momentary silence as everyone acknowledged Pierre would be standing up with him, but everyone stayed where they were. He glanced around and saw Sam and Leah standing by his cousins, and standing away from the crowd but close enough to see and hear the ceremony were all the servants and slaves from the Baumgartners' plantation.

A violin began to play a sweet tune just as Helen and Josie stepped between their guests and started walking toward him.

North's eyes met Helen's as she drew closer to him, and he felt his heart swell with love and thankfulness. God had given him so much, and that included his heart's desire—Helen Nichols.

When she'd reached him, he eagerly took her hand and tucked it in his arm. He smiled down at her, not really hearing what the preacher was saying until he got to the part about anyone objecting to the marriage.

When they heard someone clear their throat as if they were about to say something, North whispered a name at the same time as Helen, "Sam!"

Horrified, they glanced back to look at the Indian, only to see him smiling benignly at them with a look of mock innocence. Leah had her face covered and was shaking her head in obvious embarrassment.

North quickly turned around and found the young preacher frowning at him. "May I continue?" he asked, apparently perturbed that North seemed to not be paying attention.

North glimpsed at Helen and found her trying to hold back a giggle. "Yes, please do," he stressed, relieved that Sam had behaved himself.

Except for the fact that North heard someone whisper that, as a duke, he *could* have provided benches or chairs for his guests, the rest of the day went off without a problem.

⌒⌒⌒

Five Months Later—London, England

"The Duke and Duchess of Northingshire!" the wiry butler announced to the ballroom at large, causing every person in attendance to stop what they were doing and stare at the couple standing at the top of the stairs.

"Oh dear! They're all looking as if they've received the shock of their lives. Wasn't it posted in the *Times* some while back?" Helen whispered nervously, gripping her husband's arm as if her life depended on it. Even though they were in the familiar surroundings of Kenswick Hall, she still felt like an outsider.

She looked up to see North smiling as if he had no cares in the world. "Of course they know. It's been the talk of the town, if not the entire country. Smile and pretend you don't notice them."

"That will be a little difficult," she said between a clenched-teeth smile.

Carefully they walked down the stairway, and Helen prayed she wouldn't fall, giving them something more to gossip about! They'd spent a wonderful week in North's Bronwyn Castle in Scotland, and though Helen knew that attending her best friend's ball was important, she would have rather stayed up in the Scottish hills with North.

They had just cleared the last of the steps when Christina, her best friend and the Countess of Kenswick, appeared through the crowd with her husband, Nicholas, in tow.

"Helen!" she cried and threw her arms around Helen. "I am so glad to have you back home!"

"I am glad to see you, as well," Helen told her, as she returned the hug and stepped back to look at Christina with surprise. "You're expecting another. . ." She didn't finish her sentence but looked wide-eyed at Christina's slightly rounded tummy.

"Yes!" she nodded happily.

She turned then to greet Nicholas, while Christina warmly welcomed North. Out of the corner of her eye, Helen noticed most of the people had pretended to lose interest in them, but she could see by their glances over their fans and between their gloved fingers that they had not.

"Oh, don't be bothered by them," Christina said, waving a dismissive hand toward the crowd. "You will only be of interest to them until someone else within the ton does something to shock them even more. Then you'll be yesterday's news and merely tolerated."

"I hope so," Helen answered, only to find out later that it was better than even Christina had hoped. Perhaps they had underestimated the power that the Duke of Northingshire wielded, or perhaps it was another sign that God was looking after them.

As the couples walked about the room greeting other people, Helen was surprised to find most were, if not friendly, at least forbearing of her presence.

The one person who she was excited to see was Claudia Baumgartner. The pretty American girl was truly excited for her marriage and wanted to know all about how her family was faring in Golden Bay.

Finally North whispered into her ear, asking if she would like to step out to the terrace, and she quickly agreed, so tired was she from the stress of anticipating the evening.

"Are you glad to be back?" North asked her softly, once they had walked outside and found a nice private part of the terrace. He placed himself behind her as she leaned on the railing and linked his arms about her middle, hugging her to himself.

"I am, but I am surprised to find I miss Louisiana, too. I would love to go back one day," she sighed, as she thought of how sad everyone had been on that last Sunday there.

"Of course we'll go back. The Kent plantation is partly mine, too, so I'll want to check its progress every so often." He paused, and Helen could sense he was hesitant to ask her something. "Do you regret we married in Louisiana?"

Helen smiled and glanced up at him. "Not at all. Under the oaks with all our friends around us was perfect."

Helen had never felt such love as she walked toward North as he waited for her by Pierre, wearing a proud smile. He'd looked so handsome in his dark gray suit and white cravat, and so regal, since it was from his own collection of fine apparel.

While it was true the congregation had been saddened by the fact that North couldn't remain as their pastor, they were thankful that they'd stayed for three months while they located a new pastor.

If only the members of the ton could have seen how North and I lived those months after we were married, Helen thought fondly. They had continued to live in the little house behind the church, milking the cow and taking care of the house alone, except for the occasional help from Pierre.

It had been the perfect honeymoon, living so simply and happily together.

There, of course, had been sad moments along their way. The body of the real Hamish Campbell had been discovered by fishermen, and North had the unhappy duty of writing his sister and telling her the bad news.

All in all, Helen believed North had enjoyed his time away from the some-times stressful job of being the Duke of Northingshire, yet she had worried he would somehow change when he returned to that position.

But she should have known he wouldn't. Even though they were back in England and living in luxury and style, North remained the same as he had been when he thought he was a simple preacher.

"What are you thinking about?" North asked as a breeze blew by, cooling their faces and ruffling their hair.

"I'm trying to picture how your mother would look if she saw you milking our cow."

North chuckled and then placed a kiss on her ear. "I miss Queen Mary. We were just beginning to get along," he teased. "Now my mother is another story." North's mother had still not come around to accepting Helen for a daughter-in-law. But Helen had faith that one day she would.

In fact, Helen's faith had grown tremendously in all aspects as she and North studied the Bible and prayed together. It united and strengthened them so much that Helen knew God could help them overcome anything.

Even the English ton.

Even North's mother, the dowager Duchess of Northingshire!

Helen turned her head slightly to smile up at North and to possibly steal a kiss, but she became distracted when she saw a woman walk to the other side of the terrace and look up into the sky. As the moon caught the curves of her delicate features, Helen could see sadness in her expression and the slump of her shoulders.

The woman was Claudia Baumgartner.

"Now what are you thinking?" North asked as he often did when she became quiet and introspective. He never wanted to be left out of anything. . .even her mind.

"I'm just thinking about a friend who might need my help." Already her mind was whirling with ideas about what she could do to lift Claudia's spirits and help her feel more comfortable with life in England. She'd just finished reading a novel called *Emma*, about a matchmaker who found love herself. Perhaps that's what she could do for Claudia.

North brushed her lips, bringing her thoughts back to him. "You are a very thoughtful friend," he complimented her, smiling into her eyes.

As North looked at her, all previous thoughts jumped out of her head as she reflected again on just how much she loved him. She turned in his arms and placed her arms around his neck. "Now what are *you* thinking about?" she asked, teasingly.

"You," he whispered huskily, as he slowly lowered his head to prove his answer true.

A Letter to Our Readers

Dear Readers:

In order that we might better contribute to your reading enjoyment, we would appreciate your taking a few minutes to respond to the following questions. When completed, please return to the following: Fiction Editor, Barbour Publishing, Inc., P.O. Box 719, Uhrichsville, OH 44683.

1. Did you enjoy reading *Regency Brides*?
   ❏ Very much—I would like to see more books like this.
   ❏ Moderately—I would have enjoyed it more if _____
   _____
   _____

2. What influenced your decision to purchase this book?
   (Check those that apply.)
   ❏ Cover   ❏ Back cover copy   ❏ Title   ❏ Price
   ❏ Friends   ❏ Publicity   ❏ Other

3. Which story was your favorite?
   ❏ *The Vicar's Daughter*   ❏ *Remember Me*
   ❏ *The Engagement*

4. Please check your age range:
   ❏ Under 18   ❏ 18–24   ❏ 25–34
   ❏ 35–45   ❏ 46–55   ❏ Over 55

5. How many hours per week do you read? _____

Name _____

Occupation _____

Address _____

City_____ State_____ Zip_____

E-mail_____